JONATHAN SWIFT

Gulliver's Travels

*This limited edition
is published by
The Franklin Library
exclusively for subscribers to*

THE COLLECTED STORIES OF
THE WORLD'S GREATEST WRITERS

JONATHAN SWIFT
by Chet Jezierski

JONATHAN SWIFT

Gulliver's Travels

ILLUSTRATED BY JERRY PINKNEY

A Limited Edition

THE FRANKLIN LIBRARY
Franklin Center, Pennsylvania
1977

The Publisher to the Reader

The author of these Travels, Mr. Lemuel Gulliver, is my ancient and intimate friend; there is likewise some relation between us on the mother's side. About three years ago, Mr. Gulliver, growing weary of the concourse of curious people coming to him at his house in Redriff, made a small purchase of land, with a convenient house, near Newark, in Nottinghamshire, his native country, where he now lives retired, yet in good esteem among his neighbours.

Although Mr. Gulliver was born in Nottinghamshire, where his father dwelt, yet I have heard him say his family came from Oxfordshire; to confirm which, I have observed in the churchyard at Banbury, in that county, several tombs and monuments of the Gullivers.

Before he quitted Redriff he left the custody of the following papers in my hands, with the liberty to dispose of them as I should think fit. I have carefully perused them three times. The style is very plain and simple; and the only fault I find is that the author, after the manner of travellers, is a little too circumstantial. There is an air of truth apparent through the whole; and, indeed, the author was so distinguished for his veracity, that it became a sort of proverb among his neighbours at Redriff, when any one affirmed a thing, to say, "it was as true as if Mr. Gulliver had spoken it."

By the advice of several worthy persons, to whom, with the author's permission, I communicated these papers, I now venture to send them into the world, hoping they may be, at least for some time, a better entertainment to our young noblemen than the common scribbles of politics and party.

This volume would have been at least twice as large, if I had not made bold to strike out innumerable passages relating to the winds and tides, as well as to the variations and bearings in the several voyages, together with the minute descriptions of the management of the ship in storms, in the style of sailors; likewise the account of longitudes and latitudes; wherein I have reason to apprehend that Mr. Gulliver may be a little dissatisfied: but I was resolved to fit the work as much as possible to the general capacity of readers. However, if my own ignorance in sea affairs shall have led me to commit some mistakes, I alone am answerable for them: and if any traveller has a curiosity to see the whole work at large, as it came from the hands of the author, I will be ready to gratify him.

As for any farther particulars relating to the author, the reader will receive satisfaction from the first pages of the book.

London, 1726

RICHARD SYMPSON

A Letter from Capt. Gulliver
to his Cousin Sympson

I hope you will be ready to own publicly, whenever you shall be called to it, that, by your great and frequent urgency, you prevailed on me to publish a very loose and uncorrect account of my travels, with direction to hire some young gentleman of either university to put them in order, and correct the style, as my cousin Dampier did, by my advice, in his book called *A Voyage Round the World,* but I do not remember I gave you power to consent that anything should be omitted, and much less that anything should be inserted: therefore, as to the latter, I do here renounce everything of that kind, particularly a paragraph about her majesty Queen Anne, of most pious and glorious memory, although I did reverence and esteem her more than any of the human species. But you, or your interpolator, ought to have considered, that as it was not my inclination, so was it not decent to praise any animal of our composition before my master *Houyhnhnm:* and, besides, the fact was altogether false; for to my knowledge, being in England during some part of her majesty's reign, she did govern by a chief minister; nay, even by two successively; the first whereof was the lord of Godolphin, and the second the lord of Oxford; so that you have made me *say the thing that was not.* Likewise, in the account of the academy of projectors, and several passages of my discourse to my master *Houyhnhnm,* you have either omitted some material circumstances, or minced or changed them in such a manner, that I do hardly know my own work. When I formerly hinted to you something of this in a letter, you were pleased to answer, that you were afraid of giving offence; that people in power were very watchful over the press, and apt not only to interpret, but to punish everything which looked like an innuendo, (as I think you call it). But, pray, how could that which I spoke so many years ago, and at above five thousand leagues' distance, in another reign, be applied to any one of the *Yahoos* who now are said to govern the herd: especially at a time when I little thought on or feared the unhappiness of living under them? Have not I the most reason to complain, when I see these very *Yahoos* carried by *Houyhnhnms* in a vehicle, as if these were brutes, and those the rational creatures? And, indeed, to avoid so monstrous and detestable a sight was one principal motive of my retirement hither.

Thus much I thought proper to tell you in relation to yourself, and to the trust I reposed in you.

I do, in the next place, complain of my own great want of judgment, in being prevailed upon, by the entreaties and false reasonings of you and some others, very much against my own opinion, to suffer my travels to be published. Pray bring to your mind how often I desired you to consider, when you insisted on the motive of public good, that the *Yahoos* were a species of animals utterly incapable of amendment by precepts or example, and so it has proved; for, instead of seeing a full stop put to all abuses and corruptions, at least in this little island, as I had reason to expect,—behold, after above six months' warning, I cannot learn that my book has produced one single effect according to my intentions. I desired you would let me know, by a letter, when party and faction were extinguished; judges learned and upright; pleaders honest and modest, with some tincture of common sense, and Smithfield blazing with pyramids of law books; the young nobility's education entirely changed; the physicians banished; the female *Yahoos* abounding in virtue, honour, truth, and good sense; courts and levees of great ministers thoroughly weeded and swept; wit, merit, and learning rewarded; all disgracers of the press, in prose and verse, condemned to eat nothing but their own cotton, and quench their thirst with their own ink. These and a thousand other reformations, I firmly counted upon by your encouragement; as, indeed, they were plainly deducible from the precepts delivered in my book. And it must be owned, that seven months were a sufficient time to correct every vice and folly to which *Yahoos* are subject, if their natures had been capable of the least disposition to virtue or wisdom. Yet, so far have you been from answering my expectation in any of your letters, that, on the contrary, you are loading our carrier every week with libels, and keys, and reflections, and memoirs, and second parts; wherein I see myself accused of reflecting upon great state folks; of degrading human nature, (for so they have still the confidence to style it), and of abusing the female sex. I find, likewise, that the writers of those bundles are not agreed among themselves; for some of them will not allow me to be the author of my own travels, and others make me author of books to which I am wholly a stranger.

I find, likewise, that your printer has been so careless as to confound the times, and mistake the dates, of my several voyages and returns; neither assigning the true year, nor the true month, nor day of the month: and I hear the original manuscript is all destroyed since the publication of my book; neither have I any copy left. However, I have sent you some corrections, which you may insert, if ever there should be a second edition: and yet I cannot stand to them, but shall leave that matter to my judicious and candid readers, to adjust it as they please.

I hear some of our sea *Yahoos* find fault with my sea language, as not proper in many parts, nor now in use. I cannot help it. In my first voyages, while I was young, I was instructed by the oldest mariners, and learned to speak as they did. But I have since found that the sea *Yahoos* are apt, like the land ones, to become new-fangled in their words, which the latter change every year; insomuch, as I remember, upon each return to my own country, their old dialect was so altered, that I could hardly understand the new. And I observe, when any *Yahoo* comes from London, out of curiosity, to visit me at my house, we neither of us are able to deliver our conceptions in a manner intelligible to the other.

If the censure of the *Yahoos* could anyway affect me, I should have great reason to complain that some of them are so bold as to think my book of travels a mere fiction out of mine own brain; and have gone so far as to drop hints, that the *Houyhnhnms* and *Yahoos* have no more existence than the inhabitants of Utopia.

Indeed I must confess, that as to the people of *Lilliput, Brobdingrag,* (for so the word should have been spelt, and not, erroneously, *Brobdingnag,*) and *Laputa,* I have never yet heard of any *Yahoo* so presumptuous as to dispute their being, or the facts I have related concerning them; because the truth immediately strikes every reader with conviction. And is there less probability in my account of the *Houyhnhnms* or *Yahoos,* when it is manifest, as to the latter, there are so many thousands, even in this country, who only differ from their brother brutes in *Houyhnhnm-land* because they use a sort of jabber, and do not go naked? I wrote for their amendment, and not their approbation. The united praise of the whole race would be of less consequence to me than the neighing of those two degenerate *Houyhnhnms* I keep in my stable; because from these, degenerate as they are, I still improve in some virtues, without any mixture of vice.

Do these miserable animals presume to think that I am so degenerated as to defend my veracity? *Yahoo* as I am, it is well known through all *Houyhnhnm-land,* that, by the instructions and example of my illustrious master, I was able, in the compass of two years, (although, I confess, with the utmost difficulty), to remove that infernal habit of lying, shuffling, deceiving, and equivocating, so deeply rooted in the very souls of all my species, especially the Europeans.

I have other complaints to make upon this vexatious occasion; but I forbear troubling myself or you any farther. I must freely confess, that since my last return, some corruptions of my *Yahoo* nature have revived in me, by conversing with a few of your species, and particularly those of my own family, by an unavoidable necessity; else I should never have attempted so absurd a project as that of reforming the *Yahoo* race in this kingdom; but I have now done with all such visionary schemes for ever.

April 27, 1727

CONTENTS

A VOYAGE TO

Lilliput

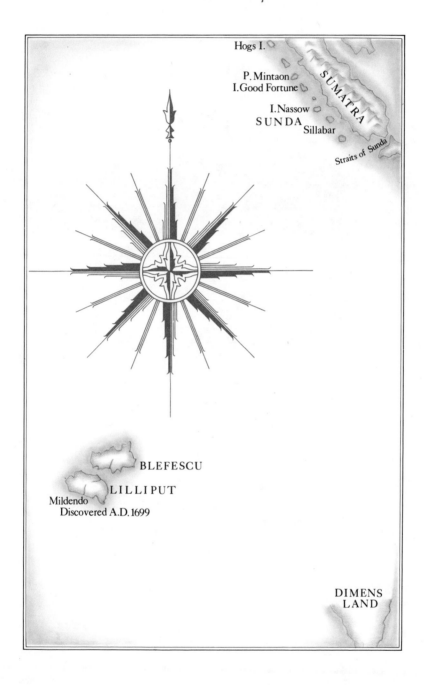

Hogs I.

P. Mintaon
I. Good Fortune

I. Nassow
SUNDA
Sillabar
SUMATRA

Straits of Sunda

BLEFESCU
LILLIPUT
Mildendo
Discovered A.D. 1699

DIMENS
LAND

CHAPTER I

The author gives some account of himself and family. His first inducements to travel. He is shipwrecked, and swims for his life. Gets safe on shore in the country of Lilliput. Is made a prisoner, and carried up the country.

My FATHER had a small estate in Nottinghamshire; I was the third of five sons. He sent me to Emanuel College in Cambridge, at fourteen years old, where I resided three years, and applied myself close to my studies; but the charge of maintaining me, although I had a very scanty allowance, being too great for a narrow fortune, I was bound apprentice to Mr. James Bates, an eminent surgeon in London, with whom I continued four years; my father now and then sending me small sums of money, I laid them out in learning navigation, and other parts of the mathematics, useful to those who intend to travel, as I always believed it would be, sometime or other, my fortune to do. When I left Mr. Bates, I went down to my father, where, by the assistance of him and my uncle John, and some other relations, I got forty pounds, and a promise of thirty pounds a year to maintain me at Leyden: there I studied physic two years and seven months, knowing it would be useful in long voyages.

Soon after my return from Leyden, I was recommended by my good master, Mr. Bates, to be surgeon to the *Swallow*, Captain Abraham Pannel, commander; with whom I continued three years and a half, making a voyage or two into the Levant, and some other parts. When I came back, I resolved to settle in London; to which Mr. Bates my master encouraged me; and by him I was recommended to several patients. I took part of a small house in the Old Jewry; and, being advised to alter my condition, I married Mrs. Mary Burton, second daughter to Mr. Edmund Burton, hosier, in Newgate Street, with whom I received four hundred pounds for a portion.

But my good master Bates dying in two years after, and I having few friends, my business began to fail; for my conscience would not suffer me to imitate the bad practice of too many among my brethren. Having therefore consulted with my wife and some of my acquaintance, I determined to go again to sea. I was surgeon successively in two ships, and made several voyages, for six years, to the East and West Indies, by which I got some addition to my fortune. My hours of leisure I spent in reading the best authors, ancient and modern, being always provided with a good number of books; and when I was ashore, in observing the manners and dispositions of the people, as well as learning their language; wherein I had a great facility, by the strength of my memory.

The last of these voyages not proving very fortunate, I grew weary of the sea, and intended to stay at home with my wife and family. I removed from the Old Jewry to Fetter Lane, and from thence to Wapping, hoping to get business among the sailors; but it would not turn to account. After three years' expectation that things would mend, I accepted an advantageous offer from Captain William Prichard, master of the *Antelope,* who was making a voyage to the South Sea. We set sail from Bristol, May 4, 1699, and our voyage at first was very prosperous.

It would not be proper, for some reasons, to trouble the reader with the particulars of our adventures in those seas: let it suffice to inform him, that, in our passage from thence to the East Indies, we were driven by a violent storm to the north-west of Van Diemen's Land. By an observation, we found ourselves in the latitude of 30 degrees 2 minutes south. Twelve of our crew were dead by immoderate labour and ill food; the rest were in a very weak condition. On the 5th of

November, which was the beginning of summer in those parts, the weather being very hazy, the seamen spied a rock within half a cable's length of the ship; but the wind was so strong, that we were driven directly upon it, and immediately split. Six of the crew, of whom I was one, having let down the boat into the sea, made a shift to get clear of the ship and the rock. We rowed, by my computation, about three leagues, till we were able to work no longer, being already spent with labour while we were in the ship. We therefore trusted ourselves to the mercy of the waves, and in about half an hour the boat was overset by a sudden flurry from the north. What became of my companions in the boat, as well as of those who escaped on the rock, or were left in the vessel, I cannot tell, but conclude they were all lost. For my own part, I swam as Fortune directed me, and was pushed forward by wind and tide. I often let my legs drop, and could feel no bottom; but when I was almost gone, and able to struggle no longer, I found myself within my depth, and by this time the storm was much abated. The declivity was so small, that I walked near a mile before I got to the shore, which I conjectured was about eight o'clock in the evening. I then advanced forward near half a mile, but could not discover any sign of houses or inhabitants; at least I was in so weak a condition that I did not observe them. I was extremely tired, and with that, and the heat of the weather, and about half a pint of brandy that I drank as I left the ship, I found myself much inclined to sleep. I lay down on the grass, which was very short and soft, where I slept sounder than ever I remembered to have done in my life, and, as I reckoned, about nine hours, for when I awaked, it was just daylight. I attempted to rise, but was not able to stir; for, as I happened to lie on my back, I found my arms and legs were strongly fastened on each side to the ground, and my hair which was long and thick, tied down in the same manner. I likewise felt several slender ligatures across my body, from

my arm-pits to my thighs. I could only look upwards; the sun
began to grow hot, and the light offended my eyes. I heard a
confused noise about me, but, in the posture I lay, could see
nothing except the sky. In a little time I felt something alive
moving on my left leg, which, advancing gently forward over
my breast, came almost up to my chin; when, bending my eyes
downward as much as I could, I perceived it to be a human
creature not six inches high, with a bow and arrow in his
hands, and a quiver at his back. In the meantime, I felt at least
forty more of the same kind (as I conjectured) following the
first. I was in the utmost astonishment, and roared so loud,
that they all ran back in a fright; and some of them, as I was
afterwards told, were hurt with the falls they got by leaping
from my sides upon the ground. However, they soon returned; and one of them, who ventured so far as to get a full
sight of my face, lifting up his hands and eyes by way of admiration, cried out, in a shrill but distant voice, *Hekinah degul;*
the others repeated the same words several times; but I then
knew not what they meant. I lay all this while, as the reader
may believe, in great uneasiness. At length, struggling to get
loose, I had the fortune to break the strings, and wrench out
the pegs that fastened my left arm to the ground; for, by lifting it to my face, I discovered the methods they had taken to
bind me, and, at the same time, with a violent pull, which gave
me excessive pain, I a little loosened the strings that tied down
my hair on the left side, so that I was just able to turn my head
about two inches. But the creatures ran off a second time before I could seize them; whereupon there was a great shout, in
a very shrill accent, and, after it ceased, I heard one of them
cry aloud, *Tolgo phonac;* when, in an instant, I felt above an
hundred arrows discharged on my left hand, which pricked
me like so many needles; and, besides, they shot another flight
into the air, as we do bombs in Europe, whereof many, I suppose, fell on my body, (though I felt them not,) and some on

my face, which I immediately covered with my left hand.
When this shower of arrows was over, I fell a-groaning with
grief and pain; and then, striving again to get loose, they discharged another volley, larger than the first, and some of
them attempted, with spears, to stick me in the sides; but by
good luck, I had on me a buff jerkin, which they could not
pierce. I thought it the most prudent method to lie still; and
my design was to continue so till night, when, my left hand
being already loose, I could easily free myself: and as for the
inhabitants, I had reason to believe I might be a match for
the greatest army they could bring against me, if they were
all of the same size with him that I saw. But fortune disposed
otherwise of me. When the people observed I was quiet,
they discharged no more arrows; but by the noise I heard, I
knew their numbers increased; and about four yards from
me, over against my right ear, I heard a knocking for above
an hour, like that of people at work, when, turning my head
that way, as well as the pegs and strings would permit me, I
saw a stage erected about a foot and a half from the ground,
capable of holding four of the inhabitants, with two or three
ladders to mount it; from whence one of them who seemed to
be a person of quality, made me a long speech whereof I understood not one syllable. But I should have mentioned, that
before the principal person began his oration, he cried out
three times, *Langro dehul san;* (these words and the former
were afterwards repeated and explained to me;) whereupon,
immediately, about fifty of the inhabitants came and cut the
strings that fastened the left side of my head, which gave me
the liberty of turning it to the right, and of observing the person and gesture of him that was to speak. He appeared to be
of a middle age, and taller than any of the other three who
attended him; whereof one was a page, that held up his train,
and seemed to be somewhat longer than my middle finger; the
other two stood one on each side to support him. He acted

every part of an orator, and I could observe many periods of
threatenings, and others of promise, pity, and kindness. I answered in a few words, but in the most submissive manner,
lifting up my left hand and both my eyes to the sun, as calling
him for a witness: and being almost famished with hunger,
having not eaten a morsel for some hours before I left the
ship, I found the demands of nature so strong upon me, that I
could not forbear shewing my impatience, (perhaps against
the strict rules of decency,) by putting my finger frequently
to my mouth, to signify that I wanted food. The *hurgo* (for
so they call a great lord, as I afterwards learnt) understood
me very well. He descended from the stage, and commanded
that several ladders should be applied to my sides, on which
above a hundred of the inhabitants mounted, and walked
towards my mouth, laden with baskets full of meat, which had
been provided and sent thither by the king's orders, upon the
first intelligence he received of me. I observed there was the
flesh of several animals, but could not distinguish them by the
taste. There were shoulders, legs, and loins, shaped like those
of mutton, and very well dressed, but smaller than the wings
of a lark. I eat them by two or three at a mouthful, and took
three loaves at a time, about the bigness of musket-bullets.
They supplied me as fast as they could, shewing a thousand
marks of wonder and astonishment at my bulk and appetite.
I then made another sign, that I wanted drink. They found
by my eating that a small quantity would not suffice me; and,
being a most ingenious people, they slung up, with great
dexterity, one of their largest hogsheads, then rolled it towards my hand, and beat out the top: I drank it off at a
draught, which I might well do, for it did not hold half a pint,
and tasted like a small wine of Burgundy, but much more
delicious. They brought me a second hogshead, which I drank
in the same manner, and made signs for more; but they had
none to give me. When I had performed these wonders, they

shouted for joy, and danced upon my breast, repeating several times, as they did at first, *Hekinah degul.* They made
me a sign that I should throw down the two hogsheads, but
first warning the people below to stand out of the way, crying
aloud, *Borach mevolah;* and when they saw the vessels in the
air, there was a universal shout of, *Hekinah degul.* I confess
I was often tempted, while they were passing backwards and
forwards on my body, to seize forty or fifty of the first that
came in my reach, and dash them against the ground. But the
remembrance of what I had felt, which probably might not be
the worst they could do, and the promise of honour I made
them,—for so I interpreted my submissive behaviour,—
soon drove out these imaginations. Besides, I now considered
myself as bound by the laws of hospitality to a people who had
treated me with so much expense and magnificence. However,
in my thoughts I could not sufficiently wonder at the intrepidity of these diminutive mortals, who durst venture to
mount and walk upon my body, while one of my hands was at
liberty, without trembling at the very sight of so prodigious a
creature as I must appear to them. After some time, when
they observed that I made no more demands for meat, there
appeared before me a person of high rank from his Imperial
Majesty. His Excellency, having mounted on the small of
my right leg, advanced forwards up to my face, with about
a dozen of his retinue; and producing his credentials, under
the signet-royal, which he applied close to my eyes, spoke
about ten minutes without any signs of anger, but with a kind
of determined resolution, often pointing forwards, which, as
I afterwards found, was towards the capital city, about half
a mile distant; whither it was agreed by his Majesty in council
that I must be conveyed. I answered in few words, but to no
purpose, and made a sign with my hand that was loose, putting
it to the other, (but over his Excellency's head, for fear of
hurting him or his train,) and then to my own head and

body, to signify that I desired my liberty. It appeared that he understood me well enough, for he shook his head by way of disapprobation, and held his hand in a posture to shew that I must be carried as a prisoner. However he made other signs, to let me understand that I should have meat and drink enough, and very good treatment. Whereupon, I once more thought of attempting to break my bonds; but again, when I felt the smart of their arrows upon my face and hands, which were all in blisters, and many of the darts still sticking in them, and observing likewise that the number of my enemies increased, I gave tokens to let them know that they might do with me what they pleased. Upon this, the *hurgo* and his train withdrew, with much civility, and cheerful countenances. Soon after, I heard a general shout, with frequent repetitions of the words, *Peplom selan;* and I felt great numbers of people on my left side, relaxing the cords to such a degree, that I was able to turn upon my right, and to ease myself with making water, which I very plentifully did, to the great astonishment of the people; who, conjecturing by my motion what I was going to do, immediately opened to the right and left on that side, to avoid the torrent which fell with much noise and violence from me. But before this, they had daubed my face and both my hands with a sort of ointment, very pleasant to the smell, which, in a few minutes, removed all the smart of their arrows. These circumstances, added to the refreshment I had received by their victuals and drink, which were very nourishing, disposed me to sleep. I slept about eight hours, as I was afterwards assured; and it was no wonder, for the physicians, by the Emperor's order, had mingled a sleeping potion in the hogsheads of wine.

It seems, that upon the first moment I was discovered sleeping on the ground, after my landing, the Emperor had early notice of it by an express, and determined, in council, that I should be tied in the manner I have related, (which was done in the night, while I slept), that plenty of meat and drink should be sent to me, and a machine prepared to carry me to the capital city.

This resolution, perhaps, may appear very bold and dangerous, and I am confident would not be imitated by any prince in Europe on the like occasion. However, in my opinion, it was extremely prudent, as well as generous; for, supposing these people had endeavoured to kill me with their spears and arrows while I was asleep, I should certainly have awaked with the first sense of smart, which might so far have roused my rage and strength, as to have enabled me to break the strings wherewith I was tied; after which, as they were not able to make resistance, so they could expect no mercy.

These people are most excellent mathematicians, and arrived to a great perfection in mechanics, by the countenance and encouragement of the Emperor, who is a renowned patron of learning. This prince has several machines fixed on wheels, for the carriage of trees and other great weights. He often builds his largest men-of-war, whereof some are nine feet long, in the woods where the timber grows, and has them carried on these engines three or four hundred yards to the sea. Five hundred carpenters and engineers were immediately set at work to prepare the greatest engine they had. It was a frame of wood raised three inches from the ground, about seven feet long, and four wide, moving upon twenty-two wheels. The shout I heard was upon the arrival of this engine, which, it seems, set out in four hours after my landing. It was brought parallel to me as I lay. But the principal difficulty was to raise and place me in this vehicle. Eighty poles, each of one foot high, were erected for the purpose, and very strong cords, of the bigness of pack-thread, were fastened by hooks to many bandages, which the workmen had girt round my neck, my hands, my body, and my legs. Nine hundred of the strongest men were employed to draw up these cords, by many pulleys fastened on the poles; and thus, in less than three hours I was raised and slung into the engine, and there tied fast. All this I was told; for, while the whole operation was performing, I lay in a profound sleep, by the force of that soporiferous medicine infused into my liquor. Fifteen hundred of the Emperor's largest horses, each about four inches and a half high, were employed to draw me towards the metropolis, which, as I said, was half a mile distant.

About four hours after we began our journey, I awaked by a very ridiculous accident; for the carriage being stopped awhile, to adjust something that was out of order, two or three of the young natives had the curiosity to see how I looked when I was asleep; they climbed up into the engine, and advancing very softly to my face, one of them an officer in the guards, put the sharp end of his half-pike a good way up into my left nostril, which tickled my nose like a straw, and made me sneeze violently; whereupon they stole off unperceived, and it was three weeks before I knew the cause of my waking so suddenly. We made a long march the remaining part of the day, and rested at night with five hundred guards on each side of me, half with torches, and half with bows and arrows, ready to shoot me if I should offer to stir. The next morning at sunrise we continued our march, and arrived within two hundred yards of the city-gates about noon. The Emperor, and all his court, came out to meet us, but his great officers would by no means suffer his Majesty to endanger his person, by mounting on my body.

At the place where the carriage stopped there stood an ancient temple, esteemed to be the largest in the whole kingdom; which, having been polluted some years before by an unnatural murder, was according to the zeal of those people, looked upon as profane, and therefore had been applied to common use, and all the ornaments and furniture carried away. In this edifice it was determined I should lodge. The great gate fronting to the north, was about four feet high, and almost two feet wide, through which I could easily creep. On each side of the gate was a small window, not above six inches from the ground: into that on the left side, the king's smith conveyed fourscore and eleven chains, like those that hang to a lady's watch in Europe, and almost as large, which were locked to my left leg with six-and-thirty padlocks. Over against this temple, on the other side of the great highway, at twenty feet distance, there was a turret at least five feet high. Here the Emperor ascended, with many principal lords of his court, to have an opportunity of viewing me, as I was told, for I could not see them. It was reckoned that above a hundred thousand inhabitants came out of the town upon the same errand; and, in spite of my guards, I believe there could not be fewer than ten thousand at several times, who mounted my body by the help of ladders. But a proclamation was soon issued, to forbid it upon pain of death. When the workmen found it was impossible for me to break loose, they cut all the strings that bound me; whereupon I rose up, with as melancholy a disposition as ever I had in my life. But the noise and astonishment of the people, at seeing me rise and walk, are not to be expressed. The chains that held my left leg were about two yards long, and gave me not only liberty of walking backwards and forwards in a semicircle, but being fixed within four inches of the gate, allowed me to creep in, and lie at my full length in the temple.

CHAPTER 2

The Emperor of Lilliput, attended by several of the nobility, comes to see the author in his confinement. The Emperor's person and habit described. Learned men appointed to teach the author their language. He gains favour by his mild disposition. His pockets are searched, and his sword and pistols taken from him.

WHEN I FOUND myself on my feet, I looked about me, and must confess I never beheld a more entertaining prospect. The country around appeared like a continued garden, and the enclosed fields, which were generally forty feet square, resembled so many beds of flowers. These fields were intermingled with woods of half a *stang,* and the tallest trees, as I could judge, appeared to be seven feet high. I viewed the town on my left hand, which looked like the painted scene of a city in a theatre.

I had been for some hours extremely pressed by the necessities of nature; which was no wonder, it being almost two days since I had last disburdened myself. I was under great difficulties between urgency and shame. The best expedient I could think on, was to creep into my house, which I accordingly did; and, shutting the gate after me, I went as far as the length of my chain would suffer, and discharged my body of that uneasy load. But this was the only time I was ever guilty of so uncleanly an action; for which I cannot but hope the candid reader will give some allowance, after he has maturely and impartially considered my case, and the distress I was in. From this time my constant practice was, as soon as I rose, to perform that business in open air, at the full extent of my chain; and due care was taken every morning before company came, that the offensive matter should be carried off in wheel-

barrows, by two servants appointed for that purpose. I would
not have dwelt so long upon a circumstance, that perhaps, at
first sight, may appear not very momentous, if I had not
thought it necessary to justify my character, in point of cleanliness, to the world; which, I am told, some of my maligners
have been pleased, upon this and other occasions, to call in
question.

When this adventure was at an end, I came back out of
my house, having occasion for fresh air. The Emperor was
already descending from the tower, and advancing on horseback towards me, which had like to have cost him dear; for
the beast, though very well trained, yet wholly unused to such
a sight, which appeared as if a mountain moved before him,
reared up on his hinder feet: but that prince, who is an excellent horseman, kept his seat, till his attendants ran in, and
held the bridle, while his Majesty had time to dismount.
When he alighted, he surveyed me around with great admiration; but kept beyond the length of my chain. He ordered his
cooks and butlers who were already prepared, to give me
victuals and drink, which they pushed forward in a sort of
vehicles upon wheels, till I could reach them. I took these
vehicles, and soon emptied them all; twenty of them were
filled with meat, and ten with liquor; each of the former afforded me two or three good mouthfuls; and I emptied the
liquor of ten vessels, which was contained in earthen vials,
into one vehicle, drinking it off at a draught; and so I did with
the rest. The Empress and young princes of the blood of both
sexes, attended by many ladies, sat at some distance in their
chairs; but upon the accident that happened to the Emperor's
horse, they alighted, and came near his person, which I am
now going to describe. He is taller, by almost the breadth of
my nail, than any of his court; which alone is enough to strike
an awe into the beholders. His features are strong and masculine, with an Austrian lip and arched nose, his complexion

olive, his countenance erect, his body and limbs well proportioned, all his motions graceful, and his deportment majestic.
He was then past his prime, being twenty-eight years and
three quarters old, of which he had reigned about seven in
great felicity, and generally victorious. For the better convenience of beholding him, I lay on my side, so that my face was
parallel to his, and he stood but three yards off: however, I
have had him since many times in my hand, and therefore cannot be deceived in the description. His dress was very plain
and simple, and the fashion of it between the Asiatic and the
European: but he had on his head a light helmet of gold,
adorned with jewels, and a plume on the crest. He held his
sword drawn in his hand to defend himself, if I should happen
to break loose; it was almost three inches long; the hilt and
scabbard were gold enriched with diamonds. His voice was
shrill, but very clear and articulate; and I could distinctly hear
it when I stood up. The ladies and courtiers were all most
magnificently clad; so that the spot they stood upon seemed
to resemble a petticoat spread on the ground, embroidered
with figures of gold and silver. His Imperial Majesty spoke
often to me, and I returned answers: but neither of us could
understand a syllable. There were several of the priests and
lawyers present, (as I conjectured by their habits,) who were
commanded to address themselves to me; and I spoke to them
in as many languages as I had the least smattering of, which
were High and Low Dutch, Latin, French, Spanish, Italian,
and Lingua Franca, but all to no purpose. After about two
hours the court retired, and I was left with a strong guard,
to prevent the impertinence, and probably the malice of the
rabble, who were very impatient to crowd about me as near
as they durst; and some of them had the impudence to shoot
their arrows at me, as I sat on the ground by the door of my
house, whereof one very narrowly missed my left eye. But the
colonel ordered six of the ringleaders to be seized, and

thought no punishment so proper, as to deliver them bound
into my hands; which some of his soldiers accordingly did,
pushing them forward with the butt-ends of their pikes into
my reach. I took them all in my right hand, put five of them
into my coat-pocket, and as to the sixth, I made a countenance
as if I would eat him alive. The poor man squalled terribly,
and the colonel and his officers were in much pain, especially
when they saw me take out my pen-knife: but I soon put them
out of fear; for, looking mildly, and immediately cutting the
strings he was bound with, I set him gently on the ground,
and away he ran. I treated the rest in the same manner, taking
them one by one out of my pocket; and I observed both the
soldiers and people were highly delighted at this mark of my
clemency, which was represented very much to my advantage
at court.

Towards night I got with some difficulty into my house,
where I lay on the ground, and continued to do so about a
fortnight; during which time, the Emperor gave orders to
have a bed prepared for me. Six hundred beds of the common
measure were brought in carriages, and worked up in my
house; a hundred and fifty of their beds, sewn together, made
up the breadth and length; and these were four double;
which, however, kept me but very indifferently from the hardness of the floor, that was of smooth stone. By the same computation, they provided me with sheets, blankets, and cover-
lets, tolerable enough for one who had been so long inured
to hardships.

As the news of my arrival spread through the kingdom,
it brought prodigious numbers of rich, idle, and curious people to see me; so that the villages were almost emptied; and
great neglect of tillage and household affairs must have ensued, if his Imperial Majesty had not provided, by several
proclamations and orders of state, against this inconveniency.
He directed, that those who had already beheld me should

return home, and not presume to come within fifty yards of my house, without licence from the court; whereby the secretaries of state got considerable fees.

In the meantime the Emperor held frequent councils, to debate what course should be taken with me; and I was afterwards assured by a particular friend, a person of great quality, who was as much in the secret as any, that the court was under many difficulties concerning me. They apprehended my breaking loose: that my diet would be very expensive, and might cause a famine. Sometimes they determined to starve me, or at least to shoot me in the face and hands with poisoned arrows, which would soon dispatch me; but again they considered, that the stench of so large a carcase might produce a plague in the metropolis, and probably spread through the whole kingdom. In the midst of these consultations, several officers of the army went to the door of the great council chamber, and two of them being admitted, gave an account of my behaviour to the six criminals above-mentioned, which made so favourable an impression in the breast of his Majesty and the whole board, in my behalf, that an imperial commission was issued out, obliging all the villages, nine hundred yards round the city, to deliver in every morning six beeves, forty sheep, and other victuals, for my sustenance; together with a proportionable quantity of bread, and wine, and other liquors; for the due payment of which his Majesty gave assignments upon his treasury:—for this prince lives chiefly upon his own demesnes, seldom, except upon great occasions, raising any subsidies upon his subjects, who are bound to attend him in his wars at their own expense. An establishment was also made of six hundred persons to be my domestics, who had broad wages allowed for their maintenance, and tents built for them, very conveniently on each side of my door. It was likewise ordered, that three hundred tailors should make me a suit of clothes, after the fashion of

the country; that six of his Majesty's greatest scholars should
be employed to instruct me in their language: and, lastly,
that the Emperor's horses, and those of the nobility and
troops of guards, should be frequently exercised in my sight,
to accustom themselves to me. All these orders were duly put
in execution; and in about three weeks I made a great progress in learning their language; during which time the Emperor frequently honoured me with his visits, and was pleased
to assist my masters in teaching me. We began already to
converse together in some sort; and the first words I learnt,
were to express my desire that he would please to give me my
liberty; which I every day repeated on my knees. His answer, as I could apprehend it, was that this must be a work
of time, not to be thought on without the advice of his
council, and that first I must *lumos kelmin pesso desmar lon
emposo;* that is, swear a peace with him and his kingdom.
However, that I should be used with all kindness, and he
advised me to acquire, by my patience and discreet behaviour,
the good opinion of himself and his subjects. He desired I
would not take it ill, if he gave orders to certain proper officers to search me; for probably I might carry about me several weapons which must needs be dangerous things, if they
answered the bulk of so prodigious a person. I said his Majesty should be satisfied; for I was ready to strip myself, and
turn up my pockets before him. This I delivered part in words
and part in signs. He replied that by the laws of the kingdom,
I must be searched by two of his officers: that he knew this
could not be done without my consent and assistance; and
he had so good an opinion of my generosity and justice, as
to trust their persons in my hands: that whatever they took
from me, should be returned when I left the country, or paid
for at the rate which I would set upon them. I took up the
two officers in my hands, put them first into my coat-pockets
and then into every other pocket about me, except my two

fobs, and another secret pocket which I had no mind should
be searched, wherein I had some little necessaries that were
of no consequence to any but myself. In one of my fobs there
was a silver watch, and in the other a small quantity of gold
in a purse. These gentlemen, having pen, ink, and paper about
them, made an exact inventory of everything they saw; and
when they had done, desired I would set them down, that they
might deliver it to the Emperor. This inventory I afterwards
translated into English, and is, word for word, as follows:—

  "*Imprimis*, In the right coat-pocket of the Great Man-
Mountain, (for so I interpret the words *Quinbus Flestrin*,)
after the strictest search, we found only one great piece of
coarse cloth, large enough to be a footcloth for your Majesty's chief room of state. In the left pocket we saw a huge
silver chest, with a cover of the same metal, which we the
searchers were not able to lift. We desired it should be
opened, and one of us stepping into it, found himself up to
the mid-leg in a sort of dust, some part whereof flying up to
our faces, set us both a-sneezing for several times together.
In his right waistcoat pocket we found a prodigious bundle
of white thin substances, folded one over another, about the
bigness of three men, tied with a strong cable, and marked
with black figures, which we humbly conceive to be writings,
every letter almost half as large as the palm of our hands.
In the left there was a sort of engine, from the back of which
were extended twenty long poles, resembling the palisadoes
before your Majesty's court; wherewith we conjecture the
Man-Mountain combs his head; for we did not always trouble him with questions, because we found it a great difficulty
to make him understand us. In the large pocket, on the right
side of his middle cover, (so I translate the word *ranfulo,* by
which they meant my breeches,) we saw a hollow pillar of
iron, about the length of a man, fastened to a strong piece
of timber larger than the pillar; and upon one side of the

pillar were huge pieces of iron sticking out, cut into strange
figures, which we know not what to make of. In the left
pocket, another engine of the same kind. In the smaller
pocket, on the right side, were several round flat pieces of
white and red metal, of different bulk; some of the white,
which seemed to be silver, were so large and heavy, that my
comrade and I could hardly lift them. In the left pocket were
two black pillars irregularly shaped; we could not, without
difficulty, reach the top of them, as we stood at the bottom of
his pocket. One of them was covered, and seemed all of a
piece; but at the upper end of the other there appeared a
white round substance, about twice the bigness of our heads.
Within each of these was enclosed a prodigious plate of steel;
which, by our orders, we obliged him to shew us, because we
apprehended they might be dangerous engines. He took
them out of their cases, and told us, that, in his own country,
his practice was to shave his beard with one of these, and
cut his meat with the other. There were two pockets which
we could not enter: these he called his fobs; they were two
large slits cut into the top of his middle cover, but squeezed
close by the pressure of his belly. Out of the right fob hung
a great silver chain, with a wonderful kind of engine at the
bottom. We directed him to draw out whatever was at the
end of that chain, which appeared to be a globe, half silver,
and half of some transparent metal; for, on the transparent
side, we saw certain strange figures circularly drawn, and
thought we could touch them, till we found our fingers
stopped by that lucid substance. He put this engine to our
ears, which made an incessant noise, like that of a watermill:
and we conjecture it is either some unknown animal, or the
god that he worships; but we are more inclined to the latter
opinion, because he assured us, (if we understood him right,
for he expressed himself very imperfectly,) that he seldom
did anything without consulting it. He called it his oracle,

and said, it pointed out the time for every action of his life. From the left fob he took out a net, almost large enough for a fisherman, but contrived to open and shut like a purse, and served him for the same use: we found therein several massy pieces of yellow metal, which, if they be real gold, must be of immense value.

"Having thus, in obedience to your Majesty's commands, diligently searched all his pockets, we observed a girdle about his waist, made of the hide of some prodigious animal, from which, on the left side, hung a sword of the length of five men; and on the right, a bag or pouch divided into two cells, each cell capable of holding three of your Majesty's subjects. In one of these cells were several globes, or balls, of a most ponderous metal, about the bigness of our heads, and required a strong hand to lift them: the other cell contained a heap of certain black grains, but of no great bulk or weight, for we could hold above fifty of them in the palms of our hands.

"This is an exact inventory of what we found about the body of the Man-Mountain, who used us with great civility, and due respect to your Majesty's commission. Signed and sealed on the fourth day of the eighty-ninth moon of your Majesty's auspicious reign.

"CLEFRIN FRELOCK, MARSI FRELOCK."

When this inventory was read over to the Emperor, he directed me, although in very gentle terms, to deliver up the several particulars. He first called for my scimitar, which I took out, scabbard and all. In the meantime he ordered three thousand of his choicest troops, (who then attended him,) to surround me, at a distance, with their bows and arrows just ready to discharge; but I did not observe it, for mine eyes were wholly fixed upon his Majesty. He then desired me to draw my scimitar, which, although it had got some rust by the seawater, was in most parts exceeding bright. I did so, and immediately all the troops gave me a shout between terror and surprise; for the sun shone clear, and the reflection dazzled their eyes, as I waved the scimitar to and fro in my hand. His Majesty, who is a most magnanimous prince, was less daunted than I could expect; he ordered me to return it into the scabbard, and cast it on the ground as gently as I could, about six feet from the end of my chain. The next thing he demanded was one of the hollow pillars; by which he meant my pocket pistols. I drew it out, and, at his desire, as well as I could, expressed to him the use of it; and charging it only with powder, which, by the closeness of my pouch, happened to escape wetting in the sea (an inconvenience against which all prudent mariners take special care to provide), I first cautioned the Emperor not to be afraid, and then I let it off in the air. The astonishment here was much greater than at the sight of my scimitar. Hundreds fell down as if they had been struck dead; and even the Emperor, although he stood his ground, could not recover himself for some time. I delivered up both my pistols in the same manner as I had done my scimitar, and then my pouch of powder and bullets; begging him that the former might be kept from fire, for it would kindle with the smallest spark, and blow up his imperial palace into the air. I likewise delivered up my watch, which the Emperor was very curious to see, and commanded two of his tallest yeomen of the guards to bear it on a pole upon their shoulders, as draymen in England do a barrel of ale. He was amazed at the continual noise it made, and the motion of the minute-hand, which he could easily discern; for their sight is much more acute than ours; he asked the opinions of his learned men about it, which were various and remote, as the reader may well imagine without my repeating; although indeed I could not very perfectly understand them. I then gave up my silver and copper money, my purse with nine large pieces of gold, and some smaller ones; my knife and razor, my comb and silver snuff box, my handkerchief and journal-book. My scimitar, pistols, and pouch, were conveyed in carriages to his Majesty's stores; but the rest of my goods were returned me.

I had, as I before observed, one private pocket, which escaped their search, wherein there was a pair of spectacles, (which I sometimes use for the weakness of mine eyes,) a pocket perspective, and some other little conveniences; which being of no consequence to the Emperor, I did not think myself bound in honour to discover, and I apprehended they might be lost or spoiled if I ventured them out of my possession.

CHAPTER 3

The author diverts the Emperor, and his nobility of both sexes, in a very uncommon manner. The diversions of the court of Lilliput described. The author has his liberty granted him upon certain conditions.

My GENTLENESS and good behaviour had gained so far upon the Emperor and his court, and indeed upon the army and people in general, that I began to conceive hopes of getting my liberty in a short time. I took all possible methods to cultivate this favourable disposition. The natives came, by degrees, to be less apprehensive of any danger from me. I would sometimes lie down, and let five or six of them dance on my hand; and at last the boys and girls would venture to come and play at hide-and-seek in my hair. I had now made a good progress in understanding and speaking the language. The Emperor had a mind one day to entertain me with several of the country shows, wherein they exceed all nations I have known, both for dexterity and magnificence. I was diverted with none so much as that of the rope-dancers, performed upon a slender white thread, extended about two feet, and twelve inches from the ground. Upon which I shall desire liberty, with the reader's patience, to enlarge a little.

This diversion is only practised by those persons who are candidates for great employments, and high favour at court. They are trained in this art from their youth, and are not always of noble birth, or liberal education. When a great office is vacant, either by death or disgrace (which often happens), five or six of those candidates petition the Emperor to entertain his Majesty and the court with a dance on the rope; and whoever jumps the highest, without falling, succeeds in the office. Very often the chief ministers themselves are commanded to shew their skill, and to convince the Emperor that they have not lost their faculty. Flimnap, the treasurer, is allowed to cut a caper on the straight rope, at least an inch higher than any other lord in the whole empire. I have seen him do the summerset several times together, upon a trencher fixed on a rope, which is no thicker than a common pack-thread in England. My friend Reldresal, principal secretary for private affairs, is, in my opinion, if I am not partial, the second after the treasurer; the rest of the great officers are much upon a par.

These diversions are often attended with fatal accidents, whereof great numbers are on record. I myself have seen two or three candidates break a limb. But the danger is much greater, when the ministers themselves are commanded to shew their dexterity; for, by contending to excel themselves and their fellows, they strain so far, that there is

hardly one of them who has not received a fall, and some of them two or three. I was assured, that, a year or two before my arrival, Flimnap would infallibly have broke his neck, if one of the king's cushions, that accidentally lay on the ground, had not weakened the force of his fall.

There is likewise another diversion, which is only shewn before the Emperor and Empress, and first minister, upon particular occasions. The Emperor lays on the table three fine silken threads of six inches long; one is blue, the other red, and the third green. These threads are proposed as prizes for those persons whom the Emperor has a mind to distinguish by a peculiar mark of his favour. The ceremony is performed in his Majesty's great chamber of state where the candidates are to undergo a trial of dexterity, very different from the former, and such as I have not observed the least resemblance of in any other country of the new or old world. The Emperor holds a stick in his hands, both ends parallel to the horizon, while the candidates advancing, one by one, sometimes leap over the stick, sometimes creep under it, backward and forward, several times, according as the stick is advanced or depressed. Sometimes the Emperor holds one end of the stick, and the first minister the other; sometimes the minister has it entirely to himself. Whoever performs his part with most agility, and holds out the longest in leaping and creeping, is rewarded with the blue-coloured silk; the red is given to the next, and the green to the third, which they all wear girt twice round about the middle; and you see few great persons about this court who are not adorned with one of these girdles.

The horses of the army, and those of the royal stables, having been daily led before me, were no longer shy, but would come up to my very feet without starting. The riders would leap them over my hand, as I held it on the ground; and one of the Emperor's huntsmen, upon a large courser, took my foot, shoe and all; which was indeed a prodigious leap. I had the good fortune to divert the Emperor one day after a very extraordinary manner. I desired he would order several sticks of two feet high, and the thickness of an ordinary cane, to be brought me; whereupon his Majesty commanded the master of his woods to give directions accordingly; and the next morning six woodmen arrived with as many carriages, drawn by eight horses to each. I took nine of these sticks, and fixing them firmly in the ground in a quadrangular figure, two feet and a half square, I took four other sticks, and tied them parallel at each corner, about two feet from the ground; then I fastened my handkerchief to the nine sticks that stood erect; and extended it on all sides, till it was tight as the top of a drum; and the four parallel sticks, rising about five inches higher than the handkerchief, served as ledges on each side. When I had finished my work, I desired the Emperor to let a troop of the best horse, twenty-four in number, come and exercise upon this plain. His Majesty approved of the proposal, and I took them up, one by one, in my hands, ready mounted and armed, with the proper officers to exercise them. As soon as they got into order, they divided into two parties, performed mock skirmishes, discharged blunt arrows, drew their swords, fled and pursued, attacked and retired, and, in short, discovered the best military discipline I ever beheld. The parallel sticks secured them and their horses from falling over the stage; and the Emperor was so much delighted, that he ordered this entertainment to be repeated several days, and once was pleased to be lifted up and give the word of command; and with great difficulty persuaded even the Empress herself to let me hold her in her close chair within two yards of the stage, when she was able to take a full view of the whole performance. It was my good fortune, that no ill accident happened in these entertainments; only once a fiery horse, that belonged to one of the captains, pawing with his hoof, struck a hole in my handkerchief, and his foot slipping, he overthrew his rider and himself; but I immediately relieved them both, and covering the hole with one hand, I set down the troop with the other, in the same manner as I took them up. The horse that fell was strained in the left shoulder, but the rider got no hurt; and I repaired my handkerchief as well as I could: however, I would not trust to the strength of it any more, in such dangerous enterprizes.

About two or three days before I was set at liberty, as I was entertaining the court with these kinds of feats, there arrived an express to inform his Majesty, that some of his subjects, riding near the place where I was first taken up, had seen a great black substance lying on the ground, very oddly shaped, extending its edges round, as wide as his Majesty's bed-chamber, and rising up in the middle as high as a man; that it was no living creature, as they at first apprehended, for it lay on the grass without motion, and some of them had walked round it several times; that, by mounting upon each other's shoulders, they had got to the top, which was flat and even, and stamping upon it, they found that it was hollow within; that they humbly conceived it might be something belonging to the Man-Mountain; and, if his Majesty pleased, they would undertake to bring it with only five horses. I presently knew what they meant, and was glad at heart to receive this intelligence. It seems, upon my first reaching the shore after our shipwreck, I was in such confusion, that, before I came to the place where I went to sleep, my hat, which I had fastened with a string to my head while I was rowing, and had stuck on all the time I was swimming, fell off after I came to land; the string, as I conjecture, breaking by some accident, which I never observed, but thought my hat had been lost at sea. I entreated his Imperial Majesty to give orders it might be brought to me as soon as possible, describing to him the use and the nature of it; and the next day the waggoners arrived with it, but not in a very good condition; they had bored two holes in the brim, within an inch and half of the edge, and fastened two hooks in the holes; these hooks were tied by a long cord to the harness, and thus my hat was dragged along for above half an English mile; but, the ground in that country being extremely smooth and level, it received less damage than I expected.

Two days after this adventure, the Emperor, having ordered that part of his army which quarters in and about his metropolis, to be in readiness, took a fancy of diverting himself in a very singular manner. He desired I would stand like a Colossus, with my legs as far asunder as I conveniently could. He then commanded his general (who was an old experienced leader, and a great patron of mine) to draw up the troops in close order, and march them under me; the foot by twenty-four in a breast, and the horse by sixteen, with drums beating, colours flying, and pikes advanced. This body consisted of three thousand foot, and a thousand horse. His Majesty gave orders, upon pain of death, that every soldier in his march should observe the strictest decency with regard to my person; which, however, could not prevent some of the younger officers from turning up their eyes as they passed under me: and, to confess the truth, my breeches were at that time in so ill a condition, that they afforded some opportunities for laughter and admiration.

I had sent so many memorials and petitions for my liberty, that his Majesty at length mentioned the matter, first in the cabinet, and then in a full council, where it was opposed by none, except Skyresh Bolgolam, who was pleased, without any provocation, to be my mortal enemy. But it was carried against him by the whole board, and confirmed by the Emperor. That minister was *Galbet,* or Admiral of the Realm, very much in his master's confidence, and a person well versed in affairs, but of a morose and sour complexion. However, he was at length persuaded to comply, but prevailed that the articles and conditions upon which I should be set free, and to which I must swear, should be drawn up by himself. These articles were brought to me by Skyresh Bolgolam in person, attended by two undersecretaries, and several persons of distinction. After they were read, I was demanded to swear to the performance of them; first in the manner of my own country, and afterwards in the method prescribed by their laws, which was, to hold my right foot in my left hand, and to place the middle finger of my right hand on the crown of my head, and my thumb on the tip of my right ear. But because the reader may be curious to have some idea of the style and manner of expression peculiar to that people, as well as to know the articles upon which I recovered my liberty, I have made a translation of the whole instrument, word for word, as near as I was able, which I here offer to the public. —

"Golbasto Momarem Evlame Gurdilo Shefin Mully Ully Gue, most mighty Emperor of Lilliput, delight and terror of the universe, whose dominions extend five thousand *blustrugs* (about twelve miles in circumference) to the extremities of the globe; monarch of all monarchs, taller than the sons of men; whose feet press down to the centre, and whose head strikes against the sun; at whose nod the princes of the earth shake their knees; pleasant as the spring, comfortable as the summer, fruitful as autumn, dreadful as winter. His most sublime Majesty proposes to the Man-Mountain, lately arrived at our celestial dominions, the following articles, which, by a solemn oath, he shall be obliged to perform: —

"1st, The Man-Mountain shall not depart from our dominions, without our licence under our great seal.

"2d, He shall not presume to come into our metropolis without our express order; at which time the inhabitants shall have two hours' warning to keep within doors.

"3d, The said Man-Mountain shall confine his walks to our principal high-roads, and not offer to walk, or lie down, in a meadow or field of corn.

"4th, As he walks the said roads, he shall take the utmost care not to trample upon the bodies of any of our loving subjects, their horses, or carriages, nor take any of our subjects into his hands without their own consent.

"5th, If an express requires extraordinary dispatch, the Man-Mountain shall be obliged to carry, in his pocket, the messenger and horse a six day's journey, once in every moon, and return the said messenger back, (if so required,) safe to our Imperial Presence.

"6th, He shall be our ally against our enemies in the Island of Blefuscu, and do his utmost to destroy their fleet, which is now preparing to invade us.

"7th, That the said Man-Mountain shall, at his times of leisure, be aiding and assisting to our workmen, in helping to raise certain great stones towards covering the wall of the principal park, and other of our royal buildings.

"8th, That the said Man-Mountain shall, in two moons' time, deliver in an exact survey of the circumference of our dominions, by a computation of his own paces round the coast.

"Lastly, That, upon his solemn oath to observe all the above articles, the said Man-Mountain shall have a daily allowance of meat and drink sufficient for the support of 1724 of our subjects, with free access to our Royal Person, and other marks of our favour. Given at our palace at Belfaborac, the twelfth day of the ninety-first moon of our reign."

I swore and subscribed to these articles with great cheerfulness and content, although some of them were not so honourable as I could have wished, which proceeded wholly from the malice of Skyresh Bolgolam, the High Admiral; whereupon my chains were immediately unlocked, and I was at full liberty. The Emperor himself, in person, did me the

honour to be by at the whole ceremony. I made my acknowledgments by prostrating myself at his Majesty's feet; but he
commanded me to rise; and after many gracious expressions,
which, to avoid the censure of vanity, I shall not repeat, he
added, that he hoped I should prove a useful servant, and
well deserve all the favours he had already conferred upon
me, or might do for the future.

The reader may please to observe, that, in the last article for the recovery of my liberty, the Emperor stipulates to
allow me a quantity of meat and drink sufficient for the support of 1724 Lilliputians. Some time after, asking a friend
at court how they came to fix on that determined number, he
told me that his Majesty's mathematicians, having taken the
height of my body by the help of a quadrant, and finding it
to execeed theirs in the proportion of twelve to one, they
concluded, from the similarity of their bodies, that mine must
contain at least 1724 of theirs, and consequently would require as much food as was necessary to support that number
of Lilliputians. By which the reader may conceive an idea of
the ingenuity of that people, as well as the prudent and exact
economy of so great a prince.

CHAPTER 4

Mildendo, the metropolis of Lilliput, described, together with the Emperor's palace. A conversation between the author and principal secretary, concerning the affairs of that empire. The author's offer to serve the Emperor in his wars.

THE FIRST REQUEST I made, after I had obtained my liberty, was, that I might have licence to see Mildendo, the metropolis; which the Emperor easily granted me, but with a special charge to do no hurt either to the inhabitants or their houses. The people had notice, by proclamation, of my design to visit the town. The wall, which encompasses it, is two feet and a half high, and at least eleven inches broad, so that a coach and horses may be driven very safely round it; and it is flanked with strong towers, at ten feet distance. I stepped over the great western gate, and passed very gently and sideling through the two principal streets, only in my short waistcoat, for fear of damaging the roofs and eaves of the houses with the skirts of my coat. I walked with the utmost circumspection, to avoid treading on any stragglers who might remain on the streets, although the orders were very strict that all people should keep in their houses, at their own peril. The garret windows and tops of houses were so crowded with spectators, that I thought in all my travels I had not seen a more populous place. The city is an exact square, each side of the wall being five hundred feet long. The two great streets, which run across, and divide it into four quarters, are five feet wide. The lanes and alleys, which I could not enter, but viewed them as I passed, are from twelve to eighteen inches. The town is capable of holding five hundred thousand souls: the houses are from three to five stories: the shops and markets well provided.

The Emperor's palace is in the centre of the city, where
the two great streets meet. It is enclosed by a wall of two
feet high, and twenty feet distance from the buildings. I had
his Majesty's permission to step over this wall; and the space
being so wide between that and the palace, I could easily view
it on every side. The outward court is a square of forty feet,
and includes two other courts: in the inmost are the royal
apartments, which I was very desirous to see, but found it
extremely difficult: for the great gates, from one square into
another, were but eighteen inches high, and seven inches wide.
Now the buildings of the outer court were at least five feet
high, and it was impossible for me to stride over them without
infinite damage to the pile, though the walls were strongly
built of hewn stone, and four inches thick. At the same time
the Emperor had a great desire that I should see the magnificence of his palace; but this I was not able to do till three
days after, which I spent in cutting down with my knife some
of the largest trees in the royal park, about a hundred yards'
distance from the city. Of these trees I made two stools, each
about three feet high, and strong enough to bear my weight.
The people having received notice a second time, I went again
through the city to the palace with my two stools in my hands.
When I came to the side of the outer court, I stood upon
one stool, and took the other in my hand; this I lifted over
the roof, and gently set it down on the space between the
first and second court, which was eight feet wide. I then stept
over the building very conveniently from one stool to the
other, and drew up the first after me with a hooked stick. By
this contrivance I got into the inmost court; and, lying down
upon my side, I applied my face to the windows of the middle
stories, which were left open on purpose, and discovered the
most splendid apartments that can be imagined. There I saw
the Empress and the young princes, in their several lodgings,
with their chief attendants about them. Her Imperial Maj-

esty was so pleased to smile very graciously upon me, and
gave me out of the window her hand to kiss.

But I shall not anticipate the reader with farther descriptions of this kind, because I reserve them for a greater work,
which is now almost ready for the press; containing a general
description of this empire, from its first erection, through a
long series of princes; with a particular account of their wars
and politics, laws, learning, and religion; their plants and
animals, their peculiar manners and customs, with other matters very curious and useful; my chief design at present being
only to relate such events and transactions as happened to
the public or to myself during a residence of about nine
months in that empire.

One morning, about a fortnight after I had obtained my
liberty, Reldresal, principal secretary (as they style him) for
private affairs, came to my house attended only by one servant. He ordered his coach to wait at a distance, and desired
I would give him an hour's audience; which I readily consented to, on account of his quality and personal merits, as
well as of the many good offices he had done me during my
solicitations at court. I offered to lie down, that he might the
more conveniently reach my ear; but he chose rather to let
me hold him in my hand during our conversation. He began
with compliments on my liberty; said he might pretend to
some merit in it; but, however, added that if it had not been
for the present situation of things at court, perhaps I might
not have obtained it so soon. "For," said he, "as flourishing
a condition as we may appear to be in to foreigners, we
labour under two mighty evils; a violent faction at home, and
the danger of an invasion, by a most potent enemy, from
abroad. As to the first, you are to understand, that for above
seventy moons past there have been two struggling parties
in this empire, under the names of *Tramecksan* and *Slameck-
san,* from the high and low heels of their shoes, by which

they distinguish themselves. It is alleged, indeed, that the
high heels are most agreeable to our ancient constitution;
but, however this be, his Majesty has determined to make
use only of low heels in the administration of the government,
and all offices in the gift of the crown, as you cannot but observe; and particularly, that his Majesty's imperial heels are
lower at least by a *drurr,* than any of his court: (*drurr* is a
measure about the fourteenth part of an inch.) The animosi-
ties between these two parties run so high, that they will
neither eat, nor drink, nor talk with each other. We compute
the *Tramecksan,* or high heels, to exceed us in number; but
the power is wholly on our side. We apprehend his Imperial
Highness, the heir to the crown, to have some tendency
towards the high heels; at least, we can plainly discover that
one of his heels is higher than the other, which gives him a
hobble in his gait. Now, in the midst of these intestine disquiets, we are threatened with an invasion from the Island
of Blefuscu, which is the other great empire of the universe,
almost as large and powerful as this of his Majesty. For, as
to what we have heard you affirm, that there are other kingdoms and states in the world, inhabited by human creatures
as large as yourself, our philosophers are in much doubt,
and would rather conjecture that you dropped from the
moon, or one of the stars: because it is certain, that a hundred
mortals of your bulk would in a short time destroy all the
fruits and cattle of his Majesty's dominions: besides, our
histories of six thousand moons make no mention of any other
regions than the two great empires of Lilliput and Blefuscu.
Which two mighty powers have, as I was going to tell you,
been engaged in a most obstinate war for six-and-thirty moons
past. It began upon the following occasion: it is allowed on
all hands, that the primitive way of breaking eggs, before
we eat them, was upon the larger end; but his present Majesty's grandfather, while he was a boy, going to eat an egg,

and breaking it according to the ancient practice, happened
to cut one of his fingers. Whereupon the Emperor his father
published an edict, commanding all his subjects, upon great
penalties, to break the smaller ends of their eggs. The people
so highly resented this law, that our histories tell us, there
have been six rebellions raised on that account; wherein one
emperor lost his life, and another his crown. These civil
commotions were constantly fomented by the monarchs of
Blefuscu; and when they were quelled, the exiles always fled
for refuge to that empire. It is computed that eleven thousand persons have at several times suffered death, rather than
submit to break their eggs at the smaller end. Many hundred large volumes have been published upon this controversy: but the books of the Big-endians have been long forbidden, and the whole party rendered incapable by law of
holding employments. During the course of these troubles,
the emperors of Blefuscu did frequently expostulate by their
ambassadors, accusing us of making a schism in religion, by
offending against a fundamental doctrine of our great
prophet Lustrog, in the fifty-fourth chapter of the Blun-
decral, (which is their Alcoran.) This, however, is thought
to be a mere strain upon the text; for the words are these:
that all true believers break their eggs at the convenient end.
And which is the convenient end, seems, in my humble opinion, to be left to every man's conscience, or at least in the
power of the chief magistrate to determine. Now, the Big-
endian exiles have found so much credit in the Emperor of
Blefuscu's court, and so much private assistance and encouragement from their party here at home, that a bloody war
has been carried on between the two empires for six-and-
thirty moons, with various success: during which time we
have lost forty capital ships, and a much greater number of
smaller vessels, together with thirty thousand of our best
seamen and soldiers; and the damage received by the enemy

is reckoned to be somewhat greater than ours. However, they have now equipped a numerous fleet, and are just preparing to make a descent upon us; and his Imperial Majesty, placing great confidence in your valour and strength, has commanded me to lay this account of his affairs before you."

I desired the secretary to present my humble duty to the Emperor; and to let him know, that I thought it would not become me, who was a foreigner, to interfere with parties; but I was ready, with the hazard of my life, to defend his person and state against all invaders.

CHAPTER 5

The author, by an extraordinary stratagem, prevents an invasion. A high title of honour is conferred upon him. Ambassadors arrive from the Emperor of Blefuscu, and sue for peace. The Empress's apartment on fire by an accident; the author instrumental in saving the rest of the palace.

THE EMPIRE OF Blefuscu is an island situated to the north-east of Lilliput, from which it is parted only by a channel of eight hundred yards wide. I had not yet seen it, and upon this notice of an intended invasion, I avoided appearing on that side of the coast, for fear of being discovered by some of the enemy's ships, who had received no intelligence of me; all intercourse between the two empires having been strictly forbidden during the war, upon pain of death, and an embargo laid by our Emperor upon all vessels whatsoever. I communicated to his Majesty a project I had formed of seizing the enemy's whole fleet; which, as

our scouts assured us, lay at anchor in the harbour, ready to
sail with the first fair wind. I consulted the most experienced
seamen upon the depth of the channel, which they had often
plumbed; who told me, that in the middle, at high water, it
was seventy *glumgluffs* deep, which is about six feet of European measure; and the rest of it fifty *glumgluffs* at most. I
walked toward the north-east coast, over against Blefuscu,
where, lying down behind a hillock, I took out my small perspective glass, and viewed the enemy's fleet at anchor, consisting of about fifty men-of-war, and a great number of
transports: I then came back to my house, and gave orders
(for which I had a warrant) for a great quantity of the
strongest cable and bars of iron. The cable was about as
thick as packthread, and the bars of the length and size of a
knitting-needle. I trebled the cable to make it stronger, and
for the same reason I twisted three of the iron bars together,
bending the extremities into a hook. Having thus fixed fifty
hooks to as many cables, I went back to the north-east coast,
and, putting off my coat, shoes, and stockings, walked into
the sea, in my leathern jerkin, about half an hour before high
water. I waded with what haste I could, and swam in the middle about thirty yards, till I felt ground. I arrived at the fleet
in less than half an hour. The enemy was so frightened when
they saw me, that they leaped out of their ships, and swam to
shore, where there could not be fewer than thirty thousand
souls: I then took my tackling, and, fastening a hook to the
hole at the prow of each, I tied all the cords together at the
end. While I was thus employed, the enemy discharged several thousand arrows, many of which stuck in my hands and
face; and, besides the excessive smart, gave me much disturbance in my work. My greatest apprehension was for mine
eyes, which I should have infallibly lost, if I had not suddenly
thought of an expedient. I kept, among other little necessaries, a pair of spectacles in a private pocket, which, as I

observed before, had escaped the Emperor's searchers. These
I took out, and fastened as strongly as I could upon my nose,
and thus armed, went on boldly with my work, in spite of the
enemy's arrows, many of which struck against the glasses of
my spectacles, but without any other effect farther than a
little to discompose them. I had now fastened all the hooks,
and taking the knot in my hand, began to pull; but not a ship
would stir, for they were all too fast held by their anchors,
so that the boldest part of my enterprise remained. I therefore let go the cord, and, leaving the hooks fixed to the ships,
I resolutely cut with my knife the cables that fastened the
anchors, receiving about two hundred shots in my face and
hands; then I took up the knotted end of the cables, to which
my hooks were tied, and with great ease drew fifty of the
enemy's largest men-of-war after me.

The Blefuscudians, who had not the least imagination
of what I intended, were at first confounded with astonishment. They had seen me cut the cables, and thought my design
was only to let the ships run a-drift, or fall foul on each other;
but when they perceived the whole fleet moving in order, and
saw me pulling at the end, they set up such a scream of grief
and despair, as it is almost impossible to describe or conceive.
When I had got out of danger, I stopped awhile to pick out
the arrows that stuck in my hands and face; and rubbed on
some of the same ointment that was given me at my first
arrival, as I formerly mentioned. I then took off my spectacles, and, waiting about an hour, till the tide was a little fallen,
I waded through the middle with my cargo, and arrived safe
at the royal port of Lilliput.

The Emperor and his whole court stood on the shore,
expecting the issue of this great adventure. They saw the
ships move forward in a large half-moon, but could not discern me, who was up to my breast in water. When I advanced to the middle of the channel, they were yet more in

pain, because I was under water to my neck. The Emperor concluded me to be drowned, and that the enemy's fleet was approaching in a hostile manner: but he was soon eased of his fears; for the channel growing shallower every step I made, I came in a short time within hearing, and, holding up the end of the cable, by which the fleet was fastened, I cried in a loud voice, "Long live the most puissant Emperor of Lilliput!" This great prince received me at my landing with all possible encomiums, and created me a *Nardac* upon the spot, which is the highest title of honour among them.

His Majesty desired I would take some other opportunity of bringing all the rest of his enemy's ships into his ports. And so unmeasurable is the ambition of princes, that he seemed to think of nothing less than reducing the whole empire of Blefuscu into a province, and governing it by a viceroy; of destroying the Big-endian exiles, and compelling that people to break the smaller end of their eggs, by which he would remain the sole monarch of the whole world. But I endeavoured to divert him from this design, by many arguments drawn from the topics of policy as well as justice; and I plainly protested, that I would never be an instrument of bringing a free and brave people into slavery. And, when the matter was debated in council, the wisest part of the ministry were of my opinion.

This open, bold declaration of mine was so opposite to the schemes and politics of his Imperial Majesty, that he could never forgive me. He mentioned it in a very artful manner at council, where I was told that some of the wisest appeared, at least by their silence, to be of my opinion; but others, who were my secret enemies, could not forbear some expressions, which, by a sidewind, reflected on me. And from this time began an intrigue between his Majesty and a junto of ministers, maliciously bent against me, which broke out in less than two months, and had like to have ended in my utter destruction. Of so little weight are the greatest services to princes, when put into the balance with a refusal to gratify their passions.

About three weeks after this exploit, there arrived a solemn embassy from Blefuscu, with humble offers of a peace; which was soon concluded, upon conditions very advantageous to our Emperor, wherewith I shall not trouble the reader. There were six ambassadors, with a train of about five hundred persons: and their entry was very magnificent, suitable to the grandeur of their master, and the importance of their business. When their treaty was finished, wherein I did them several good offices by the credit I now had, or at least appeared to have, at court, their Excellencies, who were privately told how much I had been their friend, made me a visit in form. They began with many compliments upon my valour and generosity, invited me to that kingdom in the Emperor their master's name, and desired me to shew them some proofs of my prodigious strength, of which they had heard so many wonders; wherein I readily obliged them, but shall not trouble the reader with the particulars.

When I had for some time entertained their Excellencies, to their infinite satisfaction and surprise, I desired they would do me the honour to present my most humble respects to the Emperor their master, the renown of whose virtues had so justly filled the whole world with admiration, and whose royal person I resolved to attend, before I returned to my own country. Accordingly, the next time I had the honour to see our Emperor, I desired his general licence to wait on the Blefuscudian monarch, which he was pleased to grant me, as I could plainly perceive, in a very cold manner; but could not guess the reason, till I had a whisper from a certain person, "that Flimnap and Bolgolam had represented my intercourse with those ambassadors as a mark of disaffection;" from which I am sure my heart was wholly free. And this was the first time I began to conceive some imperfect idea of courts and ministers.

It is to be observed, that these ambassadors spoke to me by an interpreter, the languages of both empires differing as much from each other as any two in Europe, and each nation priding itself upon the antiquity, beauty, and energy of their own tongues, with an avowed contempt for that of their neighbour: yet our Emperor, standing upon the advantage he had got by the seizure of their fleet, obliged them to deliver their credentials, and make their speech in the Lilliputian tongue. And it must be confessed, that, from the great intercourse of trade and commerce between both realms, from the continual reception of exiles, which is mutual among them, and from the custom in each empire to send their young nobility and richer gentry to the other, in order to polish themselves by seeing the world, and understanding men and manners, there are few persons of distinction, or merchants, or seamen, who dwell in the maritime parts, but what can hold conversation in both tongues; as I found some weeks after, when I went to pay my respects to the Emperor of Blefuscu, which, in the midst of great misfortunes, through the malice of my enemies, proved a very happy adventure to me, as I shall relate in its proper place.

The reader may remember, that when I signed those articles upon which I recovered my liberty, there were some which I disliked, upon account of their being too servile; neither could anything but an extreme necessity have forced me to submit. But being now a *Nardac* of the highest rank in that empire, such offices were looked upon as below my dignity, and the Emperor, (to do him justice) never once mentioned them to me. However, it was not long before I had an opportunity of doing his Majesty, at least as I then thought, a most signal service. I was alarmed at midnight with the cries of many hundred people at my door; by which being suddenly awakened, I was in some kind of terror. I heard the word *burglum* repeated incessantly: several of the Emperor's court making their way through the crowd, entreated me to come immediately to the palace where her Imperial Majesty's apartment was on fire, by the carelessness of a maid of honour, who fell asleep while she was reading a romance. I got up in an instant; and orders being given to clear the way before me, and it being likewise a moonshine night, I made a shift to get to the palace without trampling on any of the people. I found they had already applied ladders to the walls of the apartment, and were well provided with buckets, but the water was at some distance. The buckets were about the size of large thimbles, and the poor people supplied me with them as fast as they could: but the flame was so violent, that they did little good. I might easily have stifled it with my coat, which I unfortunately left behind me for haste, and came away only in my leathern jerkin. The case seemed wholly desperate and deplorable: and this magnificent palace would have infallibly been burnt down to the ground, if, by a presence of mind unusual to me, I had not suddenly thought of an expedient. I had the evening before drunk plentifully of a most delicious wine called *glimigrim,* (the Blefuscudians call it *flunec,* but ours is esteemed the better sort,) which is very diuretic. By the luckiest chance in the world, I had not discharged myself of any part of it. The heat I had contracted by coming very near the flames, and by my labouring to quench them, made the wine begin to operate by urine; which I voided in such a quantity, and applied so well to the proper places, that in three minutes the fire was wholly extinguished, and the rest of that noble pile, which had cost so many ages in erecting, preserved from destruction.

It was now day-light, and I returned to my house without waiting to congratulate with the Emperor; because, although I had done a very eminent piece of service, yet I

could not tell how his Majesty might resent the manner by
which I had performed it: for, by the fundamental laws of
the realm, it is capital in any person, of what quality soever,
to make water within the precincts of the palace. But I was
a little comforted by a message from his Majesty, that he
would give orders to the grand justiciary for passing my
pardon in form: which, however, I could not obtain. And I
was privately assured that the Empress, conceiving the greatest abhorrence of what I had done, removed to the most distant side of the court, firmly resolved that those buildings
should never be repaired for her use; and, in the presence of
her chief confidants, could not forbear vowing revenge.

CHAPTER 6

*Of the inhabitants of Lilliput; their learning, laws, and cus-
toms: the manner of educating their children. The author's
way of living in that country. His vindication of a great lady.*

ALTHOUGH I intend to leave
the description of this empire to a particular treatise, yet in
the meantime, I am content to gratify the curious reader
with some general ideas. As the common size of the natives
is somewhat under six inches high, so there is an exact proportion in all other animals, as well as plants and trees: for
instance, the tallest horses and oxen are between four and
five inches in height, the sheep an inch and half, more or less;
their geese about the bigness of a sparrow, and so the several
gradations downwards, till you come to the smallest, which,
to my sight, were almost invisible; but nature has adapted

the eyes of the Lilliputians to all objects proper for their view: they see with great exactness but at no great distance. And, to shew the sharpness of their sight towards objects that are near, I have been much pleased with observing a cook pulling a lark, which was not so large as a common fly; and a young girl threading an invisible needle with invisible silk. Their tallest trees are about seven feet high; I mean some of those in the royal park, the tops whereof I could but just reach with my fist clinched. The other vegetables are in the same proportion; but this I leave to the reader's imagination.

I shall say but little at present of their learning, which for many ages has flourished in all its branches among them; but their manner of writing is very peculiar, being neither from the left to the right, like the Europeans; nor from the right to the left, like the Arabians; nor from up to down like the Chinese: but aslant from one corner of the paper to the other, like ladies in England.

They bury their dead with their heads directly downward, because they hold an opinion, that in eleven thousand moons they are all to rise again; in which period the earth (which they conceive to be flat) will turn upside down, and by this means they shall at their resurrection be found ready standing on their feet. The learned among them confess the absurdity of this doctrine; but the practice still continues, in compliance to the vulgar.

There are some laws and customs in this empire very peculiar, and if they were not so directly contrary to those of my own dear country, I should be tempted to say a little in their justification. It is only to be wished they were as well executed. The first I shall mention, relates to informers. All crimes against the state are punished here with the utmost severity; but, if the person accused makes his innocence plainly to appear upon his trial, the accuser is immediately put to an ignominious death; and out of his goods or lands the innocent person is quadruply recompensed for the loss of his time, for the danger he underwent, for the hardship of his imprisonment, and for all the charges he has been at of making his defence. Or, if that fund be deficient, it is largely supplied by the crown. The Emperor also confers on him some public mark of his favour, and proclamation is made of his innocence through the whole city.

They look upon fraud as a greater crime than theft, and therefore seldom fail to punish it with death; for they allege, that care and vigilance, with a very common understanding, may preserve a man's goods from thieves, but honesty has no fence against superior cunning; and, since it is necessary that there should be a perpetual intercourse of buying and selling, and dealing upon credit, where fraud is permitted and connived at, or has no law to punish it, the honest dealer is always undone, and the knave gets the advantage. I remember, when I was once interceding with the king for a criminal who had wronged his master of a great sum of money, which he had received by order, and ran away with; and happening to tell his Majesty, by way of extenuation, that it was only a breach of trust, the Emperor thought it monstrous in me to offer as a defence the greatest aggravation of the crime; and truly I had little to say in return, farther than the common answer, that different nations had different customs; for I confess, I was heartily ashamed.

Although we usually call reward and punishment the two hinges upon which all government turns, yet I could never observe this maxim to be put in practice by any nation, except that of Lilliput. Whoever can there bring sufficient proof, that he has strictly observed the laws of his country for seventy-three moons, has a claim to certain privileges, according to his quality or condition of life, with a proportionable sum of money out of a fund appropriated for that use: he likewise acquires the title of *Snilpall,* or Legal, which is added to his name, but does not descend to his posterity. And these people thought it a prodigious defect of policy among us, when I told them that our laws were enforced only by penalties, without any mention of reward. It is upon this account that the image of Justice, in their courts of judicature, is formed with six eyes, two before, as many behind, and on each side one, to signify circumspection; with a bag of gold open in her right hand, and a sword sheathed in her left, to shew she is more disposed to reward than to punish.

In choosing persons for all employments, they have more regard to good morals than to great abilities; for, since government is necessary to mankind, they believe that the common size of human understanding is fitted to some station or other; and that Providence never intended to make the management of public affairs a mystery to be comprehended only by a few persons of sublime genius, of which there seldom are three born in an age: but they suppose truth, justice, temperance, and the like, to be in every man's power; the practice of which virtues, assisted by experience and a good intention, would qualify any man for the service of his country, except where a course of study is required. But they thought the want of moral virtues was so far from being supplied by superior endowments of the mind, that employments could never be put into such dangerous hands as those of persons so qualified; and, at least, that the mistakes committed by ignorance, in a virtuous disposition, would never be of such fatal consequence to the public weal, as the practices of a man, whose inclinations led him to be corrupt, and who had great abilities to manage, to multiply, and defend his corruptions.

In like manner, the disbelief of a Divine Providence renders a man incapable of holding any public station; for, since kings avow themselves to be the deputies of Providence, the

Lilliputians think nothing can be more absurd than for a prince to employ such men as disown the authority under which he acts.

In relating these and the following laws, I would only be understood to mean the original institutions, and not the most scandalous corruptions, into which these people are fallen by the degenerate nature of man. For, as to that infamous practice of acquiring great employments by dancing on the ropes, or badges of favour and distinction, by leaping over sticks and creeping under them, the reader is to observe, that they were first introduced by the grandfather of the Emperor now reigning, and grew to the present height by the gradual increase of party and faction.

Ingratitude is among them a capital crime, as we read it to have been in some other countries; for they reason thus, that whoever makes ill returns to his benefactor, must needs be a common enemy to the rest of mankind, from whom he has received no obligation, and therefore such a man is not fit to live.

Their notions relating to the duties of parents and children differ extremely from ours. For, since the conjunction of male and female is founded upon the great law of nature, in order to propagate and continue the species, the Lilliputians will needs have it that men and women are joined together, like other animals, by the motives of concupiscence; and that their tenderness towards their young proceeds from the like natural principle: for which reason, they will never allow that a child is under any obligation to his father for begetting him, or to his mother for bringing him into the world; which, considering the miseries of human life, was neither a benefit in itself, nor intended so by his parents, whose thoughts, in their love encounters, were otherwise employed. Upon these, and the like reasonings, their opinion is, that parents are the last of all others to be trusted with the education of their own children: and therefore, they have in every town public nurseries, where all parents, except cottagers and labourers, are obliged to send their infants of both sexes to be reared and educated, when they come to the age of twenty moons, at which time they are supposed to have some rudiments of docility. These schools are of several kinds, suited to different qualities, and to both sexes. They have certain professors, well skilled in preparing children for such a condition of life as befits the rank of their parents, and their own capacities, as well as inclinations. I shall first say something of the male nurseries, and then of the female.

The nurseries for males of noble or eminent birth, are provided with grave and learned professors, and their several deputies. The clothes and food of the children are plain and simple. They are bred up in the principles of honour, justice, courage, modesty, clemency, religion, and love of their country; they are always employed in some business, except in times of eating and sleeping, which are very short, and two hours for diversions consisting of bodily exercises. They are dressed by men till four years of age, and then are obliged to dress themselves, although their quality be ever so great; and the women attendants, who are aged proportionably to ours at fifty, perform only the most menial offices. They are never suffered to converse with servants, but go together in smaller or greater numbers to take their diversions, and always in the presence of a professor, or one of his deputies; whereby they avoid those early bad impressions of folly and vice, to which our children are subject. Their parents are suffered to see them only twice a-year; the visit is to last but an hour; they are allowed to kiss the child at meeting and parting; but a professor, who always stands by on those occasions, will not suffer them to whisper, or use any fondling expressions, or bring any presents of toys, sweetmeats, and the like.

The pension from each family for the education and

entertainment of a child, upon failure of due payment, is levied by the Emperor's officers.

The nurseries for children of ordinary gentlemen, merchants, traders, and handicrafts, are managed proportionably after the same manner; only those designed for trades are put out apprentices at eleven years old; whereas those of persons of quality continue in their exercises till fifteen, which answers to twenty-one with us; but the confinement is gradually lessened for the last three years.

In the female nurseries, the young girls of quality are educated much like the males, only they are dressed by orderly servants of their own sex: but always in the presence of a professor or deputy, till they come to dress themselves, which is at five years old. And if it be found, that these nurses ever presume to entertain the girls with frightful or foolish stories, or the common follies practised by chamber-maids among us, they are publicly whipped thrice about the city, imprisoned for a year, and banished for life to the most desolate part of the country. Thus, the young ladies there are as much ashamed of being cowards and fools as the men; and despise all personal ornaments, beyond decency and cleanliness: neither did I perceive any difference in their education, made by their difference of sex, only that the exercises of the females were not altogether so robust; and that some rules were given them relating to domestic life, and a smaller compass of learning was enjoined them: for their maxim is, that among people of quality, a wife should be always a reasonable and agreeable companion, because she cannot always be young. When the girls are twelve years old, which among them is the marriageable age, their parents or guardians take them home, with great expressions of gratitude to the professors, and seldom without tears of the young lady and her companions.

In the nurseries of females of the meaner sort, the children are instructed in all kinds of works proper for their sex, and their several degrees; those intended for apprentices are dismissed at seven years old, the rest are kept to eleven.

The meaner families, who have children at these nurseries, are obliged, beside their annual pension, which is as low as possible, to return to the steward of the nursery small monthly share of their gettings, to be a portion for the child; and therefore all parents are limited in their expenses by the law. For the Lilliputians think nothing can be more unjust than for people, in subservience to their own appetites, to bring children into the world, and leave the burden of supporting them on the public. As to persons of quality, they give security to appropriate a certain sum for each child, suitable to their condition; and these funds are always managed with good husbandry, and the most exact justice.

The cottagers and labourers keep their children at home, their business being only to till and cultivate the earth, and therefore their education is of little consequence to the public; but the old and diseased among them are supported by hospitals, for begging is a trade unknown in this empire.

And here it may perhaps divert the curious reader, to give some account of my domestics, and my manner of living in this country, during a residence of nine months and thirteen days. Having a head mechanically turned, and being likewise forced by necessity, I had made for myself a table and chair convenient enough, out of the largest trees in the royal park. Two hundred sempstresses were employed to make me shirts, and linen for my bed and table, all of the strongest and coarsest kind they could get; which however they were forced to quilt together in several folds, for the thickest was some degrees finer than lawn. Their linen is usually three inches wide, and three feet make a piece. The sempstresses took my measure as I lay on the ground, one standing at my neck, and another at my midleg, with a strong cord extended, that each held by the end, while a third measured the length of the cord with a rule of an inch long. Then they measured my right thumb, and desired no more; for, by a mathematical computation, that twice round the thumb is once round the wrist, and so on to the neck and the waist; and by the help of my old shirt, which I displayed on the ground before them for a pattern, they fitted me exactly. Three hundred tailors were employed in the same manner to make me clothes, but they had another contrivance for taking my measure. I kneeled down, and they raised a ladder from the ground to my neck; upon this ladder one of them mounted, and let fall a plumb-line from my collar to the floor, which just answered the length of my coat, but my waist and arms I measured myself. When my clothes were finished, which was done in my house, (for the largest of theirs would not have been able to hold them,) they looked like the patch-work made by the ladies in England, only that mine were all of a colour.

I had three hundred cooks to dress my victuals, in little convenient huts built about my house, where they and their families lived, and prepared me two dishes apiece. I took up twenty waiters in my hand, and placed them on the table: a hundred more attended below on the ground, some with dishes of meat, and some with barrels of wine, and other liquors, slung on their shoulders; all which the waiters above drew up, as I wanted, in a very ingenious manner, by certain cords, as we draw the bucket up a well in Europe. A dish of their meat was a good mouthful, and a barrel of their liquor a reasonable draught. Their mutton yields to ours, but their beef is excellent. I have had a sirloin so large, that I have been forced to make three bites of it, but this is rare. My servants were astonished to see me eat it, bones and all, as in our country we do the leg of a lark. Their geese and turkeys I usu-ally eat at a mouthful, and I confess they far exceed ours. Of their smaller fowl, I could take up twenty or thirty at the end of my knife.

One day his Imperial Majesty, being informed of my way of living, desired that himself and his royal consort,

with the young princes of the blood of both sexes, might have
the happiness, as he was pleased to call it, of dining with
me. They came accordingly, and I placed them in chairs of
state, upon my table, just over against me, with their guards
about them. Flimnap, the lord high treasurer, attended there
likewise with his white staff; and I observed he often looked
on me with a sour countenance, which I would not seem to
regard, but eat more than usual, in honour to my dear country, as well as to fill the court with admiration. I have some
private reasons to believe that this visit from his Majesty
gave Flimnap an opportunity of doing me ill offices to his
master. That minister had always been my secret enemy,
though he outwardly caressed me more than was usual to the
moroseness of his nature. He represented to the Emperor the
low condition of his treasury; that he was forced to take up
money at a great discount; that exchequer bills would not
circulate under nine per cent. below par; that I had cost his
Majesty above a million and a half of *sprugs,* (their greatest
gold coin, about the bigness of a spangle;) and, upon the
whole, that it would be advisable in the Emperor to take the
first fair occasion of dismissing me.

I am here obliged to vindicate the reputation of an
excellent lady, who was an innocent sufferer upon my account.
The treasurer took a fancy to be jealous of his wife, from the
malice of some evil tongues, who informed him that her grace
had taken a violent affection for my person; and the court
scandal ran for some time, that she once came privately to
my lodging. This I solemnly declare to be a most infamous
falsehood, without any grounds, farther than that her grace
was pleased to treat me with all innocent marks of freedom
and friendship. I own she often came to my house, but always
publicly, nor even without three more in the coach, who were
usually her sister and young daughter, and some particular
acquaintance; but this was common to many other ladies of
the court. And I still appeal to my servants round, whether

they at any time saw a coach at my door without knowing what persons were in it. On those occasions, when a servant had given me notice, my custom was to go immediately to the door, and after paying my respects, to take up the coach and two horses very carefully in my hands, (for, if there were six horses, the postillion always unharnessed four,) and placed them on a table, where I had fixed a moveable rim quite round, of five inches high, to prevent accidents. And I have often had four coaches and horses at once on my table, full of company, while I sat in my chair, leaning my face towards them; and when I was engaged with one set, the coachmen would gently drive the others round my table. I have passed many an afternoon very agreeably in these conversations. But I defy the treasurer, or his two informers, (I will name them, and let them make the best of it,) Clustril and Drunlo, to prove that any person ever came to me *incognito,* except the Secretary Reldresal, who was sent by express command of his Imperial Majesty, as I have before related. I should not have dwelt so long upon this particular, if it had not been a point wherein the reputation of a great lady is so nearly concerned, to say nothing of my own; though I then had the honour to be a *Nardac,* which the treasurer himself is not; for all the world knows, that he is only a *Glumglum,* a title inferior by one degree, as that of a marquis is to a duke in England; yet I allow he preceded me, in right of his post. These false informations, which I afterwards came to the knowledge of by an accident not proper to mention, made the treasurer shew his lady for some time an ill countenance, and me a worse; and although he was at last undeceived and reconciled to her, yet I lost all credit with him, and found my interest decline very fast with the Emperor himself, who was indeed too much governed by that favourite.

CHAPTER 7

The author, being informed of a design to accuse him of high treason, makes his escape to Blefuscu. His reception there.

Before I proceed to give an account of my leaving this kingdom, it may be proper to inform the reader of a private intrigue, which had been for two months forming against me.

I had been hitherto, all my life, a stranger to courts, for which I was unqualified by the meanness of my condition. I had indeed heard and read enough of the dispositions of great princes and ministers, but never expected to have found such terrible effects of them, in so remote a country, governed, as I thought, by very different maxims from those in Europe.

When I was just preparing to pay my attendance on the Emperor of Blefuscu, a considerable person at court (to whom I had been very serviceable, at a time when he lay under the highest displeasure of his Imperial Majesty) came to my house very privately at night, in a close chair, and, without sending his name, desired admittance. The chairmen were dismissed: I put the chair, with his Lordship in it, into my coat-pocket: and, giving orders to a trusty servant to say I was indisposed and gone to sleep, I fastened the door of my house, placed the chair on the table, according to my usual custom, and sat down by it. After the common salutations were over, observing his Lordship's countenance full of concern, and inquiring into the reason, he desired "I would hear him with patience, in a matter that highly concerned my honour and life." His speech was to the following effect, for I took notes of it as soon as he left me:—

"You are to know," said he, "that several committees of council have been lately called, in the most private manner, on your account; and it is but two days since his Majesty came to a full resolution.

"You are very sensible that Skyresh Bolgolam, (*Galbet,* or High-Admiral,) has been your mortal enemy, almost ever since your arrival. His original reasons I know not; but his hatred is increased since your great success against Blefuscu, by which his glory as Admiral is much obscured. This lord in conjunction with Flimnap the High-Treasurer, whose enmity against you is notorious, on account of his lady, Limtoc the General, Lalcon the Chamberlain, and Blamuff the Grand Justiciary, have prepared articles of impeachment against you, for treason and other capital crimes."

This preface made me so impatient, being conscious of my own merits and innocence, that I was going to interrupt him, when he entreated me to be silent, and thus proceeded:—

"Out of gratitude for the favours you have done me, I procured information of the whole proceedings, and a copy of the articles, wherein I venture my head for your service.

Articles of Impeachment against QUINBUS FLESTRIN, *the Man-Mountain*

ARTICLE I

"Whereas, by a statute made in the reign of his Imperial Majesty Calin Deffar Plune, it is enacted, that whoever shall make water within the precincts of the royal palace, shall be liable to the pains and penalties of high treason; notwithstanding, the said Quinbus Flestrin, in open breach of the said law, under colour of extinguishing the fire kindled in the apartment of his Majesty's most dear imperial consort, did maliciously, traitorously, and devilishly, by discharge of his urine, put out the said fire kindled in the said apartment, lying and being within the precincts of the said royal palace, against the statute in that case provided, *etc.,* against the duty, *etc.*

ARTICLE II

"That the said Quinbus Flestrin, having brought the imperial fleet of Blefuscu into the royal port, and being afterwards commanded by his Imperial Majesty to seize all the other ships of the said empire of Blefuscu, and reduce that empire to a province, to be governed by a viceroy from hence, and to destroy and put to death, not only all the Big-endian exiles, but likewise all the people of that empire who would not immediately forsake the Big-endian heresy; he, the said Flestrin, like a false traitor against his most Auspicious, Serene, Imperial Majesty, did petition to be excused from the said service, upon pretence of unwillingness to force the consciences, or destroy the liberties and lives, of an innocent people.

ARTICLE III

"That, whereas certain ambassadors arrived from the court of Blefuscu, to sue for peace in his Majesty's court; he, the said Flestrin, did, like a false traitor, aid, abet, comfort, and divert the said ambassadors, although he knew them to be servants to a prince who was lately an open enemy to his Imperial Majesty, and in an open war against his said Majesty.

ARTICLE IV

"That the said Quinbus Flestrin, contrary to the duty of a faithful subject, is now preparing to make a voyage to the court and empire of Blefuscu, for which he has received only verbal licence from his Imperial Majesty and, under colour of the said license, does falsely and traitorously intend to take the said voyage, and thereby to aid, comfort, and abet the emperor of Blefuscu, so lately an enemy, and in open war with his Imperial Majesty aforesaid."

"There are some other articles; but these are the most important, of which I have read you an abstract.

"In the several debates upon this impeachment, it must be confessed, that his Majesty gave many marks of his great lenity; often urging the services you have done him, and endeavouring to extenuate your crimes. The Treasurer and Admiral insisted that you should be put to the most painful and ignominious death, by setting fire to your house at night; and the General was to attend with twenty thousand men, armed with poisoned arrows, to shoot you on the face and hands. Some of your servants were to have private orders to strew a poisonous juice on your shirts and sheets, which would soon make you tear your own flesh, and die in the utmost torture. The General came into the same opinion; so that for a long time there was a majority against you; but his Majesty resolving, if possible, to spare your life, at last brought off the Chamberlain.

"Upon this incident, Reldresal, Principal Secretary for Private Affairs, who always approved himself your true friend, was commanded by the Emperor to deliver his opinion, which he accordingly did; and therein justified the good thoughts you have of him. He allowed your crimes to be great, but that still there was room for mercy, the most commendable virtue in a prince, and for which his Majesty was so justly celebrated. He said, the friendship between you and him was so well known to the world, that perhaps the most honourable board might think him partial; however, in obedience to the command he had received, he would freely offer his sentiments. That if his Majesty, in consideration of your services, and pursuant to his own merciful disposition, would please to spare your life, and only give orders to put out both your eyes, he humbly conceived, that, by this expedient, justice might in some measure be satisfied, and all the world would applaud the lenity of the Emperor, as well as the fair and

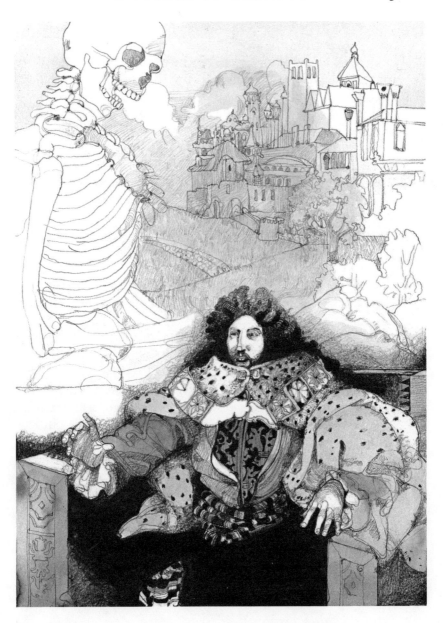

generous proceedings of those who have the honour to be his counsellors. That the loss of your eyes would be no impediment to your bodily strength, by which you might still be useful to his Majesty: that blindness is an addition to courage, by concealing dangers from us; that the fear you had for your eyes was the greatest difficulty in bringing over the enemy's fleet; and it would be sufficient for you to see by the eyes of the ministers, since the greatest princes could do no more.

"This proposal was received with the utmost disapprobation by the whole board. Bolgolam, the Admiral, could not preserve his temper; but, rising up in a fury, said, he wondered how the Secretary durst presume to give his opinion for preserving the life of a traitor: that the services you had performed were, by all true reasons of state, the great aggravation of your crimes; that you, who were able to extinguish the fire by discharge of urine in her Majesty's apartment, (which he mentioned with horror,) might at another time raise an inundation by the same means, to drown the whole palace; and the same strength, which enabled you to bring over the enemy's fleet, might serve, upon the first discontent, to carry it back: that he had good reasons to think you were a Big-endian in your heart; and as treason begins in the heart, before it appears in overt acts, so he accused you as a traitor on that account, and therefore insisted you should be put to death.

"The Treasurer was of the same opinion: he shewed to what straits his Majesty's revenue was reduced, by the charge of maintaining you, which would soon grow insupportable: that the Secretary's expedient of putting out your eyes was so far from being a remedy against this evil, that it would probably increase it, as is manifest from the common practice of blinding some kinds of fowls, after which they fed the faster, and grew sooner fat: that his sacred Majesty and the council, who are your judges, were in their own consciences fully convinced of your guilt, which was a sufficient argument to condemn you to death, without the formal proofs required by the strict letter of the law.

"But his Imperial Majesty, fully determined against capital punishment, was graciously pleased to say, that since the counsel thought the loss of your eyes too easy a censure, some other may be inflicted hereafter. And your friend the Secretary, humbly desiring to be heard again, in answer to what the Treasurer had objected, concerning the great charge his Majesty was at in maintaining you, said, that his Excellency, who had the sole disposal of the Emperor's revenue, might easily provide against that evil, by gradually lessening your establishment; by which, for want of sufficient food, you will grow weak and faint, and lose your appetite, and consume in a few months; neither would the stench of your carcase be then so dangerous, when it should become more than half diminished; and immediately upon your death, five or six thousand of his Majesty's subjects might, in two or three days, cut the flesh from your bones, take it away by cartloads, and bury it in distant parts, to prevent infection, leaving the skeleton as a monument of admiration to posterity.

"Thus, by the great friendship of the Secretary, the whole affair was compromised. It was strictly enjoined, that the project of starving you by degrees should be kept a secret; but the sentence of putting out your eyes was entered on the books; none dissenting, except Bolgolam the Admiral, who, being a creature of the Empress, was perpetually instigated by her Majesty to insist upon your death, she having borne perpetual malice against you on account of that infamous and illegal method you took to extinguish the fire in her apartment.

"In three days your friend the Secretary will be directed to come to your house, and read before you the articles of

impeachment; and then to signify the great lenity and favour
of his Majesty and council, whereby you are only condemned
to the loss of your eyes, which his Majesty does not question
you will gratefully and humbly submit to; and twenty of his
Majesty's surgeons will attend, in order to see the operation
well performed, by discharging very sharp-pointed arrows
into the balls of your eyes, as you lie on the ground.

"I leave to your prudence what measures you will take;
and, to avoid suspicion, I must immediately return, in as
private a manner as I came."

His Lordship did so; and I remained alone, under many
doubts and perplexities of mind.

It was a custom introduced by this prince and his ministry, (very different, as I have been assured, from the practice of former times,) that after the court had decreed any
cruel execution, either to gratify the monarch's resentment,
or the malice of a favourite, the Emperor always made a
speech to his whole council, expressing his great lenity and
tenderness, as qualities known and confessed by all the world.
This speech was immediately published throughout the kingdom; nor did anything terrify the people so much as those
encomiums on his Majesty's mercy; because it was observed,
that the more these praises were enlarged and insisted on,
the more inhuman was the punishment, and the sufferer more
innocent. Yet, as to myself, I must confess, having never
been designed for a courtier, either by my birth or education,
I was so ill a judge of things, that I could not discover the
lenity and favour of this sentence, but conceived it (perhaps
erroneously) rather to be rigorous than gentle. I sometimes
thought of standing my trial; for, although I could not deny
the facts alleged in the several articles, yet I hoped they
would admit of some extenuation. But, having in my life
perused many state-trials, which I ever observed to terminate
as the judges thought fit to direct, I durst not rely on so

dangerous a decision, in so critical a juncture, and against such powerful enemies. Once I was strongly bent upon resistance; for, while I had liberty, the whole strength of that empire could hardly subdue me, and I might easily with stones pelt the metropolis to pieces; but I soon rejected that project with horror, by remembering the oath I had made to the Emperor, the favours I received from him, and the high title of *Nardac* he conferred upon me. Neither had I so soon learned the gratitude of courtiers, to persuade myself, that his Majesty's present severities acquitted me of all past obligations.

At last, I fixed upon a resolution for which it is probable I may incur some censure, and not unjustly; for I confess I owe the preserving of my eyes, and consequently my liberty, to my own great rashness and want of experience; because, if I had then known the nature of princes and ministers, which I have since observed in many other courts, and their methods of treating criminals less obnoxious than myself, I should, with great alacrity and readiness, have submitted to so easy a punishment. But, hurried on by the precipitancy of youth, and having his Imperial Majesty's licence to pay my attendance upon the Emperor of Blefuscu, I took this opportunity, before the three days were elapsed, to send a letter to my friend the Secretary, signifying my resolution of setting out that morning for Blefuscu, pursuant to the leave I had got; and without waiting for an answer, I went to that side of the island where our fleet lay. I seized a large man-of-war, tied a cable to the prow, and, lifting up the anchors, I stripped myself, put my clothes (together with my coverlet, which I carried under my arm) into the vessel, and, drawing it after me, between wading and swimming, arrived at the royal port of Blefuscu, where the people had long expected me: they lent me two guides to direct me to the capital city, which is of the same name. I held them in my hands, till I came within two hundred yards of the gate, and desired them "to signify my arrival to one of the secretaries, and let him know, I there waited his Majesty's command." I had an answer in about an hour, "that his Majesty, attended by the royal family, and great officers of the court, was coming out to receive me." I advanced a hundred yards. The Emperor and his train alighted from their horses, the Empress and ladies from their coaches, and I did not perceive they were in any fright or concern. I lay on the ground to kiss his Majesty's and the Empress's hands. I told his Majesty, "that I was come, according to my promise, and with the licence of the Emperor my master, to have the honour of seeing so mighty a monarch, and to offer him any service in my power, consistent with my duty to my own prince;" not mentioning a word of my disgrace, because I had hitherto no regular information of it, and might suppose myself wholly ignorant of any such design; neither could I reasonably conceive that the Emperor would discover the secret, while I was out of his power; wherein, however, it soon appeared I was deceived.

I shall not trouble the reader with the particular account of my reception at this court, which was suitable to the generosity of so great a prince; nor of the difficulties I was in for want of a house and bed, being forced to lie on the ground, wrapped up in my coverlet.

CHAPTER 8

The author, by a lucky accident, finds means to leave Ble-
fuscu; and, after some difficulties, returns safe to his native
country.

THREE DAYS after my arrival, walking out of curiosity to the north-east coast of the island, I observed, about half a league off in the sea, somewhat that looked like a boat overturned. I pulled off my shoes and stockings, and, wading two or three hundred yards, I found the object to approach nearer by force of the tide; and then plainly saw it to be a real boat, which I supposed might by some tempest have been driven from a ship; whereupon I returned immediately towards the city, and desired his Imperial Majesty to lend me twenty of the tallest vessels he had left, after the loss of his fleet, and three thousand seamen, under the command of his Vice-Admiral. This fleet sailed round, while I went back the shortest way to the coast; where I first discovered the boat. I found the tide had driven it still nearer. The seamen were all provided with cordage, which I had beforehand twisted to a sufficient strength. When the ships came up, I stripped myself, and waded till I came within a hundred yards of the boat, after which I was forced to swim till I got up to it. The seamen threw me the end of the cord, which I fastened to a hole in the forepart of the boat, and the other end to a man-of-war; but I found all my labour to little purpose; for, being out of my depth, I was not able to work. In this necessity, I was forced to swim behind, and push the boat forward, as often as I could, with one of my hands; and the tide favouring me, I advanced so far that I could just hold up my chin and feel the ground. I rested two or three minutes, and then gave the boat another shove, and so on, till the sea was no higher than my arm-pits; and now, the most laborious part being over, I took out my other cables, which were stowed in one of the ships, and fastened them first to the boat, and then to nine of the vessels which attended me; the wind being favourable, the seamen towed and I shoved, until we arrived within forty yards of the shore; and, waiting till the tide was out, I got dry to the boat, and by the assistance of two thousand men, with ropes and engines, I made a shift to turn it on its bottom, and found it was but little damaged.

I shall not trouble the reader with the difficulties I was under, by the help of certain paddles, which cost me ten days making, to get my boat to the royal port of Blefuscu, where a mighty concourse of people appeared upon my arrival, full of wonder at the sight of so prodigious a vessel. I told the Emperor that my good fortune had thrown this boat in my way, to carry me to some place whence I might return into my native country; and begged his Majesty's orders for getting materials to fit it up, together with his licence to depart, which, after some kind expostulations, he was pleased to grant.

I did very much wonder, in all this time, not to have heard of any express relating to me from our Emperor to the court of Blefuscu. But I was afterward given privately to understand, that his Imperial Majesty, never imagining I had the least notice of his designs, believed I was only gone to Blefuscu in performance of my promise, according to the licence he had given me, which was well known at our court, and would return in a few days, when the ceremony was ended. But he was at last in pain at my long absence; and, after consulting with the Treasurer and the rest of that cabal, a person of quality was dispatched with the copy of the articles against me. This envoy had instructions to repre-sent to the monarch of Blefuscu, "the great lenity of his master, who was content to punish me no farther than with the loss of mine eyes; that I had fled from justice; and if I did not return in two hours, I should be deprived of my title of *Nardac,* and declared a traitor." The envoy farther added, "that in order to maintain the peace and amity between both empires, his master expected that his brother of Blefuscu would give orders to have me sent back to Lilliput, bound hand and foot, to be punished as a traitor."

The Emperor of Blefuscu, having taken three days to consult, returned an answer consisting of many civilities and excuses. He said that, as for sending me bound, his brother knew it was impossible; that although I had deprived him of his fleet, yet he owed great obligations to me for many good offices I had done him in making the peace. That, however, both their majesties would soon be made easy; for I had found a prodigious vessel on the shore, able to carry me on the sea, which he had given orders to fit up, with my own assistance and direction; and he hoped, in a few weeks, both empires would be freed from so insupportable an incumbrance.

With this answer the envoy returned to Lilliput; and the monarch of Blefuscu related to me all that had passed; offering me, at the same time, (but under the strictest confidence,) his gracious protection, if I would continue in his service, wherein although I believed him sincere, yet I resolved never more to put any confidence in princes or ministers, where I could possibly avoid it; and therefore, with all due acknowledgments for his favourable intentions, I humbly begged to be excused. I told him that, since fortune, whether good or evil, had thrown a vessel in my way, I was resolved to venture myself on the ocean, rather than be an occasion of difference between two such mighty monarchs. Neither did I find the Emperor at all displeased; and I discovered, by a certain accident, that he was very glad of my resolution, and so were most of his ministers.

These considerations moved me to hasten my departure somewhat sooner than I intended; to which the court, impatient to have me gone, very readily contributed. Five hundred workmen were employed to make two sails to my boat, according to my directions, by quilting thirteen folds of their strongest linen together. I was at the pains of making ropes and cables, by twisting ten, twenty, or thirty, of the thickest and strongest of theirs. A great stone that I happened to find, after a long search, by the sea-shore, served me for an anchor. I had the tallow of three hundred cows, for greasing my boat, and other uses. I was at incredible pains in cutting down some of the largest timber-trees, for oars and masts, wherein I was, however, much assisted by his Majesty's ship-carpenters, who helped me in smoothing them, after I had done the rough work.

In about a month, when all was prepared, I sent to receive his Majesty's commands, and to take my leave. The Emperor and royal family came out of the palace; I lay down on my face to kiss his hand, which he very graciously gave me; so did the Empress and young princes of the blood. His Majesty presented me with fifty purses of two hundred *sprugs* apiece, together with his picture at full length, which I put immediately into one of my gloves, to keep it from being hurt. The ceremonies at my departure were too many to trouble the reader with at this time.

I stored the boat with the carcases of an hundred oxen, and three hundred sheep, with bread and drink proportionable, and as much meat ready dressed as four hundred cooks could provide. I took with me six cows and two bulls alive, with as many ewes and rams, intending to carry them into my own country, and propagate the breed. And to feed them on board, I had a good bundle of hay, and a bag of corn. I would gladly have taken a dozen of the natives, but this was a thing the Emperor would by no means permit; and, besides a diligent search into my pockets, his Majesty engaged my honour not to carry away any of his subjects, although with their own consent and desire.

Having thus prepared all things as well as I was able, I set sail on the twenty-fourth day of September, 1701, at six in the morning; and when I had gone about four leagues to the northward, the wind being at south-east, at six in the evening I descried a small island, about half a league to the northwest. I advanced forward, and cast anchor on the lee-side of the island, which seemed to be uninhabited. I then took some refreshment, and went to my rest. I slept well, and, as I conjecture, at least six hours, for I found the day broke in two hours after I awaked. It was a clear night. I ate my breakfast before the sun was up; and heaving anchor, the wind being favourable, I steered the same course that I had done the day before, wherein I was directed by my pocket compass. My intention was to reach, if possible, one of those islands which I had reason to believe lay to the north-east of Van Diemen's Land. I discovered nothing all that day; but upon the next, about three in the afternoon, when I had, by my computation, made twenty-four leagues from Blefuscu, I descried a sail steering to the south-east; my course was due east. I hailed her, but could get no answer; yet I found I gained upon her, for the wind slackened. I made all the sail I could, and in half an hour she spied me, then hung out her ancient, and discharged a gun. It is not easy to express the joy I was in, upon the unexpected hope of once more seeing my beloved country, and the dear pledges I left in it. The ship slackened her sails, and I came up with her between five and six in the evening, September 26; but my heart leapt within me to see her English colours. I put my cows and sheep into my coat-pockets, and got on board with all my little cargo of provisions. The vessel was an English merchantman, returning from Japan by the North and South Seas; the captain,

Mr. John Biddel of Deptford, a very civil man, and an excellent sailor. We were now in the latitude of 30 degrees south;
there were about fifty men in the ship; and here I met an old
comrade of mine, one Peter Williams, who gave me a good
character to the captain. This gentleman treated me with
kindness, and desired I would let him know what place I came
from last, and whither I was bound; which I did in a few
words, but he thought I was raving, and that the dangers I
had underwent had disturbed my head; whereupon I took
my black cattle and sheep out of my pocket, which, after
great astonishment, clearly convinced him of my veracity.
I then shewed him the gold given me by the Emperor of
Blefuscu, together with his Majesty's picture at full length,
and some other rarities of that country. I gave him two
purses of two hundred *sprugs* each, and promised, when we
arrived in England, to make him a present of a cow and a
sheep big with young.

I shall not trouble the reader with a particular account
of this voyage, which was very prosperous for the most part.
We arrived in the Downs on the 13th of April, 1702. I had
only one misfortune, that the rats on board carried away
one of my sheep; I found her bones in a hole, picked clean
from the flesh. The rest of my cattle I got safe ashore, and
set them a-grazing in a bowling-green at Greenwich, where
the fineness of the grass made them feed very heartily, though
I had always feared the contrary; neither could I possibly
have preserved them in so long a voyage, if the captain had
not allowed me some of his best biscuit, which rubbed to
powder, and mingled with water, was their constant food.
The short time I continued in England, I made a considerable profit by shewing my cattle to many persons of quality
and others; and, before I began my second voyage, I sold
them for six hundred pounds. Since my last return I find the
breed is considerably increased, especially the sheep, which

I hope will prove much to the advantage of the woollen manu-
facture, by the fineness of the fleeces.

I stayed but two months with my wife and family; for
my insatiable desire of seeing foreign countries would suffer
me to continue no longer. I left fifteen hundred pounds with
my wife, and fixed her in a good house at Redriff. My remaining stock I carried with me, part in money, and part in goods,
in hopes to improve my fortunes. My eldest uncle John had
left me an estate in land, near Epping, of about thirty pounds
a-year; and I had a long lease of the Black Bull in Fetter-
lane, which yielded me as much more; so that I was not in any
danger of leaving my family upon the parish. My son
Johnny, named so after his uncle, was at the grammar-school,
and a towardly child. My daughter Betty (who is now well
married, and has children) was then at her needle-work. I
took my leave of my wife, and boy and girl, with tears on
both sides, and went on board the *Adventure,* a merchant
ship of three hundred tons, bound for Surat, Captain John
Nicholas, of Liverpool, commander. But my account of this
voyage must be referred to the second part of my travels.

THE END OF
A VOYAGE TO LILLIPUT

A VOYAGE TO

Brobdingnag

BROBDINGNAG

Flanflasnic

Lorbrulgrud

Discovered A.D. 1703

NORTH

AMERICA

Straits of Annian

C. Blanco

St. Sebastian

NEW

ALBION

C. Mendocino

P. Sir Francis Drake

Mount
St. Martin

P. Monterey

CHAPTER I

*A great storm described, the long-boat sent to fetch water,
the author goes with it to discover the country. He is left on
shore, is seized by one of the natives, and carried to a farmer's
house. His reception, with several accidents that happened
there. A description of the inhabitants.*

Having been condemned, by
nature and fortune, to an active and restless life, in two
months after my return, I again left my native country, and
took shipping in the Downs on the 20th day of June, 1702,
in the *Adventure,* Captain John Nicholas, a Cornish man,
commander, bound for Surat. We had a very prosperous gale,
till we arrived at the Cape of Good Hope, where we landed
for fresh water; but, discovering a leak, we unshipped our
goods, and wintered there; for the Captain falling sick of an
ague, we could not leave the Cape till the end of March. We
then set sail, and had a good voyage till we passed the Straits
of Madagascar; but having got northward of that island,
and to about five degrees south latitude, the winds, which in
those seas are observed to blow a constant equal gale between
the north and west, from the beginning of December to the
beginning of May, on the 19th of April began to blow with
much greater violence, and more westerly than usual, continuing so for twenty days together: during which time, we
were driven a little to the east of the Molucca Islands, and
about three degrees northward of the line, as our Captain
found by an observation he took the 2d of May, at which
time the wind ceased, and it was a perfect calm, whereat I
was not a little rejoiced. But he, being a man well experienced in the navigation of those seas, bid us all prepare
against a storm, which accordingly happened the day fol-

lowing: for the southern wind, called the southern monsoon, began to set in.

Finding it was likely to overblow, we took in our sprit-sail, and stood by to hand the fore-sail; but making foul weather, we looked the guns were all fast, and handed the mizzen. The ship lay very broad off, so we thought it better spooning before the sea, than trying or hulling. We reefed the fore-sail, and set him, and hauled aft the fore-sheet; the helm was hard a-weather. The ship wore bravely. We be-layed the fore downhaul; but the sail was split, and we hauled down the yard, and got the sail into the ship, and unbound all the things clear of it. It was a very fierce storm; the sea broke strange and dangerous. We hauled off upon the lanyard of the whipstaff, and helped the man at the helm. We would not get down our top-mast, but let all stand, because she scudded before the sea very well, and we knew that the top-mast being aloft the ship was the wholesomer, and made better way through the sea, seeing we had sea-room. When the storm was over, we set fore-sail and main-sail, and brought the ship to. Then we set the mizzen, main-top-sail, and the fore-top-sail. Our course was east-north-east, the wind was at south-west. We got the starboard tacks aboard, we cast off our weather-braces and lifts; we set-in the lee-braces, and hauled forward by the weather-bowlings, and hauled them tight, and belayed them, and hauled over the mizzen-tack to windward, and kept her full and by as near as she would lie.

During this storm, which was followed by a strong wind west-south-west, we were carried, by my computation, about five hundred leagues to the east, so that the oldest sailor on board could not tell in what part of the world we were. Our provisions held out well, our ship was staunch, and our crew all in good health; but we lay in the utmost dis-tress for water. We thought it best to hold on the same course, rather than turn more northerly, which might have brought us to the north-west part of Great Tartary, and into the Frozen Sea.

On the 16th day of June, 1703, a boy on the top-mast discovered land. On the 17th, we came in full view of a great island, or continent, (for we knew not whether;) on the south side whereof was a small neck of land jutting out into the sea, and a creek too shallow to hold a ship of above one hundred tons. We cast anchor within a league of this creek, and our captain sent a dozen of his men well armed in the long-boat, with vessels for water, if any could be found. I desired his leave to go with them, that I might see the country, and make what discoveries I could. When we came to land, we saw no river or spring, nor any sign of inhabitants. Our men therefore wandered on the shore to find out some fresh water near the sea, and I walked alone about a mile on the other side, where I observed the country all barren and rocky. I now began to be weary, and, seeing nothing to entertain my curiosity, I returned gently down towards the creek; and the sea being full in my view, I saw our men already got into the boat, and rowing for life to the ship. I was going to holla after them, although it had been to little purpose, when I observed a huge creature walking after them in the sea, as fast as he could: he waded not much deeper than his knees, and took prodigious strides: but our men had the start of him half a league, and, the sea thereabouts being full of sharp-pointed rocks, the monster was not able to overtake the boat. This I was afterwards told, for I durst not stay to see the issue of the adventure; but ran as fast as I could the way I first went, and then climbed up a steep hill, which gave me some prospect of the country. I found it fully cultivated; but that which first surprised me was the length of the grass, which, in those grounds that seemed to be kept for hay, was about twenty feet high.

I fell into a high road, for so I took it to be, though it
served to the inhabitants only as a foot-path through a field
of barley. Here I walked on for some time, but could see
little on either side, it being now near harvest, and the corn
rising at least forty feet. I was an hour walking to the end of
this field, which was fenced in with a hedge of at least one
hundred and twenty feet high, and the trees so lofty that I
could make no computation of their altitude. There was a
stile to pass from this field into the next. It had four steps, and
a stone to cross over when you came to the uppermost. It was
impossible for me to climb this stile, because every step was
six feet high, and the upper stone about twenty. I was endeavouring to find some gap in the hedge, when I discovered one of
the inhabitants in the next field, advancing towards the stile,
of the same size with him whom I saw in the sea pursuing our
boat. He appeared as tall as an ordinary spire-steeple, and
took about ten yards at every stride, as near as I could guess.
I was struck with the utmost fear and astonishment, and ran
to hide myself in the corn, whence I saw him at the top of
the stile, looking back into the next field on the right hand,
and heard him call in a voice many degrees louder than a
speaking-trumpet; but the noise was so high in the air, that
at first I certainly thought it was thunder. Whereupon seven
monsters, like himself, came towards him with reaping-hooks
in their hands, each hook about the largeness of six scythes.
These people were not so well clad as the first, whose servants
or labourers they seemed to be; for, upon some words he
spoke, they went to reap the corn in the field where I lay. I
kept from them at as great a distance as I could, but was
forced to move with extreme difficulty, for the stalks of the
corn were sometimes not above a foot distant, so that I could
hardly squeeze my body betwixt them. However, I made a
shift to go forward, till I came to a part of the field where the
corn had been laid by the rain and wind. Here it was impossi-

ble for me to advance a step; for the stalks were so interwoven, that I could not creep through, and the beards of the fallen ears so strong and pointed, that they pierced through my clothes into my flesh. At the same time I heard the reapers not above a hundred yards behind me. Being quite dispirited with toil, and wholly overcome by grief and despair, I lay down between two ridges, and heartily wished I might there end my days. I bemoaned my desolate widow and fatherless children. I lamented my own folly and wilfulness, in attempting a second voyage, against the advice of all my friends and relations. In this terrible agitation of mind, I could not forbear thinking of Lilliput, whose inhabitants looked upon me as the greatest prodigy that ever appeared in the world; where I was able to draw an imperial fleet in my hand, and perform those other actions which will be recorded for ever in the chronicles of that empire, while posterity shall hardly believe them, although attested by millions. I reflected what a mortification it must prove to me, to appear as inconsiderable in this nation as one single Lilliputian would be among us. But this I conceived was to be the least of my misfortunes; for, as human creatures are observed to be more savage and cruel in proportion to their bulk, what could I expect but to be a morsel in the mouth of the first among these enormous barbarians that should happen to seize me? Undoubtedly philosophers are in the right, when they tell us that nothing is great or little otherwise than by comparison. It might have pleased fortune, to have let the Lilliputians find some nation, where the people were as diminutive with respect to them, as they were to me. And who knows but that even this prodigious race of mortals might be equally overmatched in some distant part of the world, whereof we have yet no discovery.

Scared and confounded as I was, I could not forbear going on with these reflections, when one of the reapers, approaching within ten yards of the ridge where I lay, made me

apprehend that with the next step I should be squashed to
death under his foot, or cut in two with his reaping-hook.
And, therefore, when he was again about to move, I screamed
as loud as fear could make me : whereupon the huge creature
trod short, and looking round about under him for some time,
at last espied me as I lay on the ground. He considered a
while, with the caution of one who endeavours to lay hold
on a small dangerous animal in such a manner that it shall
not be able either to scratch or to bite him, as I myself have
sometimes done with a weasel in England. At length he ventured to take me behind, by the middle, between his fore-
finger and thumb, and brought me within three yards of his
eyes, that he might behold my shape more perfectly. I guessed
his meaning, and my good fortune gave me so much presence
of mind, that I resolved not to struggle in the least as he held
me in the air above sixty feet from the ground, although he
grievously pinched my sides, for fear I should slip through
his fingers. All I ventured was to raise mine eyes towards the
sun, and place my hands together in a supplicating posture,
and to speak some words in an humble melancholy tone,
suitable to the condition I then was in, for I apprehended
every moment that he would dash me against the ground, as
we usually do any little hateful animal, which we have a mind
to destroy. But my good star would have it, that he appeared
pleased with my voice and gestures, and began to look upon
me as a curiosity, much wondering to hear me pronounce
articulate words, although he could not understand them. In
the meantime, I was not able to forbear groaning and shed-
ding tears, and turning my head towards my sides ; letting
him know, as well as I could, how cruelly I was hurt by the
pressure of his thumb and finger. He seemed to apprehend
my meaning ; for, lifting up the lappet of his coat, he put me
gently into it, and immediately ran along with me to his master, who was a substantial farmer, and the same person I had
first seen in the field.

The farmer having (as I suppose by their talk) received such an account of me as his servant could give him, took a piece of a small straw, about the size of a walking staff, and therewith lifted up the lappets of my coat; which, it seems, he thought to be some kind of covering that nature had given me. He blew my hairs aside to take a better view of my face. He called his hands about him, and asked them, as I afterwards learned, whether they had ever seen in the fields any little creature that resembled me. He then placed me softly on the ground upon all four, but I got immediately up, and walked slowly backward and forward, to let those people see I had no intent to run away. They all sat down in a circle about me, the better to observe my motions. I pulled off my hat, and made a low bow towards the farmer. I fell on my knees, and lifted up my hands and eyes, and spoke several words as loud as I could: I took a purse of gold out of my pocket, and humbly presented it to him. He received it on the palm of his hand, then applied it close to his eye to see what it was, and afterwards turned it several times with the point of a pin, (which he took out of his sleeve,) but could make nothing of it. Whereupon I made a sign that he should place his hand on the ground. I then took the purse, and opening it, poured all the gold into his palm. There were six Spanish pieces of four pistoles each, beside twenty or thirty smaller coins. I saw him wet the tip of his little finger upon his tongue, and take up one of my largest pieces, and then another; but he seemed to be wholly ignorant what they were. He made me a sign to put them again into my purse, and the purse again into my pocket, which after offering it to him several times, I thought it best to do.

The farmer, by this time, was convinced I must be a rational creature. He spoke often to me; but the sound of his voice pierced my ears like that of a water-mill, yet his words were articulate enough. I answered as loud as I could in several languages, and he often laid his ear within two yards

of me; but all in vain, for we were wholly unintelligible to
each other. He then sent his servants to their work, and taking his handkerchief out of his pocket, he doubled, and spread
it on his left hand, which he placed flat on the ground, with
the palm upward, making me a sign to step into it, as I could
easily do, for it was not above a foot in thickness. I thought
it my part to obey; and, for fear of falling, laid myself at
full length upon the handkerchief, with the remainder of
which he lapped me up to the head for farther security, and in
this manner carried me home to his house. There he called
his wife, and shewed me to her; but she screamed and ran
back, as women in England do at the sight of a toad or a
spider. However, when she had awhile seen my behaviour,
and how well I observed the signs her husband made, she
was soon reconciled, and by degrees grew extremely tender
of me.

It was about twelve at noon, and a servant brought in
dinner. It was only one substantial dish of meat (fit for the
plain condition of a husbandman,) in a dish of about four-
and-twenty feet diameter. The company were the farmer and
his wife, three children, and an old grandmother. When they
were sat down, the farmer placed me at some distance from
him on the table, which was thirty feet high from the floor. I
was in a terrible fright, and kept as far as I could from the
edge, for fear of falling. The wife minced a bit of meat, then
crumbled some bread on a trencher, and placed it before me.
I made her a low bow, took out my knife and fork, and fell to
eat, which give them exceeding delight. The mistress sent her
maid for a small dramcup, which held about two gallons, and
filled it with drink; I took up the vessel with much difficulty
in both hands, and in a most respectful manner drank to her
ladyship's health, expressing the words as loud as I could
in English, which made the company laugh so heartily, that I
was almost deafened with the noise. This liquor tasted like

a small cider, and was not unpleasant. Then the master made me a sign to come to his trencher side; but as I walked on the table, being in great surprise all the time, as the indulgent reader will easily conceive and excuse, I happened to stumble against a crust, and fell flat on my face, but received no hurt. I got up immediately, and observing the good people to be in much concern, I took my hat, (which I held under my arm out of good manners,) and waving it over my head, made three huzzas, to shew I had got no mischief by my fall. But advancing forward towards my master (as I shall henceforth call him) his youngest son, who sat next to him, an arch boy of about ten years old, took me up by the legs, and held me so high in the air, that I trembled every limb; but his father snatched me from him, and at the same time gave him such a box on the left ear as would have felled an European troop of horse to the earth, ordering him to be taken from the table. But, being afraid the boy might owe me a spite, and well remembering how mischievous all children among us naturally are to sparrows, rabbits, young kittens, and puppy-dogs, I fell on my knees, and pointing to the boy, made my master to understand, as well as I could, that I desired his son might be pardoned. The father complied, and the lad took his seat again, whereupon I went to him, and kissed his hand, which my master took, and made him stroke me gently with it.

In the midst of dinner, my mistress's favourite cat leaped into her lap. I heard a noise behind me like that of a dozen stocking-weavers at work; and turning my head I found it proceeded from the purring of that animal, who seemed to be three times larger than an ox, as I computed by the view of her head, and one of her paws, while her mistress was feeding and stroking her. The fierceness of this creature's countenance altogether discomposed me; though I stood at the farther end of the table, above fifty feet off; and although my mistress held her fast, for fear she might give a spring, and seize me in her talons. But it happened there was no danger; for the cat took not the least notice of me when my master placed me within three yards of her. And, as I have been always told, and found true by experience in my travels, that flying or discovering fear before a fierce animal, is a certain way to make it pursue or attack you, so I resolved, in this dangerous juncture, to shew no manner of concern. I walked with intrepidity five or six times before the very head of the cat, and came within half a yard of her; whereupon she drew herself back, as if she were more afraid of me. I had less apprehension concerning the dogs, whereof three or four came into the room, as it is usual in farmers' houses; one of which was a mastiff, equal in bulk to four elephants, and a greyhound, somewhat taller than the mastiff, but not so large.

When dinner was almost done, the nurse came in with a child of a year old in her arms, who immediately spied me, and began a squall that you might have heard from London Bridge to Chelsea, after the usual oratory of infants, to get me for a plaything. The mother, out of pure indulgence, took me up, and put me towards the child, who presently seized me by the middle, and got my head into his mouth, where I roared so loud that the urchin was frighted, and let me drop, and I should infallibly have broke my neck, if the mother had not held her apron under me. The nurse, to quiet her babe, made use of a rattle, which was a kind of hollow vessel filled with great stones, and fastened by a cable to the child's waist: but all in vain, so that she was forced to apply the last remedy by giving it suck. I must confess no object ever disgusted me so much as the sight of her monstrous breast, which I cannot tell what to compare with, so as to give the curious reader an idea of its bulk, shape, and colour. It stood prominent six feet, and could not be less than sixteen in circumference. The nipple was about half the bigness of my head, and the hue, both of that and the dug, so varied with spots, pimples, and freckles, that nothing could appear more nauseous: for I had a near sight of her, she sitting down the more conveniently to give suck, and I standing on the table. This made me reflect upon the fair skins of our English ladies, who appear so beautiful to us, only because they are of our own size, and their defects not to be seen but through a magnifying glass; where we find by experiment, that the smoothest and whitest skins look rough, and coarse, and ill-coloured.

I remember, when I was at Lilliput, the complexions of those diminutive people appeared to me the fairest in the world; and talking upon this subject with a person of learning there, who was an intimate friend of mine, he said that my face appeared much fairer and smoother when he looked on me from the ground, than it did upon a nearer view, when I took him up in my hand, and brought him close, which he confessed was at first a very shocking sight. He said he could discover great holes in my skin; that the stumps of my beard were ten times stronger than the bristles of a boar, and my complexion made up of several colours altogether disagreeable; although I must beg leave to say for myself, that I am as fair as most of my sex and country, and very little sunburnt by all my travels. On the other side, discoursing of the ladies in that emperor's court, he used to tell me one had freckles, another too wide a mouth, a third too large a nose; nothing of which I was able to distinguish. I confess, this reflection was obvious enough; which, however, I could not forbear, lest the reader might think those vast creatures were actually deformed; for I must do them justice to say, they are a comely race of people; and particularly the features of my master's countenance, although he were but a farmer, when I beheld him from the height of sixty feet, appeared very well proportioned.

When dinner was done, my master went out to his labourers, and, as I could discover by his voice and gesture, gave his wife a strict charge to take care of me. I was very much tired, and disposed to sleep, which my mistress perceiving, she put me on her own bed, and covered me with a clean white handkerchief, but larger and coarser than the main-sail of a man-of-war.

I slept about two hours, and dreamt I was at home with my wife and children, which aggravated my sorrows when I awaked, and found myself alone in a vast room, between two and three hundred feet wide, and above two hundred high, lying in a bed twenty yards wide. My mistress was gone about her household affairs, and had locked me in. The bed was eight yards from the floor. Some natural necessities required me to get down; I durst not presume to call; and if I had, it would have been in vain, with such a voice as mine, at so great a distance as from the room where I lay to the kitchen where the family kept. While I was under these circumstances two rats crept up the curtains, and ran smelling backwards and forwards on the bed. One of them came up almost to my face, whereupon I rose in a fright, and drew out my hanger to defend myself. These horrible animals had the boldness to attack me on both sides, and one of them held his forefeet at my collar; but I had the good fortune to rip up his belly, before he could do me any mischief. He fell down at my feet; and the other, seeing the fate of his comrade, made his escape, but not without one good wound on the back, which I gave him as he fled, and made the blood run trickling from him. After this exploit, I walked gently to and fro on the bed, to recover my breath and loss of spirits. These creatures were of the size of a large mastiff, but infinitely more nimble and fierce; so that, if I had taken off my belt, before I went to sleep, I must have infallibly been torn to pieces and devoured. I measured the tail of the dead rat, and found it to be two yards long, wanting an inch; but it went against my stomach to drag the carcase off the bed, where it lay still bleeding; I observed it had yet some life, but with a strong slash across the neck, I thoroughly dispatched it.

Soon after my mistress came into the room, who, seeing me all bloody, ran and took me up in her hand. I pointed to the dead rat, smiling, and making other signs to shew I was not hurt; whereat she was extremely rejoiced, calling the maid to take up the dead rat with a pair of tongs, and throw it out of the window. Then she set me on a table, where I shewed her my hanger all bloody, and, wiping it on the lappet of my coat, returned it to the scabbard. I was pressed to do more than one thing which another could not do for me, and therefore endeavoured to make my mistress understand, that I desired to be set down on the floor; which, after she had done, my bashfulness would not suffer me to express myself farther, than by pointing to the door, and bowing several times. The good woman, with much difficulty, at last perceived what I would be at, and, taking me up again in her hand, walked into the garden, where she set me down. I went on one side about two hundred yards, and beckoning to her not to look or to follow me, I hid myself between two leaves of sorrel, and there discharged the necessities of nature.

I hope the gentle reader will excuse me for dwelling on these and the like particulars, which, however insignificant they may appear to grovelling vulgar minds, yet will certainly help a philosopher to enlarge his thoughts and imagination, and apply them to the benefit of public as well as private life, which was my sole design in presenting this and other accounts of my travels to the world; wherein I have been chiefly studious of truth, without affecting any ornaments of learning or of style. But the whole scene of this voyage made so strong an impression on my mind, and is so deeply fixed in my mem-

ory, that, in committing it to paper, I did not omit one material circumstance: however, upon a strict review, I blotted
out several passages of less moment, which were in my first
copy, for fear of being censured as tedious and trifling,
whereof travellers are often, perhaps not without justice,
accused.

CHAPTER 2

*A description of the farmer's daughter. The author carried to
a market-town, and then to the metropolis. The particulars
of his journey.*

M<small>Y MISTRESS</small> had a daughter
of nine years old, a child of towardly parts for her age, very
dexterous at her needle, and skilful in dressing her baby. Her
mother and she contrived to fit up the baby's cradle for me
against night; the cradle was put into a small drawer of a
cabinet, and the drawer placed upon a hanging shelf for fear
of the rats. This was my bed all the time I staid with those
people, though made more convenient by degrees as I began
to learn their language, and make my wants known. This
young girl was so handy, that, after I had once or twice
pulled off my clothes before her, she was able to dress and
undress me, though I never gave her that trouble when she
would let me do either myself. She made me seven shirts, and
some other linen, of as fine cloth as could be got, which indeed
was coarser than sackcloth; and these she constantly washed
for me with her own hands. She was likewise my schoolmis-
tress, to teach me the language: when I pointed to anything,

she told me the name of it in her own tongue, so that in a few days I was able to call for whatever I had a mind to. She was very good-natured, and not above forty feet high, being little for her age. She gave me the name of *Grildrig,* which the family took up, and afterwards the whole kingdom. The word imports what the Latins call *nanunculus,* the Italians *homunceletino,* and the English *mannikin.* To her I chiefly owe my preservation in that country: we never parted while I was there; I called her my *Glumdalclitch,* or little nurse; and should be guilty of great ingratitude, if I omitted this honourable mention of her care and affection towards me, which I heartily wish it lay in my power to requite as she deserves, instead of being the innocent, but unhappy instrument of her disgrace, as I have too much reason to fear.

It now began to be known and talked of in the neighbourhood, that my master had found a strange animal in the field, about the bigness of a *splacnuck,* but exactly shaped in every part like a human creature, which it likewise imitated in all its actions, seemed to speak in a little language of its own, had already learned several words of theirs, went erect upon two legs, was tame and gentle, would come when it was called, do whatever it was bid, had the finest limbs in the world, and a complexion fairer than a nobleman's daughter of three years old. Another farmer, who lived hard by, and was a particular friend of my master, came on a visit on purpose to inquire into the truth of this story. I was immediately produced, and placed upon a table, where I walked as I was commanded, drew my hanger, put it up again, made my reverence to my master's guest, asked him, in his own language, how he did, and told him *he was welcome,* just as my little nurse had instructed me. This man, who was old and dim-sighted, put on his spectacles to behold me better, at which I could not forbear laughing very heartily, for his eyes appeared like the full moon shining into a chamber at two windows. Our

people, who discovered the cause of my mirth, bore me company in laughing, at which the old fellow was fool enough to
be angry and out of countenance. He had the character of
a great miser; and, to my misfortune, he well deserved it, by
the cursed advice he gave my master, to shew me as a sight
upon a market-day in the next town, which was half an
hour's riding, about two-and-twenty miles from our house.
I guessed there was some mischief contriving, when I observed my master and his friend whispering long together,
sometimes pointing at me; and my fears made me fancy that
I overheard and understood some of their words. But the
next morning Glumdalclitch, my little nurse, told me the
whole matter, which she had cunningly picked out from her
mother. The poor girl laid me on her bosom, and fell
a-weeping with shame and grief. She apprehended some mischief would happen to me from rude vulgar folks, who might
squeeze me to death, or break one of my limbs by taking me
in their hands. She had also observed how modest I was in
my nature, how nicely I regarded my honour, and what an
indignity I should conceive it, to be exposed for money as a
public spectacle to the meanest of the people. She said, her
papa and mamma had promised that Grildrig should be hers;
but now she found they meant to serve her as they did last
year, when they pretended to give her a lamb, and yet, as
soon as it was fat, sold it to a butcher. For my own part, I may
truly affirm, that I was less concerned than my nurse. I had a
strong hope, which never left me, that I should one day recover my liberty; and, as to the ignominy of being carried
about for a monster, I considered myself to be a perfect
stranger in the country, and that such a misfortune could
never be charged upon me as a reproach, if ever I should return to England, since the King of Great Britain himself, in
my condition, must have undergone the same distress.

My master, pursuant to the advice of his friend, carried

me in a box the next market-day to the neighbouring town, and took along with him his little daughter, my nurse, upon a pillion behind him. The box was close on every side, with a little door for me to go in and out, and a few gimlet-holes to let in air. The girl had been so careful as to put the quilt of her baby's bed into it, for me to lie down on. However, I was terribly shaken and discomposed in this journey, though it were but of half an hour; for the horse went about forty feet at every step, and trotted so high, that the agitation was equal to the rising and falling of a ship in a great storm, but much more frequent. Our journey was somewhat farther than from London to St. Alban's. My masted alighted at an inn which he used to frequent; and, after consulting a while with the innkeeper, and making some necessary preparations, he hired the *grultrud,* or crier, to give notice through the town of a strange creature to be seen at the sign of the Green Eagle, not so big as a *splacnuck,* (an animal in that country very finely shaped, about six feet long,) and in every part of the body resembling a human creature, could speak several words, and perform a hundred diverting tricks.

I was placed upon a table in the largest room of the inn, which might be near three hundred feet square. My little nurse stood on a low stool close to the table, to take care of me, and direct what I should do. My master, to avoid a crowd, would suffer only thirty people at a time to see me. I walked about on the table as the girl commanded; she asked me questions, as far as she knew my understanding of the language reached, and I answered them as loud as I could. I turned about several times to the company, paid my humble respects, said *they were welcome,* and used some other speeches I had been taught. I took up a thimble filled with liquor, which Glumdalclitch had given me for a cup, and drank their health. I drew out my hanger, and flourished with it after the manner of fencers in England. My nurse gave me a part of a straw, which I exercised as a pike, having learnt the art in my youth. I was that day shewn to twelve sets of company, and as often forced to act over again the same fopperies, till I was half dead with weariness and vexation; for those who had seen me made such wonderful reports, that the people were ready to break down the doors to come in. My master, for his own interest, would not suffer any one to touch me except my nurse; and, to prevent danger, benches were set round the table, at such a distance as to put me out of everybody's reach. However, an unlucky schoolboy aimed a hazel-nut directly at my head, which very narrowly missed me, otherwise, it came with so much violence, that it would have infallibly knocked out my brains, for it was almost as large as a small pumpion; but I had the satisfaction to see the young rogue well beaten, and turned out of the room.

My master gave public notice that he would shew me again the next market-day; and in the meantime he prepared a more convenient vehicle for me, which he had reason enough to do; for I was so tired with my first journey, and with entertaining company for eight hours together, that I could hardly stand upon my legs, or speak a word. It was at least three days before I recovered my strength; and, that I might have no rest at home, all the neighbouring gentlemen, from a hundred miles round, hearing of my fame, came to see me at my master's own house. There could be no fewer than thirty persons, with their wives and children (for the country is very populous;) and my master demanded the rate of a full room whenever he shewed me at home, although it were only to a single family; so that, for some time, I had but little ease every day of the week, (except Wednesday, which is their Sabbath,) although I were not carried to the town.

My master, finding how profitable I was likely to be, resolved to carry me to the most considerable cities of the kingdom. Having therefore provided himself with all things

necessary for a long journey, and settled his affairs at home,
he took leave of his wife; and upon the 17th of August, 1703,
about two months after my arrival, we set out for the metropolis, situate near the middle of that empire, and about
three thousand miles' distance from our house. My master
made his daughter Glumdalclitch ride behind him. She carried me on her lap, in a box tied about her waist. The girl
had lined it on all sides with the softest cloth she could get,
well quilted underneath, furnished it with her baby's bed, provided me with linen and other necessaries, and made everything as convenient as she could. We had no other company
but a boy of the house, who rode after us with the luggage.

My master's design was to shew me in all the towns
by the way, and to step out of the road, for fifty or a hundred
miles, to any village, or person of quality's house, where he
might expect custom. We made easy journeys, of not above
seven or eight score miles a-day, for Glumdalclitch, on purpose to spare me, complained she was tired with the trotting
of the horse. She often took me out of my box, at my own
desire, to give me air, and shew me the country, but always
held me fast by a leading-string. We passed over five or six
rivers, many degrees broader and deeper than the Nile or
the Ganges; and there was hardly a rivulet so small as the
Thames at London Bridge. We were ten weeks in our journey, and I was shewn in eighteen large towns, besides many
villages and private families.

On the 26th day of October, we arrived at the metropolis, called in their language *Lorbrulgrud,* or Pride of the Universe. My master took a lodging in the principal street of the
city, not far from the royal palace, and put out bills in the
usual form, containing an exact description of my person and
parts. He hired a large room between three and four hundred
feet wide. He provided a table sixty feet in diameter, upon
which I was to act my part, and palisadoed it round three

feet from the edge, and as many high, to prevent my falling over. I was shewn ten times a day, to the wonder and satisfaction of all people. I could now speak the language tolerably well, and perfectly understood every word that was spoken to me. Besides, I had learnt their alphabet, and could make a shift to explain a sentence here and there; for Glumdalclitch had been my instructor, while we were at home, and at leisure hours during our journey. She carried a little book in her pocket, not much larger than a Sanson's Atlas; it was a common treatise for the use of young girls, giving a short account of their religion: out of this she taught me my letters and interpreted the words.

CHAPTER 3

The author is sent for to court. The Queen buys him of his master the farmer, and presents him to the King. He disputes with his Majesty's great scholars. An apartment at court provided for the author. He is in high favour with the Queen. He stands up for the honour of his own country. His quarrels with the Queen's dwarf.

THE FREQUENT labours I underwent every day, made in a few weeks a very considerable change in my health: the more my master got by me, the more insatiable he grew. I had quite lost my stomach, and was almost reduced to a skeleton. The farmer observed it, and concluding I must soon die, resolved to make as good a hand of me as he could. While he was thus reasoning and resolving with himself, a *sardral,* or gentleman-usher, came from court, commanding my master to carry me immediately thither for the diversion of the Queen and her ladies. Some of the latter had already been to see me, and reported strange things of my beauty, behaviour, and good sense. Her Majesty, and those who attended her, were beyond measure delighted with my demeanour. I fell on my knees, and begged the honour of kissing her imperial foot; but this gracious princess held out her little finger towards me, after I was set on the table, which I embraced in both my arms, and put the tip of it with the utmost respect to my lip. She made me some general questions about my country and my travels, which I answered as distinctly and in as few words as I could. She asked, "Whether I would be content to live at court?" I bowed down to the board of the table, and humbly answered that I was my master's slave; but, if I were at my own disposal, I should be proud to devote my life to her Majesty's service. She then asked my master whether he was willing to sell me at a good price. He, who apprehended I could not live a month, was ready enough to part with me, and demanded a thousand pieces of gold, which were ordered him on the spot, each piece being about the bigness of eight hundred moidores: but allowing for the proportion of all things between that country and Europe, and the high price of gold among them, was hardly so great a sum as a thousand guineas would be in England. I then said to the Queen, since I was now her Majesty's most humble creature and vassal, I must beg the favour that Glumdalclitch, who had always tended me with so much care and kindness, and understood to do it so well, might be admitted into her service, and continue to be my nurse and instructor.

Her Majesty agreed to my petition, and easily got the farmer's consent, who was glad enough to have his daughter preferred at court, and the poor girl herself was not able to hide her joy. My late master withdrew, bidding me farewell, and saying he had left me in good service; to which I replied not a word, only making him a slight bow.

The Queen observed my coldness: and, when the farmer was gone out of the apartment, asked me the reason. I made bold to tell her Majesty that I owed no other obligation to my late master, than his not dashing out the brains of a poor harmless creature, found by chance in his field: which obligation was amply recompensed by the gain he had made in shewing me through half the kingdom, and the price he had now sold me for. That the life I had since led was laborious enough to kill an animal of ten times my strength. That my health was much impaired, by the continual drudgery of entertaining the rabble every hour of the day; and that, if my master had not thought my life in danger, her Majesty would not have got so cheap a bargain. But as I was out of all fear of being ill-treated, under the protection of so great and good an empress, the ornament of nature, the darling of the world, the delight of her subjects, the phoenix of the creation; so, I hoped my late master's apprehensions would appear to be groundless; for I already found my spirits to revive by the influence of her august presence.

This was the sum of my speech, delivered with great improprieties and hesitation. The latter part was altogether framed in the style peculiar to that people, whereof I learned some phrases from Glumdalclitch, while she was carrying me to court.

The Queen, giving great allowance for my defectiveness in speaking, was, however, surprised at so much wit and good sense, in so diminutive an animal. She took me in her own hand, and carried me to the King, who was then retired to his cabinet. His Majesty, a prince of much gravity and austere countenance, not well observing my shape at first view, asked the Queen after a cold manner, "How long it was since she grew fond of a *splacnuck?*" for such, it seems, he took me to be, as I lay upon my breast in her Majesty's right hand. But this princess, who has an infinite deal of wit and humour, set me gently on my feet upon the scrutoire, and commanded me to give his Majesty an account of myself, which I did in a very few words: and Glumdalclitch, who attended at the cabinet door, and could not endure I should be out of her sight, being admitted, confirmed all that had passed from my arrival at her father's house.

The King, although he be as learned a person as any in his dominions, had been educated in the study of philosophy, and particularly mathematics; yet when he observed my shape exactly, and saw me walk erect, before I began to speak, conceived I might be a piece of clock-work (which is in that country arrived to a very great perfection) contrived by some ingenious artist. But, when he heard my voice, and found what I delivered to be regular and rational, he could not conceal his astonishment. He was by no means satisfied with the relation I gave him of the manner I came into his kingdom, but thought it a story concerted between Glumdalclitch and her father, who had taught me a set of words, to make me sell at a better price. Upon this imagination, he put several other questions to me, and still received rational answers; no otherwise defective, than by a foreign accent, and an imperfect knowledge in the language, with some rustic phrases which I had learned at the farmer's house, and did not suit the polite style of a court.

His Majesty sent for three great scholars, who were then in their weekly waiting, according to the custom in that country. These gentlemen, after they had awhile examined my shape with much nicety, were of different opinions concerning me. They all agreed, that I could not be produced according to the regular laws of nature, because I was not framed with a capacity of preserving my life, either by swiftness, or climbing of trees, or digging holes in the earth. They

observed by my teeth, which they viewed with great exactness, that I was a carnivorous animal; yet, most quadrupeds
being an overmatch for me, and field-mice, with some others,
too nimble, they could not imagine how I should be able to
support myself, unless I fed upon snails and other insects,
which they offered, by many learned arguments, to evince
that I could not possibly do. One of these virtuosi seemed to
think that I might be an embryo, or abortive birth. But this
opinion was rejected by the other two, who observed my limbs
to be perfect and finished; and that I had lived several years,
as it was manifest from my beard, the stumps whereof they
plainly discovered through a magnifying glass. They would
not allow me to be a dwarf, because my littleness was beyond
all degrees of comparison; for the Queen's favourite dwarf,
the smallest ever known in that kingdom, was near thirty feet
high. After much debate, they concluded unanimously, that
I was only *relplum scalcath,* which is interpreted literally
lusus naturæ; a determination exactly agreeable to the modern philosophy of Europe, whose professors, disdaining the
old evasion of occult causes, whereby the followers of Aristotle endeavoured in vain to disguise their ignorance, have
invented this wonderful solution of all difficulties, to the un-
speakable advancement of human knowledge.

After this decisive conclusion, I entreated to be heard
a word or two. I applied myself to the King, and assured his
Majesty, "that I came from a country which abounded with
several millions of both sexes, and of my own stature; where
the animals, trees, and houses, were all in proportion, and
where, by consequence, I might be as able to defend myself,
and to find sustenance, as any of his Majesty's subjects could
do here; which I took for a full answer to those gentlemen's
arguments." To this they only replied with a smile of contempt, saying, "that the farmer had instructed me very well
in my lesson." The King, who had a much better understand-

ing, dismissing his learned men, sent for the farmer, who, by good fortune, was not yet gone out of town. Having, therefore, first examined him privately, and then confronted him with me and the young girl, his Majesty began to think that what we told him might possibly be true. He desired the Queen to order that a particular care should be taken of me; and was of opinion that Glumdalclitch should still continue in her office of tending me, because he observed we had a great affection for each other. A convenient apartment was provided for her at court; she had a sort of governess appointed to take care of her education, a maid to dress her, and two other servants for menial offices; but the care of me was wholly appropriated to herself. The Queen commanded her own cabinet-maker to contrive a box, that might serve me for a bedchamber, after the model that Glumdalclitch and I should agree upon. This man was a most ingenious artist, and according to my direction, in three weeks, finished for me a wooden chamber of sixteen feet square, and twelve high, with sash-windows, a door, and two closets, like a London bedchamber. The board that made the ceiling was to be lifted up and down by two hinges, to put in a bed, ready furnished by her Majesty's upholsterer, which Glumdalclitch took out every day to air, made it with her own hands, and letting it down at night, locked up the roof over me. A nice workman, who was famous for little curiosities, undertook to make me two chairs, with backs and frames of a substance not unlike ivory, and two tables, with a cabinet to put my things in. The room was quilted on all sides, as well as the floor and ceiling, to prevent any accident from the carelessness of those who carried me, and to break the force of a jolt, when I went in a coach. I desired a lock for my door, to prevent rats and mice from coming in. The smith, after several attempts, made the smallest that ever was seen among them, for I have known a larger at the gate of a gentleman's house in England.

I made a shift to keep the key in a pocket of my own, fearing Glumdalclitch might lose it. The Queen likewise ordered the thinnest silks that could be gotten, to make me clothes, not much thicker than an English blanket, very cumbersome till I was accustomed to them. They were after the fashion of the kingdom, partly resembling the Persian, and partly the Chinese, and are a very grave and decent habit.

The Queen became so fond of my company, that she could not dine without me. I had a table placed upon the same at which her Majesty eat, just at her left elbow, and a chair to sit on. Glumdalclitch stood on a stool on the floor near to my table, to assist and take care of me. I had an entire set of silver dishes and plates, and other necessaries, which, in proportion to those of the Queen, were not much bigger than what I have seen in London toy-shops, for the furniture of a baby-house: these my little nurse kept in her pocket in a silver box, and gave me at meals as I wanted them, always cleaning them herself. No person dined with the Queen but the two princesses royal, the elder sixteen years old, and the younger at that time thirteen and a month. Her Majesty used to put a bit of meat upon one of my dishes, out of which I carved for myself, and her diversion was to see me eat in miniature; for the Queen (who had, indeed, but a weak stomach) took up, at one mouthful, as much as a dozen English farmers could eat at a meal, which to me was, for some time, a very nauseous sight. She would cranch the wing of a lark, bones and all, between her teeth, although it were nine times as large as that of a full-grown turkey; and put a bit of bread in her mouth as big as two twelve-penny loaves. She drank out of a golden cup, above a hogshead at a draught. Her knives were twice as long as a scythe, set straight upon the handle. The spoons, forks, and other instruments, were all in the same proportion. I remember when Glumdalclitch carried me, out of curiosity, to see some of the tables at court, where ten or a dozen of these enormous knives and forks were lifted up together. I thought I had never, till then, beheld so terrible a sight.

It is the custom, that every Wednesday (which, as I have before observed, is their Sabbath) the King and Queen, with the royal issue of both sexes, dine together in the apartment of his Majesty, to whom I was now become a great favourite; and at these times, my little chair and table were placed at his left hand, before one of the salt-cellars. This prince took a pleasure in conversing with me, inquiring into the manners, religion, laws, government, and learning of Europe; wherein I gave him the best account I was able. His apprehension was so clear, and his judgment so exact, that he made very wise reflections and observations upon all I said. But, I confess, that, after I had been a little too copious in talking of my own beloved country, of our trade, and wars by sea and land, of our schisms in religion, and parties in the state, the prejudices of his education prevailed so far, that he could not forbear taking me up in his right hand, and stroking me gently with the other, after a hearty fit of laughter, asked me whether I was a Whig or Tory. Then turning to his first minister, who waited behind him with a white staff, near as tall as the main-mast of the Royal Sovereign, he observed, "How contemptible a thing was human grandeur, which could be mimicked by such diminutive insects as I : and yet," says he, "I dare engage, these creatures have their titles and distinctions of honour; they contrive little nests and burrows, that they call houses and cities; they make a figure in dress and equipage; they love, they fight, they dispute, they cheat, they betray!" And thus he continued on, while my colour came and went several times, with indignation, to hear our noble country, the mistress of arts and arms, the scourge of France, the arbitress of Europe, the seat of virtue, piety, honour, and truth, the pride and envy of the world, so contemptuously treated.

But as I was not in a condition to resent injuries, so, upon mature thoughts, I began to doubt whether I was injured or no. For, after having been accustomed several months to the sight and converse of this people, and observed every object upon which I cast mine eyes to be of proportionable magnitude, the horror I had at first conceived from their bulk and aspect was so far worn off, that, if I had then beheld a company of English lords and ladies in their finery and birthday clothes, acting their several parts in the most courtly manner of strutting, and bowing, and prating; to say the truth, I should have been strongly tempted to laugh as much at them as the King and his grandees did at me. Neither, indeed, could I forbear smiling at myself, when the Queen used to place me upon her hand towards a looking-glass, by which both our persons appeared before me in full view together; and there could be nothing more ridiculous than the comparison : so that I really began to imagine myself dwindled many degrees below my usual size.

Nothing angered and mortified me so much as the Queen's dwarf; who, being of the lowest stature that was ever in that country, (for I verily think he was not full thirty feet high,) became so insolent at seeing a creature so much beneath him, that he would always affect to swagger and look big as he passed by me in the Queen's antechamber, while I was standing on some table talking with the lords or ladies of the court, and he seldom failed of a smart word or two upon my *littleness;* against which I could only revenge myself by calling him *brother,* challenging him to wrestle, and such repartees as are usually in the mouths of court pages. One day, at dinner, this malicious little cub was so nettled with something I had said to him, that, raising himself upon the frame of her Majesty's chair, he took me up by the middle, as I was sitting down, not thinking any harm, and let me drop into a large silver bowl of cream, and then ran away as fast as he could. I fell over head and ears, and, if I had not been a good swimmer, it might have gone very hard with me; for Glumdalclitch in that instant happened to be at the other end of the room, and the Queen was in such a fright, that she wanted presence of mind to assist me. But my little nurse ran to my relief, and took me out, after I had swallowed above a quart of cream. I was put to bed: however, I received no other damage than the loss of a suit of clothes, which was utterly spoiled. The dwarf was soundly whipped, and, as a farther punishment, forced to drink up the bowl of cream into which he had thrown me: neither was he ever restored to favour; for soon after the Queen bestowed him on a lady of high quality, so that I saw him no more, to my very great satisfaction; for I could not tell to what extremity such a malicious urchin might have carried his resentment.

He had before served me a scurvy trick, which set the Queen a-laughing, although at the same time she was heartily vexed, and would have immediately cashiered him, if I had not been so generous as to intercede. Her Majesty had taken a marrow-bone upon her plate, and, after knocking out the marrow, placed the bone again in the dish erect, as it stood before; the dwarf, watching his opportunity while Glumdalclitch was gone to the sideboard, mounted the stool that she stood on to take care of me at meals, took me up in both hands, and squeezing my legs together, wedged them into the marrow-bone above my waist, where I stuck for some time, and made a very ridiculous figure. I believe it was near a minute before any one knew what was become of me; for I thought it below me to cry out. But as princes seldom get their meat hot, my legs were not scalded, only my stockings and breeches in a sad condition. The dwarf, at my entreaty, had no other punishment than a sound whipping.

I was frequently rallied by the Queen upon account of my fearfulness; and she used to ask me whether the people of my country were as great cowards as myself? The occasion

was this: the kingdom is much pestered with flies in summer; and these odious insects, each of them as big as a Dunstable lark, hardly gave me any rest while I sat at dinner, with their continual humming and buzzing about mine ears. They would sometimes alight upon my victuals, and leave their loathsome excrement or spawn behind, which to me was very visible, though not to the natives of that country, whose large optics were not so acute as mine, in viewing smaller objects. Sometimes they would fix upon my nose or forehead, where they stung me to the quick, smelling very offensively; and I could easily trace that viscous matter, which, our naturalists tell us, enables those creatures to walk with their feet upwards upon a ceiling. I had much ado to defend myself against these detestable animals, and could not forbear starting when they came on my face. It was the common practice of the dwarf, to catch a number of these insects in his hand, as school-boys do among us, and let them out suddenly under my nose, on purpose to frighten me, and divert the Queen. My remedy was to cut them in pieces with my knife, as they flew in the air, wherein my dexterity was much admired.

I remember, one morning, when Glumdalclitch had set me in my box upon a window, as she usually did in fair days to give me air (for I durst not venture to let the box be hung on a nail out of the window, as we do with cages in England,) after I had lifted up one of my sashes, and sat down at my table to eat a piece of sweet cake for my breakfast, above twenty wasps, allured by the smell, came flying into the room, humming louder than the drones of as many bagpipes. Some of them seized my cake, and carried it piecemeal away: others flew about my head and face, confounding me with the noise, and putting me in the utmost terror of their stings. However, I had the courage to rise and draw my hanger, and attack them in the air. I dispatched four of them, but the rest got away, and I presently shut my window. These insects were as large as partridges: I took out their stings, found them an inch and a half long, and as sharp as needles. I carefully preserved them all; and having since shewn them, with some other curiosities, in several parts of Europe, upon my return to England I gave three of them to Gresham College, and kept the fourth for myself.

CHAPTER 4

The country described. A proposal for correcting modern maps. The King's palace, and some account of the metropolis. The author's way of travelling. The chief temple described.

I NOW INTEND to give the reader a short description of this country, as far as I travelled in it, which was not above two thousand miles round Lorbrulgrud the metropolis, for the Queen, whom I always attended, never went farther when she accompanied the King in his progresses, and there staid till his Majesty returned from viewing his frontiers. The whole extent of this prince's dominions reaches about six thousand miles in length, and from three to five in breadth: whence I cannot but conclude, that our geographers of Europe are in a great error, by supposing nothing but sea between Japan and California; for it was ever my opinion, that there must be a balance of earth to counterpoise the great continent of Tartary; and, therefore, they ought to correct their maps and charts, by joining this vast tract of land to the north-west parts of America, wherein I shall be ready to lend them my assistance.

The kingdom is a peninsula terminated to the northeast by a ridge of mountains thirty miles high, which are altogether impassable, by reason of the volcanoes upon the tops: neither do the most learned know what sort of mortals inhabit beyond those mountains, or whether they be inhabited at all. On the three other sides it is bounded by the ocean. There is not one seaport in the whole kingdom: and those parts of the coasts into which the rivers issue, are so full of pointed rocks, and the sea generally so rough, that there is no venturing with the smallest of their boats; so that these people are wholly excluded from any commerce with the rest of the world. But the large rivers are full of vessels, and abound with excellent fish; for they seldom get any from the sea, because the sea-fish are of the same size with those in Europe, and consequently not worth catching; whereby it is manifest, that nature in the production of plants and animals of so extraordinary a bulk, is wholly confined to this continent, of which I leave the reasons to be determined by philosophers. However, now and then they take a whale that happens to be dashed against the rocks, which the common people feed on heartily. These whales I have known so large, that a man could hardly carry one upon his shoulders; and sometimes, for curiosity, they are brought in hampers to Lorbrulgrud: I saw one of them in a dish at the King's table, which passed for a rarity, but I did not observe he was fond of it; for I think, indeed, the bigness disgusted him, although I have seen one somewhat larger in Greenland.

The country is well inhabited, for it contains fifty-one cities, near a hundred walled towns, and a great number of villages. To satisfy my curious reader, it may be sufficient to describe Lorbrulgrud. This city stands upon almost two equal parts, on each side the river that passes through. It contains above eighty thousand houses, and about six hundred thousand inhabitants. It is in length three *glomglungs,* (which make about fifty-four English miles,) and two and a half in breadth; as I measured it myself in the royal map, made by the King's order, which was laid on the ground on purpose for me, and extended a hundred feet: I paced the diameter and circumference several times bare foot, and, computing by the scale, measured it pretty exactly.

The King's palace is no regular edifice, but a heap of building, about seven miles round; the chief rooms are generally two hundred and forty feet high, and broad and long in proportion. A coach was allowed to Glumdalclitch and me, wherein her governess frequently took her out to see the town, or go among the shops; and I was always of the party, carried in my box; although the girl, at my own desire, would often take me out, and hold me in her hand, that I might more conveniently view the houses and the people, as we passed along the streets. I reckoned our coach to be about a square of Westminster-hall, but not altogether so high; however, I cannot be very exact. One day the governess ordered our coachman to stop at several shops, where the beggars, watching their opportunity, crowded to the sides of the coach, and gave me the most horrible spectacles that ever a European eye beheld. There was a woman with a cancer in her breast, swelled to a monstrous size, full of holes, in two or three of which I could have easily crept and covered my whole body. There was a fellow with a wen in his neck, larger than five wool-packs; and another with a couple of wooden legs, each about twenty feet high. But the most hateful sight of all, was the lice crawling on their clothes. I could see distinctly the limbs of these vermin with my naked eye, much better than those of an European louse through a microscope, and their snouts, with which they rooted like swine. They were the first I had ever beheld, and I should have been curious enough to dissect one of them, if I had had proper instruments, which I unluckily left behind me in the ship, although, indeed, the sight was so nauseous, that it perfectly turned my stomach.

Besides the large box in which I was usually carried, the

Queen ordered a smaller one to be made for me, of about
twelve feet square, and ten high, for the convenience of
travelling: because the other was somewhat too large for
Glumdalclitch's lap, and cumbersome in the coach; it was
made by the same artist, whom I directed in the whole contrivance. This travelling-closet was an exact square, with a
window in the middle of three of the squares, and each window was latticed with iron wire on the outside, to prevent
accidents in long journeys. On the fourth side, which had no
window, two strong staples were fixed, through which the
person that carried me, when I had a mind to be on horseback, put a leathern belt, and buckled it about his waist. This
was always the office of some grave trusty servant in whom
I could confide, whether I attended the King and Queen
in their progresses, or were disposed to see the gardens, or
pay a visit to some great lady or minister of state in the court,
when Glumdalclitch happened to be out of order; for I soon
began to be known and esteemed among the greatest officers;
I suppose more upon account of their Majesties' favour, than
any merit of my own. In journeys, when I was weary of the
coach, a servant on horseback would buckle on my box, and
place it upon a cushion before him; and there I had a full
prospect of the country on three sides, from my three windows. I had, in this closet, a field-bed and a hammock hung
from the ceiling, two chairs and a table, neatly screwed to the
floor, to prevent being tossed about by the agitation of the
horse or the coach. And having been long used to sea voyages, those motions, although sometimes very violent, did
not much discompose me.

Whenever I had a mind to see the town, it was always
in my travelling closet, which Glumdalclitch held in her lap
in a kind of open sedan, after the fashion of the country,
borne by four men, and attended by two others in the Queen's
livery. The people who had often heard of me, were very

curious to crowd about the sedan, and the girl was complaisant enough to make the bearers stop, and to take me in
her hand, that I might be more conveniently seen.

I was very desirous to see the chief temple, and particularly the tower belonging to it, which is reckoned the highest
in the kingdom. Accordingly one day my nurse carried me
thither, but I may truly say I came back disappointed; for the
height is not above three thousand feet, reckoning from the
ground to the highest pinnacle top; which, allowing for the
difference between the size of those people and us in Europe,
is no great matter for admiration, nor at all equal in proportion (if I rightly remember) to Salisbury steeple. But not to
detract from a nation, to which, during my life, I shall acknowledge myself extremely obliged, it must be allowed that
whatever this famous tower wants in height, it is amply made
up in beauty and strength. For the walls are near a hundred
feet thick, built of hewn stone, whereof each is about forty
feet square, and adorned on all sides with statues of gods and
emperors, cut in marble, larger than the life, placed in their
several niches, I measured a little finger which had fallen
down from one of these statues, and lay unperceived among
some rubbish, and found it exactly four feet and an inch in
length. Glumdalclitch wrapped it up in her handkerchief; and
carried it home in her pocket, to keep among other trinkets,
of which the girl was very fond, as children at her age usually
are.

The King's kitchen is indeed a noble building, vaulted at
top, and about six hundred feet high. The great oven is not
so wide, by ten paces, as the cupola at St. Paul's: for I measured the latter on purpose after my return. But if I should
describe the kitchen grate, the prodigious pots and kettles,
the joints of meat turning on the spits, with many other particulars, perhaps I should be hardly believed; at least a severe
critic would be apt to think I enlarged a little, as travellers

are often suspected to do. To avoid which censure, I fear I have run too much into the other extreme; and that, if this treatise should happen to be translated into the language of Brobdingnag (which is the general name of that kingdom,) and transmitted thither, the King and his people would have reason to complain that I had done them an injury by a false and diminutive representation.

His Majesty seldom keeps above six hundred horses in his stables: they are generally from fifty-four to sixty feet high. But when he goes abroad on solemn days, he is attended, for state, by a militia guard of five hundred horse, which indeed I thought was the most splendid sight that could be ever beheld, till I saw part of his army in battalia, whereof I shall find another occasion to speak.

CHAPTER 5

Several adventures that happened to the author. The execution of a criminal. The author shews his skill in navigation.

I SHOULD HAVE lived happy enough in that country, if my littleness had not exposed me to several ridiculous and troublesome accidents; some of which I shall venture to relate. Glumdalclitch often carried me into the gardens of the court in my smaller box, and would sometimes take me out of it, and hold me in her hand, or set me down to walk. I remember, before the dwarf left the Queen, he followed us one day into those gardens, and my nurse having set me down, he and I being close together, near some dwarf apple trees, I must need shew my wit, by a silly allusion between him and the trees, which happens to hold in their language as it does in ours. Whereupon the malicious rogue, watching his opportunity, when I was walking under one of them, shook it directly over my head, by which a dozen of apples, each of them near as large as a Bristol barrel, came tumbling about my ears; one of them hit me on the back as I chanced to stoop, and knocked me down flat on my face; but I received no other hurt, and the dwarf was pardoned at my desire, because I had given the provocation.

Another day Glumdalclitch left me on a smooth grass-plot to divert myself, while she walked at some distance with her governess. In the meantime, there suddenly fell such a violent shower of hail, that I was immediately, by the force of it, struck to the ground: and when I was down, the hail-stones gave me such cruel bangs all over the body, as if I had been pelted with tennis-balls; however, I made a shift to creep on all four, and shelter myself by lying flat on my face, on the lee-side of a border of lemon-thyme; but so bruised from head to foot, that I could not go abroad in ten days. Neither is this at all to be wondered at, because nature, in that country, observing the same proportion through all her operations, a hailstone is near eighteen hundred times as large as one in Europe; which I can assert upon experience, having been so curious to weigh and measure them.

But a more dangerous accident happened to me in the same garden, when my little nurse, believing she had put me in a secure place (which I often entreated her to do, that I might enjoy my own thoughts,) and having left my box at home, to avoid the trouble of carrying it, went to another part of the garden with her governess and some ladies of her acquaintance. While she was absent and out of hearing, a small white spaniel that belonged to one of the chief gardeners, having got by accident into the garden, happened to range near the place where I lay: the dog followed the scent, came directly up, and taking me in his mouth, ran straight to his master, wagging his tail, and set me gently on the ground. By good fortune he had been so well taught, that I was carried between his teeth without the least hurt, or even tearing my clothes. But the poor gardener, who knew me well, and had a great kindness for me, was in a terrible fright: he gently took me up in both his hands, and asked me how I did? but I was so amazed and out of breath, that I could not speak a word. In a few minutes I came to myself, and he carried me safe to my little nurse, who by this time had returned to the place where she left me, and was in cruel agonies when I did not appear, nor answer when she called. She severely reprimanded the gardener on account of his dog. But the thing was hushed up, and never known at court, for the girl was afraid of the Queen's anger; and truly, as to myself, I thought it would not be for my reputation, that such a story should go about.

This accident absolutely determined Glumdalclitch never to trust me abroad for the future, out of her sight. I had been long afraid of this resolution, and therefore concealed from her some little unlucky adventures, that happened in those times when I was left by myself. Once a kite, hovering over the garden, made a stoop at me, and if I had not resolutely drawn my hanger, and run under a thick espalier, he would have certainly carried me away in his talons. Another time, walking to the top of a fresh mole-hill, I fell to my neck in the hole, through which that animal cast up the earth, and coined some lie, not worth remembering, to excuse myself for spoiling my clothes. I likewise broke my right shin against the shell of a snail, which I happened to stumble over, as I was walking alone and thinking on poor England.

I cannot tell whether I were more pleased or mortified to observe, in those solitary walks, that the smaller birds did not appear to be at all afraid of me, but would hop about within a yard's distance, looking for worms and other food, with as much indifference and security as if no creature at all were near them. I remember, a thrush had the confidence to snatch out of my hand, with his bill, a piece of cake that Glumdalclitch had just given me for my breakfast. When I attempted to catch any of these birds, they would boldly turn against me, endeavouring to peck my fingers, which I durst not venture within their reach; and then they would hop back unconcerned, to hunt for worms or snails, as they did before. But one day I took a thick cudgel, and threw it with all my strength so luckily at a linnet, that I knocked him down, and seizing him by the neck with both my hands, ran with him in triumph to my nurse. However, the bird, who had only been stunned, recovering himself, gave me so many boxes with his wings on both sides of my head and body, though I held him at arm's length, and was out of the reach of his claws, that I was twenty times thinking to let him go. But I was soon relieved by one of our servants, who wrung off the bird's neck, and I had him next day for dinner, by the Queen's command. This linnet, as near as I can remember, seemed to be somewhat larger than an English swan.

The maids of honour often invited Glumdalclitch to their apartments, and desired she would bring me along with her, on purpose to have the pleasure of seeing and touching me. They would often strip me naked from top to toe, and lay me at full length in their bosoms, wherewith I was much disgusted, because, to say the truth, a very offensive smell came from their skins, which I do not mention, or intend, to the disadvantage of those excellent ladies, for whom I have all manner of respect; but I conceive that my sense was more acute in proportion to my littleness, and that those illustrious persons were no more disagreeable to their lovers, or to each other, than people of the same quality are with us in England. And, after all, I found their natural smell was much more supportable, than when they used perfumes, under which I immediately swooned away. I cannot forget, that an intimate friend of mine in Lilliput, took the freedom in a warm day, when I had used a good deal of exercise, to complain of a strong smell about me, although I am as little faulty that way as most of my sex; but I suppose his faculty of smelling was as nice with regard to me, as mine was to that of this people. Upon this point, I cannot forbear doing justice to the Queen my mistress, and Glumdalclitch my nurse, whose persons were as sweet as those of any lady in England.

That which gave me the most uneasiness among these maids of honour (when my nurse carried me to visit them) was, to see them use me without any manner of ceremony, like a creature who had no sort of consequence, for they would strip themselves to the skin, and put on their smocks in my presence, while I was placed on their toilet directly before their naked bodies, which I am sure to me was very far from being a tempting sight, or giving me any other emotion than those of horror and disgust; their skins appeared so coarse and uneven, so variously coloured, when I saw them near, with a mole here and there as broad as a trencher, and hairs hanging from it thicker than packthreads, to say nothing farther concerning the rest of their persons. Neither did they at all scruple, while I was by, to discharge what they had drank, to the quantity of at least two hogsheads in a vessel that held above three tuns. The handsomest among these maids of honour, a pleasant, frolicsome girl of sixteen, would sometimes set me astride upon one of her nipples, with many other tricks, wherein the reader will excuse me for not being over particular. But I was so much displeased, that I entreated Glumdalclitch to contrive some excuse for not seeing that young lady any more.

One day, a young gentleman, who was nephew to my nurse's governess, came and pressed them both to see an exe-

cution. It was of a man who had murdered one of that gentleman's intimate acquaintance. Glumdalclitch was prevailed
on to be of the company, very much against her inclination,
for she was naturally tender-hearted: and as for myself
although I abhorred such kind of spectacles, yet my curiosity
tempted me to see something that I thought must be extraordinary. The malefactor was fixed on a chair upon a scaffold
erected for that purpose, and his head cut off at one blow,
with a sword of about forty feet long. The veins and arteries
spouted up such a prodigious quantity of blood, and so high
in the air, that the great *jet-d'eau* at Versailles was not equal
for the time it lasted; and the head, when it fell on the scaffold floor, gave such a bounce as made me start, although I
were at least half an English mile distant.

The Queen, who often used to hear me talk of my sea-
voyages, and took all occasions to divert me when I was
melancholy, asked me whether I understood how to handle
a sail or an oar, and whether a little exercise of rowing might
not be convenient for my health? I answered, that I understood both very well; for although my proper employment
had been to be surgeon or doctor to the ship, yet often,
upon a pinch, I was forced to work like a common mariner.
But I could not see how this could be done in their country,
where the smallest wherry was equal to a first-rate man-of-
war among us; and such a boat as I could manage would
never live in any of their rivers. Her Majesty said if I would
contrive a boat, her own joiner should make it, and she would
provide a place for me to sail in. The fellow was an ingenious
workman, and by my instructions, in ten days, finished a
pleasure-boat, with all its tackling, able conveniently to hold
eight Europeans. When it was finished, the Queen was so
delighted, that she ran with it in her lap to the King, who
ordered it to be put into a cistern full of water, with me in it,
by way of trial, where I could not manage my two sculls, or

little oars, for want of room. But the Queen had before contrived another project: she ordered the joiner to make a
wooden trough of three hundred feet long, fifty broad, and
eight deep, which, being well pitched, to prevent leaking,
was placed on the floor, along the wall, in an outer room of
the palace. It had a cock near the bottom to let out the
water, when it began to grow stale; and two servants could
easily fill it in half an hour. Here I often used to row for my
own diversion as well as that of the Queen and her ladies,
who thought themselves well entertained with my skill and
agility. Sometimes I would put up my sail, and then my business was only to steer, while the ladies gave me a gale with
their fans; and, when they were weary, some of their pages
would blow my sail forward with their breath, while I
shewed my art by steering starboard or larboard as I pleased.
When I had done, Glumdalclitch always carried back my boat
into her closet, and hung it on a nail to dry.

In this exercise, I once met an accident, which had like
to have cost me my life; for, one of the pages having put my
boat into the trough, the governess who attended Glumdalclitch very officiously lifted me up, to place me in the boat;
but I happened to slip through her fingers, and should infallibly have fallen down forty feet, upon the floor, if, by the
luckiest chance in the world, I had not been stopped by a
corking-pin that stuck the good gentlewoman's stomacher;
the head of the pin passed between my shirt and the waistband
of my breeches, and thus I was held by the middle in the air,
till Glumdalclitch ran to my relief.

Another time, one of the servants, whose office it was
to fill my trough every third day with fresh water, was so
careless as to let a huge frog (not perceiving it) slip out of
his pail. The frog lay concealed till I was put into my boat,
but then, seeing a resting-place, climbed up, and made it lean
so much on one side, that I was forced to balance it with all

my weight on the other, to prevent overturning. When the frog was got in, it hopped at once half the length of the boat, and then over my head, backward and forward, daubing my face and clothes with its odious slime. The largeness of its features made it appear the most deformed animal that can be conceived. However, I desired Glumdalclitch to let me deal with it alone. I banged it a good while with one of my sculls, and at last forced it to leap out of the boat.

But the greatest danger I ever underwent in that kingdom, was from a monkey, who belonged to one of the clerks of the kitchen. Glumdalclitch had locked me up in her closet, while she went somewhere upon business or a visit. The weather being very warm, the closet-window was left open, as well as the windows and the door of my bigger box, in which I usually lived, because of its largeness and conveniency. As I sat quietly meditating at my table, I heard something bounce in at the closet-window, and skip about from one side to the other; whereat although I was much alarmed, yet I ventured to look out, but not stirring from my seat; and then I saw this frolicsome animal frisking and leaping up and down, till at last he came to my box, which he seemed to view with great pleasure and curiosity, peeping in at the door and every window, I retreated to the farther corner of my room, or box; but the monkey, looking in at every side, put me into such a fright, that I wanted presence of mind to conceal myself under the bed, as I might easily have done. After some time spent in peeping, grinning, and chattering, he at last espied me; and reaching one of his paws in at the door, as a cat does when she plays with a mouse, although I often shifted place to avoid him, he at length seized the lappet of my coat, (which, being made of that country silk, was very thick and strong,) and dragged me out. He took me up in his right fore-foot, and held me as a nurse does a child she is going to suckle, just as I have seen the same sort of creature do with a kitten in Europe; and when I offered to struggle, he squeezed me so hard, that I thought it more prudent to submit. I have good reason to believe, that he took me for a young one of his own species, by his often stroking my face very gently with his other paw. In these diversions he was interrupted by a noise at the closet-door, as if somebody were opening it; whereupon he suddenly leaped up to the window, at which he had come in, and thence upon the leads and gutters, walking upon three legs, and holding me in the fourth, till he clambered up to a roof that was next to ours. I heard Glumdalclitch give a shriek at the moment he was carrying me out. The poor girl was almost distracted; that quarter of the palace was all in an uproar; the servants ran for ladders; the monkey was seen by hundreds in the court, sitting upon the ridge of a building, holding me like a baby in one of his forepaws, and feeding me with the other, by cramming into my mouth some victuals he had squeezed out of the bag on one side of his chaps, and patting me when I would not eat; whereat many of the rabble below could not forbear laughing; neither do I think they justly ought to be blamed, for without question the sight was ridiculous enough to everybody but myself. Some of the people threw up stones, hoping to drive the monkey down; but this was strictly forbidden, or else, very probably my brains had been dashed out.

The ladders were now applied, and mounted by several men; which the monkey observing, and finding himself almost encompassed, not being able to make speed enough with his three legs, let me drop on a ridge tile, and made his escape. Here I sat for some time, five hundred yards from the ground, expecting every moment to be blown down by the wind, or to fall by my own giddiness, and come tumbling over and over from the ridge to the eaves; but an honest lad, one of my nurse's footmen, climbed up, and, putting me into his breeches-pocket, brought me down safe.

I was almost choked with the filthy stuff the monkey had crammed down my throat; but my dear little nurse picked it out of my mouth with a small needle, and then I fell a-vomiting, which gave me great relief. Yet I was so weak, and bruised in the sides with the squeezes given me by this odious animal, that I was forced to keep my bed a fortnight. The King, Queen, and all the court, sent every day to enquire after my health; and her Majesty made me several visits during my sickness. The monkey was killed, and an order made, that no such animal should be kept about the palace.

When I attended the King after my recovery, to return him thanks for his favours, he was pleased to rally me a good deal upon this adventure. He asked me, "what my thoughts and speculations were, while I lay in the monkey's paw; how I liked the victuals he gave me; his manner of feeding; and whether the fresh air on the roof had sharpened my stomach?" He desired to know, "what I would have done upon such an occasion in my own country?" I told his majesty, "that in Europe, we had no monkeys, except such as were brought for curiosities from other places, and so small, that I could deal with a dozen of them together, if they presumed to attack me. And as for that monstrous animal, with whom I was so lately engaged, (it was indeed as large as an elephant,) if my fears had suffered me to think so far as to make use of my hanger, (looking fiercely, and clapping my hand upon the hilt, as I spoke,) when he poked his paw into my chamber, perhaps I should have given him such a wound, as would have made him glad to withdraw it with more haste than he put it in." This I delivered in a firm tone, like a person who was jealous lest his courage should be called in question. However, my speech produced nothing else beside a loud laughter, which all the respect due to his Majesty from those about him, could not make them contain. This made me reflect how vain an attempt it is, for a man to endeavour to do himself honour among those who are out of all degree of equality or comparison with him. And yet I have seen the moral of my own behaviour very frequent in England since my return; where a little contemptible varlet, without the least title to birth, person, wit, or common sense, shall presume to look with importance, and put himself upon a foot with the greatest persons of the kingdom.

I was every day furnishing the court with some ridiculous story; and Glumdalclitch, although she loved me to excess, yet was arch enough to inform the Queen, whenever I committed any folly that she thought would be diverting to her Majesty. The girl, who had been out of order, was carried by her governess to take the air about an hour's distance, or thirty miles from town. They alighted out of the coach near a small footpath in a field, and Glumdalclitch setting down my travelling box, I went out of it to walk. There was a cow-dung in the path, and I must need try my activity by attempting to leap over it. I took a run, but unfortunately jumped short, and found myself just in the middle, up to my knees. I waded through with some difficulty, and one of the footmen wiped me as clean as he could with his handkerchief, for I was filthily bemired; and my nurse confined me to my box till we returned home; where the Queen was soon informed of what had passed, and the footmen spread it about the court; so that all the mirth for some days was at my expense.

CHAPTER 6

Several contrivances of the author to please the King and
Queen. He shews his skill in music. The King inquires into
the state of England, which the author relates to him. The
King's observations thereon.

I USED TO ATTEND the King's
levee once or twice a-week, and had often seen him under
the barber's hand, which, indeed, was at first very terrible to
behold; for the razor was almost twice as long as an ordinary
scythe. His Majesty, according to the custom of the country,
was only shaved twice a-week. I once prevailed on the barber
to give me some of the suds or lather, out of which I picked
forty or fifty of the strongest stumps of hair. I then took a
piece of fine wood, and cut it like the back of a comb, making
several holes in it, at equal distances, with as small a needle
as I could get from Glumdalclitch. I fixed in the stumps so
artificially, scraping and sloping them with my knife towards
the points, that I made a very tolerable comb; which was a
seasonable supply, my own being so much broken in the
teeth, that it was almost useless; neither did I know any
artist in that country so nice and exact, as would undertake
to make me another.

And this puts me in mind of an amusement, wherein I
spent many of my leisure hours. I desired the Queen's woman
to save for me the combings of her Majesty's hair, whereof
in time I got a good quantity; and consulting with my friend
the cabinet-maker, who had received general orders to do
little jobs for me, I directed him to make two chair-frames,
no larger than those I had in my box, and then to bore little
holes with a fine awl, round those parts where I designed the
backs and seats; through these holes I wove the strongest

hairs I could pick out, just after the manner of cane chairs in England. When they were finished, I made a present of them to her Majesty, who kept them in her cabinet, and used to shew them for curiosities, as indeed they were the wonder of every one that beheld them. The Queen would have me sit upon one of these chairs, but I absolutely refused to obey her, protesting I would rather die a thousand deaths, than place a dishonourable part of my body on those precious hairs that once adorned her Majesty's head. Of these hairs (as I had always a mechanical genius) I likewise made a neat little purse, about five feet long, with her Majesty's name deciphered in gold letters, which I gave to Glumdalclitch by the Queen's consent. To say the truth, it was more for show than use, being not of strength to bear the weight of the larger coins, and therefore she kept nothing in it but some little toys that girls are fond of.

The King, who delighted in music, had frequent concerts at court, to which I was sometimes carried, and set in my box on a table to hear them: but the noise was so great that I could hardly distinguish the tunes. I am confident that all the drums and trumpets of a royal army, beating and sounding together just at your ears, could not equal it. My practice was to have my box removed from the place where the performers sat, as far as I could, then to shut the doors and windows of it, and draw the window-curtains; after which I found their music not disagreeable.

I had learned in my youth to play a little upon the spinet. Glumdalclitch kept one in her chamber, and a master attended twice a-week to teach her: I called it a spinet, because it somewhat resembled that instrument, and was played upon in the same manner. A fancy came into my head, that I would entertain the King and Queen with an English tune upon this instrument. But this appeared extremely difficult: for the spinet was near sixty feet long, each key being

almost a foot wide, so that with my arms extended I could
not reach to above five keys, and to press them down required a good smart stroke with my fist, which would be too
great a labour, and to no purpose. The method I contrived
was this: I prepared two round sticks about the bigness of
common cudgels; they were thicker at one end than the other,
and I covered the thicker ends with pieces of a mouse's skin,
that by rapping on them I might neither damage the tops of
the keys, nor interrupt the sound. Before the spinet a bench
was placed, about four feet below the keys, and I was put upon
the bench. I ran sideling upon it, that way and this, as fast
as I could, banging the proper keys with my two sticks, and
made a shift to play a jig, to the great satisfaction of both
their Majesties; but it was the most violent exercise I ever
underwent: and yet I could not strike above sixteen keys, nor
consequently play the bass and treble together, as other artists
do; which was a great disadvantage to my performance.

The King, who, as I before observed, was a prince of
excellent understanding, would frequently order that I should
be brought in my box, and set upon the table in his closet:
he would then command me to bring one of my chairs out
of the box, and sit down within three yards' distance upon
the top of the cabinet, which brought me almost to a level
with his face. In this manner I had several conversations
with him. I one day took the freedom to tell his Majesty,
"that the contempt he discovered towards Europe, and the
rest of the world, did not seem answerable to those excellent
qualities of mind that he was master of: that reason did not
extend itself with the bulk of the body; on the contrary, we
observed in our country, that the tallest persons were usually
the least provided with it: that among other animals, bees
and ants had the reputation of more industry, art, and sagacity, than many of the larger kinds; and that, as inconsiderable
as he took me to be, I hoped I might live to do his Majesty

some signal service." The King heard me with attention, and began to conceive a much better opinion of me than he had ever before. He desired "I would give him as exact an account of the government of England as I possibly could; because, as fond as princes commonly are of their own customs, (for so he conjectured of other monarchs by my former discourses,) he should be glad to hear of anything that might deserve imitation."

Imagine with thyself, courteous reader, how often I then wished for the tongue of Demosthenes or Cicero, that might have enabled me to celebrate the praise of my own dear native country, in a style equal to its merits and felicity.

I began my discourse by informing his Majesty, that our dominions consisted of two islands, which composed three mighty kingdoms, under one sovereign, besides our plantations in America. I dwelt long upon the fertility of our soil, and the temperature of our climate. I then spoke at large upon the constitution of an English parliament; partly made up of an illustrious body, called the House of Peers; persons of the noblest blood, and of the most ancient and ample patrimonies. I described that extraordinary care always taken of their education in arts and arms, to qualify them for being counsellors both to the king and kingdom; to have a share in the legislature; to be members of the highest court of judicature, whence there can be no appeal; and to be champions always ready for the defence of their prince and country, by their valour, conduct, and fidelity. That these were the ornament and bulwark of the kingdom, worthy followers of their most renowned ancestors, whose honour had been the reward of their virtue, from which their posterity were never once known to degenerate. To these were joined several holy persons, as part of that assembly, under the title of bishops; whose peculiar business it is to take care of religion, and of those who instruct the people therein. These were searched and sought out through the whole nation, by the prince and his wisest counsellors, among such of the priesthood as were most deservedly distinguished by the sanctity of their lives, and the depth of their erudition; who were indeed the spiritual fathers of the clergy and the people.

That the other part of the parliament consisted of an assembly, called the House of Commons, who were all principal gentlemen, freely picked and culled out by the people themselves, for their great abilities and love of their country, to represent the wisdom of the whole nation. And that these two bodies made up the most august assembly in Europe; to whom, in conjunction with the prince, the whole legislature is committed.

I then descended to the courts of justice; over which, the judges, those venerable sages and interpreters of the law, presided, for determining the disputed rights and properties of men, as well as for the punishment of vice and protection of innocence. I mentioned the prudent management of our treasury; the valour and achievements of our forces, by sea and land. I computed the number of our people, by reckoning how many millions there might be of each religious sect, or political party, among us. I did not omit even our sports and pastimes, or any other particular which I thought might redound to the honour of my country. And I finished all with a brief historical account of affairs and events in England for about a hundred years past.

This conversation was not ended under five audiences, each of several hours; and the King heard the whole with great attention, frequently taking notes of what I spoke, as well as memorandums of what questions he intended to ask me.

When I had put an end to these long discourses, his Majesty, in a sixth audience, consulting his notes, proposed many doubts, queries, and objections, upon every article. He asked, what methods were used to cultivate the minds and bodies of our young nobility, and in what kind of business they commonly spent the first and teachable part of their lives. What course was taken to supply that assembly, when any noble family became extinct. What qualifications were necessary in those who are to be created new lords: whether the humour of the prince, a sum of money to a court lady, or a prime minister, or a design of strengthening a party opposite to the public interest, ever happened to be the motives in those advancements. What share of knowledge these lords had in the laws of their country, and how they came by it, so as to enable them to decide the properties of their fellow-subjects in the last resort. Whether they were always so free from avarice, partialities, or want, that a bribe, or some other sinister view, could have no place among them. Whether those holy lords I spoke of were always promoted to that rank upon account of their knowledge in religious matters, and the sanctity of their lives; had never been compliers with the times, while they were common priests; or slavish prostitute chaplains to some nobleman, whose opinions they continued servilely to follow, after they were admitted into that assembly.

He then desired to know what arts were practised in electing those whom I called Commoners: whether a stranger, with a strong purse, might not influence the vulgar voters, to choose him before their own landlord, or the most considerable gentleman in the neighbourhood. How it came to pass, that people were so violently bent upon getting into this assembly, which I allowed to be a great trouble and expense, often to the ruin of their families, without any salary or pension; because this appeared such an exalted strain of virtue and public spirit, that his Majesty seemed to doubt it might possibly not be always sincere. And he desired to know whether such zealous gentlemen could have any views of refunding themselves for the charges and trouble they were at,

by sacrificing the public good to the designs of a weak and
vicious prince, in conjunction with a corrupted ministry. He
multiplied his questions, and sifted me thoroughly upon every
part of this head, proposing numberless inquiries and objections, which I think it not prudent or convenient to repeat.

Upon what I said in relation to our courts of justice, his
Majesty desired to be satisfied in several points: and this I
was the better able to do, having been formerly almost ruined
by a long suit in Chancery, which was decreed for me with
costs. He asked what time was usually spent in determining
between right and wrong, and what degree of expense.
Whether advocates and orators had liberty to plead in causes
manifestly known to be unjust, vexatious, or oppressive.
Whether party, in religion or politics, were observed to be
of any weight in the scale of justice. Whether those pleading
orators were persons educated in the general knowledge of
equity, or only in provincial, national and other local customs.
Whether they or their judges had any part in penning those
laws, which they assumed the liberty of interpreting and
glossing upon at their pleasure. Whether they had ever, at
different times, pleaded for and against the same cause, and
cited precedents to prove contrary opinions. Whether they
received any pecuniary reward for pleading, or delivering
their opinions. And particularly, whether they were ever admitted as members in the lower senate.

He fell next upon the management of our treasury, and
said he thought my memory had failed me, because I computed our taxes at about five or six millions a year, and when
I came to mention the issues, he found they sometimes
amounted to more than double; for the notes he had taken
were very particular in this point, because he hoped, as he
told me, that the knowledge of our conduct might be useful to
him, and he could not be deceived in his calculations. But, if
what I told him were true, he was still at a loss how a king-

dom could run out of its estate, like a private person. He asked me who were our creditors, and where we found money to pay them. He wondered to hear me talk of such chargeable and expensive wars; that certainly we must be a quarrelsome people, or live among very bad neighbours, and that our generals must needs be richer than our kings. He asked what business we had out of our own islands, unless upon the score of trade, or treaty, or to defend the coasts with our fleet. Above all, he was amazed to hear me talk of a mercenary standing army, in the midst of peace, and among a free people. He said, if we were governed by our own consent, in the persons of our representatives, he could not imagine of whom we were afraid, or against whom we were to fight; and would hear my opinion, whether a private man's house might not better be defended by himself, his children and family, than by half a dozen rascals, picked up at a venture in the streets for small wages, who might get a hundred times more by cutting their throats.

He laughed at my "odd kind of arithmetic," as he was pleased to call it, in reckoning the numbers of our people by a computation drawn from the several sects among us, in religion and politics. He said he knew no reason why those who entertain opinions prejudicial to the public, should be obliged to change, or should not be obliged to conceal them. And, as it was tyranny in any government to require the first, so it was weakness not to enforce the second; for a man may be allowed to keep poisons in his closet, but not to vend them about for cordials.

He observed that, among the diversions of our nobility and gentry, I had mentioned gaming: he desired to know, at what age this entertainment was usually taken up, and when it was laid down; how much of their time it employed; whether it ever went so high as to affect their fortunes; whether mean, vicious people, by their dexterity in that art, might not arrive at great riches, and sometimes keep our very nobles in dependence, as well as habituate them to vile companions; wholly take them from the improvement of their minds, and force them, by the losses they received, to learn and practise that infamous dexterity upon others.

He was perfectly astonished with the historical account I gave him of our affairs during the last century; protesting, it was only a heap of conspiracies, rebellions, murders, massacres, revolutions, banishments, the very worst effects that avarice, faction, hypocrisy, perfidiousness, cruelty, rage, madness, hatred, envy, lust, malice, and ambition, could produce.

His Majesty, in another audience, was at the pains to recapitulate the sum of all I had spoken; compared the questions he made with the answers I had given; then, taking me into his hands, and stroking me gently, delivered himself in these words, which I shall never forget, nor the manner he spoke them in: "My little friend Grildrig, you have made a most admirable panegyric upon your country; you have clearly proved, that ignorance, idleness, and vice, are the proper ingredients for qualifying a legislator; that laws are best explained, interpreted, and applied, by those whose interest and abilities lie in perverting, confounding, and eluding them. I observe among you some lines of an institution, which, in its original, might have been tolerable, but these half erased, and the rest wholly blurred and blotted by corruptions. It does not appear, from all you have said, how any one perfection is required toward the procurement of any one station among you; much less, that men are ennobled on account of their virtue; that priests are advanced for their piety or learning; soldiers, for their conduct or valour; judges, for their integrity; senators, for the love of their country; or counsellors, for their wisdom. As for yourself," continued the King, "who have spent the greatest part of your life in travelling, I am well disposed to hope you may hitherto have escaped many vices of your country. But, by what I have gathered from your own relation, and the answers I have with much pains wringed and extorted from you, I cannot but conclude the bulk of your natives to be the most pernicious race of little odious vermin, that nature ever suffered to crawl upon the surface of the earth."

CHAPTER 7

The author's love of his country. He makes a proposal of much advantage to the King, which is rejected. The King's great ignorance in politics. The learning of that country very imperfect and confined. The laws, and military affairs, and parties in the state.

NOTHING BUT an extreme love of truth could have hindered me from concealing this part of my story. It was in vain to discover my resentments, which were always turned into ridicule; and I was forced to rest with patience, while my noble and beloved country was so injuriously treated. I am as heartily sorry as any of my readers can possibly be, that such an occasion was given: but this prince happened to be so curious and inquisitive upon every particular, that it could not consist either with gratitude or good manners, to refuse giving him what satisfaction I was able. Yet thus much I may be allowed to say in my own vindication, that I artfully eluded many of his questions, and gave to every point a more favourable turn, by many degrees, that the strictness of truth would allow; for I have always borne that laudable partiality to my own country, which Dionysius Halicarnassensis, with so much justice, recommends to an historian: I would hide the frailties and deformities of my political mother, and place her virtues and beauties in the most advantageous light. This was my sincere endeavour, in those many discourses I had with that monarch, although it unfortunately failed of success.

But great allowances should be given to a King who lives wholly secluded from the rest of the world, and must, therefore, be altogether unacquainted with the manners and customs that must prevail in other nations: the want of which knowledge will ever produce many prejudices, and a certain narrowness of thinking, from which we, and the politer countries of Europe, are wholly exempted. And it would be hard indeed, if so remote a prince's notions of virtue and vice were to be offered as a standard for all mankind.

To confirm what I have now said, and farther to shew the miserable effects of a confined education, I shall here insert a passage which will hardly obtain belief. In hopes to ingratiate myself farther into his Majesty's favour, I told him of an invention, discovered between three and four hundred years ago, to make a certain powder, into a heap of which, the smallest spark of fire falling, would kindle the whole in a moment, although it were as big as a mountain, and make it all fly up in the air together, with a noise and agitation greater than thunder. That a proper quantity of this powder, rammed into a hollow tube of brass or iron, according to its bigness, would drive a ball of iron or lead with such violence and speed, as nothing was able to sustain its force. That the largest balls, thus discharged, would not only destroy whole ranks of an army at once, but batter the strongest walls to the ground, sink down ships, with a thousand men in each, to the bottom of the sea; and when linked together by a chain, would cut through masts and rigging, divide hundreds of bodies in the middle, and lay all waste before them. That we often put this powder into large, hollow balls of iron, and discharged them by an engine into some city we were besieging, which would rip up the pavements, tear the houses to pieces, burst, and throw splinters on every side, dashing out the brains of all who came near. That I knew the ingredients very well, which were cheap and common; I understood the manner of compounding them, and could direct his workmen how to make those tubes, of a size proportionable to all other things in his Majesty's kingdom, and the largest need not be above a hundred feet long; twenty or thirty of which tubes, charged with the proper quantity of powder and balls, would batter down the walls of the strongest town in his dominions in a few hours, or destroy the whole metropolis, if ever it should pretend to dispute his absolute commands. This I humbly offered to his Majesty, as a small tribute of acknowledgment, in return of so many marks that I had received of his royal favour and protection.

The King was struck with horror at the description I had given of these terrible engines, and the proposal I had made. He was amazed, how so impotent and grovelling an insect as I, (these were his expressions,) could entertain such inhuman ideas, and in so familiar a manner, as to appear wholly unmoved at all the scenes of blood and desolation which I had painted, as the common effects of those destructive machines; whereof, he said, some evil genius, enemy to mankind, must have been the first contriver. As for himself, he protested, that although few things delighted him so much as new discoveries in art or in nature, yet he would rather lose half his kingdom than be privy to such a secret; which he commanded me, as I valued my life, never to mention any more.

A strange effect of narrow principles and views! that a prince, possessed of every quality which procures veneration, love, and esteem; of strong parts, great wisdom, and pro-

found learning, endued with admirable talents, and almost
adored by his subjects, should, from a nice, unnecessary
scruple, whereof in Europe we can have no conception, let
slip an opportunity put into his hands, that would have made
him absolute master of the lives, the liberties, and the fortunes of his people! Neither do I say this with the least intention to detract from the many virtues of that excellent king,
whose character, I am sensible, will, on this account, be very
much lessened in the opinion of an English reader; but, I
take this defect among them to have risen from their ignorance, by not having hitherto reduced politics into a science, as
the more acute wits of Europe have done. For, I remember
very well, in a discourse one day with the King, when I happened to say, "there were several thousand books among us
written upon the art of government," it gave him (directly
contrary to my intention) a very mean opinion of our under-
standings. He professed both to abominate and despise all
mystery, refinement, and intrigue, either in a prince or a minister. He could not tell what I meant by secrets of state,
where an enemy, or some rival nation, were not in the case.
He confined the knowledge of governing within very narrow
bounds, to common sense and reason, to justice and lenity, to
the speedy determination of civil and criminal causes; with
some other obvious topics, which are not worth considering.
And he gave it for his opinion, "That whoever could make
two ears of corn, or two blades of grass, to grow upon a spot
of ground where only one grew before, would deserve better
of mankind, and do more essential service to his country, than
the whole race of politicians put together."

The learning of this people is very defective, consisting
only in morality, history, poetry, and mathematics, wherein
they must be allowed to excel. But the last of these is wholly
applied to what may be useful in life, to the improvement of
agriculture, and all mechanical arts, so that, among us, it

would be little esteemed. And, as to ideas, entities, abstractions, and transcendentals, I could never drive the least conception into their heads.

No law of that country must exceed in words the number of letters in their alphabet, which consists only of two-and-twenty. But, indeed, few of them extend even to that length. They are expressed in the most plain and simple terms, wherein those people are not mercurial enough to discover above one interpretation; and to write a comment upon any law is a capital crime. As to the decision of civil cases, or proceedings against criminals, their precedents are so few, that they have little reason to boast of any extraordinary skill in either.

They have had the art of printing, as well as the Chinese, time out of mind: but their libraries are not very large; for that of the King, which is reckoned the largest, does not amount to above a thousand volumes, placed in a gallery of twelve hundred feet long, whence I had liberty to borrow what books I pleased. The Queen's joiner had contrived, in one of Glumdalclitch's rooms, a kind of wooden machine, five-and-twenty feet high, formed like a standing ladder; the steps each fifty feet long. It was indeed a movable pair of stairs, the lowest end placed at ten feet distance from the wall of the chamber. The book I had a mind to read was put up leaning against the wall; I first mounted to the upper step of the ladder, and turning my face towards the book, began at the top of the page, and so walking to the right and left about eight or ten paces, according to the length of the lines, till I had gotten a little below the level of mine eyes, and then descending gradually till I came to the bottom; after which I mounted again, and began the other page in the same manner, and so turned over the leaf, which I could easily do with both my hands, for it was as thick and stiff as a pasteboard, and in the largest folios not above eighteen or twenty feet long.

Their style is clear, masculine, and smooth, but not florid; for they avoid nothing more than multiplying unnecessary words, or using various expressions. I have perused many of their books, especially those in history and morality. Among the rest, I was much diverted with a little old treatise, which always lay in Glumdalclitch's bedchamber, and belonged to her governess, a grave elderly gentlewoman, who dealt in writings of morality and devotion. The book treats of the weakness of human kind, and is in little esteem, except among the women and the vulgar. However, I was curious to see what an author of that country could say upon such a subject. This writer went through all the usual topics of European moralists, shewing how diminutive, contemptible, and helpless an animal was man in his own nature; how unable to defend himself from inclemencies of the air, or the fury of wild beasts: how much he was excelled by one creature in strength, by another in speed, by a third in foresight, by a fourth in industry. He added that nature was degenerated in these latter declining ages of the world, and could now produce only small abortive births, in comparison of those in ancient times. He said it was very reasonable to think, not only that the species of men were originally much larger, but also that there must have been giants in former ages; which, as it is asserted by history and tradition, so it has been confirmed by huge bones and skulls, casually dug up in several parts of the kingdom, far exceeding the common dwindled race of men in our days. He argued that the very laws of nature absolutely required we should have been made, in the beginning, of a size more large and robust; not so liable to destruction from every little accident, of a tile falling from a house, or a stone cast from the hand of a boy, or being drowned in a little brook. From this way of reasoning, the author drew several moral applications, useful in the conduct of life, but needless here to repeat. For my own part, I could not avoid reflecting how universally this talent was spread, of drawing lectures in morality, or indeed rather matter of discontent and repining, from the quarrels we raise with nature. And I believe, upon a strict inquiry, those quarrels might be shewn as ill-grounded among us as they are among that people.

As to their military affairs, they boast that the King's army consists of a hundred and seventy-six thousand foot, and thirty-two thousand horse: if they may be called an army, which is made up of tradesmen in the several cities, and farmers in the country, whose commanders are only the nobility and gentry, without pay or reward. They are indeed perfect enough in their exercises, and under very good discipline, wherein I saw no great merit: for how should it be otherwise, where every farmer is under the command of his own landlord, and every citizen under that of the principal men in his own city, chosen after the manner of Venice, by ballot?

I have often seen the militia of Lorbrulgrud drawn out to exercise in a great field near the city, of twenty miles square. They were in all not above twenty-five thousand foot, and six thousand horse; but it was impossible for me to compute their number, considering the space of ground they took up. A cavalier, mounted on a large steed, might be about ninety feet high. I have seen this whole body of horse, upon a word of command, draw their swords at once, and brandish them in the air. Imagination can figure nothing so grand, so surprising, and so astonishing! It looked as if ten thousand flashes of lightning were darting at the same time from every quarter of the sky.

I was curious to know how this prince, to whose dominions there is no access from any other country, came to think of armies, or to teach his people the practice of military discipline. But I was soon informed, both by conversation and reading their histories; for, in the course of many ages, they have been troubled with the same disease to which the whole race of mankind is subject: the nobility often contending for power, the people for liberty, and the King for absolute dominion. All which, however happily tempered by the laws of that kingdom, have been sometimes violated by each of the three parties, and have more than once occasioned civil wars; the last whereof was happily put an end to by this prince's grandfather, in a general composition; and the militia, then settled with common consent, has been ever since kept in the strictest duty.

CHAPTER 8

The King and Queen make a progress to the frontiers. The author attends them. The manner in which he leaves the country very particularly related. He returns to England.

I HAD ALWAYS a strong impulse, that I should some time recover my liberty, though it was impossible to conjecture by what means, or to form any project with the least hope of succeeding. The ship in which I sailed was the first known to be driven within sight of that coast, and the King had given strict orders that if at any time another appeared, it should be taken ashore, and, with all its crew and passengers, brought in a tumbril to Lorbrulgrud. He was strongly bent to get me a woman of my own size, by whom I might propagate the breed; but I think I should rather have died than undergone the disgrace of leaving a posterity to be kept in cages, like tame canary birds, and perhaps, in time, sold about the kingdom, to persons of quality, for curiosities. I was indeed treated with much kindness; I was the favourite of a great king and queen, and the delight of the whole court; but it was upon such a foot as ill became the dignity of human kind. I could never forget those domestic pledges I had left behind me. I wanted to be among people with whom I could converse upon even terms, and walk about the streets and fields without being afraid of being trod to death like a frog or a young puppy. But my deliverance came sooner than I expected, and in a manner not very common; the whole story and circumstances of which I shall faithfully relate.

I had now been two years in the country; and about the beginning of the third, Glumdalclitch and I attended the King and Queen in a progress to the south coast of the kingdom. I was carried, as usual, in my travelling box, which, as I have already described, was a very convenient closet, of twelve feet wide. And I had ordered a hammock to be fixed, by silken ropes, from the four corners at the top, to break the jolts, when a servant carried me before him on horseback, as I sometimes desired; and would often sleep in my hammock, while we were upon the road. On the roof of my closet, not directly over the middle of the hammock, I ordered the joiner to cut out a hole of a foot square, to give me air in hot weather, as I slept: which hole I shut at pleasure with a board that drew backward and forward through a groove.

When we came to our journey's end, the King thought proper to pass a few days at a palace he has near Flanflasnic, a city within eighteen English miles of the seaside. Glumdalclitch and I were much fatigued: I had gotten a small cold, but the poor girl was so ill as to be confined to her chamber. I longed to see the ocean, which must be the only scene of my escape, if ever it should happen. I pretended to be worse than I really was, and desired leave to take the fresh air of the sea, with a page I was very fond of, and who had been sometimes trusted with me. I shall never forget with what unwillingness Glumdalclitch consented, nor the strict charge she gave the page to be careful of me, bursting at the same time into a flood of tears, as if she had some foreboding of what was to happen. The boy took me out in my box, about half an hour's walk from the palace, towards the rocks on the seashore. I ordered him to set me down, and lifting up one of the sashes, cast many a wistful melancholy look towards the sea. I found myself not very well, and told the page that I had a mind to take a nap in my hammock, which I hoped would do me good. I got in, and the boy shut the window close down to keep out the cold. I soon fell asleep, and all I can conjecture is that while I slept, the page, thinking no danger could happen, went among the rocks to look for birds' eggs, having before observed him from my window searching about and picking up one or two in the clefts. Be that as it will, I found myself suddenly awakened with a violent pull upon the ring, which was fastened at the top of my box for the conveniency of carriage. I felt my box raised very high in the air, and then borne forward with prodigious speed. The first jolt had like to have shaken me out of my hammock, but afterwards the motion was easy enough. I called out several times, as loud as I could raise my voice, but all to no purpose. I looked towards my windows, and could see nothing but the clouds and sky. I heard a noise over my head, like the clapping of wings, and then began to perceive the woeful condition I was in; that some eagle had got the ring of my box in his beak, with an intent to let it fall on a rock, like a tortoise in a shell, and then pick out my body and devour it: for the sagacity and smell of this bird enabled him to discover his quarry at a great distance, though better concealed than I could be within a two-inch board.

In a little time, I observed the noise and flutter of wings

to increase very fast, and my box was tossed up and down like a sign in a windy day. I heard several bangs or buffets, as I thought, given to the eagle (for such I am certain it must have been that held the ring of my box in his beak), and then, all on a sudden, felt myself falling perpendicularly down, for above a minute, but with such incredible swiftness that I almost lost my breath. My fall was stopped by a terrible squash that sounded louder to my ears than the cataract of Niagara; after which, I was quite in the dark for another minute, and then my box began to rise so high, that I could see light from the tops of the windows. I new perceived I was fallen into the sea. My box, by the weight of my body, the goods that were in, and the broad plates of iron fixed for strength at the four corners of the top and bottom, floated about five feet deep in water. I did then, and do now, suppose that the eagle who flew away with my box, was pursued by two or three others, and forced to let me drop, while he defended himself against the rest, who hoped to share in the prey. The plates of iron fastened at the bottom of the box (for those were the strongest) preserved the balance while it fell, and hindered it from being broken on the surface of the water. Every joint of it was well grooved; and the door did not move on hinges, but up and down like a sash, which kept my closet so tight, that very little water came in. I got with much difficulty out of my hammock, having first ventured to draw back the slip-board on the roof already mentioned, contrived on purpose to let in air, for want of which I found myself almost stifled.

How often did I then wish myself with my dear Glumdalclitch, from whom one single hour had so far divided me! And I may say with truth, that, in the midst of my own misfortunes, I could not forbear lamenting my poor nurse, the grief she would suffer for my loss, the displeasure of the Queen, and the ruin of her fortune. Perhaps many travellers have not been under greater difficulties and distress than I was at this juncture, expecting every moment to see my box dashed to pieces, or at least overset by the first violent blast, or rising wave. A breach in one single pane of glass would have been immediate death: nor could anything have preserved the windows, but the strong lattice wires placed on the outside, against accidents in travelling. I saw the water ooze in at several crannies, although the leaks were not considerable, and I endeavoured to stop them as well as I could. I was not able to lift up the roof of my closet, which otherwise I certainly should have done, and sat on the top of it; where I might at least preserve myself some hours longer, than by being shut up (as I may call it) in the hold. Or, if I escaped these dangers for a day or two, what could I expect but a miserable death of cold and hunger? I was for four hours under these circumstances, expecting, and indeed wishing, every moment to be my last.

I have already told the reader, that there were two strong staples fixed upon that side of my box which had no window, and into which the servant, who used to carry me on horseback, would put a leathern belt, and buckle it about his waist. Being in this disconsolate state, I heard, or at least thought I heard, some kind of grating noise on that side of my box where the staples were fixed; and soon after I began to fancy, that the box was pulled or towed along the sea; for I now and then felt a sort of tugging, which made the waves rise near the tops of my windows, leaving me almost in the dark. This gave me some faint hopes of relief, although I was not able to imagine how it could be brought about. I ventured to unscrew one of my chairs, which were always fastened to the floor; and having made a hard shift to screw it down again, directly under the slipping-board that I had lately opened, I mounted on the chair, and, putting my mouth as near as I could to the hole, I called for help in a loud voice, and in all the languages I understood. I then fastened my handkerchief to a stick I usually carried, and, thrusting it up the hole, waved it several times in the air, that, if any boat or ship were near, the seamen might conjecture some unhappy mortal to be shut up in the box.

I found no effect from all I could do, but plainly perceived my closet to be moved along; and in the space of an hour, or better, that side of the box where the staples were, and had no windows, struck against something that was hard. I apprehended it to be a rock, and found myself tossed more than ever. I plainly heard a noise upon the cover of my closet, like that of a cable, and the grating of it as it passed through the ring. I then found myself hoisted up by degrees, at least three feet higher than I was before. Whereupon I again thrust up my stick and handkerchief, calling for help till I was almost hoarse. In return to which, I heard a great shout repeated three times, giving me such transports of joy as are not to be conceived but by those who feel them. I now heard a trampling over my head, and somebody calling through the hole with a loud voice, in the English tongue, "If there be anybody below, let them speak." I answered I was an Englishman, drawn by ill fortune into the greatest calamity that ever any creature underwent, and begged, by all that was moving, to be delivered out of the dungeon I was in. The voice replied I was safe, for my box was fastened to their ship; and the carpenter should immediately come and saw a hole in the cover, large enough to pull me out. I answered, that was needless, and would take up too much time; for there was no more to be done, but let one of the crew put his finger into the ring and take the box out of the sea into the ship, and so into the captain's cabin. Some of them, upon hearing me talk so wildly, thought I was mad; others laughed; for indeed it never came into my head that I was now got among people of my own stature and strength. The carpenter came, and in a few minutes sawed a passage about four feet square, then let down a small ladder, upon which I mounted, and thence was taken into the ship in a very weak condition.

The sailors were all in amazement, and asked me a thousand questions, which I had no inclination to answer. I was equally confounded at the sight of so many pigmies, for such I took them to be, after having so long accustomed mine eyes to the monstrous objects I had left. But the captain, Mr. Thomas Wilcocks, an honest worthy Shropshire man, observing I was ready to faint, took me into his cabin, gave me a cordial to comfort me, and made me turn in upon his own bed, advising me to take a little rest, of which I had great need. Before I went to sleep, I gave him to understand that I had some valuable furniture in my box, too good to be lost; a fine hammock; a handsome fieldbed, two chairs, a table, and a cabinet. That my closet was hung on all sides, or rather quilted, with silk and cotton: that, if he would let one of the crew bring up my closet into his cabin, I would open it there before him, and shew him my goods. The captain, hearing me utter these absurdities, concluded I was raving: however (I suppose to pacify me), he promised to give order as I desired, and going upon deck, sent some of his men down into my closet, whence (as I afterwards found) they drew up all my goods, and stripped off the quilting; but the chairs, cabinet, and bedstead, being screwed to the floor, were much damaged by the ignorance of the seamen, who tore them up by force. Then, they knocked off some of the boards for the use of the ship, and, when they got all they had a mind for, let the hull drop into the sea, which, by reason of many breaches made in the bottom and sides, sunk to rights. And, indeed, I was glad not to have been a spectator of the havoc they made, because I am confident it would have sensibly touched me, by bringing former passages into my mind, which I would rather have forgot.

I slept some hours, but perpetually disturbed with

dreams of the place I had left, and the dangers I had escaped. However, upon waking, I found myself much recovered. It was now about eight o'clock at night, and the captain ordered supper immediately, thinking I had already fasted too long. He entertained me with great kindness, observing me not to look wildly, or talk inconsistently; and, when we were left alone, desired I would give him a relation of my travels, and by what accident I came to be set adrift in that monstrous wooden chest. He said that about twelve o'clock at noon, as he was looking through his glass, he spied it at a distance, and thought it was a sail, which he had a mind to make, being not much out of his course, in hopes of buying some biscuit, his own beginning to fall short. That, upon coming nearer, and finding his error, he sent out his long-boat to discover what it was; that his men came back in a fright, swearing they had seen a swimming house. That he laughed at their folly, and went himself in the boat, ordering his men to take a strong cable along with them. That the weather being calm, he rowed round me several times, observed my windows, and wire lattices that defended them. That he discovered two staples upon one side, which was all of boards without any passage for light. He then commanded his men to row up to that side, and fastening a cable to one of the staples, ordered them to tow my chest, as they called it, towards the ship. When it was there, he gave directions to fasten another cable to the ring fixed in the cover, and to raise up my chest with pulleys, which all the sailors were not able to do above two or three feet. He said, they saw my stick and handker-chief thrust out of the hole, and concluded that some un-happy man must be shut up in the cavity. I asked whether he or the crew had seen any prodigious birds in the air about the time he first discovered me. To which he answered, that discoursing this matter with the sailors while I was asleep, one of them said he had observed three eagles flying towards

the north, but remarked nothing of their being larger than
the usual size; which I suppose must be imputed to the great
height they were at; and he could not guess the reason of my
question. I then asked the captain how far he reckoned we
might be from land. He said by the best computation he
could make, we were at least a hundred leagues. I assured
him that he must be mistaken by almost half, for I had not
left the country whence I came above two hours before I
dropped into the sea. Whereupon, he began again to think
that my brain was disturbed, of which he gave me a hint,
and advised me to go to bed in a cabin he had provided. I assured him I was well refreshed with his good entertainment
and company, and as much in my senses as ever I was in my
life. He then grew serious, and desired to ask me freely
whether I were not troubled in my mind by the consciousness
of some enormous crime, for which I was punished, at the
command of some prince, by exposing me in that chest; as
great criminals, in other countries, have been forced to sea in
a leaky vessel, without provisions: for, although he should
be sorry to have taken so ill a man into his ship, yet, he would
engage his word to set me safe ashore, in the first port where
we arrived. He added that his suspicions were much increased
by some very absurd speeches I had delivered at first to his
sailors, and afterwards to himself, in relation to my closet or
chest, as well as by my odd looks and behaviour, while I was
at supper.

I begged his patience to hear me tell my story, which I
faithfully did, from the last time I left England, to the
moment he first discovered me. And, as truth always forces
its way into rational minds, so this honest, worthy gentleman, who had some tincture of learning, and very good sense,
was immediately convinced of my candour and veracity. But
farther, to confirm all I have said, I entreated him to give
order that my cabinet should be brought, of which I had the

key in my pocket; for he had already informed me how the
seamen disposed of my closet. I opened it in his own presence,
and shewed him the small collection of rarities I made in the
country from which I had been so strangely delivered. There
was the comb I had contrived out of the stumps of the King's
beard, and another of the same materials, but fixed into a
paring of her Majesty's thumb-nail, which served for the
back. There was a collection of needles and pins, from a foot
to half a yard long; four wasps' stings, like joiners' tacks;
some combings of the Queen's hair; a gold ring, which one
day she made me a present of, in a most obliging manner,
taking it from her little finger, and throwing it over my head
like a collar. I desired the captain would please to accept
this ring in return of his civilities, which he absolutely refused.
I shewed him a corn that I had cut off, with my own hand,
from a maid of honour's toe; it was about the bigness of a
Kentish pippin, and grown so hard, that, when I returned to
England, I got it hollowed into a cup, and set in silver. Lastly,
I desired him to see the breeches I had then on, which were
made of a mouse's skin.

I could force nothing on him but a footman's tooth,
which I observed him to examine with great curiosity, and
found he had a fancy for it. He received it with abundance
of thanks, more than such a trifle could deserve. It was drawn
by an unskilful surgeon, in a mistake, from one of Glumdalclitch's men, who was afflicted with the toothache, but it was
as sound as any in his head. I got it cleaned, and put it into my
cabinet. It was about a foot long, and four inches in
diameter.

The captain was very well satisfied with this plain relation I had given him, and said he hoped, when we returned
to England, I would oblige the world by putting it on paper,
and making it public. My answer was that I thought we were
overstocked with books of travels: that nothing could now

pass which was not extraordinary; wherein I doubted some authors less consulted truth than their own vanity, or interest, or the diversion of ignorant readers; that my story could contain little beside common events, without those ornamental descriptions of strange plants, trees, birds, and other animals; or, of the barbarous customs and idolatry of savage people, with which most writers abound. However, I thanked him for his good opinion, and promised to take the matter into my thoughts.

He said he wondered at one thing very much, which was, to hear me speak so loud; asking me whether the king or queen of that country were thick of hearing. I told him it was what I had been used to for above two years past, and that I admired as much at the voices of him and his men, who seemed to me only to whisper, and yet I could hear them well enough. But, when I spoke in that country, it was like a man talking in the streets to another looking out from the top of a steeple, unless when I was placed on a table, or held in any person's hand. I told him I had likewise observed another thing, that when I first got into the ship, and the sailors stood all about me, I thought they were the most little contemptible creatures I had ever beheld. For, indeed, while I was in that prince's country, I could never endure to look in a glass after mine eyes had been accustomed to such prodigious objects, because the comparison gave me so despicable a conceit of myself. The captain said that, while we were at supper, he observed me to look at everything with a sort of wonder, and that I often seemed hardly able to contain my laughter, which he knew not well how to take, but imputed it to some disorder in my brain. I answered it was very true; and I wondered how I could forbear, when I saw his dishes of the size of a silver three-pence, a leg of pork hardly a mouthful, a cup not so big as a nut-shell; and so I went on, describing the rest of his household stuff and provisions, after the same manner. For, although the Queen had ordered a little equipage of all things necessary for me, while I was in her service, yet my ideas were wholly taken up with what I saw on every side of me, and I winked at my own littleness, as people do at their own faults. The captain understood my raillery very well, and merrily replied with the old English proverb, that he doubted mine eyes were bigger than my belly, for he did not observe my stomach so good, although I had fasted all day; and, continuing in his mirth, protested he would have gladly given a hundred pounds, to have seen my closet in the eagle's bill, and afterwards in its fall from so great a height into the sea; which would certainly have been a most astonishing object, worthy to have the description of it transmitted to future ages: and the comparison of Phaeton was so obvious, that he could not forbear applying it, although I did not much admire the conceit.

The captain, having been at Tonquin, was, in his return to England, driven north-eastward to the latitude of 44 degrees, and longitude of 143. But meeting a trade-wind two days after I came on board him, we sailed southward a long time, and coasting New Holland, kept our course west-south-west, and then south-south-west, till we doubled the Cape of Good Hope. Our voyage was very prosperous, but I shall not trouble the reader with a journal of it. The captain called in at one or two ports, and sent in his long-boat for provisions and fresh water; but I never went out of the ship till we came into the Downs, which was on the third day of June, 1706, about nine months after my escape. I offered to leave my goods in security for payment of my freight; but the captain protested he would not receive one farthing. We took a kind leave of each other, and I made him promise that he would come to see me at my house in Redriff. I hired a horse and guide for five shillings, which I borrowed of the captain.

As I was on the road, observing the littleness of the

houses, the trees, the cattle, and the people, I began to think myself in Lilliput. I was afraid of trampling on every traveller I met, and often called aloud to have them stand out of the way, so that I had like to have gotten one or two broken heads for my impertinence.

When I came to my own house, for which I was forced to inquire, one of the servants opening the door, I bent down to go in, (like a goose under a gate,) for fear of striking my head. My wife ran out to embrace me, but I stooped lower than her knees, thinking she could otherwise never be able to reach my mouth. My daughter kneeled to ask my blessing, but I could not see her till she arose, having been so long used to stand with my head and eyes erect to above sixty feet; and then I went to take her up with one hand by the waist. I looked down upon the servants, and one or two friends who were in the house, as if they had been pigmies and I a giant. I told my wife she had been too thrifty, for I found she had starved herself and her daughter to nothing. In short, I behaved myself so unaccountably, that they were all of the captain's opinion when he first saw me, and concluded I had lost my wits. This I mention as an instance of the great power of habit and prejudice.

In a little time, I and my family and friends came to a right understanding; but my wife protested, I should never go to sea any more; although my evil destiny so ordered, that she had not power to hinder me, as the reader may know hereafter. In the meantime, I here conclude the second part of my unfortunate voyages.

THE END OF
A VOYAGE TO BROBDINGNAG

A VOYAGE TO

Laputa

Balnibarbi, Glubbdubdrib, Luggnagg, & Japan

Parts
Unknown

LAND C.Patience
OF St.James
Bay
IESSO
Salmon
Bay
C.Canal

COMPANY'S
LAND

LAPUTA

BALNIBARBI
Lagado

Straits of the Vries

Stats I.

Sea of Corea
Torpui Toy
Yedo Red Pt.
JAPAN Bosho Pt.
Xamoschi Barnevelts
Tonsa I. Ongeluckig I.
Bungo I. South I.
Dineris Straits

Maldonada

GLUBBDUBDRIB
Discovered A.D.1701

LUGGNAGG

Traldragdubh

I.Tanaxima

Sialo
Glangurn

Clumegnig

Glanguenstald

I.Deserta

Urac
Timal

CHAPTER I

The author sets out on his third voyage. Is taken by pirates.
The malice of a Dutchman. His arrival at an island. He is
received into Laputa.

I HAD NOT BEEN at home
above ten days, when Captain William Robinson, a Cornish
man, commander of the *Hopewell,* a stout ship of three hundred tons, came to my house. I had formerly been surgeon of
another ship, where he was master and a fourth part owner,
in a voyage to the Levant. He had always treated me more
like a brother than an inferior officer; and, hearing of my
arrival, made me a visit, as I apprehended, only out of friendship, for nothing passed more than what is usual after long
absences. But, repeating his visits often, expressing his joy to
find me in good health, asking whether I were now settled
for life, adding that he intended a voyage to the East Indies
in two months; at last he plainly invited me, though with
some apologies, to be surgeon of the ship; that I should have
another surgeon under me, beside our two mates; that my
salary should be double to the usual pay; and that, having
experienced my knowledge in sea-affairs to be at least equal
to his, he would enter into any engagement to follow my advice, as much as if I had shared in the command.

He said so many other obliging things, and I knew him
to be so honest a man, that I could not reject his proposal;
the thirst I had of seeing the world, notwithstanding my past
misfortunes, continuing as violent as ever. The only difficulty
that remained, was to persuade my wife, whose consent, however, I at last obtained, by the prospect of advantage she
proposed to her children.

We set out the 5th day of August, 1706, and arrived at

Fort St. George the 11th of April, 1707. We staid there three weeks to refresh our crew, many of whom were sick. From thence we went to Tonquin, where the captain resolved to continue some time, because many of the goods he intended to buy were not ready, nor could he expect to be dispatched in several months. Therefore, in hopes to defray some of the charges he must be at, he bought a sloop, loaded it with several sorts of goods, wherewith the Tonquinese usually trade to the neighbouring islands, and putting fourteen men on board, whereof three were of the country, he appointed me master of the sloop, and gave me power to traffic, while he transacted his affairs at Tonquin.

We had not sailed above three days, when, a great storm arising, we were driven five days to the north-north-east, and then to the east; after which we had fair weather, but still with a pretty strong gale from the west. Upon the tenth day we were chased by two pirates, who soon overtook us; for my sloop was so deep laden, that she sailed very slow, neither were we in a condition to defend ourselves.

We were boarded about the same time by both the pirates, who entered furiously at the head of their men; but, finding us all prostrate upon our faces, (for so I gave order,) they pinioned us with strong ropes, and, setting a guard upon us, went to search the sloop.

I observed among them a Dutchman, who seemed to be of some authority, though he was not commander of either ship. He knew us by our countenances to be Englishmen, and, jabbering to us in his own language, swore we should be tied back to back, and thrown into the sea. I spoke Dutch tolerably well; I told him who we were, and begged him, in consideration of our being Christians and Protestants, of neighbouring countries in strict alliance, that he would move the captains to take some pity on us. This inflamed his rage; he repeated his threatenings, and, turning to his companions, spoke with great vehemence in the Japanese language, as I suppose, often using the word *Christianos*.

The largest of the two pirate ships was commanded by a Japanese captain, who spoke a little Dutch, but very imperfectly. He came up to me, and, after several questions, which I answered in great humility, he said we should not die. I made the captain a very low bow, and then, turning to the Dutchman, said I was sorry to find more mercy in a heathen than in a brother Christian. But I had soon reason to repent those foolish words; for that malicious reprobate, having often endeavoured in vain to persuade both the captains that I might be thrown into the sea (which they would not yield to, after the promise made me that I should not die), however, prevailed so far, as to have a punishment inflicted on me, worse, in all human appearance, than death itself. My men were sent by an equal division into both the pirate ships, and my sloop new manned. As to myself, it was determined that I should be set adrift in a small canoe, with paddles and a sail, and four days' provisions; which last, the Japanese captain was so kind to double out of his own stores, and would permit no man to search me. I got down into the canoe, while the Dutchman, standing upon the deck, loaded me with all the curses and injurious terms his language could afford.

About an hour before we saw the pirates, I had taken an observation, and found we were in the latitude of 46 N. and longitude of 183. When I was at some distance from the pirates, I discovered, by my pocket-glass, several islands to the south-east. I set up my sail, the wind being fair, with a design to reach the nearest of those islands, which I made a shift to do in about three hours. It was all rocky; however, I got many birds' eggs; and, striking fire, I kindled some heath and dry sea-weed, by which I roasted my eggs. I ate no other supper, being resolved to spare my provisions as much as I could. I passed the night under the shelter of a rock, strewing some heath under me, and slept pretty well.

The next day I sailed to another island, and thence to a third and fourth, sometimes using my sail, and sometimes my paddles. But not to trouble the reader with a particular account of my distresses, let it suffice that on the fifth day I arrived at the last island in my sight, which lay south-south-east to the former.

This island was at a greater distance than I expected, and I did not reach it in less than five hours. I encompassed it almost round, before I could find a convenient place to land in; which was a small creek, about three times the wideness of my canoe. I found the island to be all rocky, only a little intermingled with tufts of grass, and sweet-smelling herbs. I took out my small provisions, and, after having refreshed myself, I secured the remainder in a cave, whereof there were great numbers; I gathered plenty of eggs upon the rocks, and got a quantity of dry sea-weed and parched grass, which I designed to kindle the next day, and roast my eggs as well as I could; for I had about me my flint, steel, match, and burning-glass. I lay all night in the cave where I had lodged my provisions. My bed was the same dry grass and sea-weed which I intended for fuel. I slept very little, for the disquiets of my mind prevailed over my weariness, and kept me awake. I considered how impossible it was to preserve my life in so desolate a place, and how miserable my end must be; yet found myself so listless and desponding, that I had not the heart to rise: and, before I could get spirits enough to creep out of my cave, the day was far advanced. I walked a while among the rocks: the sky was perfectly clear, and the sun so hot, that I was forced to turn my face from it; when, all on a sudden, it became obscure, as I thought, in a manner very different from what happens by the interposition of a cloud. I turned back, and perceived a vast opaque body between me and the sun, moving forwards towards the island: it seemed to me about two miles high, and hid the sun six or seven minutes, but I did not observe the air to be much colder, or the sky more darkened, than if I had stood under the shade of a mountain. As it approached nearer over the place where I was, it appeared to be a firm substance, the bottom flat, smooth, and shining very bright, from the reflection of the sea below. I stood upon a height about two hundred yards from the shore, and saw this vast body descending almost to a parallel with me, at less than an English mile distance. I took out my pocket perspective, and could plainly discover numbers of people moving up and down the sides of it, which appeared to be sloping; but what those people were doing, I was not able to distinguish.

The natural love of life gave me some inward motion of joy, and I was ready to entertain a hope, that this adventure might, some way or other, help to deliver me from the desolate place and condition I was in. But, at the same time, the reader can hardly conceive my astonishment, to behold an island in the air, inhabited by men, who were able (as it should seem) to rise or sink, or put it into progressive motion, as they pleased. But not being at that time in a disposition to philosophize upon this phenomenon, I rather chose to observe what course the island would take, because it seemed for a while to stand still. Yet, soon after, it advanced nearer, and I could see the sides of it encompassed with several gradations of galleries, and stairs, at certain intervals, to descend from one to the other. In the lowest gallery, I beheld some people fishing with long angling rods, and others looking on. I waved my cap (for my hat was long since worn out) and my handkerchief towards the island; and upon its nearer approach, I called and shouted with the utmost strength of my voice: and then looking circumspectly, I beheld a crowd gather to that side which was most in my view. I found, by their pointing towards me and to each other, that they plainly discovered me, although they made no return to my shouting. But I could see four or five men running in great haste, up the stairs to the top of the island, who then disappeared. I happened rightly to conjecture that these were sent for orders, to some person in authority upon this occasion.

The number of people increased, and in less than half an hour, the island was moved and raised in such a manner, that the lowest gallery appeared in a parallel of less than a hundred yards' distance from the height where I stood. I then put myself in the most supplicating postures, and spoke in the humblest accent, but received no answer. Those who stood nearest over against me seemed to be persons of distinction, as I supposed by their habit. They conferred earnestly with each other, looking often upon me. At length, one of them called out in a clear, polite, smooth dialect, not unlike in sound to the Italian; and, therefore, I returned an answer in that language, hoping, at least, that the cadence might be more agreeable to his ears. Although neither of us understood the other, yet my meaning was easily known, for the people saw the distress I was in.

They made signs for me to come down from the rock, and go towards the shore, which I accordingly did; and the flying island being raised to a convenient height, the verge directly over me, a chain was let down from the lowest gallery, with a seat fastened to the bottom, to which I fixed myself, and was drawn up by the pulleys.

CHAPTER 2

The humours and dispositions of the Laputians described. An account of their learning. Of the King and his court. The author's reception there. The inhabitants subject to fear and disquietudes. An account of the women.

AT MY ALIGHTING, I was surrounded with a crowd of people, but those who stood nearest seemed to be of better quality. They beheld me with all the marks and circumstances of wonder, neither, indeed, was I much in their debt; having never till then seen a race of mortals so singular in their shapes, habits, and countenances. Their heads were all reclined, either to the right or the left; one of their eyes turned inward, and the other directly up to the zenith. Their outward garments were adorned with the figures of suns, moons, and stars; interwoven with those of fiddles, flutes, harps, trumpets, guitars, harpsichords, and many other instruments of music unknown to us in Europe. I observed, here and there, many in the habit of servants, with a brown bladder, fastened like a flail to the end of a stick, which they carried in their hands. In each bladder was a small quantity of dried pease, or little pebbles, as I was afterwards informed. With these bladders they now and then flapped the mouths and ears of those who stood near them, of which practice I could not then conceive the meaning. It seems the minds of these people are so taken up with intense speculations, that they neither can speak, nor attend to the discourses of others, without being roused by some external taction upon the organs of speech and hearing; for which reason, those persons who are able to afford it, always keep a flapper, (the original is *climenole,*) in their family, as one of their domestics; nor ever walk abroad, or make visits, without him. And the business of this officer is, when

two, three, or more persons are in company, gently to strike
with his bladder the mouth of him who is to speak, and the
right ear of him or them to whom the speaker addresses himself. This flapper is likewise employed diligently to attend
his master in his walks, and upon occasion to give him a soft
slap on his eyes; because he is always so wrapped up in cogi-
tation, that he is in manifest danger of falling down every
precipice, and bouncing his head against every post; and in
the streets, of justling others, or being justled himself into
the kennel.

It was necessary to give the reader this information,
without which he would be at the same loss with me to understand the proceedings of these people, as they conducted me
up the stairs to the top of the island, and from thence to the
royal palace. While we were ascending, they forgot several
times what they were about, and left me to myself, till their
memories were again roused by their flappers; for they appeared altogether unmoved by the sight of my foreign habit
and countenance, and by the shouts of the vulgar, whose
thoughts and minds were more disengaged.

At last we entered the palace, and proceeded into the
chamber of presence, where I saw the King seated on his
throne, attended on each side by persons of prime quality.
Before the throne, was a large table filled with globes and
spheres, and mathematical instruments of all kinds. His
Majesty took not the least notice of us, although our entrance
was not without sufficient noise, by the concourse of all persons belonging to the court. But he was then deep in a prob-
lem; and we attended at least an hour before he could solve
it. There stood by him, on each side, a young page with flaps
in their hands, and when they saw he was at leisure, one of
them gently struck his mouth, and the other his right ear;
at which he startled like one awaked on the sudden, and
looking towards me and the company I was in, recollected the

occasion of our coming, whereof he had been informed before. He spoke some words, whereupon immediately a young man with a flap came up to my side, and flapped me gently on the right ear; but I made signs, as well as I could, that I had no occasion for such an instrument; which, as I afterwards found, gave his Majesty, and the whole court, a very mean opinion of my understanding. The King, as far as I could conjecture, asked me several questions, and I addressed myself to him in all the languages I had. When it was found I could neither understand nor be understood, I was conducted by his order to an apartment in his palace, (this prince being distinguished above all his predecessors for his hospitality to strangers,) where two servants were appointed to attend me. My dinner was brought, and four persons of quality, whom I remembered to have seen very near the King's person, did me the honour to dine with me. We had two courses, of three dishes each. In the first course, there was a shoulder of mutton cut into an equilateral triangle, a piece of beef into a rhomboides, and a pudding into a cycloid. The second course was two ducks trussed up in the form of fiddles; sausages and puddings, resembling flutes and hautboys, and a breast of veal in the shape of a harp. The servants cut our bread into cones, cylinders, parallelograms, and several other mathematical figures.

While we were at dinner, I made bold to ask the names of several things in their language, and those noble persons, by the assistance of their flappers, delighted to give me answers, hoping to raise my admiration of their great abilities, if I could be brought to converse with them. I was soon able to call for bread or drink, or whatever else I wanted.

After dinner my company withdrew, and a person was sent to me by the King's order, attended by a flapper. He brought with him pen, ink, and paper, and three or four books, giving me to understand by signs, that he was sent to teach me the language. We sat together four hours, in which time I wrote down a great number of words in columns; with the translations over-against them; I likewise made a shift to learn several short sentences. For my tutor would order one of my servants to fetch something, to turn about, to make a bow, to sit, or to stand, or walk, and the like. Then I took down the sentence in writing. He shewed me also, in one of his books, the figures of the sun, moon, and stars, the zodiac, the tropics, and polar circles, together with the denominations of many planes and solids. He gave me the names and descriptions of all the musical instruments, and the general terms of art in playing on each of them. After he had left me, I placed all my words, with their interpretation, in alphabetical order. And thus, in a few days, by the help of a very faithful memory, I got some insight into their language.

The word which I interpret the Flying or Floating Island, is in the original *Laputa,* whereof I could never learn the right etymology. *Lap,* in the old obsolete language, signifies high; and *untuh,* a governor; from which they say, by corruption, was derived *Laputa,* from *Lapuntuh.* But I do not approve of this derivation, which seems to be a little strained. I ventured to offer to the learned among them, a conjecture of my own, that Laputa was *quasi lap outed; lap* signifying properly the dancing of the sun-beams in the sea, and *outed* a wing; which, however, I shall not obtrude, but submit to the judicious reader.

Those to whom the King had entrusted me, observing how ill I was clad, ordered a tailor to come next morning and take measure for a suit of clothes. This operator did his office after a different manner from those of his trade in Europe. He first took my altitude by a quadrant, and then, with rule and compasses, described the dimensions and outlines of my whole body, all which he entered upon paper; and, in six days, brought my clothes very ill made, and quite out of shape, by happening to mistake a figure in the calculation. But my comfort was, that I observed such accidents very frequent, and little regarded.

During my confinement for want of clothes, and by an indisposition that held me some days longer, I much enlarged my dictionary; and when I went next to court, was able to understand many things the King spoke, and to return him some kind of answers. His Majesty had given orders, that the island should move north-east and by east, to the vertical point over Lagado, the metropolis of the whole kingdom below, upon the firm earth. It was about ninety leagues distant, and our voyage lasted four days and a half. I was not in the least sensible of the progressive motion made in the air by the island. On the second morning, about eleven o'clock, the King himself in person, attended by his nobility, courtiers, and officers, having prepared all their musical instruments, played on them for three hours without intermission, so that I was quite stunned with the noise; neither could I possibly guess the meaning, till my tutor informed me. He said, "that the people of their island had their ears always adapted to hear the music of the spheres, which always played at certain periods, and the court was now prepared to bear their part, in whatever instrument they most excelled."

In our journey towards Lagado, the capital city, his Majesty ordered that the island should stop over certain towns and villages, from whence he might receive the petitions of his subjects. And, to this purpose, several pack-threads were let down, with small weights at the bottom. On these packthreads the people strung their petitions, which mounted up directly, like the scraps of paper fastened by schoolboys at the end of the string that holds their kite. Sometimes we received wine and victuals from below, which were drawn up by pulleys.

The knowledge I had in mathematics gave me great assistance in acquiring their phraseology, which depended much
upon that science, and music; and in the latter I was not un-
skilled. Their ideas are perpetually conversant in lines and
figures. If they would, for example, praise the beauty of a
woman, or any other animal, they describe it by rhombs, circles, parallelograms, ellipses, and other geometrical terms,
or by words of art drawn from music, needless here to repeat.
I observed, in the King's kitchen, all sorts of mathematical
and musical instruments, after the figures of which they cut
up the joints that were served to his Majesty's table.

Their houses are very ill-built, the walls bevel, without
one right angle in any apartment; and this defect arises from
the contempt they bear to practical geometry, which they
despise as vulgar and mechanic; those instructions they give
being too refined for the intellects of their workmen, which
occasions prepetual mistakes. And although they are dexterous enough upon a piece of paper, in the management of
the rule, the pencil, and the divider, yet in the common actions
and behaviour of life, I have not seen a more clumsy, awk-
ward, and unhandy people, nor so slow and perplexed in
their conceptions upon all other subjects, except those of
mathematics and music. They are very bad reasoners, and
vehemently given to opposition, unless when they happen to
be of the right opinion, which is seldom their case. Imagination, fancy, and invention, they are wholly strangers to, nor
have any words in their language, by which those ideas can be
expressed; the whole compass of their thoughts and mind
being shut up within the two formentioned sciences.

Most of them, and especially those who deal in the
astronomical part, have great faith in judicial astrology,
although they are ashamed to own it publicly. But what I
chiefly admired, and thought altogether unaccountable, was
the strong disposition I observed in them towards news and

politics, perpetually inquiring into public affairs, giving their judgments in matters of state, and passionately disputing every inch of a party opinion. I have indeed observed the same disposition among most of the mathematicians I have known in Europe, although I could never discover the least analogy between the two sciences; unless those people suppose, that because the smallest circle has as many degrees as the largest, therefore the regulation and management of the world require no more abilities than the handling and turning of a globe: but I rather take this quality to spring from a very common infirmity of human nature, inclining us to be most curious and conceited in matters where we have least concern, and for which we are least adapted by study or nature.

These people are under continual disquietudes, never enjoying a minute's peace of mind; and their disturbances proceed from causes which very little affect the rest of mortals. Their apprehensions arise from several changes they dread in the celestial bodies. For instance, that the earth, by the continual approaches of the sun towards it, must, in course of time, be absorbed, or swallowed up. That the face of the sun will, by degrees, be encrusted with its own effluvia, and give no more light to the world. That the earth very narrowly escaped a brush from the tail of the last comet, which would have infallibly reduced it to ashes; and that the next, which they have calculated for one-and-thirty years hence, will probably destroy us. For if, in its perihelion, it should approach within a certain degree of the sun (as by their calculations they have reason to dread), it will receive a degree of heat ten thousand times more intense than that of red-hot glowing iron; and, in its absence from the sun, carry a blazing tail, ten hundred thousand and fourteen miles long; through which, if the earth should pass at the distance of one hundred thousand miles from the nucleus, or main body of the

comet, it must, in its passage, be set on fire, and reduced to
ashes. That the sun, daily spending its rays, without any
nutriment to supply them, will at last be wholly consumed
and annihilated; which must be attended with the destruction
of this earth, and of all the planets that receive their light
from it.

They are so perpetually alarmed with the apprehensions
of these, and the like impending dangers, that they can
neither sleep quietly in their beds, nor have any relish for
the common pleasures and amusements of life. When they
meet an acquaintance in the morning, the first question is
about the sun's health, how he looked at his setting and rising, and what hopes they have to avoid the stroke of the
approaching comet. This conversation they are apt to run
into with the same temper that boys discover in delighting
to hear terrible stories of spirits and hobgoblins, which they
greedily listen to, and dare not go to bed for fear.

The women of the island have abundance of vivacity;
they contemn their husbands, and are exceedingly fond of
strangers, wherof there is always a considerable number
from the continent below, attending at court, either upon
affairs of the several towns and corporations, or their own
particular occasions, but are much despised, because they
want the same endowments. Among these the ladies choose
their gallants; but the vexation is, that they act with too much
ease and security; for the husband is always so wrapt in speculation, that the mistress and lover may proceed to the greatest familiarities before his face, if he be but provided with
paper and implements, and without his flapper at his side.

The wives and daughters lament their confinement to
the island, although I think it is the most delicious spot of
ground in the world; and although they live here in the greatest plenty and magnificence, and are allowed to do whatever
they please, they long to see the world, and take the diversions

of the metropolis, which they are not allowed to do without a particular licence from the King; and this is not easy to be obtained, because the people of quality have found, by frequent experience, how hard it is to persuade their women to return from below. I was told, that a great court lady, who had several children—is married to the prime minister, the richest subject in the kingdom, a very graceful person, extremely fond of her, and lives in the finest palace of the island—went down to Lagado on the pretence of health, there hid herself for several months, till the King sent a warrant to search for her; and she was found in an obscure eating-house, all in rags, having pawned her clothes to maintain an old deformed footman, who beat her every day, and in whose company she was taken, much against her will. And, although her husband received her with all possible kindness, and without the least reproach, she soon after contrived to steal down again with all her jewels, to the same gallant, and has not been heard of since.

This may, perhaps, pass with the reader rather for an European or English story, than for one of a country so remote. But he may please to consider, that the caprices of womenkind are not limited by any climate or nation, and that they are much more uniform than can be easily imagined.

In about a month's time I had made a tolerable proficiency in their language, and was able to answer most of the King's questions, when I had the honour to attend him. His Majesty discovered not the least curiosity to inquire into the laws, government, history, religion, or manners of the countries where I had been; but confined his questions to the state of mathematics, and received the account I gave him with great contempt and indifference, though often roused by his flapper on each side.

CHAPTER 3

A phenomenon solved by modern philosophy and astronomy. The Laputians' great improvements in the latter. The King's method of suppressing insurrections.

I DESIRED LEAVE of this prince to see the curiosities of the island, which he was graciously pleased to grant, and ordered my tutor to attend me. I chiefly wanted to know, to what cause, in art or nature, it owed its several motions, whereof I will now give a philosophical account to the reader.

The flying or floating island is exactly circular, its diameter 7837 yards, or about four miles and a half, and consequently contains ten thousand acres. It is three hundred yards thick. The bottom, or under surface, which appears to those who view it below, is one even, regular plate of adamant, shooting up to the height of about two hundred yards. Above it lie the several minerals, in their usual order, and over all is a coat of rich mould, ten or twelve feet deep. The declivity of the upper surface, from the circumference to the centre, is the natural cause why all the dews and rains which fall upon the island, are conveyed in small rivulets towards the middle, where they are emptied into four large basins, each of about half a mile in circuit, and two hundred yards distant from the centre. From these basins the water is continually exhaled by the sun in the daytime, which effectually prevents their overflowing. Besides, as it is in the power of the monarch to raise the island above the region of clouds and vapours, he can prevent the falling of dews and rain whenever he pleases. For the highest clouds cannot rise above two miles, as naturalists agree, at least they were never known to do so in that country.

At the centre of the island there is a chasm, about fifty
yards in diameter, whence the astronomers descend into a
large dome, which is therefore called *flandona gagnole,* or
the astronomers' cave, situated at the depth of a hundred
yards beneath the upper surface of the adamant. In this cave
are twenty lamps continually burning, which, from the reflection of the adamant, cast a strong light into every part. The
place is stored with great variety of sextants, quadrants, telescopes, astrolabes, and other astronomical instruments. But
the greatest curiosity, upon which the fate of the island de-
pends, is a loadstone of a prodigious size, in shape resembling
a weaver's shuttle. It is in length six yards, and in the thickest
part at least three yards over. This magnet is sustained by a
very strong axle of adamant passing through its middle, upon
which it plays, and is poised so exactly, that the weakest hand
can turn it. It is hooped round with a hollow cylinder of adamant, four feet deep, as many thick, and twelve yards in diameter, placed horizontally, and supported by eight adamantine feet, each six yards high. In the middle of the concave
side, there is a groove twelve inches deep, in which the extremities of the axles are lodged, and turned round as there
is occasion.

The stone cannot be moved from its place by any force,
because the hoop and its feet are one continued piece with
that body of adamant which constitutes the bottom of the
island.

By means of this loadstone, the island is made to rise
and fall, and move from one place to another. For, with respect to that part of the earth over which the monarch pre-
sides, the stone is endued at one of its sides with an attractive
power, and at the other with a repulsive. Upon placing the
magnet erect, with its attracting end towards the earth, the
islands descends; but, when the repelling extremity points
downwards, the island mounts directly upwards. When the

position of the stone is oblique, the motion of the island is so too; for, in this magnet, the forces always act in lines parallel to its direction.

By this oblique motion, the island is conveyed to different parts of the monarch's dominions. To explain the manner of its progress, let $A\ B$ represent a line drawn cross the dominions of Balnibarbi, let the line $c\ d$ represent the loadstone, of which let d be the repelling end, and c the attracting end, the island being over C: let the stone be placed in position $c\ d$, with its repelling end downwards; then the island will be driven upwards obliquely towards D. When it is arrived at D, let the stone be turned upon its axle, till its attracting end points towards E, and then the island will be carried obliquely towards E; where, if the stone be again turned upon its axle, till it stands in the position $E\ F$, with its repelling point downwards, the island will rise obliquely towards F, where, by directing the attracting end towards G, the island may be carried to G, and from G to H, by turning the stone, so as to make its repelling extremity point directly downward. And thus, by changing the situation of the stone, as often as there is occasion, the island is made to rise and fall by turns in an oblique direction, and by those alternate risings and fallings, (the obliquity being not considerable) is conveyed from one part of the dominions to the other.

But it must be observed, that this island cannot move beyond the extent of the dominions below, nor can it rise above the height of four miles. For which, the astronomers (who have written large systems concerning the stone) assign the following reason; that the magnetic virtue does not extend beyond the distance of four miles, and that the mineral, which acts upon the stone in the bowels of the earth, and in the sea about six leagues distant from the shore, is not diffused through the whole globe, but terminated with the limits of the King's dominions; and it was easy, from the great advantage of such a superior situation, for a prince to bring under his obedience, whatever country lay within the attraction of that magnet.

When the stone is put parallel to the plane of the horizon, the island stands still; for, in that case, the extremities of it being at equal distance from the earth, act with equal force, the one in drawing downwards, the other in pushing upwards, and consequently no motion can ensue.

This loadstone is under the care of certain astronomers, who, from time to time, give it such positions as the monarch directs. They spend the greatest part of their lives in observing the celestial bodies, which they do by the assistance of glasses, far excelling ours in goodness. For, although their largest telescopes do not exceed three feet, they magnify much more than those of a hundred with us, and shew the stars with greater clearness. This advantage has enabled them to extend their discoveries much farther than our astronomers in Europe; for they have made a catalogue of ten thousand fixed stars, whereas the largest of ours do not contain above one-third part of that number. They have likewise discovered two lesser stars, or satellites, which revolve about Mars; whereof the innermost is distant from the centre of the primary planet exactly three of his diameters, and the outermost, five; the former revolves in the space of ten hours, and the latter in twenty-one and a half; so that the squares of their periodical times are very near in the same proportion with the cubes of their distance, from the centre of Mars; which evidently shews them to be governed by the same law of gravitation that influences the other heavenly bodies.

They have observed ninety-three different comets, and settled their periods with great exactness. If this be true (and they affirm it with great confidence), it is much to be wished that their observations were made public, whereby the theory of comets, which at present is very lame and defective, might be brought to the same perfection with other parts of astronomy.

The King would be the most absolute prince in the universe, if he could but prevail on a ministry to join with him; but these having their estates below on the continent, and considering that the office of a favourite has a very uncertain tenure, would never consent to the enslaving of their country.

If any town should engage in rebellion or mutiny, fall into violent factions, or refuse to pay the usual tribute, the King has two methods of reducing them to obedience. The first, and the mildest course is, by keeping the island hovering over such a town, and the lands about it, whereby he can deprive them of the benefit of the sun and the rain, and consequently afflict the inhabitants with dearth and diseases. And if the crime deserve it, they are at the same time pelted from above with great stones, against which they have no defence but by creeping into cellars or caves, while the roofs of their houses are beaten to pieces. But if they still continue obstinate, or offer to raise insurrections, he proceeds to the last remedy, by letting the island drop directly upon their heads, which makes an universal destruction both of houses and men. However, this is an extremity to which the prince is seldom driven, neither indeed is he willing to put it in execution; nor dare his ministers advise him to an action, which, as it would render them odious to the people, so it would be a great damage to their own estates, which lie all below; for the island is the King's demesne.

But there is still indeed a more weighty reason, why the kings of this country have been always averse from executing so terrible an action, unless upon the utmost necessity. For, if the town intended to be destroyed should have in it any tall rocks, as it generally falls out in the larger cities, a situation probably chosen at first with a view to prevent such a catastrophe; or if it abound in high spires, or pillars of stone, a sudden fall might endanger the bottom or under surface of the island, which, although it consists, as I have said, of one entire adamant two hundred yards thick, might happen to crack by too great a shock, or burst, by approaching too near the fires from the houses below, as the backs both of iron and stone will often do in our chimneys. Of all this the people are well apprised, and understand how far to carry their obstinacy, where their liberty or property is concerned. And the King, when he is highest provoked, and most determined to press a city to rubbish, orders the island to descend with great gentleness, out of a pretence of tenderness to his people, but indeed for fear of breaking the adamantine bottom; in which case, it is the opinion of all their philosophers, that the loadstone could no longer hold it up, and the whole mass would fall to the ground.

By a fundamental law of this realm, neither the King, nor either of his two elder sons, are permitted to leave the island; nor the Queen, till she is past child-bearing.

CHAPTER 4

The author leaves Laputa, is conveyed to Balnibarbi, arrives at the metropolis. A description of the metropolis and the country adjoining. The author hospitably received by a great Lord. His conversation with that Lord.

ALTHOUGH I cannot say that I was ill-treated in this island, yet I must confess I thought myself too much neglected, not without some degree of contempt. For neither prince nor people appeared to be curious in any part of knowledge, except mathematics and music, wherein I was far their inferior, and upon that account very little regarded.

On the other side, after having seen all the curiosities of the island, I was very desirous to leave it, being heartily weary of those people. They were indeed excellent in two sciences, for which I have great esteem, and wherein I am not unversed; but, at the same time, so abstracted and involved in speculation, that I never met with such disagreeable companions. I conversed only with women, tradesmen, flappers, and court-pages, during two months of my abode there; by which at last I rendered myself extremely contemptible; yet these were the only people from whom I could ever receive a reasonable answer.

I had obtained, by hard study, a good degree of knowledge in their language; I was weary of being confined to an island where I received so little countenance, and resolved to leave it with the first opportunity.

There was a great lord at court, nearly related to the King, and for that reason alone used with respect. He was universally reckoned the most ignorant and stupid person among them. He had performed many eminent services for the crown, had great natural and acquired parts, adorned with integrity and honour; but so ill an ear for music, that his detractors reported he had been often known to beat time in the wrong place; neither could his tutors, without extreme difficulty, teach him to demonstrate the most easy proposition in the mathematics. He was pleased to shew me many marks of favour, often did me the honour of a visit, desired to be informed in the affairs of Europe, the laws and customs, the manners and learning of the several countries where I had travelled. He listened to me with great attention, and made very wise observations on all I spoke. He had two flappers attending him for state, but never made use of them, except at court and in visits of ceremony; and would always command them to withdraw when we were alone together.

I entreated this illustrious person to intercede in my behalf with his Majesty, for leave to depart, which he accordingly did, as he was pleased to tell me, with regret; for indeed he had made me several offers very advantageous, which, however, I refused, with expressions of the highest acknowledgment.

On the 16th of February I took leave of his Majesty and the court. The King made me a present to the value of about two hundred pounds English, and my protector his kinsman as much more; together with a letter of recommendation to a friend of his in Lagado, the metropolis. The island being then hovering over a mountain about two miles from it, I was let down from the lowest gallery, in the same manner as I had been taken up.

The continent, as far as it is subject to the monarch of the flying island, passes under the general name of *Balnibarbi;* and the metropolis, as I said before, is called *Lagado.* I felt some little satisfaction in finding myself on firm ground. I walked to the city without any concern, being clad like one of the natives, and sufficiently instructed to converse with them. I soon found out the person's house to whom I was recommended, presented my letter from his friend the grandee in the island, and was received with much kindness. This great lord, whose name was Munodi, ordered me an apartment in his own house, where I continued during my stay, and was entertained in a most hospitable manner.

The next morning after my arrival, he took me in his chariot to see the town, which is about half the bigness of London; but the houses very strangely built, and most of them out of repair. The people in the streets walked fast, looked wild, their eyes fixed, and were generally in rags. We passed through one of the town gates, and went about three miles into the country, where I saw many labourers working with several sorts of tools in the ground, but was not able to conjecture what they were about; neither did I observe any expectation either of corn or grass, although the soil appeared to be excellent. I could not forbear admiring at these odd appearances, both in town and country; and I made bold to desire my conductor, that he would be pleased to explain to me, what could be meant by so many busy heads, hands, and faces, both in the streets and the fields, because I did not discover any good effects they produced; but, on the contrary, I never knew a soil so unhappily cultivated, houses so ill contrived and so ruinous, or a people whose countenances and habit expressed so much misery and want.

This Lord Munodi was a person of the first rank, and had been some years governor of Lagado; but, by a cabal of ministers was discharged for insufficiency. However, the King treated him with tenderness, as a well-meaning man, but of a low contemptible understanding.

When I gave that free censure of the country and its inhabitants, he made no farther answer than by telling me that I had not been long enough among them to form a judgment; and that the different nations of the world had different customs; with other common topics to the same purpose. But, when we returned to his palace, he asked me how I liked the building, what absurdities I observed, and what quarrel I had with the dress or looks of his domestics. This he might safely do; because everything about him was magnificent, regular and polite. I answered that his Excellency's prudence, quality, and fortune, had exempted him from those defects which folly and beggary had produced in others. He said if I would go with him to his country-house, about twenty miles distant, where his estate lay, there would be more leisure for this kind of conversation. I told his Excellency that I was entirely at his disposal; and accordingly we set out next morning.

During our journey, he made me observe the several methods used by farmers in managing their lands; which to me were wholly unaccountable; for, except in some very few places, I could not discover one ear of corn, or blade of grass. But, in three hours' travelling, the scene was wholly altered; we came into a most beautiful country: farmers' houses, at small distances, neatly built; the fields enclosed, containing vineyards, corn-grounds, and meadows. Neither do I remember to have seen a more delightful prospect. His Excellency observed my countenance to clear up; he told me with a sigh that there his estate began, and would continue the same, till we should come to his house. That his countrymen ridiculed and despised him, for managing his affairs no better, and for setting so ill an example to the kingdom; which, however, was followed by very few, such as were old, and wilful, and weak like himself.

We came at length to the house, which was, indeed, a noble structure, built according to the best rules of ancient architecture. The fountains, gardens, walks, avenues and groves, were all disposed with exact judgment and taste. I gave due praises to everything I saw, whereof his Excellency took not the least notice till after supper; when, there being no third companion, he told me, with a very melancholy air, that he doubted he must throw down his houses in town and country, to rebuild them after the present mode; destroy all his plantations, and cast others into such a form as modern usage required, and give the same directions to his tenants, unless he would submit to incur the censure of pride, singularity, affectation, ignorance, caprice, and perhaps increase his Majesty's displeasure. That the admiration I appeared to be under would cease or diminish, when he had informed me of some particulars which, probably, I never heard of at court; the people there being too much taken up in their own speculations, to have regard to what passed here below.

The sum of his discourse was to this effect: that about forty years ago, certain persons went up to Laputa, either upon business or diversion, and after five months' continuance, came back with a very little smattering in mathematics, but full of volatile spirits acquired in that airy region. That these persons upon their return, began to dislike the management of everything below, and fell into schemes of putting all arts, sciences, languages, and mechanics, upon a new foot. To this end, they procured a royal patent for erecting an academy of projectors in Lagado; and the humour prevailed so strongly among the people, that there is not a town of any consequence in the kingdom without such an academy. In these colleges, the professors contrive new rules and methods of agriculture and building, and new instruments and tools for all trades and manufactures; whereby, as they undertake, one man shall do the work of ten; a palace may be built in a week, of materials so durable, as to last for ever without repairing. All the fruits of the earth shall come to maturity at whatever season we think fit to choose, and increase a hundred-fold more than they do at present; with innumerable other happy proposals. The only inconvenience is, that none of these projects are yet brought to perfection; and, in the meantime, the whole country lies miserably waste, the houses in ruins, and the people without food or clothes. By all which, instead of being discouraged, they are fifty times more violently bent upon prosecuting their schemes, driven equally on by hope and despair: that, as for himself, being not of an enterprizing spirit, he was content to go on in the old forms, to live in the houses his ancestors had built, and act as they did in every part of life, without innovation. That some few other persons of quality and gentry had done the same, but were looked on with an eye of contempt and ill-will, as enemies to art, ignorant, and ill commonwealth's men, preferring their own ease and sloth, before the general improvement of their country.

His Lordship added that he would not, by any farther particulars, prevent the pleasure I should certainly take in viewing the grand academy, whither he was resolved I should go. He only desired me to observe a ruined building, upon the side of a mountain about three miles distant, of which he gave me this account: that he had a very convenient mill within half a mile of his house, turned by a current from a large river, and sufficient for his own family, as well as a great number of his tenants. That about seven years ago, a club of those projectors came to him with proposals to destroy this mill, and build another on the side of that mountain on the long ridge whereof a long canal must be cut, for a repository of water, to be conveyed up by pipes and engines to supply the mill: because the wind and air upon a height agitated the water, and thereby made it fitter for motion; and because the water descending down a declivity, would turn the mill with half the current of a river, whose course is more upon a level. He said that, being then not very well with the court, and pressed by many of his friends, he complied with the proposal; and after employing a hundred men for two years, the work miscarried, the projectors went off, laying the blame entirely upon him, railing at him ever since, and putting others upon the same experiment, with equal assurance of success, as well as equal disappointment.

In a few days we came back to town; and his Excellency, considering the bad character he had in the academy, would not go with me himself, but recommended me to a friend of his, to bear me company thither. My Lord was pleased to represent me as a great admirer of projects, and a person of much curiosity, and easy belief; which, indeed, was not without truth; for I had myself been a sort of projector in my younger days.

CHAPTER 5

The author permitted to see the grand Academy of Lagado. The Academy largely described. The arts wherein the professors employ themselves.

THIS ACADEMY is not an entire single building, but a continuation of several houses on both sides of a street, which, growing waste, was purchased, and applied to that use.

I was received very kindly by the warden, and went for many days to the Academy. Every room has in it one or more projectors; and, I believe, I could not be in fewer than five hundred rooms.

The first man I saw was of a meagre aspect, with sooty hands and face, his hair and beard long, ragged, and singed in several places. His clothes, shirt, and skin, were all of the same colour. He had been eight years upon a project for extracting sun-beams out of cucumbers, which were to be put in phials hermetically sealed, and let out to warm the air in raw inclement summers. He told me he did not doubt, that, in eight years more, he should be able to supply the Governor's gardens with sunshine at a reasonable rate; but he complained that his stock was low, and entreated me "to give him something as an encouragement to ingenuity, especially since this had been a very dear season for cucumbers." I made him a small present, for my Lord had furnished me with money on purpose, because he knew their practice of begging from all who go to see them.

I went into another chamber, but was ready to hasten back, being almost overcome with a horrible stink. My conductor pressed me forward, conjuring me in a whisper to give no offence, which would be highly resented; and therefore I durst not so much as stop my nose. The projector of this cell was the most ancient student of the Academy; his face and beard were of a pale yellow; his hands and clothes daubed over with filth. When I was presented to him, he gave me a close embrace, a compliment I could well have excused. His employment, from his first coming into the Academy, was an operation to reduce human excrement to its original food, by separating the several parts, removing the tincture which it receives from the gall, making the ordure exhale, and scumming off the saliva. He had a weekly allowance from the society, of a vessel filled with human ordure, about the bigness of a Bristol barrel.

I saw another at work to calcine ice into gunpowder, who likewise shewed me a treatise he had written concerning the malleability of fire, which he intended to publish.

There was a most ingenious architect, who had contrived a new method for building houses, by beginning at the roof, and working downward to the foundation; which he justified to me by the like practice of those two prudent insects, the bee and the spider.

There was a man born blind, who had several apprentices in his own condition: their employment was to mix colours for painters, which their master taught them to distinguish, by feeling and smelling. It was indeed my misfortune to find them at that time not very perfect in their lessons, and the professor himself happened to be generally mistaken. This artist is much encouraged and esteemed by the whole fraternity.

In another apartment, I was highly pleased with a projector who had found a device of ploughing the ground with hogs, to save the charges of ploughs, cattle, and labour. The method is this: in an acre of ground, you bury, at six inches' distance, and eight deep, a quantity of acorns, dates, chestnuts, and other mast or vegetables, whereof these animals are fondest; then you drive six hundred or more of them into the field, where in a few days, they will root up the whole ground in search of their food, and make it fit for sowing, at the same time manuring it with their dung; it is true, upon experiment, they found the charge and trouble very great, and they had little or no crop. However, it is not doubted that this invention may be capable of great improvement.

I went into another room, where the walls and ceiling were all hung round with cobwebs, except a narrow passage for the artist to go in and out. At my entrance, he called aloud to me not to disturb his webs. He lamented the fatal mistake the world had been so long in, of using silk-worms, while we had such plenty of domestic insects, who infinitely excelled the former, because they understood how to weave, as well as spin. And he proposed farther that, by employing spiders, the charge of dying silks should be wholly saved; whereof I was fully convinced, when he shewed me a vast number of flies most beautifully coloured, wherewith he fed his spiders, assuring us that the webs would take a tincture from them; and, as he had them of all hues, he hoped to fit everybody's fancy, as soon as he could find proper food for the flies, of certain gums, oils, and other glutinous matter, to give a strength and consistence to the threads.

There was an astronomer, who had undertaken to place a sundial upon the great weathercock in the town-house, by adjusting the annual and diurnal motions of the earth and sun, so as to answer and coincide with all accidental turnings of the wind.

I was complaining of a small fit of the colic, upon which my conductor led me into a room where a great physician resided, who was famous for curing that disease by contrary operations from the same instrument. He had a large pair of bellows, with a long slender muzzle of ivory; this he conveyed eight inches up the anus, and drawing in the wind, he affirmed he could make the guts as lank as a dried bladder. But when the disease was more stubborn and violent, he let in the muzzle while the bellows were full of wind, which he discharged into the body of the patient; then withdrew the instrument to replenish it, clapping his thumb strongly against the orifice of the fundament; and this being repeated three or four times, the adventitious wind would rush out, bringing the noxious along with it, (like water put into a pump,) and the patient recovered. I saw him try both experiments upon a dog, but could not discern any effect from the former. After the latter, the animal was ready to burst, and made so violent a discharge as was very offensive to me and my companion. The dog died on the spot, and we left the doctor endeavouring to recover him by the same operation.

I visited many other apartments, but shall not trouble my reader with all the curiosities I observed, being studious of brevity.

I had hitherto seen only one side of the Academy, the

other being appropriated to the advancers of speculative
learning, of whom I shall say something, when I have mentioned one illustrious person more, who is called among them,
"the universal artist." He told us he had been thirty years
employing his thoughts for the improvement of human life.
He had two large rooms full of wonderful curiosities, and
fifty men at work. Some were condensing air into a dry
tangible substance, by extracting the nitre, and letting the
aqueous or fluid particles percolate; others softening marble
for pillows and pincushions; others petrifying the hoofs of a
living horse, to preserve them from foundering. The artist
himself was at that time busy upon two great designs; the
first, to sow land with chaff, wherein he affirmed the true
seminal virtue to be contained, as he demonstrated by several
experiments, which I was not skilful enough to comprehend.
The other was, by a certain composition of gums, minerals,
and vegetables, outwardly applied, to prevent the growth of
wool upon two young lambs; and he hoped, in a reasonable
time, to propagate the breed of naked sheep all over the
kingdom.

We crossed a walk to the other part of the Academy,
where, as I have already said, the projectors in speculative
learning resided.

The first professor I saw, was in a very large room, with
forty pupils about him. After salutation, observing me to
look earnestly upon a frame, which took up the greatest part
of both the length and breadth of the room, he said perhaps
I might wonder to see him employed in a project for improving speculative knowledge by practical mechanical operations. But the world would soon be sensible of its usefulness;
and he flattered himself, that a more noble exalted thought
never sprang in any other man's head. Every one knew how
laborious the usual method is of attaining to arts and sciences; whereas, by his contrivance, the most ignorant person,

at a reasonable charge, and with a little bodily labour, might write books in philosophy, poetry, politics, laws, mathematics, and theology, without the least assistance from genius or study. He then led me to the frame, about the sides whereof all his pupils stood in ranks. It was twenty feet square, placed in the middle of the room. The superficies was composed of several bits of wood, about the bigness of a die, but some larger than others. They were all linked together by slender wires. These bits of wood were covered, on every square, with paper pasted on them; and on these papers were written all the words of their language, in their several moods, tenses, and declensions, but without any order. The professor then desired me to observe, for he was going to set his engine at work. The pupils, at his command, took each of them hold of an iron handle, whereof there were forty fixed round the edges of the frame, and giving them a sudden turn, the whole disposition of the words was entirely changed. He then commanded six-and-thirty of the lads to read the several lines softly, as they appeared upon the frame; and, where they found three or four words together that might make part of a sentence, they dictated to the four remaining boys, who were scribes. This work was repeated three or four times, and, at every turn, the engine was so contrived, that the words shifted into new places, as the square bits of wood moved upside down.

Six hours a day the young students were employed in this labour; and the professor shewed me several volumes in large folio, already collected, of broken sentences, which he intended to piece together, and, out of those rich materials, to give the world a complete body of all arts and sciences; which, however, might be still improved, and much expedited, if the public would raise a fund for making and employing five hundred such frames in Lagado, and oblige the managers to contribute in common their several collections.

He assured me that this invention had employed all his thoughts from his youth; that he had emptied the whole vocabulary into his frame, and made the strictest computation of the general proportion there is in books between the numbers of particles, nouns, and verbs, and other parts of speech.

I made my humblest acknowledgment to this illustrious person, for his great communicativeness; and promised if ever I had the good fortune to return to my native country, that I would do him justice, as the sole inventor of this wonderful machine; the form and contrivance of which I desired leave to delineate on paper. I told him, although it were the custom of our learned in Europe to steal inventions from each other, who had thereby at least this advantage, that it became a controversy which was the right owner; yet I would take such caution, that he should have the honour entire, without a rival.

We next went to the school of languages, where three professors sat in consultation upon improving that of their own country.

The first project was to shorten discourse, by cutting polysyllables into one, and leaving out verbs and participles, because, in reality, all things imaginable are but nouns.

The other project was a scheme for entirely abolishing all words whatsoever, and this was urged as a great advantage in point of health, as well as brevity. For it is plain, that every word we speak is, in some degree, a diminution of our lungs by corrosion, and, consequently, contributes to the shortening of our lives. An expedient was therefore offered that, since words are only names for things, it would be more convenient for all men to carry about them such things as were necessary to express a particular business they are to discourse on. And this invention would certainly have taken place, to the great ease, as well as health of the subject, if the women, in conjunction with the vulgar and illiterate, had not threatened to raise a rebellion, unless they might be allowed the liberty to speak with their tongues, after the manner of their forefathers; such constant irreconcilable enemies to science are the common people. However, many of the most learned and wise adhere to the new scheme of expressing themselves by things, which has only this inconvenience attending it, that, if a man's business be very great, and of various kinds, he must be obliged, in proportion, to carry a greater bundle of things upon his back, unless he can afford one or two strong servants to attend him. I have often beheld two of these sages almost sinking under the weight of their packs, like pedlars among us; who, when they meet in the street, would lay down their loads, open their sacks, and hold conversation for an hour together, then put up their implements, help each other to resume their burdens, and take their leave.

But for short conversations, a man may carry implements in his pockets, and under his arms, enough to supply him; and in his house, he cannot be at a loss. Therefore the room where company meet who practise this art, is full of all things, ready at hand, requisite to furnish matter for this kind of artificial converse.

Another great advantage proposed by this invention was, that it would serve as a universal language, to be understood in all civilised nations, whose goods and utensils are generally of the same kind, or nearly resembling, so that their uses might easily be comprehended. And thus ambassadors would be qualified to treat with foreign princes, or ministers of state, to whose tongues they were utter strangers.

I was at the mathematical school, where the master taught his pupils after a method scarce imaginable to us in Europe. The proposition and demonstration were fairly written on a thin wafer, with ink composed of a cephalic tincture. This the student was to swallow upon a fasting stomach, and for three days following eat nothing but bread and water. As

the wafer digested, the tincture mounted to his brain, bearing the proposition along with it. But the success has not hitherto been answerable, partly by some error in the *quantum* or composition, and partly by the perverseness of lads, to whom this bolus is so nauseous, that they generally steal aside, and discharge it upwards, before it can operate; neither have they been yet persuaded to use so long an abstinence as the prescription requires.

CHAPTER 6

A farther account of the Academy. The author proposes some improvements, which are honourably received.

IN THE SCHOOL of political projectors, I was but ill entertained; the professors appearing, in my judgment, wholly out of their senses, which is a scene that never fails to make me melancholy. These unhappy people were proposing schemes for persuading monarchs to choose favourites upon the score of their wisdom, capacity, and virtue; of teaching ministers to consult the public good: of rewarding merit, great abilities, and eminent services; of instructing princes to know their true interest, by placing it on the same foundation with that of their people; of choosing for employments persons qualified to exercise them; with many other wild impossible chimeras, that never entered before into the heart of man to conceive; and confirmed in me the old observation that there is nothing so extravagant and irrational which some philosophers have not maintained for truth.

But, however, I shall so far do justice to this part of
the Academy, as to acknowledge that all of them were not
so visionary. There was a most ingenious doctor, who seemed
to be perfectly versed in the whole nature and system of government. This illustrious person had very usefully employed
his studies, in finding out effectual remedies for all diseases
and corruptions to which the several kinds of public administration are subject, by the vices or infirmities of those who
govern, as well as by the licentiousness of those who are to
obey. For instance, whereas all writers and reasoners have
agreed, that there is a strict universal resemblance between
the natural and the political body; can there be anything
more evident, than that the health of both must be preserved,
and the diseases cured, by the same prescriptions? It is allowed, that senates and great councils are often troubled
with redundant, ebullient, and other peccant humours; with
many diseases of the head, and more of the heart; with strong
convulsions, with grievous contractions of the nerves and
sinews in both hands, but especially the right; with spleen,
flatus, vertigoes, and deliriums; with scrofulous tumours, full
of fetid purulent matter; with sour frothy ructations; with
canine appetites, and crudeness of digestion, besides many
others, needless to mention. This doctor, therefore, proposed
that, upon the meeting of the senate, certain physicians should
attend at the three first days of their sitting, and at the close
of each day's debate feel the pulses of every senator; after
which, having maturely considered and consulted upon the
nature of the several maladies, and the methods of cure, they
should, on the fourth day, return to the senate-house, attended by their apothecaries, stored with proper medicines;
and before the members sat, administer to each of them leni-
tives, aperitives, abstersives, corrosives, restringents, palli-
atives, laxatives, cephalalgics, icterics, apophlegmatics,
acoustics, as their several cases required; and, according as

these medicines should operate, repeat, alter, or omit them, at the next meeting.

This project could not be of any great expense to the public, and might, in my poor opinion, be of much use for the dispatch of business, in those countries where senates have any share in the legislative power; beget unanimity, shorten debates, open a few mouths which are now closed, and close many more which are now open; curb the petulancy of the young, and correct the positiveness of the old; rouse the stupid, and damp the pert.

Again: because it is a general complaint that the favourites of princes are troubled with short and weak memories; the same doctor proposed that whoever attended a first minister, after having told his business, with the utmost brevity, and in the plainest words, should, at his departure, give the said minister a tweak by the nose, or a kick on the belly, or tread on his corns, or lug him thrice by both ears, or run a pin into his breach, or pinch his arm black and blue, to prevent forgetfulness: and at every levee day, repeat the same operation, till the business were done, or absolutely refused.

He likewise directed that every senator in the great council of a nation, after he had delivered his opinion, and argued in the defence of it, should be obliged to give his vote directly contrary; because, if that were done, the result would infallibly terminate in the good of the public.

When parties in a state are violent, he offered a wonderful contrivance to reconcile them. The method is this: you take a hundred leaders of each party; you dispose them into couples of such whose heads are nearest of a size; then let two nice operators saw off the occiput of each couple at the same time, in such a manner, that the brain may be equally divided. Let the occiputs, thus cut off, be interchanged, applying each to the head of his opposite party-man. It seems indeed to be a work that requires some exactness, but the professor assured us that if it were dexterously performed, the cure would be infallible. For he argued thus: that the two half brains, being left to debate the matter between themselves within the space of one skull, would soon come to a good understanding, and produce that moderation, as well as regularity of thinking, so much to be wished for in the heads of those who imagine they come into the world only to watch and govern its motion: and as to the difference of brains, in quantity or quality, among those who are directors in faction, the doctor assured us, from his own knowledge, that it was a perfect trifle.

I heard a very warm debate between two professors, about the most commodious and effectual ways and means of raising money, without grieving the subject. The first affirmed the justest method would be, to lay a certain tax upon vices and folly; and the sum fixed upon every man to be rated, after the fairest manner, by a jury of his neighbours. The second was of an opinion directly contrary to tax those qualities of body and mind, for which men chiefly value themselves; the rate to be more or less, according to the degrees of excelling; the decision whereof should be left entirely to their own breast. The highest tax was upon men who are the greatest favourites of the other sex, and the assessments, according to the number and nature of the favours they have received; for which they are allowed to be their own vouchers. Wit, valour, and politeness, were likewise proposed to be largely taxed, and collected in the same manner, by every person's giving his own word for the quantum of what he possessed. But as to honour, justice, wisdom, and learning, they should not be taxed at all, because they are qualifications of so singular a kind, that no man will either allow them in his neighbour, or value them in himself.

The women were proposed to be taxed according to their beauty and skill in dressing, wherein they had the same privilege with the men, to be determined by their own judgment. But constancy, chastity, good sense, and good nature, were not rated, because they would not bear the charge of collecting.

To keep senators in the interest of the crown, it was proposed that the members should raffle for employments; every man first taking an oath, and giving security, that he would vote for the court, whether he won or not; after which, the losers had, in their turn, the liberty of raffling upon the next vacancy. Thus, hope and expectation would be kept alive; none would complain of broken promises, but impute their disappointments wholly to fortune, whose shoulders are broader and stronger than those of a ministry.

Another professor shewed me a large paper of instructions for discovering plots and conspiracies against the government. He advised great statesmen to examine into the diet of all suspected persons; their times of eating; upon which side they lay in bed; with which hand they wiped their posteriors; take a strict view of their excrements, and from the colour, the ordure, the taste, the consistence, the crudeness, or maturity of digestion, form a judgment of their thoughts and designs; because men are never so serious, thoughtful, and intent, as when they are at stool, which he found by experience; for, in such conjectures, when he used, merely as a trial, to consider which was the best way of murdering the king, his ordure would have a tincture of green; but quite different when he thought only of raising an insurrection, or burning the metropolis.

The whole discourse was written with great acuteness, containing many observations, both curious and useful for politicians, but, as I conceived, not altogether complete. This I ventured to tell the author, and offered, if he pleased, to supply him with some additions. He received my proposition with more compliance than is usual among writers, especially

those of the projecting species; professing he would be glad
to receive farther information.

I told him that in the kingdom of Tribnia, by the natives
called Langdon, where I had sojourned some time in my
travels, the bulk of the people consist in a manner wholly of
discoverers, witnesses, informers, accusers, prosecutors, evi-
dencers, swearers, together with their several subservient and
subaltern instruments, all under the colours, the conduct, and
the pay of ministers of state, and their deputies. The plots,
in that kingdom, are usually the workmanship of those persons who desire to raise their own characters of profound
politicians; to restore new vigour to a crazy administration;
to stifle or divert general discontents; to fill their coffers with
forfeitures; and raise or sink the opinion of public credit, as
either shall best answer their private advantage. It is first
agreed and settled among them, what suspected persons shall
be accused of a plot; then, effectual care is taken to secure all
their letters and papers, and put the owners in chains. These
papers are delivered to a set of artists, very dexterous in
finding out the mysterious meanings of words, syllables, and
letters: for instance, they can discover a close-stool to signify
a privy council; a flock of geese, a senate; a lame dog, an invader; the plague, a standing army; a buzzard, a prime minister; the gout, a high priest; a gibbet, a secretary of state;
a chamber-pot, a committee of grandees; a sieve, a court
lady; a broom, a revolution; a mouse-trap, an employment; a
bottomless pit, a treasury; a sink, a court; a cap and bells,
a favourite; a broken reed, a court of justice; an empty tun,
a general; a running sore, the administration.

When this method fails, they have two others more
effectual, which the learned among them call acrostics and
anagrams. First, they can decipher all initial letters into political meanings. Thus, N shall signify a plot; B, a regiment
of horse; L, a fleet at sea: or, secondly, by transposing the let-

ters of the alphabet in any suspected paper, they can lay open the deepest designs of a discontented party. So, for example, if I should say, in a letter to a friend, 'Our brother Tom has just got the piles,' a skilful decipherer would discover, that the same letters which compose that sentence, may be analysed into the following words, 'Resist,——a plot is brought home,——the tour.' And this is the anagrammatic method.

The professor made me great acknowledgments for communicating these observations, and promised to make honourable mention of me in his treatise.

I saw nothing in this country that could invite me to a longer continuance, and began to think of returning home to England.

CHAPTER 7

The author leaves Lagado. Arrives at Maldonada. No ship ready. He takes a short voyage to Glubbdubdrib. His reception by the Governor.

THE CONTINENT, of which this kingdom is a part, extends itself, as I have reason to believe, eastward, to that unknown tract of America westward of California; and north, to the Pacific Ocean, which is not above a hundred and fifty miles from Lagado; where there is a good port, and much commerce with the great island of Luggnagg, situated to the north-west about 29 degrees north latitude, and 140 longitude. This island of Luggnagg stands south-eastward of Japan, about a hundred leagues dis-

tant. There is a strict alliance between the Japanese Emperor
and the King of Luggnagg, which affords frequent opportunities of sailing from one island to the other. I determined
therefore to direct my course this way, in order to hasten my
return to Europe. I hired two mules, with a guide, to shew
me the way, and carry my small baggage. I took leave of my
noble protector, who had shewn me so much favour, and
made me a generous present at my departure.

My journey was without any accident or adventure
worth relating. When I arrived at the port of Maldonada,
(for so it is called,) there was no ship in the harbour bound
for Luggnagg, nor likely to be in some time. The town is
about as large as Portsmouth. I soon fell into some acquaintance, and was very hospitably received. A gentleman of distinction said to me that since the ships bound for Luggnagg
could not be ready in less than a month, it might be no disagreeable amusement for me to take a trip to the little island
of Glubbdubdrib, about five leagues off to the south-west.
He offered himself and a friend to accompany me, and that
I should be provided with a small convenient bark for the
voyage.

Glubbdubdrib, as nearly as I can interpret the word,
signifies the Island of Sorcerers or Magicians. It is about one
third as large as the Isle of Wight, and extremely fruitful: it
is governed by the head of a certain tribe, who are all magicians. This tribe marries only among each other, and the
eldest in succession is prince, or governor. He has a noble
palace, and a park of about three thousand acres, surrounded
by a wall of hewn stone twenty feet high. In this park
are several small enclosures for cattle, corn, and gardening.

The Governor and his family are served and attended
by domestics of a kind somewhat unusual. By his skill in
necromancy, he has a power of calling whom he pleases from
the dead, and commanding their service for twenty-four

hours, but no longer; nor can he call the same persons up
again in less than three months, except upon very extraordinary occasions.

When we arrived at the island, which was about eleven
in the morning, one of the gentlemen who accompanied me
went to the Governor, and desired admittance for a stranger,
who came on purpose to have the honour of attending on his
Highness. This was immediately granted, and we all three
entered the gate of the palace between two rows of guards,
armed and dressed after a very antic manner, and something
in their countenances that made my flesh creep with a horror
I cannot express. We passed through several apartments,
between servants of the same sort, ranked on each side as
before, till we came to the chamber of presence; where, after
three profound obeisances, and a few general questions, we
were permitted to sit on three stools, near the lowest step of
his Highness's throne. He understood the language of Balnibarbi, although it were different from that of this island.
He desired me to give him some account of my travels; and,
to let me see that I should be treated without ceremony, he
dismissed all his attendants with a turn of his finger; at which,
to my great astonishment, they vanished in an instant, like
visions in a dream when we awake on a sudden. I could not
recover myself in some time, till the Governor assured me
that I should receive no hurt; and, observing my two companions to be under no concern, who had been often entertained in the same manner, I began to take courage, and
related to his Highness a short history of my several adventures; yet not without some hesitation, and frequently looking behind me to the place where I had seen those domestic
spectres. I had the honour to dine with the Governor, where
a new set of ghosts served up the meat, and waited at table.
I now observed myself to be less terrified than I had been
in the morning. I stayed till sunset, but humbly desired his

Highness to excuse me for not accepting his invitation of lodging in the palace. My two friends and I lay at a private house in the town adjoining, which is the capital of this little island; and the next morning we returned to pay our duty to the Governor, as he was pleased to command us.

After this manner we continued in the island for ten days, most part of every day with the Governor, and at night in our lodging. I soon grew so familiarized to the sight of spirits, that, after the third or fourth time, they gave me no emotion at all; or, if I had any apprehensions left, my curiosity prevailed over them. For his Highness the Governor ordered me to call up whatever persons I would choose to name, and in whatever numbers, among all the dead from the beginning of the world to the present time, and command them to answer any questions I should think fit to ask; with this condition, that my questions must be confined within the compass of the times they lived in. And one thing I might depend upon, that they would certainly tell me the truth, for lying was a talent of no use in the lower world.

I made my humble acknowledgments to his Highness for so great a favour. We were in the chamber, from whence there was a fair prospect into the park. And because my first inclination was to be entertained with scenes of pomp and magnificence, I desired to see Alexander the Great at the head of his army, just after the battle of Arbela; which, upon a motion of the Governor's finger, immediately appeared in a large field, under the window where we stood. Alexander was called up into the room; it was with great difficulty that I understood his Greek, and had but little of my own. He assured me upon his honour that he was not poisoned, but died of a bad fever by excessive drinking.

Next, I saw Hannibal passing the Alps, who told me he had not a drop of vinegar in his camp.

I saw Cæsar and Pompey at the head of their troops,

just ready to engage. I saw the former in his last great triumph. I desired that the senate of Rome might appear
before me in one large chamber, and a modern representative, in counterview, in another. The first seemed to be an
assembly of heroes and demi-gods; the other, a knot of pedlars, pickpockets, highwaymen, and bullies.

The Governor, at my request, gave the sign for Cæsar
and Brutus to advance towards us. I was struck with a profound veneration at the sight of Brutus, and could easily
discover the most consummate virtue, the greatest intrepidity
and firmness of mind, the truest love of his country, and general benevolence for mankind, in every lineament of his countenance. I observed with much pleasure, that these two persons were in good intelligence with each other; and Cæsar
freely confessed to me that the greatest actions of his own
life were not equal, by many degrees, to the glory of taking
it away. I had the honour to have much conversation with
Brutus; and was told that his ancestor Junius, Socrates,
Epaminondas, Cato the younger, Sir Thomas More, and
himself, were perpetually together, a sextumvirate, to which
all the ages of the world cannot add a seventh.

It would be tedious to trouble the reader with relating
what vast numbers of illustrious persons were called up, to
gratify that insatiable desire I had, to see the world in every
period of antiquity placed before me. I chiefly fed mine eyes
with beholding the destroyers of tyrants and usurpers, and
the restorers of liberty to oppressed and injured nations. But
it is impossible to express the satisfaction I received in my
own mind, after such a manner, as to make it a suitable
entertainment to the reader.

CHAPTER 8

*A farther account of Glubbdubdrib. Ancient and modern
history corrected.*

Having a desire to see those
ancients who were most renowned for wit and learning, I
set apart one day on purpose. I proposed that Homer and
Aristotle might appear at the head of all their commentators;
but these were so numerous, that some hundreds were forced
to attend in the court, and outward rooms of the palace. I
knew, and could distinguish those two heroes, at first sight,
not only from the crowd, but from each other. Homer was
the taller and comelier person of the two, walked very erect
for one of his age, and his eyes were the most quick and
piercing I ever beheld. Aristotle stooped much, and made use
of a staff. His visage was meagre, his hair lank and thin, and
his voice hollow. I soon discovered that both of them were
perfect strangers to the rest of the company, and had never
seen or heard of them before. And I had a whisper from a
ghost, who shall be nameless, that these commentators always
kept in the most distant quarters from their principals, in
the lower world, through a consciousness of shame and guilt,
because they had so horribly misrepresented the meaning of
those authors to posterity. I introduced Didymus and Eu-
stathius to Homer, and prevailed on him to treat them
better than perhaps they deserved, for he soon found they
wanted a genius to enter into the spirit of a poet. But
Aristotle was out of all patience with the account I gave him
of Scotus and Ramus, as I presented them to him; and he
asked them whether the rest of the tribe were as great dunces
as themselves.

I then desired the Governor to call up Descartes and

Gassendi, with whom I prevailed to explain their systems to Aristotle. This great philosopher freely acknowledged his own mistakes in natural philosophy, because he proceeded in many things upon conjecture, as all men must do; and he found that Gassendi, who had made the doctrine of Epicurus as palatable as he could, and the vortices of Descartes were equally to be exploded. He predicted the same fate to attraction, whereof the present learned are such zealous assertors. He said that new systems of nature were but new fashions, which would vary in every age; and even those who pretend to demonstrate them from mathematical principles, would flourish but a short period of time, and be out of vogue when that was determined.

I spent five days in conversing with many others of the ancient learned. I saw most of the first Roman emperors. I prevailed on the Governor to call up Eliogabalus's cooks to dress us a dinner, but they could not shew us much of their skill, for want of materials. A helot of Agesilaus made us a dish of Spartan broth, but I was not able to get down a second spoonful.

The two gentlemen, who conducted me to the island, were pressed by their private affairs to return in three days, which I employed in seeing some of the modern dead, who had made the greatest figure, for two or three hundred years past, in our own and other countries of Europe; and having been always a great admirer of old illustrious families, I desired the Governor would call up a dozen or two of kings, with their ancestors in order, for eight or nine generations. But my disappointment was grievous and unexpected; for, instead of a long train, with royal diadems, I saw in one family two fiddlers, three spruce courtiers, and an Italian prelate. In another, a barber, an abbot, and two cardinals. I have too great a veneration for crowned heads, to dwell any longer on so nice a subject. But as to counts, marquises, dukes, earls,

and the like, I was not so scrupulous. And I confess, it was not without some pleasure, that I found myself able to trace the particular features, by which certain families are distinguished, up to their originals. I could plainly discover whence one family derives a long chin; why a second has abounded with knaves for two generations, and fools for two more; why a third happened to be crack-brained, and a fourth to be sharpers; whence it came, what Polydore Virgil says of a certain great house, *Nec vir fortis, nec fæmina casta;* how cruelty, falsehood, and cowardice, grew to be characteristics, by which certain families are distinguished as much as by their coat of arms; who first brought the pox into a noble house, which has lineally descended in scrofulous tumours to their posterity. Neither could I wonder at all this, when I saw such an interruption of lineages by pages, lackeys, valets, coachmen, gamesters, fiddlers, players, captains, and pickpockets.

I was chiefly disgusted with modern history; for having strictly examined all the persons of greatest name in the courts of princes, for an hundred years past, I found how the world had been misled by prostitute writers to ascribe the greatest exploits in war to cowards, the wisest counsel to fools, sincerity to flatterers, Roman virtue to betrayers of their country, piety to atheists, chastity to sodomites, truth to informers; how many innocent and excellent persons had been condemned to death or banishment, by the practising of great ministers upon the corruption of judges, and the malice of factions; how many villains had been exalted to the highest places of trust, power, dignity, and profit; how great a share in the motions and events of courts, councils, and senates, might be challenged by bawds, whores, pimps, parasites, and buffoons. How low an opinion I had of human wisdom and integrity, when I was truly informed of the springs and motives of great enterprizes and revolutions in the world, and of the contemptible accidents to which they owed their success!

Here I discovered the roguery and ignorance of those who pretend to write anecdotes or secret history; who send so many kings to their graves with a cup of poison; will repeat the discourse between a prince and chief minister, where no witness was by; unlock the thoughts and cabinets of ambassadors and secretaries of state; and have the perpetual misfortune to be mistaken. Here I discovered the true cause of many great events that have surprised the world; how a whore can govern the back-stairs, the back-stairs a council, and the council a senate. A general confessed in my presence that he got a victory purely by the force of cowardice and ill conduct; and an admiral that, for want of proper intelligence, he beat the enemy, to whom he intended to betray the fleet. Three kings protested to me that in their whole reigns they never did once prefer any person of merit, unless by mistake, or treachery of some minister in whom they confided; neither would they do it if they were to live again; and they shewed, with great strength of reason, that the royal throne could not be supported without corruption, because that positive, confident, restive temper, which virtue infused into a man, was a perpetual clog to public business.

I had the curiosity to inquire, in a particular manner, by what method great numbers had procured to themselves high titles of honour, and prodigious estates; and I confined my inquiry to a very modern period; however, without grating upon present times, because I would be sure to give no offence even to foreigners; for I hope the reader need not to be told, that I do not in the least intend my own country, in what I say upon this occasion. A great number of persons concerned were called up; and, upon a very slight examination, discovered such a scene of infamy, that I cannot reflect upon it without some seriousness. Perjury, oppression, subornation, fraud, pandarism, and the like infirmities, were among the most excusable arts they had to mention; and for these I gave, as it was reasonable, great allowance. But when some confessed they owed their greatness and wealth to sodomy, or incest; others, to the prostituting of their own wives and daughters; and others to the betraying of their country or their prince; some to poisoning; more to the perverting of justice, in order to destroy the innocent; I hope I may be pardoned, if these discoveries inclined me a little to abate of that profound veneration, which I am naturally apt to pay to persons of high rank, who ought to be treated with the utmost respect due to their sublime dignity, by us their inferiors.

I had often read of some great services done to princes and states, and desired to see the persons by whom those services were performed. Upon inquiry, I was told that their names were to be found on no record, except a few of them, whom history has represented as the vilest of rogues and traitors. As to the rest, I had never once heard of them. They all appeared with dejected looks, and in the meanest habit; most of them telling me they died in poverty and disgrace, and the rest on a scaffold or a gibbet.

Among others, there was one person, whose case appeared a little singular. He had a youth about eighteen years old standing by his side. He told me he had for many years been commander of a ship; and in the sea-fight at Actium, had the good fortune to break through the enemy's great line of battle, sink three of their capital ships, and take a fourth, which was the sole cause of Antony's flight, and of the victory that ensued: that the youth standing by him, his only son, was killed in the action. He added that upon the confidence of some merit, the war being at an end, he went to Rome, and solicited at the court of Augustus to be preferred to a greater ship, whose commander had been killed; but, without any regard to his pretensions, it was given to a boy who had never seen the sea, the son of Libertina, who waited on one of the emperor's mistresses. Returning back to his own vessel, he was charged with neglect of duty, and the ship given to a favourite page of Publicola, the vice-admiral; whereupon he retired to a poor farm at a great distance from Rome, and there ended his life. I was so curious to know the truth of this story, that I desired Agrippa might be called, who was admiral in that fight. He appeared, and confirmed the whole account; but with much more advantage to the captain, whose modesty had extenuated or concealed a great part of his merit.

I was surprised to find corruption grown so high and so quick in that empire, by the force of luxury so lately introduced, which made me less wonder at many parallel cases in other countries, where vices of all kinds have reigned so much longer, and where the whole praise, as well as pillage, has been engrossed by the chief commander, who, perhaps, had the least title to either.

As every person called up made exactly the same appearance he had done in the world, it gave me melancholy reflections to observe how much the race of human kind was degenerated among us, within these hundred years past. How the pox, under all its consequences and denominations, had altered every lineament of an English countenance, shortened the size of bodies, unbraced the nerves, relaxed the sinews and muscles, introduced a sallow complexion, and rendered the flesh loose and rancid.

I descended so low as to desire some English yeomen of the old stamp might be summoned to appear, once so famous for the simplicity of their manners, diet, and dress; for justice in their dealings; for their true spirit of liberty; for their valour, and love of their country. Neither could I be wholly unmoved, after comparing the living with the dead, when I considered how all these pure native virtues were prostituted for a piece of money by their grandchildren, who, in selling their votes, and managing at elections, have acquired every vice and corruption that can possibly be learned in a court.

CHAPTER 9

The author returns to Maldonada. Sails to the kingdom of Luggnagg. The author confined. He is sent for to court. The manner of his admittance. The king's great lenity to his subjects.

THE DAY OF OUR departure being come, I took leave of his Highness, the Governor of Glubbdubdrib, and returned with my two companions to Maldonada, where, after a fortnight's waiting, a ship was ready to sail for Luggnagg. The two gentlemen, and some others, were so generous and kind as to furnish me with provisions, and see me on board. I was a month in this voyage. We had one violent storm, and were under a necessity of steering westward, to get into the trade wind, which holds for above sixty leagues. On the 21st of April, 1708, we sailed into the river of Clumegnig, which is a seaport town at the south-east point of Luggnagg. We cast anchor within a league of the town, and made a signal for a pilot. Two of them came on board in less than half an hour, by whom we were guided between certain shoals and rocks, which are very dangerous in the passage, to a large basin, where a fleet may ride in safety within a cable's length of the town-wall.

Some of our sailors, whether out of treachery or inadvertence, had informed the pilots that I was a stranger and a great traveller; wherof these gave notice to a custom-house officer, by whom I was examined very strictly upon my landing. This officer spoke to me in the language of Balnibarbi, which, by the force of much commerce, is generally understood in that town, especially by seamen and those employed in the customs. I gave him a short account of some particulars, and made my story as plausible and consistent as I could; but I thought it necessary to disguise my country, and call myself a Hollander, because my intentions were for Japan, and I knew the Dutch were the only Europeans permitted to enter into that kingdom. I therefore told the officer that, having been shipwrecked on the coast of Balnibarbi, and cast on a rock, I was received up into Laputa, or the Flying Island (of which he had often heard), and was now endeavouring to get to Japan, whence I might find a convenience of returning to my own country. The officer said I must be confined till he could receive orders from court, for which he would write immediately, and hoped to receive an answer in a fortnight. I was carried to a convenient lodging, with a sentry placed at the door; however, I had the liberty of a large garden, and was treated with humanity enough, being maintained all the time at the King's charge. I was visited by several persons, chiefly out of curiosity, because it was reported that I came from countries very remote, of which they had never heard.

I hired a young man, who came in the same ship, to be an interpreter; he was a native of Luggnagg, but had lived some years at Maldonada, and was a perfect master of both languages. By his assistance, I was able to hold a conversation with those who came to visit me; but this consisted only of their questions, and my answers.

The despatch came from court about the time we expected. It contained a warrant for conducting me and my retinue to *Traldragdubh,* or *Trildrogdrib,* for it is pronounced both ways, as near as I can remember, by a party of ten horse. All my retinue was that poor lad for an interpreter, whom I persuaded into my service, and, at my humble request, we had each of us a mule to ride on. A messenger was despatched half a day's journey before us, to give the King notice of my approach, and to desire that his Majesty would please to appoint a day and hour, when it would be his gracious pleasure that I might have the honour to lick the dust before his footstool. This is the court style, and I found it to be more than matter of form. For, upon my admittance, two days after my arrival, I was commanded to crawl upon my belly, and lick the floor as I advanced; but, on account of my being a stranger, care was taken to have it made so clean, that the dust was not offensive. However, this was a peculiar grace, not allowed to any but persons of the highest rank, when they desire an admittance. Nay, sometimes the floor is strewed with dust on purpose, when the person to be admitted happens to have powerful enemies at court. And I have seen a great lord with his mouth so crammed, that when he had crept to the proper distance from the throne, he was not able to speak a word. Neither is there any remedy, because it is capital for those who receive an audience to spit or wipe their mouths in his Majesty's presence. There is indeed another custom, which I cannot altogether approve of; when the King has a mind to put any of his nobles to death in a gentle, indulgent manner, he commands the floor to be strewed with a certain brown powder of a deadly composition, which, being licked up, infallibly kills him in twenty-four hours. But in justice to this prince's great clemency, and the care he has of his subjects' lives (wherein it were much to be wished that the monarch of Europe would imitate him), it must be mentioned for his honour, that strict orders are given to have the infected parts of the floor well washed after every such execution; which, if his domestics neglect, they are in danger of incurring his royal displeasure. I myself heard him give directions that one of his pages should be whipped, whose turn it was to give notice about washing the floor after an execution, but maliciously had omitted it; by which neglect, a young lord of great hopes coming to an audience, was unfortunately poisoned, although the King at that time had no design against his life. But this good prince was so gracious as to forgive the poor page his whipping, upon promise that he would do so no more, without special orders.

To return from this digression; when I had crept within four yards of the throne, I raised myself gently upon my knees, and then striking my forehead seven times against the ground, I pronounced the following words, as they had been taught me the night before. *Inckpling gloffthrobb squut scrumm blhiop mlashnalt zwin tnodbalkuffhslhiophad gurdlubh asht.* This is the compliment, established by the laws of the land, for all persons admitted to the King's presence. It may be rendered into English thus: "May your celestial Majesty outlive the sun eleven moons and a half!" To this the King returned some answer, which, although I could not understand, yet I replied as I had been directed: *Flute drin yalerick dwuldom prastrad mirpush,* which properly signifies, "My tongue is in the mouth of my friend;" and, by this expression was meant, that I desired leave to bring my interpreter; whereupon the young man, already mentioned, was accordingly introduced, by whose intervention I answered as many questions as his Majesty could put in above an hour. I spoke in the Balnibarbian tongue, and my interpreter delivered my meaning in that of Luggnagg.

The King was much delighted with my company, and ordered his *Bliffmarklub,* or High Chamberlain, to appoint a lodging in the court for me and my interpreter, with a daily allowance for my table, and a large purse of gold for my common expenses.

I stayed three months in this country, out of perfect obedience to his Majesty, who was pleased highly to favour me, and made me very honourable offers. But I thought it more consistent with prudence and justice, to pass the remainder of my days with my wife and family.

CHAPTER 10

The Luggnaggians commended. A particular description of the Struldbrugs, with many conversations between the author and some eminent persons upon that subject.

THE LUGGNAGGIANS are a polite and generous people; and, although they are not without some share of that pride which is peculiar to all eastern countries, yet they shew themselves courteous to strangers, especially such who are countenanced by the court. I had many acquaintance, and among persons of the best fashion, and being always attended by my interpreter, the conversation we had was not disagreeable.

One day, in much good company, I was asked by a person of quality whether I had seen any of their *struldbrugs,* or immortals. I said I had not; and desired he would explain to me what he meant by such an appellation, applied to a mortal creature. He told me that sometimes, though very rarely, a child happened to be born in a family with a red circular spot in the forehead directly over the left eyebrow, which was an infallible mark that it should never die. The spot, as he described it, was about the compass of a silver threepence, but in the course of time grew larger, and changed its colour; for at twelve years old it became green, so continued till five-and-twenty, and then turned to deep blue: at five-and-forty it grew coal-black, and as large as an English shilling, but never admitted any farther alteration. He said these births were so rare that he did not believe there could be above eleven hundred *struldbrugs,* or both sexes, in the whole kingdom, of which he computed above fifty in the metropolis, and, among the rest, a young girl born about three years ago; that these productions were not peculiar to any family, but a mere effect of chance, and the children of the *struldbrugs* themselves were equally mortal with the rest of the people.

I freely own myself to have been struck with inexpressible delight upon hearing this account: and the person who gave it me happening to understand the Balnibarbian language, which I spoke very well, I could not forbear breaking out into expressions, perhaps a little too extravagant. I cried out, as in a rapture: "Happy nation, where every child has at least a chance for being immortal! Happy people, who enjoy so many living examples of ancient virtue, and have masters ready to instruct them in the wisdom of all former ages! but happiest, beyond all comparison, are those excellent *struldbrugs,* who, being born exempt from that universal calamity of human nature, have their minds free and disengaged, without the weight and depression of spirits caused by the continual apprehension of death!" I discovered my admiration that I had not observed any of these illustrious persons at court; the black spot on the forehead being so remarkable a distinction, that I could not have easily overlooked it; and it was impossible that his Majesty, a most judicious prince, should not provide himself with a good number of such wise

and able counsellors. Yet, perhaps, the virtue of those rev-
erend sages was too strict for the corrupt and libertine manners of a court. And we often find by experience, that young
men are too opinionated and volatile to be guided by the sober
dictates of their seniors. However, since the King was pleased
to allow me access to his royal person, I was resolved, upon
the very first occasion, to deliver my opinion to him on this
matter freely and at large, by the help of my interpreter; and
whether he would please to take my advice or not, yet in one
thing I was determined, that, his Majesty having frequently
offered me an establishment in this country, I would, with
great thankfulness, accept the favour, and pass my life here
in the conversation of those superior beings, the *struldbrugs*,
if they would please to admit me.

The gentleman to whom I addressed my discourse, because (as I have already observed) he spoke the language of
Balnibarbi, said to me, with a sort of smile, which usually
arises from pity to the ignorant that he was glad of any
occasion to keep me among them, and desired my permission
to explain to the company what I had spoke. He did so, and
they talked together for some time in their own language,
whereof I understood not a syllable, neither could I observe
by their countenances, what impression my discourse had
made on them. After a short silence, the same person told
me that his friends and mine (so he thought fit to express
himself) were very much pleased with the judicious remarks
I had made, on the great happiness and advantages of immortal life, and they were desirous to know, in a particular
manner, what scheme of living I should have formed to
myself, if it had fallen to my lot to have been born a
struldbrug.

I answered it was easy to be eloquent on so copious and
delightful a subject, especially to me, who had been often apt
to amuse myself with visions of what I should do, if I were

a king, a general, or a great lord: and upon this very case, I had frequently run over the whole system how I should employ myself, and pass the time, if I were sure to live for ever.

That if it had been my good fortune to come into the world a *struldbrug,* as soon as I could discover my own happiness, by understanding the difference between life and death, I would first resolve, by all arts and methods whatsoever, to procure myself riches. In the pursuit of which, by thrift and management, I might reasonably expect, in about two hundred years, to be the wealthiest man in the kingdom. In the second place, I would, from my earliest youth, apply myself to the study of arts and sciences, by which I should arrive in time to excel all others in learning. Lastly, I would carefully record every action and event of consequence, that happened in the public, impartially draw the characters of the several successions of princes and great ministers of state, with my observations on every point. I would exactly set down the several changes in customs, language, fashions of dress, diet, and diversions. By all which acquirements, I should be a living treasure of knowledge and wisdom, and certainly become the oracle of the nation.

I would never marry after threescore, but live in a hospitable manner, yet still on the saving side. I would entertain myself in forming and directing the minds of hopeful young men, by convincing them from my own remembrance, experience, and observation, fortified by numerous examples, of the usefulness of virtue in public and private life. But my choice and constant companions should be a set of my own immortal brotherhood; among whom I would elect a dozen from the most ancient, down to my own contemporaries. Where any of these wanted fortunes, I would provide them with convenient lodges round my own estate, and have some of them always at my table; only mingling a few of the most valuable

among you mortals, whom length of time would harden
me to lose with little or no reluctance, and treat your posterity
after the same manner; just as a man diverts himself with
the annual succession of pinks and tulips in his garden,
without regretting the loss of those which withered the
preceding year.

These *struldbrugs* and I would mutually communicate
our observations and memorials, through the course of time;
remark the several gradations by which corruption steals
into the world, and oppose it in every step, by giving perpetual warning and instruction to mankind; which, added to
the strong influence of our own example, would probably
prevent that continual degeneracy of human nature, so justly
complained of in all ages.

Add to this, the pleasure of seeing the various revolutions of states and empires; the changes in the lower and
upper world; ancient cities in ruins, and obscure villages become the seats of kings: famous rivers lessening into shallow
brooks; the ocean leaving one coast dry, and overwhelming
another; the discovery of many countries yet unknown; bar-
barity overrunning the politest nations, and the most barbarous become civilized. I should then see the discovery of the
longitude, the perpetual motion, the universal medicine, and
many other great inventions, brought to the utmost perfection.

What wonderful discoveries should we make in astronomy, by outliving and confirming our own predictions; by
observing the progress and returns of comets, with the
changes of motion in the sun, moon, and stars!

I enlarged upon many other topics, which the natural
desire of endless life, and sublunary happiness, could easily
furnish me with. When I had ended, and the sum of my discourse had been interpreted, as before, to the rest of the
company, there was a good deal of talk among them in the

language of the country, not without some laughter at my
expense. At last, the same gentleman who had been my interpreter, said he was desired by the rest, to set me right in a
few mistakes which I had fallen into through the common
imbecility of human nature, and upon that allowance was less
answerable for them. That this breed of *struldbrugs* was
peculiar to their country, for there were no such people
either in Balnibarbi or Japan, where he had the honour to
be ambassador from his Majesty, and found the natives in
both these kingdoms very hard to believe that the fact was
possible: and it appeared from my astonishment when he
had first mentioned the matter to me, that I received it as a
thing wholly new, and scarcely to be credited. That in the
two kingdoms above mentioned, where, during his residence,
he had conversed very much, he observed long life to be the
universal desire and wish of mankind. That whoever had one
foot in the grave, was sure to hold back the other as strongly
as he could. That the oldest had still hopes of living one day
longer, and looked on death as the greatest evil, from which
nature always prompted him to retreat. Only in this island
of Luggnagg the appetite for living was not so eager, from
the continual example of the *struldbrugs* before their eyes.

That the system of living contrived by me, was unreason-
able and unjust, because it supposed a perpetuity of youth,
health, and vigour, which no man could be foolish to hope,
however extravagant he may be in his wishes. That the question therefore was not, whether a man would choose to be
always in the prime of youth, attended with prosperity and
health; but how he would pass a perpetual life, under all the
usual disadvantages which old age brings along with it. For
although men will avow their desires of being immortal,
upon such hard conditions, yet in the two kingdoms before
mentioned, of Balnibarbi and Japan, he observed that every
man desired to put off death some time longer, let it approach

ever so late; and he rarely heard of any man who died willingly, except he were incited by the extremity of grief or torture. And he appealed to me, whether in those countries I had travelled, as well as my own, I had not observed the same general disposition.

After this preface, he gave me a particular account of the *struldbrugs* among them. He said they commonly acted like mortals, till about thirty years old; after which, by degrees they grew melancholy and dejected, increasing in both till they came to fourscore. This he learned from their own confession: for otherwise, there not being above two or three of that species born in an age, they were too few to form a general observation by. When they came to fourscore years, which is reckoned the extremity of living in this country, they had not only all the follies and infirmities of other old men, but many more, which arose from the dreadful prospect of never dying. They were not only opinionative, peevish, covetous, morose, vain, talkative, but incapable of friendship, and dead to all natural affection, which never descended below their grandchildren. Envy and impotent desires are their prevailing passions. But those objects against which their envy seems principally directed, are the vices of the younger sort, and the deaths of the old. By reflecting on the former, they find themselves cut off from all possibility of pleasure; and whenever they see a funeral, they lament and repine that others are gone to a harbour of rest to which they themselves never can hope to arrive. They have no remembrance of anything, but what they learned and observed in their youth and middle age, and even that is very imperfect. And for the truth or particulars of any fact, it is safer to depend on common tradition, than upon their best recollections. The least miserable among them, appear to be those who turn to dotage, and entirely lose their memories; these meet with more pity and assistance, because they want many bad qualities which abound in others.

If a *struldbrug* happen to marry one of his own kind, the marriage is dissolved of course, by the courtesy of the kingdom, as soon as the younger of the two comes to be fourscore. For the law thinks it a reasonable indulgence, that those who are condemned, without any faults of their own, to a perpetual continuance in the world, should not have their misery doubled by the load of a wife.

As soon as they have completed the term of eighty years, they are looked on as dead in law; their heirs immediately succeed to their estates, only a small pittance is reserved for their support; and the poor ones are maintained at the public charge. After that period, they are held incapable of any employment of trust or profit; they cannot purchase lands, or take leases; neither are they allowed to be witnesses in any cause, either civil or criminal, not even for the decision of meers and bounds.

At ninety, they lose their teeth and hair; they have at that age no distinction of taste, but eat and drink whatever they can get, without relish or appetite. The diseases they were subject to still continue, without increasing or diminishing. In talking, they forget the common appellation of things, and the names of persons, even of those who are their nearest friends and relations. For the same reason, they never can amuse themselves with reading, because their memory will not serve to carry them from the beginning of a sentence to the end; and by this defect, they are deprived of the only entertainment whereof they might otherwise be capable.

The language of this country being always upon the flux, the *struldbrugs* of one age do not understand those of another; neither are they able, after two hundred years, to hold any conversation (farther than by a few general words) with their neighbours the mortals; and thus they lie under the disadvantage of living like foreigners in their own country.

This was the account given me of the *struldbrugs,* as near

as I can remember. I afterwards saw five or six of different ages, the youngest not above two hundred years old, who were brought to me at several times by some of my friends; but although they were told that I was a great traveller, and had seen all the world, they had not the least curiosity to ask me a question; only desired I would give them *slumskudask,* or a token of remembrance; which is a modest way of begging, to avoid the law, that strictly forbids it, because they are provided for by the public, although indeed with a very scanty allowance.

They are despised and hated by all sorts of people. When one of them is born, it is reckoned ominous, and their birth is recorded very particularly; so that you may know their age by consulting the register, which, however, has not been kept above a thousand years past, or at least has been destroyed by time or public disturbances. But the usual way of computing how old they are, is, by asking them what kings or great persons they can remember, and then consulting history; for infallibly the last prince in their mind did not begin his reign after they were fourscore years old.

They were the most mortifying sight I ever beheld; and the women more horrible than the men. Besides the usual deformities in extreme old age, they acquired an additional ghastliness, in proportion to their number of years, which is not to be described; and among half a dozen, I soon distinguished which was the eldest, although there was not above a century or two between them.

The reader will easily believe that, from what I had heard and seen, my keen appetite for perpetuity of life was much abated. I grew heartily ashamed of the pleasing visions I had formed; and thought no tyrant could invent a death, into which I would not run with pleasure, from such a life. The King heard of all that had passed between me and my friends upon this occasion, and rallied me very pleasantly;

wishing I could send a couple of *struldbrugs* to my own country, to arm our people against the fear of death; but this, it
seems, is forbidden by the fundamental laws of the kingdom,
or else I should have been well content with the trouble and
expense of transporting them.

I could not but agree that the laws of this kingdom rela-
tive to the *struldbrugs,* were founded upon the strongest reasons, and such as any other country would be under the necessity of enacting in the like circumstances. Otherwise, as
avarice is the necessary consequent of old age, those immortals would in time become proprietors of the whole nation,
and engross the civil power, which, for want of abilities to
manage, must end in the ruin of the public.

CHAPTER II

*The author leaves Luggnagg, and sails to Japan. From thence
he returns in a Dutch ship to Amsterdam, and from Amsterdam to England.*

I THOUGHT this account of
the *struldbrugs* might be some entertainment to the reader,
because it seems to be a little out of the common way; at least
I do not remember to have met the like in any book of travels
that has come to my hands: and if I am deceived, my excuse
must be, that it is necessary for travellers, who describe the
same country, very often to agree in dwelling on the same
particulars, without deserving the censure of having borrowed or transcribed from those who wrote before them.

There is indeed a perpetual commerce between this

kingdom and the great empire of Japan; and it is very probable, that the Japanese authors may have given some account
of the *struldbrugs;* but my stay in Japan was so short, and I
was so entirely a stranger to the language, that I was not
qualified to make any inquiries. But I hope the Dutch, upon
this notice, will be curious and able enough to supply my
defects.

His Majesty having often pressed me to accept some
employment in his court, and finding me absolutely determined to return to my native country, was pleased to give me
his licence to depart; and honoured me with a letter of recommendation, under his own hand, to the Emperor of Japan. He
likewise presented me with four hundred and forty-four large
pieces of gold, (this nation delighting in even numbers), and
a red diamond, which I sold in England for eleven hundred
pounds.

On the 6th of May, 1709, I took a solemn leave of his
Majesty, and all my friends. This prince was so gracious, as
to order a guard to conduct me to Glanguenstald, which is
a royal port to the south-west part of the island. In six days I
found a vessel ready to carry me to Japan, and spent fifteen
days in the voyage. We landed at a small port-town called
Xamoschi, situated on the south-east part of Japan; the town
lies on the western point, where there is a narrow strait leading northward into a long arm of the sea, upon the north-
west part of which Yedo the metropolis stands. At landing, I
shewed the custom-house officers my letter from the King
of Luggnagg to his Imperial Majesty. They knew the seal
perfectly well; it was as broad as the palm of my hand. The
impression was a king lifting up a lame beggar from the
earth. The magistrates of the town, hearing of my letter,
received me as a public minister; they provided me with carriages and servants, and bore my charges to Yedo, where I
was admitted to an audience, and delivered my letter, which

was opened with great ceremony, and explained to the Emperor by an interpreter; who then gave me notice, by his Majesty's order, that I should signify my request, and, whatever it were, it should be granted, for the sake of his royal brother of Luggnagg. This interpreter was a person employed to transact affairs with the Hollanders; he soon conjectured, by my countenance, that I was an European, and therefore repeated his Majesty's commands in Low Dutch, which he spoke perfectly well. I answered, as I had before determined, that I was a Dutch merchant, shipwrecked in a very remote country, whence I had travelled by sea and land to Luggnagg, and then took shipping for Japan; where I knew my countrymen often traded, and with some of these I hoped to get an opportunity of returning into Europe: I therefore most humbly entreated his royal favour, to give order that I should be conducted in safety to Nangasac. To this I added another petition, that for the sake of my patron the King of Luggnagg, his Majesty would condescend to excuse my performing the ceremony imposed on my countrymen, of trampling upon the crucifix; because I had been thrown into this kingdom by my misfortunes, without any intention of trading. When this latter petition was interpreted to the Emperor, he seemed a little surprised; and said he believed I was the first of my countrymen who ever made any scruple in this point; and that he began to doubt whether I was a real Hollander or not; but rather suspected I must be a Christian. However, for the reasons I had offered, but chiefly to gratify the King of Luggnagg, by an uncommon mark of his favour, he would comply with the singularity of my humour; but the affair must be managed with dexterity, and his officers should be commanded to let me pass, as it were by forgetfulness. For he assured me that if the secret should be discovered by my countrymen the Dutch, they would cut my throat in the voyage. I returned my thanks, by the interpreter, for so unusual a favour; and some troops being at that time on their march to Nangasac, the commanding officer had orders to convey me safe thither, with particular instructions about the business of the crucifix.

On the 9th day of June, 1709, I arrived at Nangasac, after a very long and troublesome journey. I soon fell into the company of some Dutch sailors belonging to the *Amboyna* of Amsterdam, a stout ship of 450 tons. I had lived long in Holland, pursuing my studies at Leyden, and I spoke Dutch well. The seamen soon knew whence I came last; they were curious to inquire into my voyages and course of life. I made up a story as short and probable as I could, but concealed the greatest part. I knew many persons in Holland; I was able to invent names for my parents, whom I pretended to be obscure people in the province of Gelderland. I would have given the captain (one Theodorus Vangrult) what he pleased to ask for my voyage to Holland; but understanding I was a surgeon, he was contented to take half the usual rate, on condition that I would serve him in the way of my calling. Before we took shipping, I was often asked by some of the crew whether I had performed the ceremony above mentioned? I evaded the question by general answers; that I had satisfied the Emperor and court in all particulars. However, a malicious rogue of a skipper went to an officer, and, pointing to me, told him I had not yet trampled on the crucifix; but the other, who had received instructions to let me pass, gave the rascal twenty strokes on the shoulders with a bamboo; after which I was no more troubled with such questions.

Nothing happened worth mentioning in this voyage. We sailed with a fair wind to the Cape of Good Hope, where we stayed only to take in fresh water. On the 10th of April, 1710, we arrived safe at Amsterdam, having lost only three men by sickness in the voyage, and a fourth, who fell from the fore-mast into the sea, not far from the coast of Guinea. From Amsterdam I soon after set sail for England, in a small vessel belonging to that city.

On the 16th of April we put in at the Downs. I landed next morning, and saw once more, my native country, after an absence of five years and six months complete. I went straight to Redriff, where I arrived the same day at two in the afternoon, and found my wife and family in good health.

THE END OF
A VOYAGE TO LAPUTA

A VOYAGE TO
THE COUNTRY OF

Houyhnhnms

NUYTS LAND

EDELS LAND

I. St. Pieter

I. St. Francoi

LEWINS LAND

Sweers I.

I. Maelsuyker

De Wits I.

HOUYHNHNM'S
LAND

Discovered
A.D. 1711

CHAPTER I

The author sets out as captain of a ship. His men conspire against him; confine him a long time to his cabin; set him on shore in an unknown land. He travels up into the country. The Yahoos, a strange sort of animal, described. The author meets two Houyhnhnms.

I CONTINUED at home with my wife and children about five months, in a very happy condition, if I could have learned the lesson of knowing when I was well. I left my poor wife big with child, and accepted an advantageous offer made me to be captain of the *Adventure,* a stout merchantman of 350 tons: for I understood navigation well, and being grown weary of a surgeon's employment at sea, which, however, I could exercise upon occasion, I took a skilful young man of that calling, one Robert Purefoy, into my ship. We set sail from Portsmouth upon the 7th day of September, 1710; on the 14th, we met with Captain Peacock of Bristol, at Teneriffe, who was going to the Bay of Campeachy to cut logwood. On the 16th, he was parted from us by a storm; I heard, since my return, that his ship foundered, and none escaped but one cabin-boy. He was an honest man, and a good sailor, but a little too positive in his own opinions, which was the cause of his destruction, as it had been of several others. For, if he had followed my advice, he might have been safe at home with his family at this time, as well as myself.

I had several men died in my ship of calentures, so that I was forced to get recruits out of Barbadoes and the Leeward Islands, where I touched, by the direction of the merchants who employed me; which I had soon too much cause to repent; for I found afterwards, that most of them had been buccaneers. I had fifty hands on board; and my orders were that I should trade with the Indians in the South Sea, and make what discoveries I could. These rogues, whom I had picked up, debauched my other men, and they all formed a conspiracy to seize the ship, and secure me; which they did one morning, rushing into my cabin, and binding me hand and foot, and threatening to throw me overboard if I offered to stir. I told them I was their prisoner, and would submit. This they made me swear to do, and then they unbound me, only fastening one of my legs with a chain, near my bed, and placed a sentry at my door with his piece charged, who was commanded to shoot me dead, if I attempted my liberty. They sent me down victuals and drink, and took the government of the ship to themselves. Their design was to turn pirates, and plunder the Spaniards, which they could not do till they got more men. But first they resolved to sell the goods in the ship, and then go to Madagascar for recruits, several among them having died since my confinement. They sailed many weeks, and traded with the Indians; but I knew not what course they took, being kept a close prisoner in my cabin, and expecting nothing less than to be murdered, as they often threatened me.

Upon the 9th day of May, 1711, one James Welch came down to my cabin, and said he had orders from the captain to set me ashore. I expostulated with him, but in vain; neither would he so much as tell me who their new captain was. They forced me into the long-boat, letting me put on my best suit of clothes, which were as good as new, and take a small bundle of linen, but no arms, except my hanger; and they were so civil as not to search my pockets, into which I conveyed what money I had, with some other little necessaries. They rowed about a league, and then set me down on a strand. I desired them to tell me what country it was. They all swore they knew no more than myself, but said that the captain (as they called him) was resolved, after they had sold the lading, to get rid of me in the first place where they could discover land. They pushed off immediately, advising me to make haste for fear of being overtaken by the tide, and so bade me farewell.

In this desolate condition I advanced forward, and soon got upon firm ground, where I sat down on a bank to rest myself, and consider what I had best do. When I was a little refreshed, I went up into the country, resolving to deliver myself to the first savages I should meet, and purchase my life from them by some bracelets, glass rings, and other toys, which sailors usually provide themselves with in these voyages, and whereof I had some about me. The land was divided by long rows of trees, not regularly planted, but naturally growing; there was great plenty of grass, and several fields of oats. I walked very circumspectly, for fear of being surprised, or suddenly shot with an arrow from behind, or on either side. I fell into a beaten road, where I saw many tracks of human feet, and some of cows, but most of horses. At last I beheld several animals in a field, and one or two of the same kind sitting in trees. Their shape was very singular and deformed, which a little discomposed me, so that I lay down behind a thicket, to observe them better. Some of them coming forward near the place where I lay, gave me an opportunity of distinctly marking their form. Their heads and breasts were covered with a thick hair, some frizzled, and others lank; they had beards like goats, and a long ridge of hair down their backs, and the fore parts of their legs and feet; but the rest of their bodies was bare, so that I might see their skins, which were of a brown buff colour. They had no tails, nor any hair at all on their buttocks, except about the anus; which, I presume, nature had placed there to defend them, as they sat on the ground; for this posture they used, as well as lying down, and often stood on their hind feet. They climbed high trees as nimbly as a squirrel, for they had strong extended claws before and behind, terminating in sharp points, and hooked. They would often spring, and bound, and leap, with prodigious agility. The females were not so large as the males; they had long lank hair on their head, but none on their faces, nor anything more than a sort of down on the rest of their bodies, except about the anus and pudenda. The dugs hung between their fore-feet, and often reached almost to the ground as they walked. The hair of both sexes was of several colours, brown, red, black, and yellow. Upon the whole, I never beheld, in all my travels, so disagreeable an animal, or one against which I naturally conceived so great an antipathy. So that, thinking I had seen enough, full of contempt and aversion, I got up, and pursued the beaten road, hoping it might direct me to the cabin of some Indian. I had not got far, when I met one of these creatures full in my way, and coming up directly to me. The ugly monster, when he saw me, distorted several ways every feature of his visage, and stared, as at an object he had never seen before; then approaching nearer, lifted up his fore-paw, whether out of curiosity or mischief, I could not tell; but I drew my hanger, and gave him a good blow with the flat side of it, for I durst not strike with the edge, fearing the inhabitants might be provoked against me, if they should come to know that I had killed or maimed any of their cattle. When the beast felt the smart, he drew back, and roared so loud, that a herd of at least forty came flocking about me from the next field, howling, and making odious faces; but I ran to the body of a tree, and, leaning my back against it, kept them off by waving my hanger. Several of this cursed brood, getting hold of the branches behind, leapt up into the tree, whence they began to discharge their excrements on my head; however, I escaped pretty well by sticking close to the stem of the tree, but was almost stifled with the filth, which fell about me on every side.

In the midst of this distress, I observed them all to run away on a sudden as fast as they could; at which I ventured to leave the tree, and pursue the road, and wondering what it was that could put them into this fright. But, looking on my left hand, I saw a horse walking softly in the field, which my persecutors having sooner discovered was the cause of their flight. The horse started a little when he came near me, but soon recovering himself, looked full in my face with manifest tokens of wonder. He viewed my hands and feet, walking round me several times. I would have pursued my journey, but he placed himself directly in the way, yet looking with very mild aspect, never offering the least violence. We stood gazing at each other for some time; at last I took the boldness to reach my hand towards his neck, with a design to stroke it, using the common style and whistle of jockeys when they are going to handle a strange horse. But this animal seemed to receive my civilities with disdain, shook his head, and bent his brows, softly raising up his right fore-foot to remove my hand. Then he neighed three or four times, but in so different a cadence, that I almost began to think he was speaking to himself in some language of his own.

While he and I were thus employed, another horse came up, who applying himself to the first in a very formal manner, they gently struck each other's right hoof before, neighing several times by turns, and varying the sound, which seemed to be almost articulate. They went some paces off, as if it were to confer together, walking side by side, backward and forward, like persons deliberating upon some affair of weight, but often turning their eyes towards me, as it were to watch that I might not escape. I was amazed to see such actions and behaviour in brute beasts, and concluded with myself, that if the inhabitants of this country were endued with a proportionable degree of reason, they must needs be the wisest people upon earth. This thought gave me so much comfort, that I resolved to go forward, until I could discover some house or village, or meet with any of the natives, leaving the two horses to discourse together as they pleased. But the first, who was a dapple gray, observing me to steal off, neighed after me in so expressive a tone, that I fancied myself to understand what he meant; whereupon I turned back, and came near to him, to expect his farther commands, but concealing my fear as much as I could, for I began to be in some pain how this adventure might terminate; and the reader will easily believe I did not much like my present situation.

The two horses came up close to me, looking with great earnestness upon my face and hands. The gray steed rubbed my hat all round with his right fore-hoof, and discomposed it so much, that I was forced to adjust it better by taking it off, and settling it again; whereat both he and his companion (who was a brown bay) appeared to be much surprised: the latter felt the lappet of my coat, and finding it to hang loose about me, they both looked with new signs of wonder. He stroked my right hand, seeming to admire the softness and colour, but he squeezed it so hard between his hoof and his pastern, that I was forced to roar; after which they both touched me with all possible tenderness. They were under great perplexity about my shoes and stockings, which they felt very often, neighing to each other, and using various gestures, not unlike those of a philosopher, when he would attempt to solve some new and difficult phenomenon.

Upon the whole, the behaviour of these animals was so orderly and rational, so acute and judicious, that I at last concluded they must needs be magicians, who had thus metamorphosed themselves upon some design, and seeing a stranger in the way, resolved to divert themselves with him, or, perhaps, were really amazed at the sight of a man so very different in habit, feature and complexion, from those who might probably live in so remote a climate. Upon the strength of this reasoning, I ventured to address them in the following manner: "Gentlemen, if ye be conjurors, as I have good cause to believe, you can understand my language; therefore I make bold to let your worships know that I am a poor distressed Englishman, driven by his misfortunes upon your coast; and I entreat one of you to let me ride upon his back, as if he were a real horse, to some house or village where I can be relieved. In return of which favour, I will make you a present of this knife and bracelet," taking them out of my pocket. The two creatures stood silent while I spoke, seeming to listen with great attention; and, when I had ended, they neighed frequently towards each other, as if they were engaged in serious conversation. I plainly observed that their language expressed the passions very well, and the words might, with little pains, be resolved into an alphabet more easily than the Chinese.

I could frequently distinguish the word *Yahoo,* which was repeated by each of them several times; and although it was impossible for me to conjecture what it meant, yet, while the two horses were busy in conversation, I endeavoured to practise this word upon my tongue; and, as soon as they were silent, I boldly pronounced *Yahoo,* in a loud voice, imitating at the same time, as near as I could, the neighing of a horse, at which they were both visibly surprised; and the gray repeated the same word twice, as if he meant to teach me the right accent; wherein I spoke after him as well as I could, and found myself perceivably to improve every time, though very far from any degree of perfection. Then the bay tried me with a second word, much harder to be pronounced, but, reducing it to the English orthography, may be spelt thus, *Houyhnhnm.* I did not succeed in this so well as in the former; but, after two or three farther trials, I had better fortune, and they both appeared amazed at my capacity.

After some further discourse, which I then conjectured might relate to me, the two friends took their leaves, with the same compliment of striking each other's hoof, and the gray made me signs that I should walk before him; wherein I thought it prudent to comply, till I could find a better director. When I offered to slacken my pace, he would cry *hhuun, hhuun*. I guessed his meaning, and gave him to understand, as well as I could, that I was weary, and not able to walk faster; upon which he would stand a while to let me rest.

CHAPTER 2

The author conducted by a Houyhnhnm to his house. The house described. The author's reception. The food of the Houyhnhnms. The author in distress for want of meat. Is at last relieved. His manner of feeding in this country.

Having travelled about three miles, we came to a long kind of building, made of timber stuck in the ground, and wattled across; the roof was low, and covered with straw. I now began to be a little comforted, and took out some toys, which travellers usually carry for presents to the savage Indians of America, and other parts, in hopes the people of the house would be thereby encouraged to receive me kindly. The horse made me a sign to go in first. It was a large room, with a smooth clay floor, and a rack and manger extending the whole length on one side. There were three nags and two mares, not eating, but some of them sitting down upon their hams, which I very much wondered at, but wondered more to see the rest employed in domestic business; these seemed but ordinary cattle.

However, this confirmed my first opinion, that a people who could so far civilise brute animals, must needs excel in wisdom all the nations of the world. The gray came in just after, and thereby prevented any ill treatment which the others might have given me. He neighed to them several times in a style of authority, and received answers.

Beyond this room, there were three others reaching the length of the house, to which you passed through three doors, opposite to each other, in the manner of a vista; we went through the second room towards the third. Here the gray walked in first, beckoning me to attend: I waited in the second room, and got ready my presents for the master and mistress of the house; they were two knives, three bracelets of false pearls, a small looking-glass, and a bead necklace. The horse neighed three or four times, and I waited to hear some answers in a human voice, but I heard no other returns than in the same dialect, only one or two a little shriller than his. I began to think that this house must belong to some person of great note among them, because there appeared so much ceremony before I could gain admittance. But that a man of quality should be served all by horses, was beyond my comprehension. I feared my brain was disturbed by my sufferings and misfortunes. I roused myself, and looked about me in the room where I was left alone; this was furnished like the first, only after a more elegant manner. I rubbed my eyes often, but the same objects still occurred. I pinched my arms and sides to awake myself, hoping I might be in a dream. I then absolutely concluded that all these appearances could be nothing else but necromancy and magic. But I had no time to pursue these reflections; for the gray horse came to the door, and made me a sign to follow him into the third room, where I saw a very comely mare, together with a colt and foal, sitting on their haunches upon mats of straw, not unartfully made, and perfectly neat and clean.

The mare, soon after my entrance, rose from her mat, and coming up close, after having nicely observed my hands and face, gave me a most contemptuous look, and turning to the horse, I heard the word *Yahoo* often repeated betwixt them, the meaning of which word I could not then comprehend, although it was the first I had learned to pronounce. But I was soon better informed, to my everlasting mortification; for the horse, beckoning to me with his head, and repeating the *hhuun, hhuun,* as he did upon the road, which I understood was to attend him, led me out into a kind of court, where was another building at some distance from the house. Here we entered, and I saw three of these detestable creatures which I first met after my landing, feeding upon roots and the flesh of some animals, which I afterwards found to be that of asses and dogs, and now and then a cow, dead by accident or disease. They were all tied by the neck with strong withes fastened to a beam; they held their food between the claws of their fore-feet, and tore it with their teeth.

The master horse ordered a sorrel nag, one of his servants, to untie the largest of these animals, and take him into the yard. The beast and I were brought close together, and our countenances diligently compared, both by master and servant, who thereupon repeated several times the word *Yahoo*. My horror and astonishment are not to be described, when I observed, in this abominable animal, a perfect human figure; the face of it indeed was flat and broad, the nose depressed, the lips large, and the mouth wide; but these differences are common to all savage nations, where the lineaments of the countenance are distorted by the natives suffering their infants to lie grovelling on the earth, or by carrying them on their backs, nuzzling with their face against the mother's shoulders. The fore-feet of the *Yahoo* differed from my hands in nothing else but the length of the nails, the coarseness and brownness of the palms, and the hairiness on the backs. There was the same resemblance between our feet, with the same differences, which I knew very well, though the horses did not, because of my shoes and stockings; the same in every part of our bodies, except as to hairiness and colour, which I have already described.

The great difficulty that seemed to stick with the two horses was, to see the rest of my body so very different from that of a *Yahoo;* for which I was obliged to my clothes, whereof they had no conception. The sorrel nag offered me a root, which he held (after their manner, as we shall describe in its proper place) between his hoof and pastern. I took it in my hand, and, having smelt it, returned it to him again as civilly as I could. He brought out of the *Yahoos'* kennel a piece of ass's flesh; but it smelt so offensively, that I turned from it with loathing: he then threw it to the *Yahoo,* by whom it was greedily devoured. He afterwards shewed me a wisp of hay, and a fetlock full of oats; but I shook my head, to signify that neither of these were food for me. And indeed I now apprehended that I must absolutely starve, if I did not get to some of my own species; for as to those filthy *Yahoos,* although there were few greater lovers of mankind at that time than myself, yet I confess I never saw any sensitive being so detestable on all accounts; and the more I came near them, the more hateful they grew, while I stayed in that country. This the master horse observed by my behaviour, and therefore sent the *Yahoo* back to his kennel. He then put his fore-hoof to his mouth, at which I was much surprised, although he did it with ease, and with a motion that appeared perfectly natural; and made other signs, to know what I would eat; but I could not return him such an answer as he was able to apprehend; and if he had understood me, I did not see how it was possible to contrive any way for finding myself nourishment. While we were thus engaged, I observed a cow passing by, whereupon I pointed to her, and expressed a desire to go and milk her. This had its effect; for he led me back into the house, and ordered a mare-servant to open a room, where a good store of milk lay in earthen and wooden vessels, after a very orderly and cleanly manner. She gave me a large bowlful, of which I drank very heartily, and found myself well refreshed.

About noon I saw coming towards the house a kind of vehicle drawn like a sledge by four *Yahoos*. There was in it an old steed, who seemed to be of quality; he alighted with his hind feet forward, having by accident got a hurt in his left fore-foot. He came to dine with our horse, who received him with great civility. They dined in the best room, and had oats boiled in milk for the second course, which the old horses eat warm, but the rest cold. Their mangers were placed circular in the middle of the room, and divided into several partitions, round which they sat on their haunches, upon bosses of straw. In the middle was a large rack, with angles answering to every partition of the manger; so that each horse and mare eat their own hay, and their own mash of oats and milk, with much decency and regularity. The behaviour of the young colt and foal appeared very modest, and that of the master and mistress extremely cheerful and complaisant to their guest. The gray ordered me to stand by him; and much discourse passed between him and his friend concerning me, as I found by the stranger's often looking on me, and the frequent repetition of the word *Yahoo*.

I happened to wear my gloves, which the master gray observing, seemed perplexed, discovering signs of wonder what I had done to my fore-feet. He put his hoof three or four times to them, as if he would signify, that I should reduce them to their former shape; which I presently did, pulling off both my gloves, and putting them into my pocket. This occasioned further talk; and I saw the company was pleased with my behaviour, whereof I soon found the good effects.

I was ordered to speak the few words I understood: and
while they were at dinner, the master taught me the name for
oats, milk, fire, water, and some others, which I could readily
pronounce after him, having from my youth a great facility
in learning languages.

When dinner was done, the master horse took me aside,
and by signs and words made me understand the concern he
was in that I had nothing to eat. Oats in their tongue are
called *hlunnh*. This word I pronounced two or three times:
for although I had refused them at first, yet, upon second
thoughts, I considered that I could contrive to make of them
a kind of bread, which might be sufficient, with milk, to keep
me alive till I could make my escape to some other country,
and to creatures of my own species. The horse immediately
ordered a white mare-servant of his family to bring me a
good quantity of oats in a sort of wooden tray. These I
heated before the fire, as well as I could, and rubbed them
till the husks came off, which I made a shift to winnow from
the grain; I ground and beat them between two stones, then
took water, and made them into a paste or cake, which I
toasted at the fire, and ate warm with milk. It was at first a
very insipid diet, though common enough in many parts of
Europe, but grew tolerable by time; and having been often
reduced to hard fare in my life, this was not the first experiment I had made, how easily nature is satisfied. And I cannot
but observe, that I never had one hour's sickness while I staid
in this island. It is true, I sometimes made a shift to catch a
rabbit, or bird, by springes made of *Yahoos'* hairs; and I
often gathered wholesome herbs, which I boiled, and ate as
salads with my bread; and now and then, for a rarity, I made
a little butter, and drank the whey. I was at first at a great
loss for salt, but custom soon reconciled me to the want of
it; and I am confident that the frequent use of salt among us
is an effect of luxury, and was first introduced only as a pro-

vocative to drink, except where it is necessary for preserving flesh in long voyages, or in places remote from great markets; for we observe no animal to be fond of it but man; and as to myself, when I left this country, it was a great while before I could endure the taste of it in anything that I ate.

This is enough to say upon the subject of my diet, wherewith other travellers fill their books, as if the readers were personally concerned whether we fare well or ill. However, it was necessary to mention this matter, lest the world should think it impossible that I could find sustenance for three years, in such a country, and among such inhabitants.

When it grew towards evening, the master horse ordered a place for me to lodge in: it was but six yards from the house, and separated from the stable of the *Yahoos*. Here I got some straw, and covering myself with my own clothes, slept very sound. But I was in a short time better accommodated, as the reader shall know hereafter, when I come to treat more particularly about my way of living.

CHAPTER 3

*The author studies to learn the language. The Houyhnhnm,
his master, assists in teaching him. The language described.
Several Houyhnhnms of quality come out of curiosity to see
the author. He gives his master a short account of his voyage.*

MᴍY ᴘʀɪɴᴄɪᴘᴀʟ endeavour
was to learn the language, which my master (for so I shall
henceforth call him) and his children, and every servant of
his house, were desirous to teach me; for they looked upon
it as a prodigy that a brute animal should discover such marks
of a rational creature. I pointed to everything, and inquired
the name of it, which I wrote down in my journal-book when I
was alone; and corrected my bad accent, by desiring those of
the family to pronounce it often. In this employment a sorrel
nag, one of the under servants, was very ready to assist me.

In speaking, they pronounce through the nose and
throat; and their language approaches nearest to the High
Dutch, or German, of any I know in Europe; but is much
more graceful and significant. The Emperor Charles V made
almost the same observation, when he said that if he were to
speak to his horse, it should be in High Dutch.

The curiosity and impatience of my master were so
great, that he spent many hours of his leisure to instruct me.
He was convinced (as he afterwards told me) that I must be
a *Yahoo;* but my teachableness, civility, and cleanliness, astonished him; which were qualities altogether opposite to
those animals. He was most perplexed about my clothes, reasoning sometimes with himself, whether they were a part of
my body; for I never pulled them off till the family were
asleep, and got them on before they waked in the morning.
My master was eager to learn whence I came; how I acquired

those appearances of reason which I discovered in all my actions; and to know my story from my own mouth; which he hoped he should soon do, by the great proficiency I made in learning and pronouncing their words and sentences. To help my memory, I formed all I learned into the English alphabet, and writ the words down, with the translations. This last, after some time, I ventured to do in my master's presence. It cost me much trouble to explain to him what I was doing; for the inhabitants have not the least idea of books or literature.

In about ten weeks' time I was able to understand most of his questions, and in three months could give him some tolerable answers. He was extremely curious to know from what part of the country I came, and how I was taught to imitate a rational creature; because the *Yahoos* (whom he saw I exactly resembled in my head, hands, and face, that were only visible), with some appearance of cunning, and the strongest disposition to mischief, were observed to be the most unteachable of all brutes. I answered that I came over the sea, from a far place, with many others of my own kind, in a great hollow vessel made of the bodies of trees: that my companions forced me to land on this coast, and then left me to shift for myself. It was with some difficulty, and by the help of many signs, that I brought him to understand me. He replied that I must needs be mistaken, or that I said the thing which was not; for they have no word in their language to express lying or falsehood. He knew it was impossible that there could be a country beyond the sea, or that a parcel of brutes could move a wooden vessel whither they pleased upon water. He was sure no *Houyhnhnm* alive could make such a vessel, nor would trust *Yahoos* to manage it.

The word *Houyhnhnm,* in their tongue, signifies a *horse,* and, in its etymology, *the perfection of nature.* I told my master that I was at a loss for expression, but would improve as fast as I could; and hoped, in a short time, I should be able to tell him wonders. He was pleased to direct his own mare, his colt and foal, and the servants of the family to take all opportunities of instructing me; and every day, for two or three hours, he was at the same pains himself. Several horses and mares of quality in the neighbourhood came often to our house, upon the report spread of "a wonderful *Yahoo* that could speak like a *Houyhnhnm,* and seemed, in his words and actions, to discover some glimmerings of reason." These delighted to converse with me: they put many questions, and received such answers as I was able to return. By all these advantages I made so great a progress, that, in five months from my arrival, I understood whatever was spoken, and could express myself tolerably well.

The *Houyhnhnms,* who came to visit my master out of a design of seeing and talking with me, could hardly believe me to be a right *Yahoo,* because my body had a different covering from others of my kind. They were astonished to observe me without the usual hair or skin, except on my head, face, and hands: but I discovered that secret to my master, upon an accident, which happened about a fortnight before.

I have already told the reader, that every night, when the family were gone to bed, it was my custom to strip, and cover myself with my clothes. It happened, one morning early, that my master sent for me by the sorrel nag, who was his valet. When he came, I was fast asleep, my clothes fallen off on one side, and my shirt above my waist. I awaked at the noise he made, and observed him to deliver his message in some disorder; after which he went to my master, and, in a great fright, gave him a very confused account of what he had seen. This I presently discovered; for going as soon as I was dressed, to pay my attendance upon his honour, he asked me the meaning of what his servant had reported, that

I was not the same thing when I slept, as I appeared to be at other times: that his valet assured him some part of me was white, some yellow, at least not so white, and some brown.

I had hitherto concealed the secret of my dress, in order to distinguish myself, as much as possible, from that cursed race of *Yahoos;* but now I found it in vain to do so any longer. Besides, I considered that my clothes and shoes would soon wear out, which already were in a declining condition, and must be supplied by some contrivance, from the hides of *Yahoos,* or other brutes; whereby the whole secret would be known. I therefore told my master that in the country whence I came, those of my kind always covered their bodies with the hairs of certain animals prepared by art, as well for decency as to avoid the inclemencies of air, both hot and cold; of which, as to my own person, I would give him immediate conviction, if he pleased to command me; only desiring his excuse, if I did not expose those parts that nature taught us to conceal. He said my discourse was all very strange, but especially the last part; for he could not understand why nature should teach us to conceal what nature had given: that neither himself nor family were ashamed of any part of their bodies; but, however, I might do as I pleased. Whereupon I first unbuttoned my coat, and pulled it off: I did the same with my waistcoat: I drew off my shoes, stockings, and breeches: I let my shirt down to my waist, and drew up the bottom, fastening it like a girdle about my middle, to hide my nakedness.

My master observed the whole performance with great signs of curiosity and admiration. He took up all my clothes in his pastern, one piece after another, and examined them diligently; he then stroked my body very gently and looked round me several times; after which, he said, it was plain

I must be a perfect *Yahoo;* but that I differed very much from the rest of my species, in the softness, whiteness, and smoothness of my skin; my want of hair in several parts of my body; the shape and shortness of my claws behind and before; and my affectation of walking continually on my two hinder feet. He desired to see no more, and gave me leave to put on my clothes again, for I was shuddering with cold.

I expressed my uneasiness at his giving me so often the appellation of *Yahoo,* an odious animal, for which I had so utter a hatred and contempt: I begged he would forbear applying that word to me, and make the same order in his family, and among his friends whom he suffered to see me. I requested likewise that the secret of my having a false covering to my body might be known to none but himself, at least as long as my present clothing should last; for, as to what the sorrel nag his valet had observed, his honour might command him to conceal it.

All this my master very graciously consented to; and thus the secret was kept till my clothes began to wear out, which I was forced to supply by several contrivances that shall hereafter be mentioned. In the meantime, he desired I would go on with my utmost diligence to learn their language, because he was more astonished at my capacity for speech and reason, than at the figure of my body, whether it were covered or not; adding that he waited with some impatience to hear the wonders which I promised to tell him.

Thenceforward he doubled the pains he had been at to instruct me: he brought me into all company, and made them treat me with civility; because, as he told them privately, this would put me into good humour, and make me more diverting.

Every day, when I waited on him, besides the trouble he was at in teaching, he would ask me several questions concerning myself, which I answered as well as I could; and by these means he had already received some general ideas, though very imperfect. It would be tedious to relate the several steps by which I advanced to a more regular conversation; but the first account I gave of myself in any order and length was to this purpose:

That I came from a very far country, as I already had attempted to tell him, with about fifty more of my own species; that we travelled upon the seas in a great hollow vessel made of wood, and larger than his honour's house. I described the ship to him in the best terms I could, and explained, by the help of my handkerchief displayed, how it was driven forward by the wind. That, upon a quarrel among us, I was set on shore on this coast, where I walked forward, without knowing whither, till he delivered me from the persecution of those execrable *Yahoos*. He asked me who made the ship, and how it was possible that the *Houyhnhnms* of my country would leave it to the management of brutes? My answer was that I durst proceed no farther in my relation, unless he would give me his word and honour that he would not be offended, and then I would tell him the wonders I had so often promised. He agreed; and I went on, by assuring him that the ship was made by creatures like myself; who, in all the countries I had travelled, as well as in my own, were the only governing rational animals; and that, upon my arrival hither, I was as much astonished to see the *Houyhnhnms* act like rational beings, as he, or his friends, could be, in finding some marks of reason in a creature he was pleased to call a *Yahoo;* to which I owned my resemblance in every part, but could not account for their degenerate and brutal nature. I said farther that if good fortune ever restored me to my native country, to relate my travels hither, as I resolved to do, everybody would believe that I said the thing that was not, that I invented the story out of my own head; and (with all possible respect to himself, his family, and friends, and under his promise of not being offended,) our countrymen would hardly think it probable that a *Houyhnhnm* should be the presiding creature of a nation, and a *Yahoo* the brute.

CHAPTER 4

The Houyhnhnm's notion of truth and falsehood. The author's discourse disapproved by his master. The author gives a more particular account of himself and the accidents of his voyage.

My MASTER heard me with great appearances of uneasiness in his countenance; because doubting, or not believing, are so little known in this country, that the inhabitants cannot tell how to behave themselves under such circumstances. And I remember, in frequent discourses with my master concerning the nature of manhood in other parts of the world, having occasion to talk of lying and false representation, it was with much difficulty that he comprehended what I meant, although he had otherwise a most acute judgment; for he argued thus: that the use of speech was to make us understand one another, and to receive information of facts; now, if any one said the thing which was not, these ends were defeated, because I cannot properly be said to understand him; and I am so far from receiving information, that he leaves me worse than in ignorance; for I am led to believe a thing black, when it is white; and short, when it is long. And these were all the notions he had concerning that faculty of lying, so perfectly well understood, and so universally practised, among human creatures.

To return from this digression. When I asserted that the *Yahoos* were the only governing animals in my country, which my master said was altogether past his conception, he desired to know whether we had *Houyhnhnms* among us, and what was their employment. I told him we had great numbers; that in summer they grazed in the fields, and in winter were kept in houses with hay and oats, where *Yahoo* servants were employed to rub their skins smooth, comb their manes, pick their feet, serve them with food, and make their beds. "I understand you well," said my master, "it is now very plain, from all you have spoken, that whatever share of reason the *Yahoos* pretend to, the *Houyhnhnms* are your masters. I heartily wish our *Yahoos* would be so tractable." I begged his honour would please to excuse me from proceeding any farther, because I was very certain that the account he expected from me would be highly displeasing. But he insisted in commanding me to let him know the best and the worst. I told him he should be obeyed. I owned that the *Houyhnhnms* among us, whom we called horses, were the most generous and comely animal we had; that they excelled in strength and swiftness; and when they belonged to persons of quality, were employed in travelling, racing, or drawing chariots: they were treated with much kindness and care, till they fell into diseases, or became foundered in the feet; but then they were sold, and used to all kind of drudgery till they died: after which, their skins were stripped, and sold for what they were worth, and their bodies left to be devoured by dogs and birds of prey. But the common race of horses had not so good fortune; being kept by farmers and carriers, and other mean people, who put them to greater labour, and fed them worse. I described, as well as I could, our way of riding; the shape and use of a bridle, a saddle, a spur, and a whip; of harness and wheels. I added that we fastened plates of a certain hard substance, called iron, at the bottom of their feet, to preserve their hoofs from being broken by the stony ways, on which we often travelled.

My master, after some expressions of great indignation, wondered how we dared to venture upon a *Houyhnhnm's* back; for he was sure that the weakest servant in his house would be able to shake off the strongest *Yahoo*, or, by lying down and rolling on his back, squeeze the brute to death. I answered that our horses were trained up, from three or four years old, to the several uses we intended them for; that if any of them proved intolerably vicious, they were employed for carriages; that they were severely beaten, while they were young, for any mischievous tricks; that the males, designed for the common use of riding or draught, were generally castrated about two years after their birth, to take down their spirits, and make them more tame and gentle; that they were indeed sensible of rewards and punishments; but his honour would please to consider, that they had not the least tincture of reason, any more than the *Yahoos* in this country.

It put me to the pains of many circumlocutions, to give my master a right idea of what I spoke; for their language does not abound in variety of words, because their wants and passions are fewer than among us. But it is impossible to express his noble resentment at our savage treatment of the *Houyhnhnm* race; particularly after I had explained the manner and use of castrating horses among us, to hinder them from propagating their kind, and to render them more servile. He said if it were possible there could be any country where *Yahoos* alone were endued with reason, they certainly must be the governing animal; because reason in time will always prevail against brutal strength. But, considering the frame of our bodies, and especially of mine, he thought no creature of equal bulk was so ill contrived for employing that reason in the common offices of life; whereupon he desired to know whether those among whom I lived resembled me, or the *Yahoos* of his country. I assured him, that I was as well shaped as most of my age; but the younger, and the females, were much more soft and tender, and the skins of the latter generally as white as milk. He said I differed indeed from other *Yahoos,* being much more cleanly, and not altogether so deformed; but, in point of real advantage, he thought I differed for the worse, that my nails were of no use either to my fore or hinder feet. As to my fore-feet, he could not properly call them by that name, for he never observed me to walk upon them; that they were too soft to bear the ground; that I generally went with them uncovered; neither was the covering I sometimes wore on them of the same shape, or so strong as that on my feet behind. That I could not walk with any security, or if either of my hinder feet slipped, I must inevitably fall. He then began to find fault with other parts of my body: the flatness of my face, the prominence of my nose, mine eyes placed directly in front, so that I could not look on either side without turning my head; that I was not able to feed myself, without lifting one of my fore-feet to my mouth; and therefore nature had placed those joints to answer that necessity. He knew not what could be the use of those several clefts and division in my feet behind; that these were too soft to bear the hardness and sharpness of stones, without a covering made from the skin of some other brute; that my whole body wanted a fence against heat and cold, which I was forced to put on and off every day, with tediousness and trouble. And lastly, that he observed every animal in this country naturally to abhor the *Yahoos,* whom the weaker avoided, and the stronger drove from them. So that, supposing us to have the gift of reason, he could not see how it were possible to cure that natural antipathy which every creature discovered against us; nor consequently, how we could tame and render them serviceable. However, he would, as he said, debate the matter no farther, because he was more desirous to know my own story, the country where I was born, and the several actions and events of my life before I came hither.

I assured him how extremely desirous I was that he should be satisfied on every point; but I doubted much whether it would be possible for me to explain myself on several subjects, whereof his honour could have no conception, because I saw nothing in his country to which I could resemble them; that, however, I would do my best, and strive to express myself by similitudes, humbly desiring his assistance when I wanted proper words; which he was pleased to promise me.

I said my birth was of honest parents, in an island called England, which was remote from his country, as many days' journey as the strongest of his honour's servants could travel in the annual course of the sun; that I was bred a surgeon, whose trade it is to cure wounds and hurts in the body, gotten by accident or violence; that my country was governed by a female man, whom we called queen; that I left it to get riches, whereby I might maintain myself and family, when I should return; that, in my last voyage, I was commander of the ship, and had about fifty *Yahoos* under me, many of which died at sea, and I was forced to supply them by others picked out from several nations; that our ship was twice in danger of being sunk; the first time by a great storm, and the second by striking against a rock. Here my master interposed, by asking me how I could persuade strangers out of different countries to venture with me, after the losses I had sustained, and the hazards I had run. I said they were fellows of desperate fortunes, forced to fly from the places of their birth on account of their poverty or their crimes. Some were undone by law-suits; others spent all they had in drinking, whoring and gaming; others fled for treason; many for murder, theft, poisoning, robbery, perjury, forgery, coining false money, for committing rapes, or sodomy, for flying from their colours, or deserting to the enemy; and most of them had broken prison: none of these durst return to their native countries, for fear of being hanged or of starving in a jail; and therefore they were under a necessity of seeking a livelihood in other places.

During this discourse, my master was pleased to interrupt me several times. I had made use of many circumlocutions in describing to him the nature of the several crimes for which most of our crew had been forced to fly their country. This labour took up several days' conversation, before he was able to comprehend me. He was wholly at a loss to know what could be the use or necessity of practising those vices: to clear up which, I endeavoured to give some ideas of the desire of power and riches; of the terrible effects of lust, intemperance, malice, and envy. All this I was forced to define and describe by putting cases and making suppositions. After which, like one whose imagination was struck with something never seen or heard of before, he would lift up his eyes with amazement and indignation. Power, government, war, law, punishment, and a thousand other things, had no terms wherein that language could express them, which made the difficulty almost insuperable,to give my master any conception of what I meant. But being of an excellent understanding, much improved by contemplation and converse, he at last arrived at a competent knowledge of what human nature, in our parts of the world, is capable to perform, and desired I would give him some particular account of that land which we call Europe, but especially of my own country.

CHAPTER 5

*The author, at his master's command, informs him of the
state of England. The causes of war among the princes of Europe. The author begins to explain the English constitution.*

THE READER may please to ob-
serve, that the following extract of many conversations I had
with my master contains a summary of the most material
points which were discoursed at several times for above two
years; his honour often desiring fuller satisfaction, as I farther improved in the *Houyhnhnm* tongue. I laid before him,
as well as I could, the whole state of Europe; I discoursed of
trade and manufactures, of arts and sciences; and the answers
I gave to all the questions he made, as they arose upon several
subjects, were a fund of conversation not to be exhausted.
But I shall here only set down the substance of what passed
between us concerning my own country, reducing it in order
as well as I can, without any regard to time or other circumstances, while I strictly adhere to truth. My only concern is,
that I shall hardly be able to do justice to my master's arguments and expressions, which must needs suffer by my want of
capacity, as well as by a translation into our barbarous
English.

In obedience, therefore, to his honour's commands, I
related to him the Revolution under the Prince of Orange;
the long war with France, entered into by the said prince,
and renewed by his successor, the present queen, wherein the
greatest powers of Christendom were engaged, and which
still continued. I computed, at his request, that about a million *Yahoos* might have been killed in the whole progress of
it; and perhaps a hundred or more cities taken, and five times
as many ships burnt or sunk.

He asked me what were the usual causes or motives that made one country go to war with another. I answered they were innumerable; but I should only mention a few of the chief. Sometimes the ambition of princes, who never think they have land or people enough to govern: sometimes the corruption of ministers, who engage their master in a war in order to stifle or divert the clamour of the subjects against their evil administration. Difference in opinions has cost many millions of lives: for instance, whether flesh be bread, or bread be flesh; whether the juice of a certain berry be blood or wine; whether whistling be a vice or a virtue; whether it be better to kiss a post or throw it into the fire; what is the best colour for a coat, whether black, white, red, or gray; and whether it should be long or short, narrow or wide, dirty or clean, with many more. Neither are any wars so furious or bloody, or of so long continuance, as those occasioned by difference in opinion, especially if it be in things indifferent.

Sometimes the quarrel between two princes is to decide which of them shall dispossess a third of his dominions, where neither of them pretend to any right. Sometimes one prince quarrels with another, for fear the other should quarrel with him. Sometimes a war is entered upon because the enemy is too strong, and sometimes because he is too weak. Sometimes our neighbours want the things which we have, or have the things which we want, and we both fight till they take ours, or give us theirs. It is a very justifiable cause of a war, to invade a country after the people have been wasted by famine, destroyed by pestilence, or embroiled by factions among themselves. It is justifiable to enter into war against our nearest ally, when one of his towns lies convenient for us, or a territory of land, that would render our dominions round and compact. If a prince sends forces into a nation where the people are poor and ignorant, he may lawfully put half of them to death, and make slaves of the rest, in order to civilize and reduce them from their barbarous way of living. It is a very kingly, honourable, and frequent practice, when one prince desires the assistance of another, to secure him against an invasion, that the assistant, when he has driven out the invader, should seize on the dominions himself, and kill, imprison, or banish the prince he came to relieve. Alliance by blood or marriage is a frequent cause of war between princes; and the nearer the kindred is, the greater their disposition to quarrel. Poor nations are hungry, and rich nations are proud; and pride and hunger will ever be at variance. For these reasons, the trade of a soldier is held the most honourable of all others; because a soldier is a *Yahoo,* hired to kill, in cold blood, as many of his own species, who have never offended him, as possibly he can.

There is likewise a kind of beggarly princes in Europe, not able to make war by themselves, who hire out their troops to richer nations, for so much a day to each man; of which they keep three-fourths to themselves, and it is the best part of their maintenance: such are those in many northern parts of Europe.

"What you have told me," said my master, "upon the subject of war, does, indeed, discover most admirably the effects of that reason you pretend to: however, it is happy that the shame is greater than the danger; and that nature has left you utterly incapable of doing much mischief. For, your mouths lying flat with your faces, you can hardly bite each other to any purpose, unless by consent. Then, as to the claws upon your feet, before and behind, they are so short and tender, that one of our *Yahoos* would drive a dozen of yours before him. And therefore, in recounting the numbers of those who have been killed in battle, I cannot but think you have said the thing which is not."

I could not forbear shaking my head, and smiling a little at his ignorance. And, being no stranger to the art of war, I

gave him a description of cannons, culverins, muskets, cara-
bines, pistols, bullets, powder, swords, bayonets, battles,
sieges, retreats, attacks, undermines, countermines, bombard-
ments, sea-fights, ships sunk with a thousand men, twenty
thousand killed on each side, dying groans, limbs flying in
the air, smoke, noise, confusion, trampling to death under
horses' feet, flight, pursuit, victory; fields strewed with carcases, left for food to dogs, and wolves, and birds of prey;
plundering, stripping, ravishing, burning, and destroying.
And to set forth the valour of my own dear countrymen, I
assured him that I had seen them blow up a hundred enemies
at once in a siege, and as many in a ship; and beheld the dead
bodies drop down in pieces from the clouds, to the great
diversion of the spectators.

I was going on to more particulars, when my master
commanded me silence. He said whoever understood the
nature of *Yahoos* might easily believe it possible for so vile
an animal to be capable of every action I had named, if
their strength and cunning equalled their malice. But as my
discourse had increased his abhorrence of the whole species,
so he found it gave him a disturbance in his mind to which
he was wholly a stranger before. He thought his ears, being
used to such abominable words, might, by degrees, admit
them with less detestation: that although he hated the
Yahoos of this country, yet he no more blamed them for
their odious qualities, then he did a *gnnayh* (a bird of prey)
for its cruelty, or a sharp stone for cutting his hoof. But
when a creature pretending to reason could be capable of
such enormities, he dreaded lest the corruption of that faculty might be worse than brutality itself. He seemed therefore confident that, instead of reason, we were only possessed of some quality fitted to increase our natural vices; as
the reflection from a troubled stream returns the image of an
ill-shapen body, not only larger, but more distorted.

He added that he had heard too much upon the subject of war, both in this and some former discourses. There was another point which a little perplexed him at present. I had informed him that some of our crew left their country on account of being ruined by law; that I had already explained the meaning of the word; but he was at a loss how it should come to pass, that the law, which was intended for every man's preservation, should be any man's ruin. Therefore he desired to be farther satisfied what I meant by law, and the dispensers thereof, according to the present practice in my own country; because he thought nature and reason were sufficient guides for a reasonable animal, as we pretended to be, in shewing us what he ought to do, and what to avoid.

I assured his honour that law was a science in which I had not much conversed, farther than by employing advocates, in vain, upon some injustices that had been done me: however, I would give him all the satisfaction I was able.

I said there was a society of men among us, bred up from their youth in the art of proving, by words multiplied for the purpose, that white is black, and black is white, according as they are paid. To this society all the rest of the people are slaves. For example, if my neighbour has a mind to my cow, he has a lawyer to prove that he ought to have my cow from me. I must then hire another to defend my right, it being against all rules of law that any man should be allowed to speak for himself. Now, in this case, I, who am the right owner, lie under two great disadvantages: first, my lawyer, being practised almost from his cradle in defending falsehood, is quite out of his element when he would be an advocate for justice, which is an unnatural office he always attempts with great awkwardness, if not with ill will. The second disadvantage is, that my lawyer must proceed with great caution, or else he will be reprimanded by the judges, and abhorred by his brethren, as one that would lessen the practice of the law. And therefore I have but two methods to preserve my cow. The first is, to gain over my adversary's lawyer with a double fee, who will then betray his client, by insinuating that he has justice on his side. The second way is, for my lawyer to make my cause appear as unjust as he can, by allowing the cow to belong to my adversary; and this, if it be skilfully done, will certainly bespeak the favour of the bench. Now, your honour is to know, that these judges are persons appointed to decide all controversies of property, as well as for the trial of criminals, and picked out from the most dexterous lawyers, who are grown old or lazy; and having been biased all their lives against truth and equity, lie under such a fatal necessity of favouring fraud, perjury, and oppression, that I have known some of them refuse a large bribe from the side where justice lay, rather than injure the faculty, by doing anything unbecoming their nature or their office.

It is a maxim among these lawyers, that whatever has been done before may legally be done again; and therefore they take special care to record all the decisions formerly made against common justice and the general reason of mankind. These, under the name of precedents, they produce as authorities to justify the most iniquitous opinions; and the judges never fail of directing accordingly.

In pleading, they studiously avoid entering into the merits of the cause, but are loud, violent, and tedious in dwelling upon all circumstances which are not to the purpose. For instance, in the case already mentioned, they never desire to know what claim or title my adversary has to my cow; but whether the said cow were red or black; her horns long or short; whether the field I graze her in be round or square; whether she was milked at home or abroad; what diseases she is subject to, and the like; after which they consult precedents, adjourn the cause from time to time, and in ten, twenty, or thirty years come to an issue.

It is likewise to be observed, that this society has a peculiar cant and jargon of their own, that no other mortal can
understand, and wherein all their laws are written, which
they take special care to multiply; whereby they have wholly
confounded the very essence of truth and falsehood, of right
and wrong; so that it will take thirty years to decide whether
the field left me by my ancestors for six generations belongs
to me, or to a stranger three hundred miles off.

In the trial of persons accused for crimes against the
state, the method is much more short and commendable: the
judge first sends to sound the disposition of those in power,
after which he can easily hang or save a criminal, strictly
preserving all due forms of law.

Here my master interposing, said it was a pity that
creatures endued with such prodigious abilities of mind, as
these lawyers, by the description I gave of them, must certainly be, were not rather encouraged to be instructors of
others in wisdom and knowledge. In answer to which I assured his honour that in all points out of their own trade
they were usually the most ignorant and stupid generation
among us, the most despicable in common conversation,
avowed enemies to all knowledge and learning, and equally
disposed to pervert the general reason of mankind in every
other subject of discourse as in that of their own profession.

CHAPTER 6

A continuation of the state of England under Queen Anne.
The character of a first minister of state in European courts.

M Y MASTER was yet wholly at
a loss to understand what motives could incite this race of
lawyers to perplex, disquiet, and weary themselves, and engage in a confederacy of injustice, merely for the sake of in-
juring their fellow-animals; neither could he comprehend
what I meant in saying they did it for hire: whereupon I
was at much pains to describe to him the use of money, the
materials it was made of, and the value of the metals; that
when a *Yahoo* had got a great store of this precious substance,
he was able to purchase whatever he had a mind to; the
finest clothing, the noblest houses, great tracts of land, the
most costly meats and drinks, and have his choice of the
most beautiful females. Therefore, since money alone was
able to perform all these feats, our *Yahoos* thought they
could never have enough of it to spend, or to save, as they
found themselves inclined, from their natural bent, either
to profusion or avarice; that the rich man enjoyed the fruit
of the poor man's labour, and the latter were a thousand to
one in proportion to the former; that the bulk of our people
were forced to live miserably, by labouring every day for
small wages, to make a few live plentifully.

I enlarged myself much on these, and many other particulars to the same purpose; but his honour was still to seek;
for he went upon a supposition that all animals had a title
to their share in the productions of the earth, and especially
those who presided over the rest. Therefore he desired I
would let him know what these costly meats were, and how
any of us happened to want them. Whereupon I enumerated

as many sorts as came into my head, with the various methods of dressing them, which could not be done without sending vessels by sea to every part of the world, as well for liquors to drink as for sauces, and innumerable other conveniences. I assured him that this whole globe of earth must be at least three times gone round, before one of our better female *Yahoos* could get her breakfast, or a cup to put it in. He said that must needs be a miserable country, which cannot furnish food for its own inhabitants. But what he chiefly wondered at was how such vast tracts of ground as I described should be wholly without fresh water, and the people put to the necessity of sending over the sea for drink. I replied that England (the dear place of my nativity) was computed to produce three times the quantity of food more than its inhabitants are able to consume, as well as liquors extracted from grain, or pressed out of the fruit of certain trees, which made excellent drink, and the same proportion in every other convenience of life. But in order to feed the luxury and intemperance of the males, and the vanity of the females, we sent away the greatest part of our necessary things to other countries, whence, in return, we brought the materials of diseases, folly, and vice, to spend among ourselves. Hence it follows, of necessity, that vast numbers of our people are compelled to seek their livelihood by begging, robbing, stealing, cheating, pimping, flattering, suborning, forswearing, forging, gaming, lying, fawning, hectoring, voting, scribbling, star-gazing, poisoning, whoring, canting, libelling, free-thinking, and the like occupations: every one of which terms I was at much pains to make him understand.

That wine was not imported among us from foreign countries to supply the want of water or other drinks, but because it was a sort of liquid which made us merry, by putting us out of our senses, diverted all melancholy thoughts, begat wild, extravagant imaginations in the brain, raised our hopes and banished our fears, suspended every office of reason for a time, and deprived us of the use of our limbs, till we fell into a profound sleep; although it must be confessed that we always awaked sick and dispirited, and that the use of this liquor filled us with diseases which made our lives uncomfortable and short.

But, besides all this, the bulk of our people supported themselves by furnishing the necessities or conveniences of life to the rich, and to each other. For instance, when I am at home, and dressed as I ought to be, I carry on my body the workmanship of a hundred tradesmen, the building and furniture of my house employ as many more, and five times the number to adorn my wife.

I was going on to tell him of another sort of people who get their livelihood by attending the sick, having, upon some occasions, informed his honour that many of my crew had died of diseases. But here it was with the utmost difficulty that I brought him to apprehend what I meant. He could easily conceive that a *Houyhnhnm* grew weak and heavy a few days before his death, or by some accident, might hurt a limb; but that nature, who works all things to perfection, should suffer any pains to breed in our bodies, he thought impossible, and desired to know the reason of so unaccountable an evil.

I told him we fed on a thousand things which operated contrary to each other; that we eat when we were not hungry, and drank without the provocation of thirst; that we sat whole nights drinking strong liquors, without eating a bit, which disposed us to sloth, inflamed our bodies, and precipitated or prevented digestion; that prostitute female *Yahoos* acquired a certain malady, which bred rottenness in the bones of those who fell into their embraces; that this, and many other diseases, were propagated from father to son, so that great numbers come into the world with complicated mala-

dies upon them; that it would be endless to give him a catalogue of all diseases incident to human bodies, for they would
not be fewer than five or six hundred, spread over every limb
and joint; in short, every part, external and intestine, having
diseases appropriated to itself: To remedy which, there was
a sort of people bred up among us in the profession, or the
pretence, of curing the sick. And because I had some skill in
the faculty, I would, in gratitude to his honour, let him know
the whole mystery and method by which they proceed.

Their fundamental is, that all diseases arise from repletion, whence they conclude, that a great evacuation of
the body is necessary, either through the natural passage, or
upwards at the mouth. Their next business is from herbs,
minerals, gums, oils, shells, salts, juices, seaweed, excrements,
barks of trees, serpents, toads, frogs, spiders, dead men's
flesh and bones, birds, beasts, and fishes, to form a composition, for smell and taste, the most abominable, nauseous, and
detestable they can possibly contrive, which the stomach immediately rejects with loathing, and this they call a vomit;
or else, from the same store-house, with some other poisonous additions, they command us to take in at the orifice above
or below (just as the physician then happens to be disposed)
a medicine equally annoying and disgustful to the bowels,
which, relaxing the belly, drives down all before it; and this
they call a purge, or a clyster. For nature (as the physicians
allege) having intended the superior anterior orifice only for
the intromission of solids and liquids, and the inferior pos-
terior for ejection, these artists, ingeniously considering that
in all diseases nature is forced out of her seat, therefore, to
replace her in it, the body must be treated in a manner directly
contrary, by interchanging the use of each orifice, forcing
solids and liquids in at the anus, and making evacuations at
the mouth.

But, besides real diseases, we are subject to many that

are only imaginary, for which the physicians have invented imaginary cures: these have their several names, and so have the drugs that are proper for them; and with these our female *Yahoos* are always infested.

One great excellency in this tribe is their skill at prognostics, wherein they seldom fail; their predictions in real diseases, when they rise to any degree of malignity, generally portending death, which is always in their power, when recovery is not; and therefore, upon any unexpected signs of amendment, after they have pronounced their sentence, rather than be accused as false prophets, they know how to approve their sagacity to the world, by a seasonable dose.

They are likewise of special use to husbands and wives who are grown weary of their mates, to eldest sons, to great ministers of state, and often to princes.

I had formerly, upon occasion, discoursed with my master upon the nature of government in general, and particularly of our own excellent constitution, deservedly the wonder and envy of the whole world. But having here accidently mentioned a minister of state, he commanded me, some time after, to inform him what species of *Yahoo* I particularly meant by that appellation.

I told him that a first or chief minister of state, who was the person I intended to describe, was a creature wholly exempt from joy and grief, love and hatred, pity and anger; at least, makes use of no other passions but a violent desire of wealth, power, and titles; that he applies his words to all uses, except to the indication of his mind; that he never tells a truth but with an intent that you should take it for a lie; nor a lie, but with a design that you should take it for a truth; that those he speaks worst of behind their backs are in the surest way of preferment; and whenever he begins to praise you to others, or to yourself, you are from that day forlorn. The worst mark you can receive is a promise, especially when it is confirmed with an oath; after which every wise man retires, and gives over all hopes.

There are three methods by which a man may rise to be chief minister. The first is, by knowing how, with prudence, to dispose of a wife, a daughter, or a sister; the second by betraying or undermining his predecessor; and the third is, by a furious zeal in public assemblies, against the corruptions of the court. But a wise prince would rather choose to employ those who practise the last of these methods; because such zealots prove always the most obsequious and subservient to the will and passions of their master. That these ministers, having all employments at their disposal, preserve themselves in power by bribing the majority of a senate or great council; and at last, by an expedient, called an act of indemnity (whereof I described the nature to him), they secure themselves from after-reckonings, and retire from the public laden with the spoils of the nation.

The palace of chief minister is a seminary to breed up others in his own trade: the pages, lackeys, and porter, by imitating their master, become ministers of state in their several districts, and learn to excel in the three principal ingredients of insolence, lying, and bribery. Accordingly, they have a subaltern court paid to them by persons of the best rank; and sometimes by the force of dexterity and impudence, arrive, through several gradations, to be successors to their lord.

He is usually governed by a decayed wench, or favourite footman, who are the tunnels through which all graces are conveyed, and may properly be called, in the last resort, the governors of the kingdom.

One day, in discourse, my master having heard me mention the nobility of my country, was pleased to make me a compliment which I could not pretend to deserve: that he was sure I must have been born of some noble family, because

I far exceeded in shape, colour, and cleanliness, all the
Yahoos of his nation, although I seemed to fail in strength
and agility, which must be imputed to my different way of
living from those other brutes; and, besides, I was not only
endued with the faculty of speech, but likewise with some
rudiments of reason, to a degree that, with all his acquaintance, I passed for a prodigy.

He made me observe that among the *Houyhnhnms,* the
white, the sorrel, and the iron-gray were not so exactly
shaped as the bay, the dapple-gray, and the black; nor born
with equal talents of mind, or a capacity to improve them;
and therefore continued always in the condition of servants, without ever aspiring to match out of their own race,
which, in that country, would be reckoned monstrous and
unnatural.

I made his honour my most humble acknowledgments
for the good opinion he was pleased to conceive of me, but
assured him, at the same time, that my birth was of the lower
sort, having been born of plain honest parents, who were just
able to give me a tolerable education; that nobility among us
was altogether a different thing from the idea he had of it;
that our young noblemen are bred from their childhood in
idleness and luxury; that as soon as years will permit, they
consume their vigour, and contract odious diseases among
lewd females; and when their fortunes are almost ruined,
they marry some woman of mean birth, disagreeable person,
and unsound constitution, (merely for the sake of money,)
whom they hate and despise; that the productions of such
marriages are generally scrofulous, ricketty, or deformed
children; by which means the family seldom continues above
three generations, unless the wife takes care to provide a
healthy father, among her neighbours or domestics, in order
to improve and continue the breed; that a weak, diseased
body, a meagre countenance, and sallow complexion, are the

true marks of noble blood; and a healthy, robust appearance is so disgraceful in a man of quality, that the world concludes his real father to have been a groom or a coachman. The imperfections of his mind run parallel with those of his body, being a composition of spleen, dulness, ignorance, caprice, sensuality, and pride.

Without the consent of this illustrious body, no law can be enacted, repealed, or altered: and these nobles have likewise the decision of all our possessions, without appeal.

CHAPTER 7

The author's great love of his native country. His master's observations upon the constitution and administration of England, as described by the author, with parallel cases and comparisons. His master's observations upon human nature.

THE READER may be disposed to wonder how I could prevail on myself to give so free a representation of my own species, among a race of mortals who are already too apt to conceive the vilest opinion of human kind, from that entire congruity between me and their *Yahoos*. But I must freely confess, that the many virtues of those excellent quadrupeds, placed in opposite view to human corruptions, had so far opened my eyes, and enlarged my understanding, that I began to view the actions and passions of man in a very different light, and to think the honour of my own kind not worth managing; which, besides, it was impossible for me to do, before a person of so acute a judgment as my master, who daily convinced me of a thousand faults in myself, whereof I had not the least perception before, and which, with us, would never be numbered, even among human infirmities. I had likewise learned, from his example, an utter detestation of all falsehood or disguise; and truth appeared so amiable to me that I determined upon sacrificing everything to it.

Let me deal so candidly with the reader, as to confess that there was yet a much stronger motive for the freedom I took in my representation of things. I had not yet been a year in this country, before I contracted such a love and veneration for the inhabitants that I entered on a firm resolution never to return to human kind, but to pass the rest of my life among these admirable *Houyhnhnms,* in the contemplation and practice of every virtue, where I could have no example or incitement to vice. But it was decreed by fortune, my perpetual enemy, that so great a felicity should not fall to my share. However, it is now some comfort to reflect that in what I said of my countrymen, I extenuated their faults as much as I durst before so strict an examiner, and upon every article gave as favourable a turn as the matter would bear. For, indeed, who is there alive that will not be swayed by his bias and partiality to the place of his birth?

I have related the substance of several conversations I had with my master during the greatest part of the time I had the honour to be in his service, but have, indeed, for brevity sake, omitted much more than is here set down.

When I had answered all his questions, and his curiosity seemed to be fully satisfied, he sent for me one morning early, and commanded me to sit down at some distance (an honour which he had never before conferred upon me). He said he had been very seriously considering my whole story, as far as it related both to myself and my country; that he looked upon us as a sort of animal, to whose share, by what accident he could not conjecture, some small pittance of reason had fallen, whereof we made no other use than, by its assistance, to aggravate our natural corruptions, and to acquire new ones, which Nature had not given us; that we disarmed ourselves of the few abilities she had bestowed, had been very successful in multiplying our original wants, and seemed to spend our whole lives in vain endeavours to supply them by our own inventions; that as to myself, it was manifest I had neither the strength nor agility of a common *Yahoo;* that I walked infirmly on my hinder feet, had found out a contrivance to make my claws of no use or defence, and to remove the hair from my chin, which was intended as a shelter from the sun and the weather: lastly, that I could neither run with speed, nor climb trees like my brethren, as he called them, the *Yahoos* in his country.

That our institutions of government and law were plainly owing to our gross defects in reason, and by consequence in virtue; because reason alone is sufficient to govern a rational creature; which was, therefore, a character we had no pretence to challenge, even from the account I had given of my own people; although he manifestly perceived that in order to favour them, I had concealed many particulars, and often said the thing which was not.

He was the more confirmed in this opinion, because, he observed that, as I agreed in every feature of my body with other *Yahoos,* except where it was to my real disadvantage in point of strength, speed, and activity, the shortness of my claws, and some other particulars where nature had no part; so, from the representation I had given him of our lives, our manners, and our actions, he found as near a resemblance in the disposition of our minds. He said the *Yahoos* were known to hate one another more than they did any different species of animals, and the reason usually assigned was the odiousness of their own shapes, which all could see in the rest, but not in themselves. He had, there-

fore, begun to think it not unwise in us to cover our bodies,
and by that invention conceal many of our deformities from
each other, which would else be hardly supportable. But
he now found he had been mistaken, and that the dissensions
of those brutes in his country were owing to the same cause
with ours, as I had described them. For if, said he, you throw
among five *Yahoos* as much food as would be sufficient for
fifty, they will, instead of eating peaceably, fall together by
the ears, each single one impatient to have all to itself, and
therefore a servant was usually employed to stand by while
they were feeding abroad, and those kept at home were tied
at a distance from each other; that if a cow died of age or
accident before a *Houyhnhnm* could secure it for his own
Yahoos, those in the neighbourhood would come in herds to
seize it, and then would ensue such a battle as I had described,
with terrible wounds, made by their claws, on both sides,
although they seldom were able to kill one another, for want
of such convenient instruments of death as we had invented.
At other times the like battles have been fought between
the *Yahoos* of several neighbourhoods, without any visible
cause; those of one district watching all opportunities to surprise the next, before they are prepared. But if they find
their project has miscarried, they return home, and, for want
of enemies, engage in what I call a civil war among
themselves.

That in some fields of his country there are certain
shining stones of several colours, whereof the *Yahoos* are
violently fond; and when part of these stones is fixed in the
earth, as it sometimes happens, they will dig with their claws
for whole days to get them out: then carry them away, and
hide them by heaps, in their kennels, but still looking round
with great caution, for fear their comrades should find out
their treasure. My master said he could never discover the
reason of this unnatural appetite, or how these stones could

be of any use to a *Yahoo,* but now he believed it might proceed from the same principle of avarice which I had ascribed to mankind: that he had once, by way of experiment, privately removed a heap of these stones from the place where one of his *Yahoos* had buried it; whereupon the sordid animal, missing his treasure, by his loud lamenting brought the whole herd to the place, there miserably howled, then fell to biting and tearing the rest, began to pine away, would neither eat, nor sleep, nor work, till he ordered a servant privately to convey the stones into the same hole, and hide them as before; which, when his *Yahoo* had found, he presently recovered his spirits and good humour, but took care to remove them to a better hiding-place, and has ever since been a very serviceable brute.

My master further assured me, which I also observed myself, that in the fields where the shining stones abound, the fiercest and most frequent battles are fought, occasioned by perpetual inroads of the neighbouring *Yahoos.*

He said it was common, when two *Yahoos* discovered such a stone in a field, and were contending which of them should be the proprietor, a third would take the advantage, and carry it away from them both, which my master would needs contend to have some kind of resemblance with our suits at law; wherein I thought it for our credit not to un- deceive him, since the decision he mentioned was much more equitable than many decrees among us; because the plaintiff and defendant there lost nothing besides the stone they con- tended for, whereas our courts of equity would never have dismissed the cause, while either of them had anything left.

My master, continuing his discourse, said there was nothing that rendered the *Yahoos* more odious than their undistinguishing appetite to devour everything that came in their way, whether herbs, roots, berries, the corrupted flesh of animals, or all mingled together: and it was peculiar in their temper, that they were fonder of what they could get by rapine or stealth, at a greater distance, than much better food provided for them at home. If their prey held out, they would eat till they were ready to burst; after which, nature had pointed out to them a certain root that gave them a general evacuation.

There was also another kind of root, very juicy, but somewhat rare and difficult to be found, which the *Yahoos* sought for with much eagerness, and would suck it with great delight: it produced in them the same effects that wine has upon us. It would make them sometimes hug, and sometimes tear one another: they would howl, and grin, and chatter, and reel, and tumble, and then fall asleep in the mud.

I did indeed observe that the *Yahoos* were the only animals in this country subject to any diseases; which, however, were much fewer than horses have among us, and contracted, not by any ill treatment they meet with, but by the nastiness and greediness of that sordid brute. Neither has their language any more than a general appellation for those maladies, which is borrowed from the name of the beast, and called *hnea-yahoo* or *Yahoo's evil;* and the cure prescribed is a mixture of their own dung and urine, forcibly put down the *Yahoo's* throat. This I have since often known to have been taken with success, and do here freely recommend it to my countrymen, for the public good, as an admirable specific against all diseases produced by repletion.

As to learning, government, arts, manufactures, and the like, my master confessed he could find little or no resemblance between the *Yahoos* of that country and those in ours; for he only meant to observe what parity there was in our natures. He had heard, indeed, some curious *Houyhnhnms* observe, that in most herds there were a sort of ruling *Yahoo* (as among us there is generally some leading or principal stag in a park), who was always more deformed in body, and

mischievous in disposition, than any of the rest; that this leader had usually a favourite as like himself as he could get, whose employment was to lick his master's feet and posteriors, and drive the female *Yahoos* to his kennel; for which he was now and then rewarded with a piece of ass's flesh. This favourite is hated by the whole herd, and therefore, to protect himself, keeps always near the person of his leader. He usually continues in office till a worse can be found; but the very moment he is discarded, his successor, at the head of all the *Yahoos* in that district, young and old, male and female, come in a body, and discharge their excrements upon him from head to foot. But how far this might be applicable to our courts, and favourites, and ministers of state, my master said I could best determine.

I durst make no return to this milicious insinuation, which debased human understanding below the sagacity of a common hound, who has judgment enough to distinguish and follow the cry of the ablest dog in the pack, without being ever mistaken.

My master told me there were some qualities remarkable in the *Yahoos* which he had not observed me to mention, or at least very slightly, in the accounts I had given him of human kind. He said those animals, like other brutes, had their females in common; but in this they differed, that the she *Yahoo* would admit the males while she was pregnant; and that the hes would quarrel and fight with the females, as fiercely as with each other; both which practices were such degrees of infamous brutality, as no other sensitive creature ever arrived at.

Another thing he wondered at in the *Yahoos,* was their strange disposition to nastiness and dirt; whereas there appears to be a natural love of cleanliness in all other animals. As to the two former accusations, I was glad to let them pass without any reply, because I had not a word to offer upon

them in defence of my species, which otherwise I certainly
had done from my own inclinations. But I could have easily
vindicated human kind from the imputation of singularity
upon the last article, if there had been any swine in that country (as, unluckily for me, there was not), which, although
it may be a sweeter quadruped than a *Yahoo,* cannot, I humbly conceive, in justice pretend to more cleanliness; and so
his honour must have owned, if he had seen their filthy way
of feeding, and their custom of wallowing and sleeping in
the mud.

My master likewise mentioned another quality which
his servants had discovered in several *Yahoos,* and to him
was wholly unaccountable. He said a fancy would sometimes
take a *Yahoo* to retire into a corner, to lie down, and howl,
and groan, and spurn away all that came near him, although
he were young and fat, wanted neither food nor water; nor
did the servant imagine what could possibly ail him. And the
only remedy they found was, to set him to hard work, after
which he would infallibly come to himself. To this I was
silent, out of partiality to my own kind; yet here I could
plainly discover the true seeds of spleen, which only seizes
on the lazy, the luxurious, and the rich; who, if they were
forced to undergo the same regimen, I would undertake for
the cure.

His honour had farther observed that a female *Yahoo*
would often stand behind a bank or a bush, to gaze on the
young males passing by, and then appear, and hide, using
many antic gestures and grimaces; at which time it was observed that she had a most offensive smell; and when any
of the males advanced, would slowly retire; looking often
back, and, with a counterfeit show of fear, run off into some
convenient place, where she knew the male would follow her.

At other times, if a female stranger came among them,
three or four of her own sex would get about her, and stare,

and chatter, and grin, and smell her all over, and then turn off, with gestures that seemed to express contempt and disdain.

Perhaps my master might refine a little in these speculations, which he had drawn from what he observed himself, or had been told him by others; however, I could not reflect, without some amazement, and much sorrow, that the rudiments of lewdness, coquetry, censure, and scandal, should have place by instinct in womankind.

I expected every moment that my master would accuse the *Yahoos* of those unnatural appetites in both sexes, so common among us. But Nature, it seems, has not been so expert a school-mistress; and these politer pleasures are entirely the productions of Art and Reason on our side of the globe.

CHAPTER 8

The author relates several particulars of the Yahoos. The great virtues of the Houyhnhnms. The education and exercise of their youth. Their general assembly.

As I OUGHT to have understood human nature much better than I supposed it possible for my master to do, so it was easy to apply the character he gave of the *Yahoos* to myself and my countrymen; and I believed I could yet make farther discoveries, from my own observation. I therefore often begged his honour to let me go among the herds of *Yahoos* in the neighbourhood; to which he always very graciously consented, being perfectly

convinced that the hatred I bore these brutes would never
suffer me to be corrupted by them; and his honour ordered
one of his servants, a strong sorrel nag, very honest and
good-natured, to be my guard; without whose protection I
durst not undertake such adventures; for I have already told
the reader how much I was pestered by these odious animals
upon my first arrival; and I afterward failed very narrowly
three or four times, of falling into their clutches, when I
happened to stray at any distance without my hanger. And
I have reason to believe they had some imagination that I
was of their own species; which I often assisted myself, by
stripping up my sleeves, and shewing my naked arms and
breasts in their sight, when my protector was with me. At
which times they would approach as near as they durst, and
imitate my actions, after the manner of monkeys, but ever
with great signs of hatred; as a tame jackdaw, with cap and
stockings, is always persecuted by the wild ones, when he
happens to be got among them.

They are prodigiously nimble from their infancy. However, I once caught a young male of three years old, and
endeavoured, by all marks of tenderness, to make it quiet;
but the little imp fell a-squalling, and scratching, and biting,
with such violence, that I was forced to let it go; and it was
high time; for a whole troop of old ones came about us at
the noise; but finding the cub was safe (for away it ran),
and my sorrel nag being by, they durst not venture near us.
I observed the young animal's flesh to smell very rank, and
the stink was somewhat between a weasel and a fox, but
much more disagreeable. I forgot another circumstance (and
perhaps I might have the reader's pardon if it were wholly
omitted), that while I held the odious vermin in my hands,
it voided its filthy excrements, of a yellow liquid substance,
all over my clothes; but by good fortune there was a small
brook hard by, where I washed myself as clean as I could,

although I durst not come into my master's presence until I were sufficiently aired.

By what I could discover, the *Yahoos* appear to be the most unteachable of all animals; their capacities never reaching higher than to draw or carry burdens. Yet I am of opinion this defect arises chiefly from a perverse, restive disposition; for they are cunning, malicious, treacherous, and revengeful. They are strong and hardy, but of a cowardly spirit, and by consequence insolent, abject, and cruel. It is observed, that the red haired of both sexes are more libidinous and mischievous than the rest, whom yet they much exceed in strength and activity.

The *Houyhnhnms* keep the *Yahoos* for present use in huts not far from the house; but the rest are sent abroad to certain fields, where they dig up roots, eat several kinds of herbs, and search about for carrion, or sometimes catch weasels and *luhimuhs,* (a sort of wild rat,) which they greedily devour. Nature has taught them to dig deep holes with their nails on the side of a rising ground, wherein they lie by themselves; only the kennels of the females are larger, sufficient to hold two or three cubs.

They swim from their infancy like frogs, and are able to continue long under water, where they often take fish, which the females carry home to their young. And upon this occasion I hope the reader will pardon my relating an odd adventure.

Being one day abroad with my protector, the sorrel nag, and the weather exceeding hot, I entreated him to let me bathe in a river that was near. He consented, and I immediately stripped myself stark naked, and went down softly into the stream. It happened that a young female *Yahoo,* standing behind a bank, saw the whole proceeding, and inflamed by desire, as the nag and I conjectured, came running with all speed, and leaped into the water, within five yards of the

place where I bathed. I was never in my life so terribly frightened. The nag was grazing at some distance, not suspecting
any harm. She embraced me after a most fulsome manner.
I roared as loud as I could, and the nag came galloping
towards me, whereupon she quitted her grasp with the utmost reluctancy, and leaped upon the opposite bank, where
she stood gazing and howling all the time I was putting on
my clothes.

This was a matter of diversion to my master and his
family, as well as of mortification to myself; for now I could
no longer deny that I was a real *Yahoo* in every limb and
feature, since the females had a natural propensity to me, as
one of their own species. Neither was the hair of this brute
of a red colour (which might have been some excuse for an
appetite a little irregular), but black as a sloe, and her countenance did not make an appearance altogether so hideous
as the rest of her kind; for I think she could not be above
eleven years old.

Having lived three years in this country, the reader, I
suppose, will expect that I should, like other travellers, give
him some account of the manners and customs of its inhabitants, which it was indeed my principal study to learn.

As these noble *Houyhnhnms* are endowed by nature
with a general disposition to all virtues, and have no conceptions or ideas of what is evil in a rational creature, so their
grand maxim is to cultivate reason, and to be wholly governed by it. Neither is reason among them a point problem-
atical, as with us, where men can argue with plausibility on
both sides of the question, but strikes you with immediate
conviction, as it must needs do, where it is not mingled, obscured, or discoloured, by passion and interest. I remember
it was with extreme difficulty that I could bring my master
to understand the meaning of the word *opinion,* or how a
point could be disputable; because reason taught us to affirm

or deny only where we are certain; and beyond our knowledge we cannot do either: so that controversies, wranglings, disputes, and positiveness, in false or dubious propositions, are evils unknown among the *Houyhnhnms*. In the like manner, when I used to explain to him our several systems of natural philosophy, he would laugh that a creature pretending to reason should value itself upon the knowledge of other people's conjectures, and in things where that knowledge, if it were certain, could be of no use. Wherein he agreed entirely with the sentiments of Socrates, as Plato delivers them; which I mention as the highest honour I can do to that prince of philosophers. I have often since reflected what destruction such doctrine would make in the libraries of Europe, and how many paths of fame would be then shut up in the learned world.

Friendship and benevolence are the two principal virtues among the *Houyhnhnms,* and these are not confined to particular objects, but universal to the whole race; for a stranger, from the remotest part, is equally treated with the nearest neighbour, and wherever he goes, looks upon himself as at home. They preserve decency and civility in the highest degrees, but are altogether ignorant of ceremony. They have no fondness for their colts or foals, but the care they take in educating them proceeds entirely from the dictates of reason. And I observed my master to shew the same affection to his neighbour's issue that he had for his own. They will have it that nature teaches them to love the whole species, and it is reason only that makes a distinction of persons, where there is a superior degree of virtue.

When the matron *Houyhnhnms* have produced one of each sex, they no longer accompany with their consorts, except they lose one of their issue by some casualty, which very seldom happens; but in such a case they meet again; or, when the like accident befalls a person whose wife is past bearing, some other couple bestow on him one of their own colts, and then go together again until the mother is pregnant. This caution is necessary to prevent the country from being over-burdened with numbers. But the race of inferior *Houyhn-hnms,* bred up to be servants, is not so strictly limited upon this article: these are allowed to produce three of each sex, to be domestics in the noble families.

In their marriages they are exactly careful to choose such colours as will not make any disagreeable mixture in the breed. Strength is chiefly valued in the male, and comeli-ness in the female; not upon the account of love, but to pre-serve the race from degenerating; for where a female hap-pens to excel in strength, a consort is chosen with regard to comeliness.

Courtship, love, presents, jointures, settlements, have no place in their thoughts, or terms whereby to express them in their language. The young couple meet and are joined, merely because it is the determination of their parents and friends; it is what they see done every day, and they look upon it as one of the necessary actions of a reasonable being. But the violation of marriage, or any other unchastity, was never heard of; and the married pair pass their lives with the same friendship and mutual benevolence that they bear to all others of the same species who come in their way, without jealousy, fondness, quarrelling, or discontent.

In educating the youth of both sexes their method is admirable, and highly deserves our imitation. These are not suffered to taste a grain of oats, except upon certain days, till eighteen years old; nor milk, but very rarely; and in summer they graze two hours in the morning, and as many in the evening, which their parents likewise observe: but the ser-vants are not allowed above half that time, and a great part of their grass is brought home, which they eat at the most convenient hours, when they can be best spared from work.

Temperance, industry, exercise, and cleanliness, are the lessons equally enjoined to the young ones of both sexes; and my master thought it monstrous in us to give the females a different kind of education from the males, except in articles of domestic management; whereby, as he truly observed, one half of our natives were good for nothing but bringing children into the world; and to trust the care of our children to such useless animals, he said, was yet a greater instance of brutality.

But the *Houyhnhnms* train up their youth to strength, speed, and hardiness, by exercising them in running races up and down steep hills, and over hard stony grounds; and when they are all in a sweat, they are ordered to leap over head and ears into a pond or river. Four times a year the youth of a certain district meet to show their proficiency in running and leaping, and other feats of strength and agility, where the victor is rewarded with a song in his or her praise. On this festival the servants drive a herd of *Yahoos* into the field, laden with hay, and oats, and milk, for a repast to the *Houyhnhnms;* after which, these brutes are immediately driven back again, for fear of being noisome to the assembly.

Every fourth year, at the vernal equinox, there is a representative council of the whole nation, which meets in a plain about twenty miles from our house, and continues about five or six days. Here they inquire into the state and condition of the several districts: whether they abound to be deficient in hay or oats, or cows or *Yahoos,* and wherever there is any want (which is but seldom), it is immediately supplied by unanimous consent and contribution. Here, likewise, the regulation of children is settled; as, for instance, if a *Houyhnhnm* has two males, he changes one of them with another that has two females; and when a child has been lost by any casualty, where the mother is past breeding, it is determined what family in the district shall breed another to supply the loss.

CHAPTER 9

A grand debate at the general assembly of the Houyhnhnms,
and how it was determined. The learning of the Houyhnhnms.
Their buildings. Their manner of burials. The defectiveness
of their language.

ONE OF THESE grand assemblies was held in my time, about three months before my departure, whither my master went as the representative of our district. In this council was resumed their old debate, and indeed the only debate that ever happened in their country; whereof my master, after his return, gave me a very particular account.

The question to be debated was whether the *Yahoos* should be exterminated from the face of the earth. One of the members for the affirmative offered several arguments of great strength and weight, alleging that as the *Yahoos* were the most filthy, noisome, and deformed animal which nature ever produced, so they were the most restive and indocible, mischievous and malicious. They would privately suck the teats of the *Houyhnhnms'* cows, kill and devour their cats, trample down their oats and grass, if they were not continually watched, and commit a thousand other extravagancies. He took notice of a general tradition that *Yahoos* had not been always in their country; but that many ages ago, two of these brutes appeared together upon a mountain: whether produced by the heat of the sun upon corrupted mud and slime, or from the ooze and froth of the sea, was never known: that these *Yahoos* engendered, and their brood in a short time grew so numerous as to overrun and infest the whole nation: that the *Houyhnhnms,* to get rid of this evil, made a general hunting, and at last enclosed the whole herd; and destroying the elder, every *Houyhnhnm* kept two young ones in a kennel, and brought them to such a degree of tameness, as an animal, so savage by nature, can be capable of acquiring; using them for draught and carriage : that there seemed to be much truth in this tradition; and that those creatures could not be *ylnhniamshy*, (or *aborigines* of the land,) because of the violent hatred the *Houyhnhnms,* as well as all other animals, bore them; which, although their evil disposition sufficiently deserved, could never have arrived at so high a degree, if they had been *aborigines;* or else they would have long since been rooted out : that the inhabitants, taking a fancy to use the service of the *Yahoos,* had very imprudently neglected to cultivate the breed of asses, which are a comely animal, easily kept, more tame and orderly, without any offensive smell; strong enough for labour, although they yield to the other in agility of body; and if their braying be no agreeable sound, it is far preferable to the horrible howlings of the *Yahoos*.

Several others declared their sentiments to the same purpose, when my master proposed an expedient to the assembly, whereof he had indeed borrowed the hint from me. He approved of the tradition mentioned by the honourable member who spoke before, and affirmed, that the two *Yahoos,* said to be the first seen among them, had been driven thither over the sea; that, coming to land, and being forsaken by their companions, they retired to the mountains, and, degenerating by degrees, became, in process of time, much more savage than those of their own species in the country whence these two originals came. The reason of this assertion was, that he had now in his possession a certain wonderful *Yahoo* (meaning myself), which most of them had heard of, and many of them had seen. He then related to them how he first found me; that my body was all covered with an artificial composure of the skins and hairs of other animals, that I spoke in a language of my own, and had thoroughly learned theirs; that

I had related to him the accidents which brought me thither; that when he saw me without my covering, I was an exact *Yahoo* in every part, only of a whiter colour, less hairy, and with shorter claws. He added how I had endeavoured to persuade him that, in my own and other countries, the *Yahoos* acted as the governing, rational animal, and held the *Houyhnhnms* in servitude; that he observed in me all the qualities of a *Yahoo,* only a little more civilized by some tincture of reason; which, however, was in a degree as far inferior to the *Houyhnhnm* race, as the *Yahoos* of their country were to me; that, among other things, I mentioned a custom we had of castrating *Houyhnhnms* when they were young, in order to render them tame; that the operation was easy and safe; that it was no shame to learn wisdom from brutes, as industry is taught by the ant, and building by the swallow (for so I translate the word *lyhannh,* although it be a much larger fowl); that this invention might be practised upon the younger *Yahoos* here, which, beside rendering them tractable and fitter for use, would, in an age, put an end to the whole species, without destroying life; that in the meantime the *Houyhnhnms* should be exhorted to cultivate the breed of asses, which, as they are in all respects more valuable brutes, so they have this advantage, to be fit for service at five years old, which the others are not till twelve.

This was all my master thought fit to tell me, at that time, of what passed in the grand council. But he was pleased to conceal one particular, which related personally to myself, whereof I soon felt the unhappy effect, as the reader will know in its proper place, and whence I date all the succeeding misfortunes of my life.

The *Houyhnhnms* have no letters, and consequently their knowledge is all traditional; but there happening few events of any moment among a people so well united, naturally disposed to every virtue, wholly governed by reason, and cut off from all commerce with other nations, the historical part is easily preserved, without burdening their memories. I have already observed that they are subject to no diseases, and therefore can have no need of physicians. However, they have excellent medicines, composed of herbs, to cure accidental bruises, and cuts in the pastern or frog of the foot, by sharp stones, as well as other maims and hurts in the several parts of the body.

They calculate the year by the revolution of the sun and the moon, but use no subdivisions into weeks. They are well enough acquainted with the motions of those two luminaries, and understand the nature of eclipses; and this is the utmost progress of their astronomy.

In poetry they must be allowed to excell all other mortals, wherein the justness of their similes, and the minuteness, as well as exactness, of their descriptions, are indeed inimitable. Their verses abound very much in both of these, and usually contain either some exalted notions of friendship and benevolence, or the praises of those who were victors in races and other bodily exercises. Their buildings, although very rude and simple, are not inconvenient, but well contrived to defend them from all injuries of cold and heat. They have a kind of tree, which, at forty years old, loosens in the root, and falls with the first storm: it grows very straight, and, being pointed like stakes with a sharp stone, (for the *Houyhnhnms* know not the use of iron,) they stick them erect in the ground, about ten inches asunder, and then weave in oat-straw, or sometimes wattles, between them. The roof is made after the same manner, and so are the doors.

The *Houyhnhnms* use the hollow part, between the pastern and the hoof of the fore-feet, as we do our hands, and this with greater dexterity that I could at first imagine. I have seen a white mare of our family thread a needle (which I lent her on purpose) with that joint. They milk their cows, reap their oats, and do all the work which requires hands in the same manner. They have a kind of hard flints, which, by grinding against other stones, they form into instruments, that serve instead of wedges, axes, and hammers. With tools made of these flints, they likewise cut their hay, and reap their oats, which there grow naturally in several fields; the *Yahoos* draw home their sheaves in carriages, and the servants tread them in certain covered huts, to get out the grain, which is kept in stores. They make a rude kind of earthen and wooden vessels, and make the former in the sun.

If they can avoid casualties, they die only of old age, and are buried in the obscurest places that can be found; their friends and relations expressing neither joy nor grief at their departure; nor does the dying person discover the least regret that he is leaving the world, any more than if he were upon returning home from a visit to one of his neighbours. I remember my master having once made an appointment with a friend and his family to come to his house, upon some affair of importance; on the day fixed, the mistress and her two children came very late; she made two excuses; first for her husband, who, as she said, happened that very morning to *lhnuwnh*. The word is strongly expressive in their language, but not easily rendered into English. It signifies, "to retire to his first mother." Her excuse for not coming sooner was, that her husband dying late in the morning, she was a good while consulting her servants about a convenient place where his body should be laid; and I observed she behaved herself at our house as cheerfully as the rest. She died about three months after.

They live generally to seventy, or seventy-five years, very seldom to fourscore. Some weeks before their death they feel a gradual decay, but without pain. During this time they are much visited by their friends, because they cannot go abroad with their usual ease and satisfaction. However, about ten days before their death, which they seldom fail in computing, they return the visits that have been made them by those who are nearest in the neighbourhood, being carried in a convenient sledge, drawn by *Yahoos;* which vehicle they use, not only upon this occasion, but when they grow old, upon long journeys, or when they are lamed by any accident. And therefore when the dying *Houyhnhnms* return those visits, they take a solemn leave of their friends, as if they were going to some remote part of the country, where they designed to pass the rest of their lives.

I know not whether it may be worth observing, that the *Houyhnhnms* have no word in their language to express anything that is evil, except what they borrow from the deformities or ill qualities of the *Yahoos.* Thus they denote the folly of a servant, an omission of a child, a stone that cuts their feet, a continuance of foul or unseasonable weather, and the like, by adding to each the epithet of *Yahoo.* For instance — *hhnm Yahoo, whnaholm Yahoo, ynlhmndwihlma Yahoo,* and an all-contrived house, *ynholmhnmrohlnw Yahoo.*

I could, with great pleasure, enlarge farther upon the manners and virtues of this excellent people; but intending in a short time to publish a volume by itself, expressly upon that subject, I refer the reader thither, and in the meantime proceed to relate my own sad catastrophe.

CHAPTER 10

The author's economy and happy life among the Houyhn-hnms. His great improvement in virtue, by conversing with them. Their conversations. The author has notice given him by his master, that he must depart from the country. He falls into a swoon for grief, but submits. He contrives and finishes a canoe by the help of a fellow-servant, and puts to sea at a venture.

I HAD SETTLED my little economy to my own heart's content. My master had ordered a room to be made for me, after their manner, about six yards from the house, the sides and floors of which I plastered with clay, and covered with rush-mats of my own contriving. I had beaten hemp, which there grows wild, and made of it a sort of ticking: this I filled with the feathers of several birds I had taken with springes made of *Yahoos'* hairs, and were excellent food. I had worked two chairs with my knife, the sorrel nag helping me in the grosser and more laborious part. When my clothes were worn to rags, I made myself others with the skins of rabbits, and of a certain beautiful animal about the same size, called *nnuhnoh,* the skin of which is covered with a fine down. Of these I also made very tolerable stockings. I soled my shoes with wood, which I cut from a tree, and fitted to the upper-leather; and when this was worn out, I supplied it with the skins of *Yahoos* dried in the sun. I often got honey out of hollow trees, which I mingled with water, or eat with my bread. No man could more verify the truth of these two maxims, that nature is very easily satisfied; and that necessity is the mother of invention. I enjoyed perfect health of body and tranquillity of mind; I did not feel the treachery of inconstancy of a friend, nor the injuries of a secret or open enemy; I had no occasion of bribing, flattering, or pimping, to procure the favour of any great man, or of his minion; I wanted no fence against fraud or oppression: here was neither physician to destroy my body, nor lawyer to ruin my fortune; no informer to watch my words and actions, or forge accusations against me for hire: here were no gibers, censurers, backbiters, pickpockets, highwaymen, housebreakers, attorneys, bawds, buffoons, gamesters, politicians, wits, splenetics, tedious talkers, controvertists, ravishers, murderers, robbers, virtuosoes; no leaders or followers of party and faction; no encouragers to vice, by seducement or examples; no dungeon, axes, gibbets, whipping-posts, or pillories; no cheating shop-keepers or mechanics; no pride, vanity, or affectation; no fops, bullies, drunkards, strolling whores, or poxes; no ranting, lewd, expensive wives; no stupid, proud pedants; no importunate, over-bearing, quarrelsome, noisy, roaring, empty, conceited, swearing companions; no scoundrels raised from the dust upon the merit of their vices, or nobility thrown into it on account of their virtues; no lords, fiddlers, judges, or dancing-masters.

I had the favour of being admitted to several *Houyhnhnms* who came to visit or dine with my master, where his honour graciously suffered me to wait in the room, and listen to their discourse. Both he and his company would often descend to ask me questions, and receive my answers. I had also sometimes the honour of attending my master in his visits to others. I never presumed to speak, except in answer to a question; and then I did it with inward regret, because it was a loss of so much time for improving myself: but I was infinitely delighted with the station of an humble auditor in such conversations, where nothing passed but what was useful, expressed in the fewest and most significant words; where, as I have already said, the greatest decency was observed, without the least degree of ceremony; where no person spoke without being pleased himself, and pleasing his companions; where there was no interruption, tediousness, heat, or difference of sentiments. They have a notion that when people are met together, a short silence does much improve conversation: this I found to be true; for during those little intermissions of talk, new ideas would arise in their minds, which very much enlivened the discourse. Their subjects are generally on friendship and benevolence, on order and economy; sometimes upon the visible operations of nature, or ancient traditions; upon the bounds and limits of virtue; upon the unerring rules of reason; or upon some determinations to be taken at the next great assembly; and often upon the various excellencies of poetry. I may add, without vanity, that my presence often gave them sufficient matter for discourse, because it afforded my master an occasion of letting his friends into the history of me and my country, upon which they were all pleased to descant, in a manner not very advantageous to humankind: and for that reason I shall not repeat what they said: only, I may be allowed to observe, that his honour, to my great admiration, appeared to understand the nature of *Yahoos* much better than myself. He went through all our vices and follies, and discovered many, which I had never mentioned to him, by only supposing what qualities a *Yahoo* of their country, with a small proportion of reason, might be capable of exerting; and concluded, with too much probability, how vile, as well as miserable, such a creature must be.

I freely confess, that all the little knowledge I have, of any value, was acquired by the lectures I received from my master, and from hearing the discourses of him and his friends; to which I should be prouder to listen than to dictate to the greatest and wisest assembly in Europe. I admired the strength, comeliness, and speed of the inhabitants, and such a constellation of virtues, in such amiable persons, produced in me the highest veneration. At first, indeed, I did not feel that natural awe which the *Yahoos,* and all other animals, bear towards them; but it grew upon me by degrees, much sooner than I imagined, and was mingled with a respectful love and gratitude, that they would condescend to distinguish me from the rest of my species.

When I thought of my family, my friends, my country-men, or the human race in general, I considered them, as they really were, *Yahoos* in shape and disposition, perhaps a little more civilized, and qualified with the gift of speech, but making no other use of reason, than to improve and multiply those vices whereof their brethren in this country had only the share that nature allotted them. When I happened to behold the reflection of my own form in a lake or a fountain, I turned away my face in horror and detestation of myself, and could better endure the sight of a common *Yahoo,* than of my own person. By conversing with the *Houyhnhnms,* and looking upon them with delight, I fell to imitate their gait and gesture, which is now grown into a habit; and my friends often tell me, in a blunt way, that I trot like a horse, which however I take for a great compliment. Neither shall I dis-own, that in speaking I am apt to fall into the voice and man-ner of the *Houyhnhnms,* and hear myself ridiculed on that account, without the least mortification.

In the midst of all this happiness, and when I looked upon myself to be fully settled for life, my master sent for me one morning a little earlier than his usual hour. I observed by his countenance that he was in some perplexity, and at a loss how to begin what he had to speak. After a short silence, he told me he did not know how I would take what he was going to say. That in the last general assembly, when the affair of the *Yahoos* was entered upon, the representatives had taken offence at his keeping a *Yahoo* (meaning myself) in his family, more like a *Houyhnhnm* than a brute animal: that he was known frequently to converse with me, as if he could receive some advantage or pleasure in my company; that such a practice was not agreeable to reason or nature, or a thing ever heard of before among them. The assembly did therefore exhort him either to employ me like the rest of my species, or command me to swim back to the place whence I came. That the first of these expedients was utterly rejected by all the *Houyhnhnms* who had ever seen me at his house or their own; for they alleged, that because I had some rudiments of reason added to the natural pravity of those animals, it was to be feared I might be able to seduce them into the woody and mountainous parts of the country, and bring them in troops by night to destroy the *Houyhnhnms'* cattle, as being naturally of the ravenous kind, and averse from labour.

My master added that he was daily pressed by the *Houyhnhnms* of the neighbourhood to have the assembly's exhortation executed, which he could not put off much longer. He doubted it would be impossible for me to swim to another country, and therefore wished I would contrive some sort of vehicle, resembling those I had described to him, that might carry me on the sea; in which work I should have the assistance of his own servants, as well as those of his neighbours. He concluded that for his own part, he could have been content to keep me in his service as long as I lived, because he found I had cured myself of some bad habits and dispositions, by endeavouring, as far as my inferior nature was capable, to imitate the *Houyhnhnms*.

I should here observe to the reader, that a decree of the general assembly in this country is expressed by the word *hnhloayn,* which signifies an exhortation, as near as I can render it; for they have no conception how a rational creature can be compelled, but only advised or exhorted, because no person can disobey reason, without giving up his claim to being a rational creature.

I was struck with the utmost grief and despair at my

master's discourse; and being unable to support the agonies I was under, I fell into a swoon at his feet. When I came to myself, he told me that he concluded I had been dead; for these people are subject to no such imbecilities of nature. I answered in a faint voice that death would have been too great a happiness; that although I could not blame the assembly's exhortation, or the urgency of his friends, yet, in my weak and corrupt judgment, I thought it might consist with reason to have been less rigorous; that I could not swim a league, and probably the nearest land to theirs might be distant above a hundred; that many materials, necessary for making a small vessel to carry me off, were wholly wanting in this country; which, however, I would attempt, in obedience and gratitude to his honour, although I concluded the thing to be impossible, and therefore looked on myself as already devoted to destruction: that the certain prospect of an unnatural death was the least of my evils; for supposing I should escape with life, by some strange adventure, how could I think with temper of passing my days among *Yahoos,* and relapsing into my old corruptions, for want of examples to lead and keep me within the paths of virtue? that I knew too well upon what solid reasons all the determinations of the wise *Houyhnhnms* were founded, not to be shaken by arguments of mine, a miserable *Yahoo;* and therefore, after presenting him with my humble thanks for the offer of his servants' assistance in making a vessel, and desiring a reasonable time for so difficult a work, I told him I would endeavour to preserve a wretched being; and if ever I returned to England, was not without hopes of being useful to my own species, by celebrating the praises of the renowned *Houyhnhnms,* and proposing their virtues to the imitation of mankind.

My master, in a few words, made me a very gracious reply; allowed me the space of two months to finish my boat;

and ordered the sorrel nag, my fellow-servant (for so, at this distance, I may presume to call him), to follow my instructions; because I told my master that his help would be sufficient, and I knew he had a tenderness for me.

In his company, my first business was to go to that part of the coast where my rebellious crew had ordered me to be set on shore. I got upon a height, and looking on every side into the sea, fancied I saw a small island toward the northeast. I took out my pocket-glass, and could then clearly distinguish it, about five leagues off, as I computed; but it appeared to the sorrel nag to be only a blue cloud; for as he had no conception of any country beside his own, so he could not be as expert in distinguishing remote objects at sea, as we who so much converse in that element.

After I had discovered this island, I considered no farther, but resolved it should, if possible, be the first place of my banishment, leaving the consequence to fortune.

I returned home, and consulting with the sorrel nag, we went into a copse at some distance, where I with my knife, and he with a sharp flint, fastened very artificially, after their manner, to a wooden handle, cut down several oak wattles, about the thickness of a walking-staff, and some larger pieces. But I shall not trouble the reader with a particular description of my own mechanics: let it suffice to say, that in six weeks' time, with the help of the sorrel nag, who performed the parts that required most labour, I finished a sort of Indian canoe, but much larger, covering it with the skins of *Yahoos*, well stitched together with hempen threads of my own making. My sail was likewise composed of the skins of the same animal; but I made use of the youngest I could get, the older being too tough and thick; and I likewise provided myself with four paddles. I laid in a stock of boiled flesh, of rabbits and fowls, and took with me two vessels, one filled with milk, and the other with water.

I tried my canoe in a large pond near my master's house, and then corrected in it what was amiss, stopping all the chinks with *Yahoos'* tallow, till I found it staunch, and able to bear me and my freight; and when it was as complete as I could possibly make it, I had it drawn on a carriage very gently by *Yahoos* to the sea-side, under the conduct of the sorrel nag and another servant.

When all was ready, and the day came for my departure, I took leave of my master and lady, and the whole family; my eyes flowing with tears, and my heart quite sunk with grief. But his honour, out of curiosity, and, perhaps (if I may speak it without vanity), partly out of kindness, was determined to see me in my canoe, and got several of his neighbouring friends to accompany him. I was forced to wait above an hour for the tide; and then observing the wind very fortunately bearing towards the island to which I intended to steer my course, I took a second leave of my master; but as I was going to prostrate myself to kiss his hoof, he did me the honour to raise it gently to my mouth. I am not ignorant how much I have been censured for mentioning this last particular. Detractors are pleased to think it improbable that so illustrious a person should descend to give so great a mark of distinction to a creature so inferior as I. Neither have I forgotten how apt some travellers are to boast of extraordinary favours they have received. But if these censurers were better acquainted with the noble and courteous disposition of the *Houyhnhnms,* they would soon change their opinion.

I paid my respects to the rest of the *Houyhnhnms* in his honour's company, then getting into my canoe, I pushed off from the shore.

CHAPTER II

The author's dangerous voyage. He arrives at New Holland, hoping to settle there. Is wounded with an arrow by one of the natives. Is seized, and carried by force into a Portuguese ship. The great civilities of the captain. The author arrives at England.

I BEGAN THIS desperate voyage on February 15, 1714–15, at nine o'clock in the morning. The wind was very favourable: however, I made use at first only of my paddles; but considering I should soon be weary, and that the wind might chop about, I ventured to set up my little sail; and thus, with the help of the tide, I went at the rate of a league and a half an hour, as near as I could guess. My master and his friends continued on the shore till I was almost out of sight; and I often heard the sorrel nag (who always loved me) crying out, *"Hnuy illa nyha, majah Yahoo,"* "Take care of thyself, gentle *Yahoo."*

My design was, if possible, to discover some small island uninhabited, yet sufficient, by my labour, to furnish me with the necessaries of life, which I would have thought a greater happiness than to be first minister in the politest court of Europe; so horrible was the idea I conceived of returning to live in the society, and under the government of *Yahoos*. For, in such a solitude as I desired, I could at least enjoy my own thoughts, and reflect with delight on the virtues of those inimitable *Houyhnhnms,* without any opportunity of degenerating into the vices and corruptions of my own species.

The reader may remember what I related when my crew conspired against me, and confined me to my cabin; how I continued there several weeks, without knowing what course we took; and when I was put a-shore in the long-boat, how the sailors told me, with oaths, whether true or false, that they knew not in what part of the world we were. However, I did then believe us to be about 10 degrees southward of the Cape of Good Hope, or about 45 degrees southern latitude, as I gathered from some general words I overheard among them, being, I supposed, to the south-east in their intended voyage to Madagascar. And although this were little better than conjecture, yet I resolved to steer my course eastward, hoping to reach the south-west coast of New Holland, and perhaps some such island as I desired, lying westward of it. The wind was full west; and by six in the evening I computed I had gone eastward at least eighteen leagues, when I spied a very small island about half a league off, which I soon reached. It was nothing but a rock, with one creek, naturally arched by the force of tempests. Here I put in my canoe, and climbing a part of the rock, I could plainly discover land to the east, extending from south to north. I lay all night in my canoe, and repeating my voyage early in the morning, I arrived in seven hours to the south-east point of New Holland. This confirmed me in the opinion I have long entertained, that the maps and charts place this country at least three degrees more to the east than it really is; which thought I communicated many years ago to my worthy friend Mr. Herman Moll, and gave him my reasons for it, although he has rather chosen to follow other authors.

I saw no inhabitants in the place where I landed, and being unarmed, I was afraid of venturing far into the country. I found some shell-fish on the shore, and ate them raw, not daring to kindle a fire, for fear of being discovered by the natives. I continued three days feeding on oysters and limpets, to save my own provisions; and I fortunately found a brook of excellent water, which gave me great relief.

On the fourth day, venturing out early, a little too far, I saw twenty or thirty natives upon a height, not above five hundred yards from me. They were stark naked, men, women, and children, round a fire, as I could discover by the smoke. One of them spied me, and gave notice to the rest; five of them advanced towards me, leaving the women and children at the fire. I made what haste I could to the shore, and, getting into my canoe, shoved off; the savages, observing me retreat, ran after me, and before I could get far enough into the sea, discharged an arrow, which wounded me deeply on the inside of my left knee; I shall carry the mark to my grave. I apprehended the arrow might be poisoned; and paddling out of the reach of their darts (being a calm day), I made a shift to suck the wound, and dress it as well as I could.

I was at a loss what to do; for I durst not return to the same landing-place, but stood to the north, and was forced to paddle; for the wind, though very gentle, was against me, blowing north-west. As I was looking about for a secure landing-place, I saw a sail to the north-north-east, which appearing every minute more visible, I was in some doubt whether I should wait for them or not; but at last my detestation of the *Yahoo* race prevailed, and turning my canoe, I sailed and paddled together to the south, and got into the same creek whence I set out in the morning, choosing rather to trust myself among these barbarians, than live with European *Yahoos*. I drew up my canoe as close as I could to the shore, and hid myself behind a stone by the little brook, which, as I have already said, was excellent water.

The ship came within half a league of this creek, and sent her long-boat with vessels to take in fresh water (for the place, it seems, was very well known); but I did not observe it, till the boat was almost on shore, and it was too late to seek another hiding-place. The seamen, at their landing, observed my canoe, and, rummaging it all over, easily conjectured that the owner could not be far off. Four of them, well armed, searched every cranny and lurking-hole, till at last they found me, flat on my face, behind the stone. They gazed a while in admiration at my strange uncouth dress; my coat made of skins, my wooden soled shoes, and my furred stockings; whence, however, they concluded I was not a native of the place, who all go naked. One of the seamen, in Portuguese, bid me rise, and asked who I was. I understood that language very well, and getting upon my feet, said I was a poor *Yahoo,* banished from the *Houyhn-hnms,* and desired they would please to let me depart. They admired to hear me answer them in their own tongue, and saw by my complexion I must be a European; but were at a loss to know what I meant by *Yahoos* and *Houyhnhnms;* and, at the same time, fell a-laughing at my strange tone in speaking, which resembled the neighing of a horse. I trembled all the while, betwixt fear and hatred. I again desired leave to depart, and was gently moving to my canoe; but they laid hold of me, desiring to know what country I was of, whence I came, with many other questions. I told them I was born in England, whence I came about five years ago, and then their country and ours were at peace. I therefore hoped they would not treat me as an enemy, since I meant them no harm, but was a poor *Yahoo* seeking some desolate place where to pass the remainder of his unfortunate life.

When they began to talk, I thought I never heard or saw anything so unnatural; for it appeared to me as monstrous as if a dog or a cow should speak in England, or a *Yahoo* in *Houyhnhnmland.* The honest Portuguese were equally amazed at my strange dress, and the odd manner of delivering my words, which, however, they understood very well. They spoke to me with great humanity, and said they were sure the captain would carry me *gratis* to Lisbon, whence I might return to my own country; that two of the seamen would go back to the ship, inform the captain of what they had seen, and receive his orders; in the meantime, unless I would give my solemn oath not to fly, they would secure me by force. I thought it best to comply with their proposal. They were very curious to know my story, but I gave them very little satisfaction, and they all conjectured that my misfortunes had impaired my reason. In two hours, the boat, which went loaden with vessels of water, returned with the captain's command to fetch me on board. I fell on my knees to preserve my liberty, but all was in vain; and the men, having tied me with cords, heaved me into the boat, whence I was taken into the ship, and thence into the captain's cabin.

His name was Pedro de Mendez; he was a very courteous and generous person. He entreated me to give some account of myself, and desired to know what I would eat or drink; said I should be used as well as himself; and spoke so many obliging things, that I wondered to find such civilities from a *Yahoo*. However, I remained silent and sullen; I was ready to faint at the very smell of him and his men. At last, I desired something to eat out of my own canoe; but he ordered me a chicken, and some excellent wine, and then directed that I should be put to bed in a very clean cabin. I would not undress myself, but lay on the bedclothes, and in half an hour stole out, when I thought the crew was at dinner, and getting to the side of the ship, was going to leap into the sea, and swim for my life, rather than continue among *Yahoos*. But one of the seamen prevented me, and having informed the captain, I was chained to my cabin.

After dinner Don Pedro came to me, and desired to known my reason for so desperate an attempt; assured me he only meant to do me all the service he was able; and spoke so very movingly, that at last I descended to treat him like an animal which had some little portion of reason. I gave him a very short relation of my voyage; of the conspiracy against me by my own men; of the country where they set me on shore, and of my five years' residence there. All which he looked upon as if it were a dream or a vision; whereat I took great offence; for I had quite forgot the faculty of lying, so peculiar to *Yahoos,* in all countries where they preside, and, consequently, the disposition of suspecting the truth in others of their own species. I asked him whether it were the custom in his country to say the thing which was not. I assured him I had almost forgot what he meant by falsehood, and if I had lived a thousand years in *Houyhnhnmland,* I should never have heard a lie from the meanest servant; that I was altogether indifferent whether he believed me or not; but, however, in return for his favours, I would give so much allowance to the corruption of his nature, as to answer any objection he would please to make, and then he might easily discover the truth.

The captain, a wise man, after many endeavours to catch me tripping in some part of my story, at last began to have a better opinion of my veracity. But he added that since I professed so inviolable an attachment to truth, I must give him my word and honour to bear him company in this voyage, without attempting anything against my life; or else he would continue me a prisoner till we arrived at Lisbon. I gave him the promise he required; but at the same time protested, that I would suffer the greatest hardships, rather than return to live among *Yahoos.*

Our voyage passed without any considerable accident. In gratitude to the captain, I sometimes sat with him at his earnest request, and strove to conceal my antipathy against humankind, although it often broke out; which he suffered to pass without observation. But the greatest part of the day I confined myself to my cabin, to avoid seeing any of the crew. The captain had often entreated me to strip myself of my savage dress, and offered to lend me the best suit of clothes he had. This I would not be prevailed on to accept,

abhorring to cover myself with anything that had been on the back of a *Yahoo*. I only desired he would lend me two clean shirts, which, having been washed since he wore them, I believed would not so much defile me. These I changed every second day, and washed them myself.

We arrived at Lisbon, Nov. 5, 1715. At our landing the captain forced me to cover myself with his cloak, to prevent the rabble from crowding about me. I was conveyed to his own house; and at my earnest request he led me up to the highest room backwards. I conjured him to conceal from all persons what I had told him of the *Houyhnhnms;* because the least hint of such a story would not only draw numbers of people to see me, but probably put me in danger of being imprisoned, or burnt by the Inquisition. The captain persuaded me to accept of a suit of clothes newly made; but I would not suffer the tailor to take my measure; however, Don Pedro being almost of my size, they fitted me well enough. He accoutred me with other necessaries, all new, which I aired for twenty-four hours, before I would use them.

The captain had no wife, nor above three servants, none of which were suffered to attend at meals; and his whole deportment was so obliging, added to very good human understanding, that I really began to tolerate his company. He gained so far upon me, that I ventured to look out of the back window. By degrees I was brought into another room, whence I peeped into the street, but drew my head back in a fright. In a week's time he seduced me down to the door. I found my terror gradually lessened, but my hatred and contempt seemed to increase. I was at last bold enough to walk the street in his company, but kept my nose well stopped with rue, or sometimes with tobacco.

In ten days, Don Pedro, to whom I had given some account of my domestic affairs, put it upon me, as a matter of honour and conscience, that I ought to return to my native country, and live at home with my wife and children. He told me there was an English ship in the port just ready to sail, and he would furnish me with all things necessary. It would be tedious to repeat his arguments and my contradictions. He said it was altogether impossible to find such a solitary island as I had desired to live in; but I might command in my own house, and pass my time in a manner as recluse as I pleased.

I complied at last, finding I could not do better. I left Lisbon the 24th day of November, in an English merchant-man, but, who was the master, I never inquired. Don Pedro accompanied me to the ship, and lent me twenty pounds. He took kind leave of me, and embraced me at parting, which I bore as well as I could. During this last voyage I had no commerce with the master or any of his men; but, pretending I was sick, kept close in my cabin. On the 5th of December, 1715, we cast anchor in the Downs, about nine in the morning, and at three in the afternoon I got safe to my house at Redriff.

My wife and family received me with great surprise and joy, because they concluded me certainly dead; but I must freely confess the sight of them filled me only with hatred, disgust, and contempt; and the more, by reflecting on the near alliance I had to them. For although since my unfortunate exile from the *Houyhnhnm* country, I had compelled myself to tolerate the sight of *Yahoos,* and to converse with Don Pedro de Mendez, yet my memory and imagination were per-petually filled with the virtues and ideas of those exalted *Houyhnhnms.* And when I began to consider, that by copulat-ing with one of the *Yahoo* species I had become a parent of more, it struck me with the utmost shame, confusion, and horror.

As soon as I entered the house, my wife took me in her arms, and kissed me; at which, having not been used to the touch of that odious animal for so many years, I fell into a swoon for almost an hour. At the time I am writing, it is five years since my last return to England: during the first year, I could not endure my wife or children in my presence: the very smell of them was intolerable; much less could I suffer them to eat in the same room. To this hour they dare not presume to touch my bread, or drink out of the same cup; neither was I ever able to let one of them take me by the hand. The first money I laid out was to buy two young stone horses, which I keep in a good stable; and next to them the groom is my greatest favourite; for I feel my spirits revived by the smell he contracts in the stable. My horses understand me tolerably well; I converse with them at least four hours every day. They are strangers to bridle or saddle; they live in great amity with me, and friendship to each other.

CHAPTER 12

The author's veracity. His design in publishing this work. His censure of those travellers who swerve from the truth. The author clears himself from any sinister ends in writing. An objection answered. The method of planting colonies. His native country commended. The right of the crown to those countries described by the author, is justified. The difficulty of conquering them. The author takes his last leave of the reader; proposes his manner of living for the future; gives good advice, and concludes.

Thus, GENTLE READER, I have given thee a faithful history of my travels for sixteen years and above seven months; wherein I have not been so studious of ornament as of truth. I could perhaps, like others, have astonished thee with strange improbable tales; but I rather chose to relate plain matter of fact, in the simplest manner and style; because my principal design was to inform, and not to amuse thee.

It is easy for us who travel into remote countries, which are seldom visited by Englishmen or other Europeans, to form descriptions of wonderful animals both at sea and land. Whereas a traveller's chief aim should be to make men wiser and better, and to improve their minds by the bad, as well as good example, of what they deliver concerning foreign places.

I could heartily wish a law was enacted, that every traveller, before he were permitted to publish his voyages, should be obliged to make oath before the Lord High Chancellor, that all he intended to print was absolutely true to the best of his knowledge; for then the world would no longer be deceived, as it usually is, while some writers, to make their

works pass the better upon the public, impose the grossest
falsities on the unwary reader. I have perused several books
of travel with great delight in my younger days; but having
since gone over most parts of the globe, and been able to
contradict many fabulous accounts from my own observation,
it has given me a great disgust against this part of reading,
and some indignation to see the credulity of mankind so
impudently abused. Therefore, since my acquaintance were
pleased to think my poor endeavours might not be unaccept-
able to my country, I imposed on myself, as a maxim never to
be swerved from, that I would strictly adhere to truth;
neither indeed can I be ever under the least temptation to
vary from it, while I retain in my mind the lectures and example of my noble master and the other illustrious *Houyhnhnms,* of whom I had so long the honour to be a humble
hearer.

        ——*Nec si miserum Fortuna Sinonem
    Finxit, vanum etiam, mendacemque improba finget.*

    I know very well, how little reputation is to be got by
writings, which require neither genius nor learning, nor indeed any other talent, except a good memory, or an exact
journal. I know likewise, that writers of travels, like
dictionary-makers, are sunk into oblivion by the weight and
bulk of those who come last, and therefore lie uppermost.
And it is highly probable, that such travellers, who shall hereafter visit the countries described in this work of mine, may,
by detecting my errors (if there be any), and adding many
new discoveries of their own, jostle me out of vogue, and
stand in my place, making the world forget that ever I was
an author. This indeed would be too great a mortification, if
I wrote for fame: but as my sole intention was the public
good, I cannot be altogether disappointed. For who can
read of the virtues I have mentioned in the glorious *Houyhn-*

hnms, without being ashamed of his own vices, when he considers himself as the reasoning, governing animal of his country? I shall say nothing of those remote nations, where *Yahoos* preside; among which the least are the *Brobdingnagians;* whose wise maxims in morality and government, it would be our happiness to observe. But I forbear descanting farther, and rather leave the judicious reader to his own remarks and application.

I am not a little pleased that this work of mine can possibly meet with no censurers: for what objections can be made against a writer who relates only plain facts, that happened in such distant countries, where we have not the least interest, with respect either to trade or negotiations? I have carefully avoided every fault, with which common writers of travels are often too justly charged. Besides, I meddle not the least with any party, but write without passion, prejudice, or ill-will against any man, or number of men whatsoever. I write for the noblest end, to inform and instruct mankind; over whom I may, without breach of modesty, pretend to some superiority, from the advantages I received by conversing so long among the most accomplished *Houyhnhnms.* I write without any view to profit or praise. I never suffer a word to pass that may look like reflection, or possibly give the least offence, even to those who are most ready to take it. So that I hope I may with justice pronounce myself an author perfectly blameless; against whom the tribes of Answerers, Considerers, Observers, Reflectors, Detectors, Remarkers, will never be able to find matter for exercising their talents.

I confess it was whispered to me that I was bound in duty, as a subject of England, to have given in a memorial to a secretary of state at my first coming over; because, whatever lands are discovered by a subject, belong to the crown. But I doubt, whether our conquests, in the countries I treat of, would be as easy as those of Ferdinando Cortez over the naked Americans. The *Lilliputians,* I think, are hardly worth the charge of a fleet and army to reduce them; and I question whether it might be prudent or safe to attempt the *Brobdingnagians.* Or whether an English army would be much at their ease, with the Flying Island over the heads. *The Houyhnhnms* indeed appear not to be so well prepared for war, a science to which they are perfect strangers, and especially against missive weapons. However, supposing myself to be a minister of state, I could never give my advice for invading them. Their prudence, unanimity, unacquaintedness with fear, and their love of their country, would amply supply all defects in the military art. Imagine twenty thousand of them breaking into the midst of an European army, confounding the ranks, overturning the carriages, battering the warriors' faces into mummy by terrible yerks from their hinder hoofs; for they would well deserve the character given to Augustus, *Recalcitrat undique tutus.* But, instead of proposals for conquering that magnanimous nation, I rather wish they were in a capacity, or disposition, to send a sufficient number of their inhabitants for civilizing Europe, by teaching us the first principles of honour, justice, truth, temperance, public spirit, fortitude, chastity, friendship, benevolence, and fidelity. The names of all which virtues are still retained among us in most languages, and are to be met with in modern, as well as ancient authors; which I am able to assert from my own small reading.

But I had another reason, which made me less forward to enlarge his Majesty's dominions by my discoveries. To say the truth, I had conceived a few scruples with relation to the distributive justice of princes upon those occasions. For instance, a crew of pirates are driven by a storm they know not whither; at length a boy discovers land from the topmast; they go on shore to rob and plunder; they see a harmless people, are entertained with kindness; they give the country a new name; they take formal possession of it for their king; they set up a rotten plank, or a stone, for a memorial; they murder two or three dozen of the natives, bring away a couple more, by force, for a sample; return home, and get their pardon. Here commences a new dominion acquired with a title by divine right. Ships are sent with the first opportunity; the natives driven out or destroyed; their princes tortured to discover their gold; a free licence given to all acts of inhumanity and lust, the earth reeking with the blood of its inhabitants: and this execrable crew of butchers, employed in so pious an expedition, is a modern colony, sent to convert and civilize an idolatrous and barbarous people!

But this description, I confess, does by no means affect the British nation, who may be an example to the whole world for their wisdom, care, and justice in planting colonies; their liberal endowments for the advancement of religion and learning; their choice of devout and able pastors to propagate Christianity; their caution in stocking their provinces with people of sober lives and conversations, from this the mother kingdom; their strict regard to the distribution of justice in supplying the civil administration through all their colonies with officers of the greatest abilities, utter strangers to corruption; and, to crown all, by sending the most vigilant and virtuous governors, who have no other views than the happiness of the people over whom they preside, and the honour of the king their master.

But as those countries, which I have described, do not appear to have any desire of being conquered and enslaved, murdered or driven out by colonies; nor abound either in gold, silver, sugar, or tobacco; I did humbly conceive, they were by no means proper objects of our zeal, our valour, or our interest. However, if those whom it more concerns, think fit to be of another opinion, I am ready to depose, when I shall be lawfully called, that no European did ever visit those countries before me. I mean, if the inhabitants ought to be believed, unless a dispute may arise concerning the two *Yahoos,* said to have been seen many years ago upon a mountain in *Houyhnhnmland.*

But, as to the formality of taking possession in my sovereign's name, it never came once into my thoughts; and if it had, yet, as my affairs then stood, I should perhaps, in point of prudence and self-preservation, have put it off to a better opportunity.

Having thus answered the only objection that can ever be raised against me as a traveller, I here take a final leave of all my courteous readers, and return to enjoy my own speculations in my little garden at Redriff; to apply those excellent lessons of virtue, which I learned among the *Houyhnhnms;* to instruct the *Yahoos* of my own family, as far as I shall find them docile animals; to behold my figure often in a glass, and thus, if possible, habituate myself by time to tolerate the sight of a human creature; to lament the brutality of *Houyhnhnms* in my own country, but always treat their persons with respect, for the sake of my noble master, his family, his friends, and the whole *Houyhnhnm* race, whom these of ours have the honour to resemble in all their lineaments, however their intellectuals came to degenerate.

I began last week to permit my wife to sit at dinner with me, at the farthest end of a long table; and to answer (but with the utmost brevity) the few questions I asked her. Yet, the smell of a *Yahoo* continuing very offensive, I always keep my nose well stopped with rue, lavender, or tobacco leaves. And, although it be hard for a man late in life to remove old habits, I am not altogether out of hopes, in some time, to suffer a neighbour *Yahoo* in my company, with the apprehensions I am yet under of his teeth or his claws.

My reconcilement to the *Yahoo* kind in general might not be so difficult, if they would be content with those vices and follies only which nature has entitled them to. I am not in the least provoked at the sight of a lawyer, a pickpocket, a colonel, a fool, a lord, a gamester, a politician, a whore-monger, a physician, an evidencer, a suborner, an attorney, a traitor, or the like; this is all according to the due course of things; but when I behold a lump of deformity and diseases, both in body and mind, smitten with pride, it immediately breaks all the measures of my patience; neither shall I be ever able to comprehend how such an animal, and such a vice, could tally together. The wise and virtuous *Houyhnhnms,* who abound in all excellencies that can adorn a rational crea-ture, have no name for this vice in their language; which has no terms to express anything that is evil, except those whereby they describe the detestable qualities of their *Ya-hoos:* among which they were not able to distinguish this of pride, for want of thoroughly understanding human nature, as it shews itself in other countries, where that animal pre-sides. But I, who had more experience, could plainly observe some rudiments of it among the wild *Yahoos.*

But the *Houyhnhnms,* who live under the government of reason, are no more proud of the good qualities they pos-sess, than I should be for not wanting a leg or an arm; which no man in his wits would boast of, although he must be miser-able without them. I dwell the longer upon this subject, from the desire I have to make the society of an English *Yahoo* by any means not insupportable; and therefore I here entreat those, who have any tincture of this absurd vice, that they will not presume to come in my sight.

FINIS